EVERYMAN, I will go with thee,

and be thy guide,

In thy most need to go by thy side

Lady Julie, translated by C. D. Locock
Hannele, translated by C. H. Meltzer
The Life of the Insects, translated by Paul Selver
The Infernal Machine, translated by Carl Wildman
The Mask and the Face, translated by Noel de Vic Beamish

IN THIS VOLUME:

LADY JULIE : AUGUST STRINDBERG

HANNELE : GERHART HAUPTMANN

THE LIFE OF THE INSECTS : KAREL AND JOSEF ČAPEK

THE INFERNAL MACHINE : JEAN COCTEAU

THE MASK AND THE FACE : LUIGI CHIARELLI

International Modern Plays

EDITED WITH
AN INTRODUCTION BY
ANTHONY DENT

DENT: LONDON
EVERYMAN'S LIBRARY
DUTTON: NEW YORK

All rights reserved
Printed in Great Britain by
Biddles Ltd, Guildford, Surrey
and bound at the
Aldine Press · Letchworth · Herts
for
J. M. DENT & SONS LTD
Aldine House · Albemarle Street · London
This edition was first published in
Everyman's Library in 1950
Last reprinted 1975

Published in the U.S.A. by arrangement
with J. M. Dent & Sons Ltd

No. 989 Hardback ISBN 0 460 00989 3
No. 1989 Paperback ISBN 0 460 01989 9

INTRODUCTION

INEVITABLY such a selection as this must be a compromise, and it is fortunate for the selector that certain limitations have been imposed. For given the bounds of the field—the European theatre during the past sixty years or so, that is to say plays written within living memory—what editor would venture to produce a short list of pieces with the claim that they represent the best of their kind?

An attempt has been made to bring together some plays which shall show diversity in various ways. Thus the claim of what might be called proportional representation has been satisfied, inasmuch as no two of these pieces were originally written in the same language, but this is a rather arbitrary claim, because there may be as much diversity in one art-form in one country or language as in the whole of Europe. The scope of Everyman's Library as a whole must also be taken into account. The drama section ranges from the plays of classical times to the great English plays of all periods; and the library already contains, for example, a great part of the dramatic works of Ibsen, and a Tchekhov volume containing his chief plays.

There were also the claims of the actor and producer, amateur or professional, on the one hand, and the reader on the other, to be satisfied. This has made the task of rejection much easier, since nothing in the nature of a pure *spectacle dans un fauteuil* has been included, nor any play which depends for its effect purely in its presentation on the stage and makes no impression when read in cold blood.

Again, choice has been confined to works of which good, readable, actable translations, as opposed to adaptations or 'English stage versions,' were to be had. This perhaps more than any other factor has served to narrow the field:

'Upon my word,' said Nicholas [Nickleby], taking the manager aside, 'I don't think I can be ready by Monday.' 'Pooh, pooh,' replied Mr. Crummles. 'But really I can't,' returned Nicholas. 'What the devil's that got to do with it?' retorted the manager, with evident impatience. 'Do you understand French?' 'Perfectly well.' 'Very good,' said the manager, opening the table drawer and giving a roll of paper from it to Nicholas, 'there, just turn that into English, and put your name on the title-page. Damn me,' said Mr. Crummles angrily, 'if I haven't often said that I wouldn't have a man or woman in my company that wasn't master of the language, so that they might learn it from the original, and play it in English, and save all this trouble and expense.'

Of course we all know that it is not done that way nowadays. Yet when we consider the number of new continental plays by authors of repute which are played on the English stage, and the small proportion of such scripts that achieve print in English, does it not appear that something of the Crummelsian technique must survive?

An introduction of this length and weight is not the place to treat of influences and sources and trends, nor to argue whether any dramatist since Aeschylus has managed to do anything wholly new—which Strindberg maintained was impossible. But the intention has been to choose plays which in their day represented a new approach to the theatre, and a new line of thought or of technique which is still being worked out.

As to the epithet 'modern,' it has been taken to mean the type of play which began to be presented on the European stage at the period, say, when George Bernard Shaw was in his thirties. What is it that distinguishes this type of play, and the 'quality' play of to-day, from the general run of commercial pieces current at the end of the long night of the European theatre which followed on the garish and rather blatant day of the Romantic stage? It is not primarily the manner of the dialogue which 'lets people's brains work irregularly as they do in actual life' as opposed to the 'mathematically symmetrical construction of French dialogue' from which Strindberg wished to deliver himself. For the illusion that people speak more formally and intelligibly than they do in real life is one that the theatre can sustain along with other and greater illusions, and many of our playwrights have returned to the more formal and balanced kind of speech. 'I had noticed,' said Strindberg, 'that the psychological process is what interests the newer generation; our inquisitive souls are not content with seeing a thing happen; they must also know how it happens!' There is the difference and there is the point of departure, and that is why *Lady Julie*, together with its author's preface, which has been somewhat academically labelled the manifesto of naturalism, appears as tne first piece in this volume.

In spite of the fact that he described the dramatic art of Germany as 'dead' in 1888 Strindberg began to be played as soon and as often in Germany as in his own country; and none of his early followers in the naturalist movement has since become as famous as Gerhart Hauptmann, whose long life ended one year after the Second World War. But his long one-act play *Hannele*, more properly called *Hannele's Assumption*, is not a purely naturalist play like *Fuhrmann Henschel*, or a dialect play like *Die Weber*, but something at once more tender and more profound, like a phantasy projected on a naturalist back-cloth. The reader may see in its deliberate presentation of squalor, if he will, a forerunner of the plays of social comment à la Shaw and Galsworthy, yet its values are not merely social or temporal values.

The stage has been used as vehicle for social and political comment almost since its birth. In these islands such comment was veiled at first in the religious garb of the morality play, which it threw aside about the time of the Reformation with *Ane Satyre of the Threi Estatis*. This device of a stage allegory has been combined with the still older device of the fable set in the animal world in *The Life of the Insects* by Karel and Josef Čapek. The virtue of such comment usually can be measured by the rough standard of its virulence and bite; but though *The Life of the Insects* has an authentic sting it has also the merits of poetry and of universality; it is not a polemic against any political system so much as a plea for human beings at the mercy of political and social systems of all kinds everywhere.

Perhaps no playwright of our day has been more ardent in the search for new forms of expression than Jean Cocteau. He has not confined himself to the mere writing of plays to be interpreted by others—actors, producers, decorators; but has himself been intimately concerned with new developments in the craft of the stage—developments associated with such names as François Copeau, Arthur Honegger, Michel Saint-Denis, André Obey, and Serge Diaghileff. He has also tried his hand at forms other than, but allied to, the drama, and has written for the ballet, the music-hall, the circus, and now the films. *The Infernal Machine* is perhaps of all his works the one least dependent on technical originality, and on the interplay of other arts with that of the actor. Its originality lies in the handling of the old theme of Oedipus, the hero fated to commit in all innocence both parricide and incest through the ill-will of the gods, in such a way that the tragic inevitability of events is shown in terms of a vicious circle. The Sphinx asks: 'Why must we [the gods] always be acting without aim, without understanding?' 'Because,' answers Anubis, 'logic forces us to appear to men in the shape in which they imagine us.' It is Cocteau's art to produce the authentic shiver at the inexorable working of destiny even though it is thus rationalized, and the great figures of legend are presented as such very ordinary mortals.

The last play in the volume, Chiarelli's *The Mask and the Face*, is the only one described as a comedy, or rather as a 'grotesque,' and indeed its outward form is that of a more or less conventional social comedy. But as the action develops out of a sufficiently banal situation into a paradoxical tragic farce the whole system of conventional values, which were once good enough to provide dramatic motives under the labels 'passion,' 'honour,' 'revenge,' etc., are turned topsy-turvy, and human actions are seen to be nothing but the effects of infinitely remote causes. This atmosphere of moral confusion and doubt as to 'accepted' codes of thought and behaviour are so reminiscent of the moral atmosphere of the 1920s that it comes as somewhat of a surprise to learn that this play was first produced in 1916, and actually written in 1913. That it passed with contumely through the hands of innumerable producers and managers between these two dates is due to the fact that in the period before the First World War there was no native 'theatre of ideas' in Italy. Such plays of this kind as found their way on to the Italian stage would be translations or adaptations of northern dramatists, Ibsen, Sudermann, Hauptmann, Shaw; for the rest, only conventional comedies of French origin. Now for the first time there were presented on the stage of that country the problems of reality and illusion, of life and form. On the morrow of its first performance a critic said: '[This] marks a date in the Italian theatre. We are faced not merely with a success, but with a turning point in the road of our dramatic literature, while yet remaining strictly within the limits of the Italian tradition.' This blinding revelation that human actions and motives are 'not as simple as all that' leads inevitably to the paradoxical, bitter, but stimulating comedies of Pirandello, and to the rise of Italian drama to a position which it had not reached since the days of the great Venetians.

1950.   ANTHONY DENT.

DRAMATIC WORKS

AUGUST STRINDBERG (1849–1912)

The following are the dates of composition of Strindberg's principal dramatic works. All have been translated into English, some in several versions:

Hermione, 1869; *The Outlaw*, 1872; *Master Olof*, 1872; *The Secret of the Guild*, 1880; *Lucky Peter's Travels*, 1881–2; *Sir Bengt's Lady*, 1882; *The Father*, 1887; *The Comrades*, 1888; *Lady Julie*, 1888; *Creditors*, 1888; *Pariah*, 1889; *The First Warning*, 1892; *Mother Love*, 1892; *Facing Death*, 1892; *Debit and Credit*, 1893; *Playing with Fire*, 1893; *The Link*, 1893; *To Damascus*, Parts I and II, 1898; *There are Crimes and Crimes*, 1899; *Christmas*, 1899; *Gustavus Vasa*, 1899; *Eric XIV*, 1899; *The Saga of the Folkungs*, 1899; *Gustavus Adolphus*, 1900; *Easter*, 1900; *Midsummer*, 1900; *The Dance of Death*, Parts I and II, 1901; *Engelbrecht*, 1901; *Charles XII*, 1901; *The Bridal Crown*, 1901; *Swanwhite*, 1901; *Queen Christina*, 1901; *The Dream Play*, 1902; *Gustavus III*, 1902; *The Nightingale of Wittenberg*, 1903; *To Damascus*, Part III, 1904; *Storm*, 1907; *After the Fire*, 1907; *The Spook Sonata*, 1907; *The Pelican*, 1907; *Abu Casem's Slippers*, 1908; *The Last Knight*, 1908; *The Earl of Bjallbö*, 1908; *The National Director*, 1909; *The Black Glove*, 1909; *The Great Highway*, 1909. The present translation of *Lady Julie* was made in 1930.

GERHART HAUPTMANN (1862–1946)

The following are the plays of Gerhart Hauptmann, with dates of original publication. A collection of plays in English has been published, which is complete down to *Die Tochter der Kathedrale*:

Vor Sonnenaufgang, 1889; *Das Friedensfest*, 1890; *Einsame Menschen*, 1891; *Die Weber*, 1892; *Kollege Crampton*, 1892; *Der Biberpelz*, 1893; *Hanneles Himmelfahrt*, 1893; *Florian Geyer*, 1895; *Die Versunkene Glocke*, 1896; *Elga*, 1896; *Fuhrmann Henschel*, 1898; *Schluck und Jan*, 1900; *Michael Kramer*, 1900; *Der rote Hahn*, 1901; *Der arme Heinrich*, 1902; *Rose Bernd*, 1903; *Die Jungfern vom Bischofsberg*, 1905; *Und Pippa tanzt!*, 1906; *Gabriel Schillings Flucht*, 1907; *Kaiser Karls Geisel*, 1908; *Griselda*, 1909; *Die Ratten*, 1910; *Peter Brauer*, 1911; *Festspiel in deutschen Reimen*, 1913; *Der Bogen des Odysseus*, 1914; *Winterballade*, 1917; *Der weisse Heiland*, 1919; *Indipohdi*, 1920; *Veland*, 1925; *Dorothea Angermann*, 1926; *Spuk*, 1929; *Vor Sonnenuntergang*, 1932; *Die goldene Harfe*, 1933; *Hamlet in Wittenberg*, 1935; *Ulrich von Lichtenstein*, 1939; *Die Tochter der Kathedrale*, 1939; *Iphigenie in Delphi*, 1941; *Iphigenie in Aulis*, 1944; *Die Finsternisse*, 1947; *Agamemnons Tod*, 1948; *Elektra*, 1948. The present translation of *Hannele* was made in 1894.

JOSEF (1887–1945) AND KAREL (1890–1938) ČAPEK

Besides *The Life of the Insects* the brothers Josef and Karel Čapek wrote in collaboration *Adam Stvořitel*, translated into English as *Adam the Creator* in 1929. Karel Čapek's principal dramatic works have been published in English as follows:

Rossum's Universal Robots (R.U.R.), 1923; *Power and Glory (Bila Nemoc)*, 1938; *The Mother (Matka)*, 1939; *The Macropoulos Secret (Věc Makropulos)*, 1925.

Josef Čapek's play, *The Land of Many Names*, was published in English in 1926.

The present translation of *The Life of the Insects* was made in the year of original publication, 1923, and an adaptation was published in the same year. This edition gives the translation complete.

JEAN COCTEAU (born 1891)

The dates of original publication of Jean Cocteau's principal plays are as follows:

Les Mariés de la tour Eiffel, 1923; *Orphée*, 1927; *Le Pauvre Matelot*, 1927; *Antigone* (libretto to Honegger's opera), 1928; *Œdipe Roi* (free adaptation of Sophocles), 1928; *La Voix humaine*, 1930; *Les Chevaliers de la Table Ronde*, 1937; *Les Parents terribles*, 1939 (first London production as *Intimate Relations*, 1951); *L'Aigle à deux têtes*, 1946; *Bacchus*, 1952.

La Machine infernale was first performed at the Comédie des Champs-Élysées in April 1934. The English version was first published in 1936, and has been revised for this volume.

LUIGI CHIARELLI (1884–1947)

The following are Chiarelli's principal plays, with dates of publication:

Vita Intima, 1909; *Pasqua delle Rose*, 1910; *Astuzia*, 1910; *La Portantina*, 1911; *Extra Dry*, 1912; *Il Record*, 1913; *La Maschera ed il Volto*, 1916; *La Scala di Seta*, 1917; *Le Lacrime e le Stelle*, 1918 (produced in 1919); *Chimere*, 1920 (produced in 1919); *La Morte degli Amanti*, 1921; *Fuoco d'Artificio*, 1923 (produced in 1922); *Jolly*, 1928 (produced in 1927); *K-41*, 1929; *Carne Bianca*, 1934; *Una più Due*, 1935; *Pulcinella*, 1937; *Enrico VIII*, 1940 (first produced 1948); *Il Teatro in Fiamme*, 1944; *Essere*, 1946.

This translation of *The Mask and the Face* is hitherto unpublished. *Money, Money!*, an English translation of *Fuoco d'Artificio* by N. de V. Beamish, was produced at the Royalty Theatre, London, in 1927.

CONTENTS

xi

ACKNOWLEDGMENTS

THE plays in this volume are copyright throughout the world, and for permission to include them in this volume acknowledgments are due as follows:

> *Lady Julie.* By permission of the Anglo-Swedish Literary Foundation and Jonathan Cape Ltd., 30 Bedford Sq., London WC1B 3EL. (From *Lucky Peter's Travels and other Plays.*)

> *Hannele.* By permission of Miss Hamlen Hunt of Boston, U.S.A., on behalf of the executors of the author and translator. Apply c/o J. M. Dent & Sons Ltd., 26 Albemarle Street, London W1X 4QY.

> *The Life of the Insects.* By permission of the author's trustees and of the translator. For performing rights apply to A. M. Heath & Co. Ltd., 35 Dover Street, London, W.1.

> *The Infernal Machine.* By permission of the author and translator. For performing rights apply to Eric Glass Ltd., 28 Berkeley Square, London W1X 6HD.

> *The Mask and the Face.* By permission of the author's trustees and of the translator. For performing rights apply to the International Copyright Bureau Ltd., 11 Haymarket, London, S.W.1.

The performing rights of the plays, and parts of the plays, are fully protected, and applications for permission to perform them must be made to the agents mentioned above, or otherwise, in the first instance, to the publishers of this volume for transmission.

LADY JULIE

A NATURALISTIC TRAGEDY

BY AUGUST STRINDBERG

With a Preface by
THE AUTHOR

Translated from the Swedish by
C. D. LOCOCK

CHARACTERS

LADY JULIE, *aged 25*
JEAN, *a valet, aged 30*
KRISTIN, *a cook, aged 35*

PREFACE

DRAMATIC art, like other art in general, has long seemed to me a kind of *Biblia Pauperum*—a Bible in pictures for those who cannot read the written or printed word; and the dramatic author a lay preacher, who hawks about the ideas of his time in popular form—popular enough for the middle classes, who form the bulk of theatrical audiences, to grasp the nature of the subject without troubling their brains too much. The theatre, accordingly, has always been a board school for the young, for the half educated, and for women, who still retain the inferior faculty of deceiving themselves and allowing themselves to be deceived: that is to say, of being susceptible to illusion and to the suggestions of the author. Consequently, in these days, when the rudimentary and incompletely developed thought-process which operates through the imagination appears to be developing into reflection, investigation, and examination, it has seemed to me that the theatre, like religion, may be on the verge of being abandoned as a form which is dying out, and for the enjoyment of which we lack the necessary conditions. This supposition is confirmed by the extensive theatrical crisis which now prevails throughout the whole of Europe, and especially by the fact that in those civilized countries which have produced the greatest thinkers of the age—that is to say, England and Germany—the dramatic art, like most other fine arts, is dead.

In other countries, however, it has been thought possible to create a new drama by filling the old forms with the contents of the newer age; but, for one thing, the new thoughts have not yet had time to become sufficiently popular for the public to gain the intelligence necessary for grasping the subject; moreover, party strife has so inflamed people's minds that pure, disinterested enjoyment is out of the question. One experiences a deep sense of contradiction when an applauding or hissing majority exercises its tyranny so openly as it can in the theatre. Lastly, we have not got the new form for the new contents, and the new wine has burst the old bottles.

In the present drama I have not tried to do anything new—for that is impossible—but merely to modernize the form in accordance with what I imagined would be required from this

5

art by the younger generation. To that end I have selected, or allowed myself to be gripped by, a motive which may be said to lie outside the party strife of the day, since the question of social climbing or falling, of the higher or the lower, of better or worse, of man or woman, is, has been, and will continue to be of lasting interest. When I selected this motive from life, as it was related to me several years ago, when the incident made a deep impression on me, I found it suitable for a tragedy; for we still get a tragic impression at the sight of a fortunately situated individual going under, still more at the sight of a whole family dying out. But perhaps there will come a time when we have become so developed, so enlightened, that we shall view with indifference the spectacle presented by life, which now seems cruel, cynical, and heartless; when we shall have closed down those inferior, unreliable thought machines which are called feelings, and which become superfluous and harmful when our organs of discrimination are fully developed. The fact that the heroine arouses sympathy depends solely on our weakness in not being able to resist the feeling of fear that a similar fate may overtake us too. Nevertheless the extremely sensitive spectator will perhaps not be content with this sympathy, and the man of the future, possessed of faith, will perhaps demand some positive suggestions for remedying evil—in other words, some kind of pro-gramme. But in the first place there is no such thing as absolute evil; the ruin of one family means the good fortune of another, which is thereby enabled to rise; while the alternation of climb-ing and falling constitutes one of life's principal charms, since good fortune is merely comparative. Moreover, I should like to ask the man with the programme who wants to remedy the painful fact that the bird of prey devours the dove, and lice the bird of prey: why should it be remedied? Life is not so mathe-matically idiotic as to allow only the big to eat the small; it is just as common for the bee to kill the lion, or at any rate to drive him mad.

If my tragedy creates a sad impression on many people, that is their own fault. When we have become as strong as the pioneers of the French Revolution we shall receive an un-questionably pleasant and happy impression from viewing in the public parks the thinning out of rotten and superannuated trees, which have stood too long in the way of others equally entitled to live their day—an impression as happy as the sight of the death of an incurably sick man!

A short time ago my tragedy, *The Father*, was criticized for its sadness—as if one wanted cheerful tragedies. There is a clamorous insistence on the joy of life, and managers are sending out requests for farces, as if the joy of life consisted in being idiotic and in portraying all men as sufferers from St. Vitus's dance or congenital idiocy. Personally, I find the joy of life in its tense and cruel struggles, and my enjoyment lies in getting to know something, in getting to learn something. I have chosen for that reason an unusual case, but a very instructive one; an exception in fact, but a great exception, of the kind which confirms the rule; one which I suppose will give pain to those who love the commonplace. The simple brain will also be offended by the fact that the motives which I offer for the incident are not simple, and that the point of view is not invariably one and the same. An incident in life—and this is a fairly new discovery! —is usually caused by a whole series of more or less deeply underlying motives; but the spectator commonly selects the one which his own intellect finds the easiest to grasp, or the one which brings most credit to his powers of discernment. A suicide is committed. Business troubles! says the ordinary citizen. Unrequited love! say the women. Ill health! the invalid. Shattered hopes! the unfortunate. But it is quite possible that the motive lay in all or in none of these directions, and that the dead man concealed the main motive by putting forward a quite different one which would reflect greater lustre on his memory!

Lady Julie's tragic fate has been ascribed by me to a whole multitude of circumstances: the instincts derived from her mother; the father's faulty upbringing of the girl; her own character and the influence of her betrothed on a weak degenerate brain; further, and more directly: the festive mood of Midsummer Eve; her father's absence; her own physical condition; her interest in animals; the exciting influences of the dance; the dusk of night; the strongly aphrodisiac influence of the flowers; and finally, chance, which brings the pair together in a lonely room, plus the presumption of the excited man. Thus I have not treated the matter exclusively from a physiological, nor exclusively from a psychological point of view. I have not put the blame solely on the instincts inherited from her mother, nor solely on her physical condition, nor exclusively on 'immorality.' Nor have I merely preached a moral sermon! In the absence of a priest I have left this to the cook.

I must congratulate myself on this multiplicity of motives, as being in accordance with modern views! And if others have done the same thing before me, then I congratulate myself on not being alone in my paradoxes—as all discoveries are called.

In regard to the character-drawing, I have made my figures rather 'characterless,' for the following reasons:

The word 'character' has, in the course of the ages, assumed various meanings. Originally, I suppose, it signified the dominant characteristic of the soul-complex, and was confused with 'temperament.' Afterwards it became the middle-class expression for the automaton. An individual who had once for all become fixed in his natural disposition, or had adapted himself to some definite role in life—who, in fact, had ceased to grow —was called a 'character'; while the man who continued his development, the skilful navigator of life's river who does not sail with sheets set fast, but veers before the wind to luff again, was called 'characterless.' In a derogatory sense, of course, since he was so difficult to catch, to classify, and to keep guard over. This middle-class conception of the immobility of the soul was transferred to the stage, where the middle class has always ruled. A 'character' on the stage came to signify a gentleman who was fixed and finished: one who invariably came on the stage drunk, jesting, or mournful. For characterization nothing was required but some bodily defect—a club-foot, a wooden leg, a red nose; or the character in question was made to repeat some such phrase as 'That's capital,' 'Barkis is willin',' or the like. This simple method of regarding human beings still survives in the great Molière. Harpagon is a miser pure and simple, though Harpagon might have been not only a miser but a first-rate financier, an excellent father, and a good citizen. Worse still, his 'defect' is a distinct advantage to his son-in-law and his daughter, who are his heirs, and who should not therefore blame him, even if they do have to wait a little for their wedding night. I do not believe, therefore, in simple characters on the stage. And the summary judgments on men given by authors: this man is stupid, this one brutal, this one jealous, this one stingy, etc., should be challenged by naturalists, who know the richness of the soul-complex, and recognize that 'vice' has a reverse side very much like virtue.

Since they are modern characters, living in a transitional age more feverishly hysterical than at least its predecessor, I have pictured my figures as more vacillating, as riven asunder, a blend of the old and the new; moreover, it does not seem to me improbable that modern ideas, conveyed through newspapers and conversations, might even have soaked down to the levels where a domestic servant may live.

My souls (characters) are conglomerations from past and present stages of civilization; they are excerpts from books and newspapers, scraps of humanity, pieces torn from festive garments which have become rags—just as the soul itself is a piece of patchwork. Besides this, I have provided a little evolutionary history in making the weaker repeat phrases stolen from the stronger, and in making my souls borrow 'ideas'—suggestions, as they are called—from one another.

Lady Julie is a modern character; not that the half-woman, the man-hater, has not existed in all ages, but because she has now been discovered, has stepped to the front and made herself heard. The half-woman is a type that is thrusting itself forward, that sells itself nowadays for power, for titles, for distinctions, for diplomas, as it used to sell itself for money. And it points to degeneration. It is not a good type—for it does not last—but unfortunately it transmits its own misery to another generation; moreover, degenerate men seem unconsciously to make their choice from among them, so that they multiply and produce offspring of indeterminate sex, to whom life is a torture. Fortunately, these women perish, either through lack of harmony with reality, or through the uncontrolled mutiny of the suppressed instinct, or through the shattering of their hopes of catching up with the men. The type is tragic, offering, as it does, the spectacle of a desperate fight with nature; tragic, too, as a romantic inheritance now being dispersed by naturalism, whose sole desire is happiness; and for happiness strong and good types are required.

But Lady Julie is also a relic of that old warrior aristocracy, which is now giving place to the new aristocracy of nerve and brain. She is a victim of the discord which a mother's 'crime' has produced in a family; a victim, too, of the delusions of the day, of circumstances, of her own defective constitution—all of which together are the equivalents of the old-fashioned Fate or Universal Law. The naturalist has abolished guilt by abolishing God; but the consequences of an action—punishment, imprisonment or the fear of it—these he cannot abolish, for the simple reason that they remain, whether his verdict be acquittal or not; for an injured fellow creature is not so complaisant as an outsider, who has not been injured, can well afford to be. Even if the father, for some urgent reason, had forgone his revenge, the daughter would have to take vengeance on herself, as she does in my play, as the result of that inborn or acquired sense of honour which the upper classes inherit—from what? From barbarism, from their primitive Aryan home, from the chivalry of the Middle Ages: all very beautiful, but a disadvantage nowadays to the continuation of the type. It is the aristocrat's hara-kiri, the inner law of conscience of the Japanese, which bids him cut open his own stomach at the insult of another, and which survives in a modified form in the duel, the privilege of the aristocracy. So the valet, Jean, continues to live, while Lady Julie cannot live without honour. That is where the thrall has an advantage over the earl: he is free from this fatal prejudice about honour. Moreover, in all of us Aryans there is a trace of the nobleman, or the Don Quixote, which makes us sympathize with the suicide who has committed a dishonourable action and so lost his honour; and we are aristocrats enough to be pained at the sight of fallen greatness encumbering the ground like a dead body, yes, even though the fallen rise again and make restitution by honourable deeds. The valet, Jean, is a type-builder, one in whom the distinctive character is strongly marked. He was a labourer's child who, through self-education, is now on his way to becoming a gentleman. With his finely developed senses (smell, taste, sight), and his sense of beauty, he has found it easy to learn. He has already risen, and is strong enough to have no scruples about making use of the services of others. He is already foreign to his surroundings, which he despises as stages in a journey already passed; yet he fears them and shuns them because they know his secrets, pry into his plans, watch his rise with jealousy, and look forward with pleasure to his downfall. Hence arises his dual, indefinite character, vacillating between sympathy with high rank and hatred of those who now possess it. He is an aristocrat—he tells us so himself—has learnt the secrets of good society, is polished, though vulgar at heart, and already wears his frock-coat with taste, though we have no guarantee for his personal cleanliness.

He feels respect for the young lady, but is afraid of Kristin, since she is in possession of his dangerous secrets; he is sufficiently callous not to allow the events of the night to have any disturbing effect on his plans for the future. Uniting the cruelty of the slave with the tyrant's lack of squeamishness, he can see

blood without fainting; he can take misfortune by the neck and
hurl it to the ground. For this reason he will come out of the
fight unwounded and probably end his days as a hotel-keeper.
And if he himself does not become a Roumanian count, I expect
his son will matriculate and perhaps become a district attorney.

In other respects the light which he throws on the lower-class
conception of life, as seen from beneath, is very significant—
that is, when he speaks the truth—which is not very often, since
he prefers to say what is to his own advantage rather than what
is true. When Lady Julie puts forward the suggestion that the
lower classes must feel the pressure from above so heavily, Jean,
of course, agrees, since his object is to win her sympathy; but he
corrects his statement the moment he perceives the advantage
of separating himself from the common herd.

Apart from the fact that Jean is now on the up-grade he
stands above Lady Julie in virtue of his manhood. Sexually he
is the aristocrat by reason of his manly strength, his more finely
developed senses, and his power of initiative. His inferiority is
due mainly to the accidental social *milieu* in which he lives, and
which he can probably lay aside with his livery.

The slavish disposition expresses itself in his reverence for the
count (the boots) and in his religious superstition; but his
reverence for the count is more for the occupant of the higher
place that he himself is aiming at; and this reverence remains
even when he has won the daughter of the house and discovered
how empty was the beautiful shell.

Between souls of such different quality I do not think that
any love-relationship, in the 'higher' sense, can arise. Accordingly I make Lady Julie imagine her love to be protective or
exculpative, while I make Jean suppose that love on his part
might arise if his social position were altered. Love, I think, is
like the hyacinth, which must strike root in the dark *before* it can
produce a vigorous flower. In my play it shoots up, blossoms,
and runs to seed, all at the same time, and that is why the plant
dies so quickly.

Lastly, Kristin is a feminine slave, with the dependent nature
and slothfulness which she has acquired in front of the kitchen
fire; stuffed full of morality and religion, which she makes her
cloaks and scapegoats. She goes to church as a simple and easy
way of unloading on Jesus her household thefts, and of taking
in a fresh cargo of guiltlessness. For the rest, she is a minor
character—intentionally, therefore, sketched in the same

manner as the pastor and the doctor in *The Father*, where I wanted just everyday human beings, such as country pastors and provincial doctors usually are. And if some people think that these minor characters of mine are mere abstractions, this is due to the fact that everyday human beings *are* to a certain extent abstract in the pursuit of their calling; that is to say, they are dependent, showing only one side while they are at work. And so long as the spectator does not feel the need of seeing them from other sides, my abstract delineation of them is fairly correct.

Finally, as to the dialogue: I have rather broken with tradition in not making my characters catechists who sit asking foolish questions in order to elicit a smart reply. I have avoided the mathematically symmetrical construction of French dialogue and let people's brains work irregularly, as they do in actual life, where no topic of conversation is drained to the dregs, but one brain receives haphazard from the other a cog to engage with. Consequently, my dialogue too wanders about, providing itself in the earlier scenes with material which is afterwards worked up, admitted, repeated, developed, and built up, like the theme in a musical composition.

The plot is full of possibilities, and since it really concerns only two characters I have confined myself to these, merely introducing one minor character, the cook, and allowing the father's unfortunate spirit to hover over and behind the whole. This is because I thought I had noticed that the psychological process is what chiefly interests the newer generation; our inquisitive souls are not content with seeing a thing happen; they must also know how it happens! What we want to see is the wires, the machinery; we want to examine the box with the false bottom, to handle the magic ring and find the joint, to have a look at the cards and see how they are marked.

In this connection I have kept in view the monographic novels of the brothers de Goncourt, to my mind the most attractive of all modern literature.

Coming now to the technical side of the composition, I have made the experiment of abolishing the division into acts. The experiment is due to my belief that our decreasing capacity for illusion was possibly weakened by intervals in which the spectator has time to reflect and thereby escape from the suggestive influence of the author-mesmerist. My play will probably last an hour and a half; and since one can listen to a lecture, a sermon,

or a parliamentary debate for as long as that, or longer, I imagine
that a theatrical piece should not become fatiguing in the course
of that time. As early as 1872, in one of my first dramatic
attempts, *The Outlaw*, I tried this concentrated form, though
with very little success. The piece was written in five acts,
and was finished when I first became aware of the restless, dis-
jointed effect which it produced. I burnt it, and out of the
ashes rose a single, highly elaborated act, fifty pages of type,
and playable in one hour. The form of my play is thus by no
means new, but it seems to be my own, and under the changed
conditions of taste it may have some chance of suiting the times.
My ambition would be to get a public so educated as to be
capable of sitting through a one-act play lasting an entire evening. But this is a matter for investigation. However, in
order to provide resting points for the public and the performers
without allowing the public to escape from the illusion, I have
introduced three art forms, all of which come under the head-
ing of dramatic art, namely, the monologue, the pantomime,
and the ballet: all of which, too, in their original forms, belonged
to ancient tragedy, the monody now becoming the monologue,
and the chorus the ballet.

Our modern realists have condemned the monologue as unnatural; but if I provide a motive for it I make it natural, and so
can use it with advantage. It is natural, I suppose, for a public
speaker to walk up and down the room rehearsing his speech by
himself; it is natural for an actor to read through his part aloud,
for the servant girl to talk to her cat, for a mother to talk baby-
talk to her child, for an old maid to chatter to her parrot, for a
sleeper to talk in his sleep. Further, in order to give the actor
for once a chance of working independently—a moment's rest
from the author's pointer—it is better that the monologue be
not written in full but merely indicated. For since it does not
much matter what one says in one's sleep, or to the parrot or the
cat—since it cannot influence the action—it is quite possible
that a talented actor, who will necessarily be in touch with the
spirit of the play and its situations, may improvise this better
than the author, since the latter cannot calculate in advance
how much can be spoken, and for how long, before the public
awakens from its illusion.

It is well known that the Italian theatre on some of its stages
has gone back to improvisation, and thus produced creative
actors—always, however, in accordance with the author's plans.

This may be a step forward, or even some newly germinating form of art, which we may perhaps call *creative* art.

In cases, again, where monologue would be unnatural I have had recourse to pantomime, and in this I leave still greater scope for the actor's imagination—and for his desire to win independent honour! But to avoid trying the public beyond their powers of endurance I have allowed the music—for which here the midsummer dancing provides an excellent motive—to exercise its illusive sway during the dumb show; and I ask the musical director to give special attention to his choice of the pieces performed, so that no conflicting mood may be aroused by reminiscence from current operettas or dance repertoires, or from folk-songs of too local a character.

My ballet could not well have been replaced by a so-called 'folk-scene,' for folk-scenes are badly acted when a crowd of grinning apes try to seize the opportunity for showing off, thereby destroying the illusion. Since the 'people' do not improvise their ill-natured comments, but make use of material already to hand in which some double meaning may be found, I have not composed the lampoon, but have taken a little-known dance-song which I jotted down for myself in the Stockholm district. The words are not quite to the point: they miss the bull's-eye, but that was really my intention, since the element of cunning (i.e. weakness) in the slave prevents him from delivering a direct attack. So we must have no 'funny men' in a serious play, no coarse grinning over a situation which nails the lid on the coffin of a family.

As regards the scenery, I have borrowed from impressionist painting its asymmetry and its abruptness, and I think that I have thus succeeded in creating illusion; for the fact that one does not see the whole room and the whole of the furniture leaves scope for conjecture—in other words, the imagination is set in motion and supplements the senses. I have succeeded, too, in getting rid of those tiresome exits through doors—all the more tiresome because doors on the stage are made of canvas and swing at the lightest touch; most assuredly they cannot express the wrath of an irate father of a family when, after a bad dinner, he goes out and slams the door 'so that the whole house shakes.' (In the theatre it rocks.) I have also confined myself to a single setting, with the idea not only of letting the characters grow into their *milieu*, but of breaking away from decorative luxury. But when there is one setting only it may be demanded that it should be natural. Nothing is harder than to get a room which looks something like a room, however easy it may be for the painter to produce flaming volcanoes and waterfalls. No doubt the walls must be of canvas, but it really seems time to draw the line at painting shelves and kitchen utensils on the canvas. There is so much else on the stage that is conventional, and which we are asked to accept, that we might be spared the strain involved in believing in painted saucepans.

I have placed the backcloth and the table diagonally, so that the actors may be seen full face and in half profile when they are sitting opposite each other at the table. In the opera *Aida* I have seen a diagonally arranged background which led the eye away into unseen perspectives, and it did not seem to be due to any reaction against the wearisome straight line.

Another perhaps not unnecessary novelty would be the abolition of footlights. The object of this illumination from below is said to be to make the actors' faces look fatter. But I ask, why should all actors have fat faces? Does not this lighting from below smooth away the delicate lines in the lower part of the face, especially the jaws? Does it not falsify the shape of the nose and cast shadows over the eyes? Even if this is not so, one thing is certain: the light hurts the actors' eyes so that the effective play of their glances is lost; for the glare of the footlights strikes parts of the retina which are usually protected (except in the case of sailors, who are used to seeing the sunlight on the water); and that is the reason why one seldom sees any play of the eyes, other than showing the whites in a crude rolling sideways, or up towards the gallery. Perhaps we may trace to the same source that tiresome blinking of the eyelids which we see especially in the case of actresses. Moreover, when anybody on the stage wishes to speak with his eyes he has nothing but the unsatisfactory source of looking straight at the audience, with whom he or she thus gets into direct communication *outside* the frame of the picture—a vice which, rightly or wrongly, goes by the name of 'greeting one's friends'!

Would not the use of sufficiently powerful sidelights (aided by reflectors or the like) afford the actor this new resource—the strengthening of his powers of mimicry by means of the face's chief asset—the play of the eyes?

I can hardly have any illusions as to the possibility of getting the actor to play *to* the audience, instead of *with* it, however desirable that might be. I do not dream of ever seeing the actor turn his back completely throughout the whole of an important scene; but I do earnestly wish that crucial scenes should not be played in the vicinity of the prompter's box, as though they were duets intended to be applauded. I should like them to be given in the place indicated by the situation. No revolutions, then, but just a few small modifications; for to turn the stage into a room with the fourth wall missing, and consequently with some of the furniture placed with its back to the audience, would probably, at present, have a disturbing effect.

In speaking of making-up I hardly dare hope to be listened to by the ladies, who would rather look beautiful than natural. But the male actor might perhaps consider whether it really is an advantage for him to make up his face into some abstract character, fixed on it like a mask. Take the case of a man who puts a well-defined charcoal line between his eyes, to indicate a violent temper, and imagine that from this permanently ill-tempered face some repartee requires a laugh. What a horrible grimace will result! And how shall that false forehead, shining like a billiard ball, show a wrinkle when the old man loses his temper?

In a modern psychological drama, where the soul's most delicate emotions should be reflected from the face rather than through gestures and noise, it would probably be best to experiment with powerful side-lights, on a small stage, and with no grease-paint for the actors, or at any rate the minimum possible.

If we could then abolish the visible orchestra with the disturbing glare of its lamps, and its faces turned towards the audience; if we could have the stalls raised so that the spectator's eye would be above the level of the actor's knee; if we could do away with the boxes with their giggling diners and supper-girls; if, in addition, we could have complete darkness in the auditorium throughout the performance, and, most important of all, a *small* stage and a *small* house—then perhaps a new dramatic art might arise, and at any rate the theatre might again become an institution for the enjoyment of cultured people. While waiting for such a theatre I suppose we may as well go on writing 'for stock,' and get ready the repertoire of the future.

I have made an attempt! If it is a failure, well, there is plenty of time to try again!

The action takes place in the count's kitchen on Midsummer Eve

SCENE: *A large kitchen. The ceiling and side walls are concealed by hangings and draperies. The wall at the back runs obliquely up the stage from the left. On it, to the left, are two shelves with utensils of copper, brass, iron, and tin. The shelves are fringed with crinkled paper. A little to the right, three-fourths of the great arched doorway, with two glass doors, through which are seen a fountain with a cupid, lilac shrubs in flower, and the tops of some Italian poplars.*

To the left of the stage is the corner of a large tiled range and a part of the chimney-hood.

On the right protrudes one end of the servants' dinner table of white pine, with some chairs beside it.

The stove is decorated with birch boughs : the floor strewn with twigs of juniper.

On the end of the table is a large Japanese spice-jar filled with lilac blossoms.

A refrigerator, a scullery table, and a washstand.

A large, old-fashioned bell above the door, and on the left of the door a speaking-tube.

Kristin is standing by the stove, frying something in a frying pan. She is wearing a light cotton dress and a cook's apron. Jean comes in, dressed in livery and carrying a pair of large riding boots, with spurs, which he puts down on a conspicuous part of the floor.

JEAN. Lady Julie 's mad again to-night: absolutely mad!

KRISTIN. So you 're back again, are you?

JEAN. I took the count to the station, and as I passed the barn on my way home I went in and danced, and who should I see but the young lady leading the dance with the gamekeeper. But the moment she catches sight of me she rushes straight up to me and asks me to dance the ladies' waltz. And then she danced like—well, I 've never seen the like of it. She 's mad!

KRISTIN. That she 's always been, but never like this last fort-night since the engagement was broken off.

JEAN. I wonder what really was at the bottom of that affair! A fine fellow, wasn't he, though not well off. Oh, but they 're

17

so full of whims! [*Sits down at the end of the table.*] Anyhow,
it 's curious that a young lady—ahem!—should prefer to stay
at home with the servants—eh?—rather than go with her
father to see her relations?

KRISTIN. I expect she feels a bit shy after that set-to with her
young man.

JEAN. Very likely! Anyhow, he could hold his own—that
young fellow! Do you know how it happened, Kristin? I
saw it myself, though I didn't want to let them see I did.

KRISTIN. You saw it, did you?

JEAN. I did. They were in the stable-yard one evening and our
young lady was 'training' him, as she called it. D' you know
what that was? Why, she was making him jump over her
riding-whip the way you teach a dog to jump. Twice he
jumped, and got a cut with the whip each time; but the third
time he snatched the whip from her and broke it into a thousand pieces. And then he went off.

KRISTIN. So that 's how it was! Well, I never!

JEAN. Yes, that 's how that was! But what have you got for
me there, Kristin?

KRISTIN. [*Putting what she has cooked on a plate and placing it in
front of Jean.*] Oh, just a little kidney that I cut from the
veal!

JEAN. [*Smelling the food.*] Splendid! My great *délice*! [*Feeling
the plate.*] But you might have warmed the plate!

KRISTIN. Well, if you aren't more fussy than the count himself
—when you give your mind to it!   [*Pulls his hair gently.*

JEAN. [*Annoyed.*] Don't go pulling my hair! You know how
sensitive I am.

KRISTIN. There, there now! It was only love, you know!
            [*Jean begins to eat. Kristin opens a bottle of beer.*

JEAN. Beer? On Midsummer Eve? No, thank you! *I* 've
got something better than that! [*Opens a drawer in the table
and takes out a bottle of red wine with yellow seal.*] Yellow seal,
you observe! Now give me a glass. A wineglass, of course,
when one drinks *neat*!

KRISTIN. [*Goes back to the stove and puts a small saucepan on it.*]
Lord help the woman who gets *you* for a husband! Such an
old fusser!

JEAN. Oh nonsense! You 'd be glad enough to get such a smart
fellow as I am! I don't think it 's done you much harm *my*
being known as your sweetheart! [*Tastes the wine.*] Fine!

JEAN. *[Gallantly.]* Have the ladies some secret between them?

JULIE *[Striking him in the face with her handkerchief.]* Don't be inquisitive!

JEAN. Oh, what a lovely smell of violets!

JULIE. *[Coquettishly.]* What impudence! So you 're an expert in scents too, are you? Dancing you 're certainly good at. . . . There now, don't peep! Go away!

JEAN *[Pertly, but politely.]* Is it some witches' broth for Midsummer Eve you ladies are brewing? Something to tell one's fortune by in the star of fate, and so behold one's future love?

JULIE. *[Sharply.]* You 'd want good eyes to see *that*! *[To Kristin.]* Put it into a pint bottle and cork it well. Now come and dance a schottische with me, Jean.

JEAN. *[Hesitating.]* I don't want to be rude to anybody, but I 'd promised Kristin this dance——

JULIE. Well, but she can have another instead—can't you, Kristin? Won't you lend me Jean?

KRISTIN. That 's not for me to say. Since the young lady is so condescending it isn't for him to say no. Be off, now! And be thankful for the honour.

JEAN. Speaking frankly—no offence meant of course—I 'm wondering if it 's wise of Lady Julie to dance twice running with the same partner, especially as people here are only too ready to put their own construction on——

JULIE. *[Flaring up.]* What do you mean? What sort of construction? What are you hinting at?

JEAN. *[Submissively.]* As you won't understand I must speak more plainly. It doesn't look well to prefer one of your dependents to others who are expecting the same unusual honour——

JULIE. Prefer! What an idea! I 'm surprised at you! I, the mistress of the house, honour the servants' ball with my presence, and now that I really do want to dance I intend to dance with someone who can guide and not make me look ridiculous.

JEAN. Just as you wish, Lady Julie! I am at your service.

JULIE. *[Gently.]* Don't take it as a command! To-night we 're happy people enjoying a holiday, and all questions of rank are set aside! Now give me your arm. Don't worry, Kristin! I shan't take your sweetheart away from you!

[Jean offers her his arm and leads her out.

Remarkably fine! Might be just a shade warmer! [*Warm the glass in his hands.*] We bought this at Dijon, four fran the litre—without the bottle; and then there was the duty! What are you cooking there—making that infernal smell?

KRISTIN. Oh, some devil's stuff Lady Julie wants for Diana.

JEAN. You should be more refined in your language, Kristin! But why should you have to cook for that cur on the eve of a holiday? Is the dog ill then?

KRISTIN. Yes, she's ill! She's been sneaking about with the pug at the lodge—and now things have gone wrong—and that, you see, the young lady won't hear of.

JEAN. The young lady is too stuck up in some ways and not enough in others—just like the countess was while she was alive. She was at home in the kitchen and the cow-sheds, yet she would never go out driving with one horse only; she went about with dirty cuffs, but she would have the coronet on the buttons. Our young lady—to come back to her—doesn't take any care about herself or her person. I might almost say that she's not refined. When she was dancing in the barn just now she snatched away the gamekeeper from Anna's side and actually asked him to dance with her. We shouldn't do that sort of thing ourselves; but that's what happens when the gentry try to behave like common people: they *become* common. But she's a fine woman! Magnificent! Ah, what shoulders? And—and so on!

KRISTIN. Now then, don't overdo it! Clara has dressed her, and I know what she says.

JEAN. Oh, Clara! You're always jealous of each other! But I've been out riding with her. . . . And look at her dancing!

KRISTIN. Now then, Jean! Won't you dance with me when I'm ready?

JEAN. Of course I will.

KRISTIN. Promise?

JEAN. Promise? If I say I will, of course I will! Well, thanks for the supper. It was very nice!

[*Replaces the cork in the bottle.*

JULIE. [*In the doorway, speaking to someone outside.*] Go on. I'll join you in a minute.

[*Jean slips the bottle into the drawer and rises respectfully.*
[*Julie comes in and goes up to Kristin by the looking-glass.*
Well, have you finished it?

[*Kristin makes a sign that Jean is present.*

PANTOMIME. *Played as though the actress were really alone. When desirable she turns her back on the audience. Does not look towards the spectators. Does not hurry, as though she were afraid the audience might become impatient.*

Kristin alone. Soft violin music in the distance, in schottische time. Kristin, humming the tune, clears the table where Jean has been sitting, washes the plate at the scullery board, dries it, and puts it into a cupboard.

After that she removes her apron, takes out a small looking-glass from a table drawer, and leans it against the jar of lilac on the table. Lights a candle and heats a hairpin, with which she curls her front hair.

Then she goes to the door and listens. Comes back to the table. Discovers the handkerchief which Lady Julie had left behind; picks it up and smells it. Then she spreads it out abstractedly, pulls it straight, smooths it and folds it in four, and so on.

JEAN. [*Coming in alone.*] Well, she really *is* mad! The way she danced! With everybody standing behind the doors grinning at her. What do you think about it, Kristin?

KRISTIN. Oh, she's not very well just now. And that always makes her a bit queer. But won't you come and dance with me now?

JEAN. You aren't angry with me for throwing you over——

KRISTIN. Of course not—not for a little thing like that. Besides, I know my place——

JEAN. [*Putting his arm round her waist.*] You're a sensible girl, Kristin, and you ought to make a good wife——

JULIE. [*Comes in, unpleasantly surprised; with assumed jocularity.*] Well, you *are* a nice cavalier, running away from your lady!

JEAN. On the contrary, Lady Julie; I have, as you see, hurried back to find the one I deserted!

JULIE. [*Changing her note.*] Do you know there's not a man that can dance like you!—But why are you in livery on a holiday evening? Take it off at once!

JEAN. Then I must ask you to go away for a moment; my black coat is hanging up here.

[*Indicates the place and goes towards the right.*

JULIE. Are you shy because of me? Just changing your coat? Go into your room then, and come back. Or you can stay here, and I'll turn my back.

JEAN. With your permission, Lady Julie!
> [*Goes towards the light. One of his arms is visible while he changes his coat.*

JULIE. [*To Kristin.*] Tell me, Kristin: is Jean engaged to you that he's so intimate?

KRISTIN. Engaged? Yes, if you like! We call it that.

JULIE. Call?

KRISTIN. But you've been engaged yourself, my lady, and——

JULIE. Yes, we were properly engaged——

KRISTIN. But it didn't come to anything for all that——
> [*Jean comes in, in a black frock-coat and black bowler.*

JULIE. *Très gentil, monsieur Jean! Très gentil!*

JEAN. *Vous voulez plaisanter, madame!*

JULIE. *Et vous voulez parler français!* Where did you learn that?

JEAN. In Switzerland, while I was acting as *sommelier* at one of the largest hotels in Lucerne.

JULIE. But you look like a gentleman in that frock-coat! *Charmant!* [*Sits down at the table.*

JEAN. Oh, you flatter me!

JULIE. [*Offended.*] Flatter you?

JEAN. My natural modesty does not permit me to think that you are paying genuine compliments to one in my position. Consequently I take the liberty of assuming that you were exaggerating or, in other words, flattering.

JULIE. Where did you learn to make speeches like that? I suppose you've been to the theatre a great deal?

JEAN. I have indeed! I've been about a lot, I have!

JULIE. But you were born in this neighbourhood?

JEAN. My father was a labourer on the district attorney's estate close by. I must have seen you as a child, though you never took any notice of me!

JULIE. Well really!

JEAN. Yes, I remember one occasion especially.... No, I can't tell you about that!

JULIE. Oh, but do! Yes, just for once!

JEAN. No, I really cannot now! Another time, perhaps.

JULIE. Another time means no time. Is it so risky now?

JEAN. Not risky at all; but I'd rather not. Look at her there!
> [*Points to Kristin, who has fallen asleep on a chair by the stove.*

JULIE. She'll make a nice sort of wife! Perhaps she snores too?

JEAN. No, but she talks in her sleep.

JULIE. [*Sarcastically.*] How do you know she talks in her sleep?
JEAN. [*Impudently.*] I 've heard her!

[*A pause during which they look at each other.*

JULIE. Why don't you sit down?
JEAN. I cannot take that liberty in your presence!
JULIE. But if I order you to?
JEAN. Then I obey.
JULIE. Sit down then! No, wait! Can you give me something to drink first?
JEAN. I don't know what we 've got here in the refrigerator. I fancy it 's only beer.
JULIE. Don't say *only* beer! My tastes are simple and I prefer it to wine.
JEAN. [*Takes a bottle of beer from the refrigerator and opens it; fetches a glass and a plate from the cupboard and serves the beer.*] Allow me!
JULIE. Thank you! Won't you have some yourself?
JEAN. I am not very fond of beer, but if your ladyship commands——
JULIE. Commands? I imagine that a polite cavalier would keep his lady company.
JEAN. Very true! [*Opens a bottle and fetches a glass.*
JULIE. Drink my health now!

[*Jean hesitates.*

I really believe the fellow 's shy!
JEAN. [*Kneeling, and raising his glass with mock solemnity.*] To the health of my lady!
JULIE Bravo! Now you must kiss my shoe too, and then everything will be quite perfect.

[*Jean hesitates. Then he takes hold of her foot boldly and kisses it lightly.*

Splendid! You ought to have been an actor.
JEAN. [*Getting up.*] This can't go on any longer, my lady! Somebody may come in and see us.
JULIE. What would that matter?
JEAN. People would talk—that 's all! If you only knew how their tongues went, up there just now, you——
JULIE. What sort of things did they say? Tell me! Sit down, please.
JEAN. [*Sitting down.*] I don't want to hurt you, but they made use of expressions—which threw suspicions of a kind which . . . well, you can imagine that for yourself. You are no

longer a child, and when a lady is seen drinking alone with a
man—not to say a servant—at night—well——

JULIE. Well, what? Besides, we 're not alone. Kristin is here.

JEAN. Yes, asleep!

JULIE. Then I 'll wake her up. [*Gets up.*] Kristin! Are you
asleep?

KRISTIN. [*In her sleep.*] Bla-bla-bla-bla!

JULIE. Kristin!—What a sleeper!

KRISTIN. [*In her sleep.*] The count's boots are cleaned—put the
coffee on—in one moment—heigh-ho—pouff!

JULIE. [*Taking her by the nose.*] Do wake up!

JEAN. [*Sternly.*] One shouldn't disturb a sleeper!

JULIE. [*Sharply.*] What?

JEAN. A woman who has stood by the stove all day long may
well be tired at night. Besides, one ought to respect sleep. . . .

JULIE. [*Changing her tone.*] A pretty thought: it does you credit!
Thank you. [*Gives Jean her hand.*] Now come out and pick a
few lilacs for me.

[*During the following scene Kristin wakes up and walks
sleepily to the right on her way to bed.*

JEAN. With you, my lady?

JULIE. With me.

JEAN. That won't do! It simply won't!

JULIE. I can't understand your ideas. Is it possible that you 're
imagining something?

JEAN. Not I: the people.

JULIE. What? That I'm in love with my valet?

JEAN. I 'm not a conceited man, but one has seen such cases—
and to the people nothing is sacred!

JULIE. You 're an aristocrat, I suppose!

JEAN. Yes, I am.

JULIE. I 'm stepping down——

JEAN. Take my advice, my lady, and don't step down! No one
will believe that you step down of your own accord. People
will always say that you 're falling down.

JULIE. I have a higher opinion of the people than you have.
Come and put it to the test! Come!

[*She holds him fast with her eye.*

JEAN. You 're very strange, you know!

JULIE. Perhaps, but so are you! Besides, everything is strange!
Life, humanity, everything—slush that is whirled, whirled
along the water, till it sinks, sinks! There 's a dream of mine

which comes back to me now and then; I remember it now.
I have climbed to the top of a pillar, and am sitting there without seeing any possibility of getting down. When I look
down I get dizzy, and yet get down I must, though I haven't
the courage to throw myself down. I can't hold on, and I
long to be able to fall; but I don't fall. And yet I have no
peace till I am down, no rest till I am down, down. on the
ground! And if I did reach the ground I should want to be
down in the earth. . . . Have you ever felt like that?

JEAN. No. I usually dream that I'm lying under a tall tree in
a dark wood. I want to be up, up at the top, to look out over
the bright landscape where the sun is shining, and plunder
the bird's nest where the golden eggs lie. So I climb and
climb, but the stem of the tree is so thick and so smooth, and
it's such a long way to the first branch. But I know that if
I could only reach the first branch I should get to the top as
easily as if I were on a ladder. I have never reached it yet;
but reach it I shall, if only in my dreams!

JULIE. Here I am, chattering to you about dreams! Come now.
Just into the park.

[*She offers him her arm and they go towards the door.*

JEAN. We must sleep on nine midsummer flowers to-night: then
our dreams will come true. Lady Julie!

[*Julie and Jean turn round at the door. Jean puts his hand
up to one eye.*

JULIE. Let me see what you've got in your eye!

JEAN. Oh, it's nothing—just a speck of dust; it'll soon be gone.

JULIE. My sleeve must have brushed against it. Sit down and
I'll help you. [*She takes him by the arm and makes him sit
down ; takes hold of his head and bends it backward ; tries to
remove the dust with the corner of her handkerchief.*] Sit still
now, quite still! [*Slaps him on the hand.*] Do what I tell you
now! I do believe he's trembling, the great big fellow!
[*Feels his biceps.*] And such arms too!

JEAN. [*Warningly.*] Lady Julie!

JULIE. Yes, *Monsieur* Jean!

JEAN. *Attention ! Je ne suis qu'un homme !*

JULIE. *Will* you sit still!—There! Now it's out! Kiss my
hand and say thank you!

JEAN. [*Getting up.*] Lady Julie, listen to me. Kristin has gone
to bed now. Will you listen to me!

JULIE. Kiss my hand first!

JEAN. Listen to me!

JULIE. Kiss my hand first!

JEAN. Very well: but you'll have only yourself to blame!

JULIE. For what?

JEAN. For what? Are you a child at twenty-five? Don't you know it's dangerous to play with fire?

JULIE. Not for me; I'm insured!

JEAN. [*Bluntly.*] No, that you're not! And even if you are, there are inflammable stores close by!

JULIE. Yourself, I suppose?

JEAN. Yes. Not because it is I, but because I'm a young man——

JULIE. Of prepossessing appearance—what incredible conceit! A Don Juan perhaps? Or a Joseph! On my soul, I think you must be a Joseph!

JEAN. Do you think so?

JULIE. I almost fear it!

[*Jean goes boldly up to her and tries to clasp her round the waist to kiss her.*

[*Boxing his ears.*] Impudence!

JEAN. Is that serious or a joke?

JULIE. Serious!

JEAN. Then what happened just before was also serious! Your play is much too serious, and that's the danger of it! Now I'm tired of play and I beg leave to return to my work. The count's boots must be ready in time, and it's long past midnight.

JULIE. Put those boots away!

JEAN. No. This is my work and I must do it. I never undertook to be your playfellow, and I never can be that. I consider myself too good for it!

JULIE. You are proud!

JEAN. In some ways; in other ways not.

JULIE. Have you ever been in love?

JEAN. We don't use that word, but I've been fond of several girls, and once I got ill because I couldn't have the one I wanted; ill, mark you, like the princes in the *Thousand and One Nights* who couldn't eat or drink from sheer love!

JULIE. Who was it?

[*Jean is silent*

Who was it?

JEAN. You can't make me say that.

JULIE. If I ask you as an equal, as a—friend! Who was it?

JEAN. It was you!

JULIE. [*Sitting down.*] How priceless! . . .

JEAN. Yes, if you like! It was ridiculous! That, you see, was
the story which I wouldn't tell you just now, but now I will.

Do you know how the world looks from below? You don't.
Like hawks and falcons, whose backs one rarely sees because
they usually hover above us! I used to live in the labourer's
cottage with seven brothers and sisters and a pig, out in the
grey fields where there wasn't a single tree! But from the
windows I could see the count's park wall with apple-trees
above it. It was the Garden of Eden; and a multitude of
frowning angels with flaming swords stood there keeping
watch over it. But none the less I and some other boys
found the way to the Tree of Life.—You despise me now?

JULIE. Oh, all boys steal apples.

JEAN. You may say that now, but you despise me all the same.
No matter! One day I went into the Paradise with my
mother to weed the onion beds. Close to the garden stood a
Turkish pavilion, shaded by jasmine and overgrown with
honeysuckle. I had no idea what it might be used for, but I
had never seen such a beautiful building. People went in and
out of it, and one day the door was left open. I crept up and
saw the walls covered with pictures of kings and emperors, and
there were red curtains on the windows, with fringes on them
—now you understand what I mean. I— [*Breaks off a lilac
blossom and holds it under Julie's nose.*] I had never been inside
the castle, never seen anything but the church—but this was
more beautiful; and whatever course my thoughts took they
always went back—to that. Then gradually arose the desire
to taste, just for once, the full pleasure of—*enfin*, I crept in,
saw, and admired. Then I heard someone coming! There
was only one exit for members of the family, but for me there
was another and I had to choose that.

[*Julie, who took up the lilac blossom, lets it drop on the table.*
So I took to my heels, plunged through a raspberry bed, darted
across some strawberry beds, and came up on to the rose
terrace. There I caught sight of a pink dress and a pair of
white stockings—that was you. I lay down under a heap of
weeds—right under it, I tell you—under prickly thistles and
damp, evil-smelling earth. And I watched you going about
among the roses, and I thought to myself: 'If it's true that a

thief may enter into heaven and dwell with the angels, it 's
curious that a labourer's child here on God's earth cannot come
into the castle park and play with the count's daughter!'

JULIE. [*Sentimentally.*] Do you think all poor children think
the same as you did then?

JEAN. |*Doubtfully at first, then with conviction.*] All poor—yes—
of course! Of course!

JULIE. It must be terrible to be poor!

JEAN. |*With deep distress, much exaggerated.*] Oh, Lady Julie!
Oh!—A dog may lie on the countess's sofa, a horse be stroked
on the nose by a young lady; but a servant—[*Changes his
tone.*] Well, now and then you find a man with enough stuff
in him to pull himself up into the world; but how often does
that happen? However, do you know what I did next? I
jumped into the millstream with my clothes on, was pulled out,
and got a thrashing. But the following Sunday, when my
father and all the others went off to my grandmother's, I contrived to stay at home. So I washed with soap and hot water,
put on my best clothes, and went to church in order to see you!
I saw you and went home, determined to die; but I wanted to
die beautifully and comfortably, without pain. And then I
remembered that it was dangerous to sleep under an elder bush.
We had a large one, just then in bloom. I robbed it of all it
had, and then made my bed in the oat-chest. Have you
noticed how smooth oats are? Soft to the touch as the human
skin! . . . Well, I shut the lid and closed my eyes; then fell
asleep, and woke up feeling really ill. But I didn't die, as
you see.

What I wanted—I really don't know! There was no hope
of winning you—but you were a sign to me of the hopelessness
of getting out of the circle in which I was born.

JULIE. You tell stories charmingly, you know! Did you ever
go to school?

JEAN. Only for a short time. But I've read a good many novels,
and gone to theatres. Besides that, I've listened to the conversation of refined people; and I've learnt most from them.

JULIE. So you stand about listening to what we say!

JEAN. Certainly! And I've heard a lot, I have, sitting on the
coach-box or rowing the boat. Once I heard your ladyship
and a girl friend . . .

JULIE. Oh? And what did you hear?

JEAN. Well, it 's not very easy to tell you; but I must say I was rather surprised; I couldn't think where you'd learnt all those words. Perhaps, at bottom, there isn't so much difference as one thinks between one human being and another

JULIE. For shame! We don't behave like you when we're engaged.

JEAN. [*Looking hard at her.*] Is that a fact? Really, I shouldn't bother to make yourself out so innocent. . . .

JULIE. The man I gave my love to was a scoundrel.

JEAN. That's what you always say—afterwards.

JULIE. Always?

JEAN. Always, I believe—since I've heard the expression several times before on similar occasions.

JULIE. What sort of occasions?

JEAN. Like the one in question! The last time——

JULIE. [*Getting up.*] Stop! I won't hear any more!

JEAN. *She* didn't want to either—strange to say. Now may I go to bed?

JULIE. [*Gently.*] Go to bed on Midsummer Eve?

JEAN. Yes! Dancing with the riff-raff up there doesn't really amuse me.

JULIE. Get the key of the boat-house and take me out for a row on the lake; I want to see the sunrise!

JEAN. Is that prudent?

JULIE. That sounds as if you were anxious about your reputation!

JEAN. Why not? I don't want to be ridiculous. I don't want to be discharged without a character when I want to settle down. Moreover, I feel that I am more or less under an obligation to Kristin.

JULIE. Oh, so it's Kristin then. . . .

JEAN. Yes, but you too. Take my advice and go to bed!

JULIE. Am I to obey you?

JEAN. For once; for your own sake! I implore you! The night is far gone, sleepiness intoxicates, and one's head grows hot! Go to bed! Besides, if I'm not mistaken, I hear the people coming this way to look for me. If they find us here you're lost!

The Chorus approaches, singing:

'Two wives from the woods came walking,
   Tridiridi-ralla tridiridi-ra.
And one had a hole in her stocking,
   Tridiridi-ralla-la.

    'Their talk was of hundreds of dalers,
      Tridiridi-ralla tridiridi-ra.
    Yet between them they 'd hardly a daler,
      Tridiridi-ralla-ra.

    'No garland need I give you,
      Tridiridi-ralla-tridiridi-ra.
    For another, alas, I must leave you,
      Tridiridi-ralla, ra!'

JULIE. I know my people and I love them, as they love me. Let them come and you 'll see!

JEAN No, Lady Julie, they don't love you. They accept your food, but they spit at it! Believe me! Listen to them: just listen to what they 're singing! No, don't listen to them!

JULIE. What are they singing?

JEAN. Some scurrilous verses! About you and me!

JULIE. Abominable! How disgraceful! And how sneaking!

JEAN. The rabble are always cowardly. In this sort of fight one can only run away!

JULIE. Run away? But where? We can't go out by the door! And we can't get into Kristin's room!

JEAN. Very well! Into mine then! Necessity knows no law. Besides, you can trust me, your true, sincere, and respectful friend!

JULIE. But think—think if they should look for you there!

JEAN. I shall bolt the door, and if they try to break in I shall shoot! Come! [*On his knees.*] Come!

JULIE. [*Meaningly.*] Will you promise? . . .

JEAN. I swear it!

    [*Julie goes out quickly to the right, Jean follows her excitedly.*

BALLET. *The peasants enter, in holiday attire, with flowers in their hats. A fiddler leads the procession. A barrel of small beer and a keg of spirits, decorated with greenery, are placed on the table. Glasses are fetched and drinking begins. Then they form a circle and sing and dance to the tune ' Two wives from the woods came walking.'*

When this is finished they leave the room, singing.

Julie comes in alone ; gazes on the havoc made of the kitchen ; claps her hands together. Then she takes her powder-puff and powders her face.

JEAN. [*Comes in excitedly*.] There, you see! And you heard too!
Do you think it possible to remain here?

JULIE. No, I do not. But what are we to do?

JEAN. Run away, travel, far away from here!

JULIE. Travel? Yes, but where?

JEAN. To Switzerland, to the Italian lakes; you 've never been
there, have you?

JULIE. No. Is it nice there?

JEAN. Ah! It 's eternal summer—orange-trees, laurels! Glorious!

JULIE. But what are we to do when we get there?

JEAN. I 'll start a hotel: first-class accommodation and first-
class customers.

JULIE. A hotel?

JEAN. Yes, there 's life for you! New faces continually, and
new languages; not a minute's leisure for brooding or nerves;
no worrying about something to do—the work makes itself:
bells that ring night and day, whistling trains and buses coming and going; and gold pieces rolling along the counter.
There 's life for you!

JULIE. Yes, that is life. And what about me?

JEAN. Mistress of the house, chief ornament of the firm. With
your looks . . . and your style—oh—success is a certainty!
Magnificent! You sit like a queen in the office and set your
slaves in motion by pressing an electric button; the guests file
past your throne and shyly place their treasures on your table
—you can't imagine how people tremble when they get a bill
in their hands—I 'll salt the accounts and you shall sugar them
with your prettiest smiles—ah, let 's get away from here.
[*Takes a time-table out of his pocket*.] At once, by the next train!
We 're in Malmö at six-thirty; Hamburg eight-forty in the
morning; Frankfort–Basle in a day, and Como, by the St.
Gothard line, in—let me see—three days. Three days!

JULIE. That 's all very well! But, Jean—you must give me
courage—tell me that you love me! Come and put your arms
around me!

JEAN. [*Hesitating*.] I should like to—but I dare not! Not
again in this house. I love you, Lady Julie! Without doubt
—can you doubt it?

JULIE. [*Shyly, with true womanly feeling*.] Lady Julie! Call me
Julie! There are no longer any barriers between us two!—
Call me Julie!

JEAN. [*Uneasily*.] I cannot! There are barriers still between us, as long as we stay in this house.   There is the past, there is the count—I have never met any one for whom I felt such respect: I've only to see his gloves lying on a chair and I feel small: I've only to hear his bell upstairs and I start like a shying horse: and now when I see his boots standing there so stiff and proud, I feel my back beginning to bend! [*Kicks the boots.*] Superstition, prejudice, taught us from childhood—but as easily forgotten again.   Only come to another country, a republic, and they'll bow to the earth before my porter's livery.   Bow to the earth, I tell you! But *I* shall not! I am not born to bow to the earth; for there's stuff in me—there is character; and if only I can set my foot on the first branch you shall see me climb! To-day I'm a valet, but next year I shall be a man of property: in ten years I shall be living on my own dividends: and then I shall go to Roumania, get myself an order, and may—mark you, I say *may*—end my days as a count!

JULIE. Splendid! Splendid!

JEAN. Oh, in Roumania one can buy the title, so you'll be a countess after all! My countess!

JULIE. What does all that matter to me?   I'm putting it all behind me now! Say that you love me, or—if you don't—what am I?

JEAN. I'll say it, a thousand times—later on! But not here! And above all, no sentiment, if everything is not to be lost! We must take the matter coolly like sensible people. [*Takes a cigar, cuts it and lights it.*] Now you sit there, and I'll sit here; then we can talk as if nothing had happened.

JULIE. [*In despair.*] My God! Have you no feelings, then?

JEAN. I? No man is more full of feeling than I am; but I'm able to control myself.

JULIE. Just now you could kiss my shoe—and now?

JEAN. [*Hardly.*] Yes, then! Now we've got something else to think of.

JULIE. Don't speak cruelly to me!

JEAN. No, but sensibly. One folly has been committed—don't commit more! The count may be here any moment, and before he comes our fates must be settled. What do you think of my plans for the future? Do you approve of them?

JULIE. They seem to me quite reasonable; but just one question: so large an undertaking requires considerable capital; have you got that?

JEAN. [*Chewing his cigar.*] Have I? Certainly I have! I have my professional skill, my unrivalled experience, my knowledge of languages! That's the sort of capital that counts, I should think!

JULIE. But you can't even buy a railway ticket with that.

JEAN. No doubt; that's why I'm looking for a partner—one who can advance the capital required!

JULIE. Where can you find one at a moment's notice?

JEAN. It's for you to find one, if you want to be my partner.

JULIE. I can't do that, and I've nothing of my own. [*A pause.*

JEAN. Then the whole thing falls to the ground——

JULIE. And——

JEAN. All remains as before!

JULIE. Do you think I'm going to remain under this roof as your mistress? Do you think I'll have the people pointing their fingers at me? Do you think I can look my father in the face after this? No! Take me away from here—away from this humiliation and disgrace! O God, God, what have I done? [*Weeps.*

JEAN. So that's the tune now—what have you done? What many have done before you!

JULIE. [*Screaming hysterically.*] And now you despise me! I'm falling, I'm falling!

JEAN. Fall down to my level, and I'll lift you up again!

JULIE. What dreadful power drew me towards you? The attraction of the weak to the strong? Of the falling to the rising? Or was it love? *This* love? Do you know what love is?

JEAN. Do I? You bet I do! Do you think I've never been with a girl before?

JULIE. What a way to speak! What thoughts to have!

JEAN. That's how I've been brought up and that's what I am! Now don't be hysterical, and don't give yourself airs, for we're both in the same boat now! There, little girl, let me give you a glass of something special!

[*Opens the table drawer and takes out the bottle of wine; fills the two glasses which had been used before.*

JULIE. Where did you get that wine from?

JEAN. The wine-cellar!

JULIE. My father's burgundy!

JEAN. Isn't it good enough for his son-in-law?

JULIE. And I drink beer myself!

JEAN. That merely shows your tastes are worse than mine.

JULIE. Thief!

JEAN. Are you going to give me away?

JULIE. Oh, oh! The accomplice of a house-thief! Have I been drunk, have I been walking in dreams to-night? Midsummer Eve! The feast of innocent pleasures. . . .

JEAN. Innocent; h'm!

JULIE. [*Pacing backwards and forwards.*] Is there a human being on earth so wretched as I am now?

JEAN. Why should you be? After such a conquest! Think of Kristin in there! Can't you imagine that she has her feelings too?

JULIE. I thought so just now, but I no longer think so! No, a menial is a menial——

JEAN. And a whore 's a whore!

JULIE. [*On her knees, with hands clasped together.*] O God in heaven, put an end to my miserable life! Take me away from this filth in which I am sinking! Save me! Save me!

JEAN. I can't deny that I feel sorry for you! When I lay in the onion bed and saw you in the rose-garden, I . . . I can tell you now . . . I had the same ugly thoughts as other boys.

JULIE. You, who wanted to die because of me!

JEAN. In the oat-chest? That was all humbug.

JULIE. In other words, a lie!

JEAN. [*Beginning to feel sleepy.*] Next door to it! Probably I read the story in some paper—about a chimney-sweep who shut himself up in a wood-chest full of lilac blossoms because he was sued in some maintenance case. . . .

JULIE. So that 's the sort of man you are. . . .

JEAN. I had to invent something; it 's always the pretty speeches that capture women!

JULIE. Scoundrel!

JEAN. Filth!

JULIE. And now you 've seen the hawk's back!

JEAN. Not exactly its *back*!

JULIE. And I was to be the first branch . . .

JEAN. But the branch was rotten . . .

JULIE. I was to be the signboard at the hotel . . .

JEAN. And I the hotel . . .

JULIE. Sit inside your office, lure your customers, falsify their accounts . . .

JEAN. *I* was to do that.

JULIE. To think that a human soul could be so steeped in filth!

JEAN. Wash it then!

JULIE. You lackey, you menial, stand up when I 'm speaking!

JEAN. You mistress of a menial, you lackey's wench, hold your jaw and get out! Are you the one to come and lecture me on my coarseness? No one in my class has ever behaved so coarsely as you have to-night. Do you think any servant girl attacks a man as you did? Have you ever seen a girl of my class throw herself at a man like that? I have only seen that sort of thing among beasts and fallen women!

JULIE. [*Crushed.*] That 's right; strike me; trample on me; I deserve it all. I 'm a vile creature; but help me! Help me out of this, if there *is* any way out!

JEAN. [*More gently.*] I 've no wish to lower myself by denying my own share in the honour of being the seducer. But do you imagine that any one in my position would have dared to look at you if you hadn't invited it yourself? Even now I am astounded . . .

JULIE. And proud . . .

JEAN. Why not? Though I must confess the conquest was too easy to carry me off my feet.

JULIE. Go on striking me!

JEAN. [*Getting up.*] No! Rather forgive me for what I have said! I don't strike the defenceless—least of all a woman. I can't deny that in one way I am glad to have discovered that what dazzled us below was merely tinsel: to have discovered that the hawk's back, too, was only grey, that the delicate complexion was mere powder, that the polished nails might have black edges, that the handkerchief was dirty, scented though it was! . . . On the other hand, it pains me to find that what I myself was striving to reach was not something higher, something more substantial; it pains me to see you sunk to a level far below that of your own cook; it pains me like the sight of autumn flowers lashed to pieces by the rain and turned into mud.

JULIE. You speak as if you already stood above me?

JEAN. And so I do. I could make you a countess, you see, but you could never make me a count.

JULIE. But I am the child of a count; you can never be that!

JEAN. True; but I might be the father of counts—if . . .

JULIE. But you are a thief. I am not that.

JEAN. There are worse things than being a thief! There are

lower levels than that! Besides, when I serve in a house I regard myself to some extent as a member of the family, or one of the children; one doesn't count it theft when children filch a berry from loaded bushes! [*His passion wakens again.*] Lady Julie, you 're a splendid woman, far too good for a man like me! You 've been the prey of an intoxication, and you want to conceal the mistake by persuading yourself that you love me! That you do not do, unless possibly my outward appearance attracts you—in which case your love is no higher than mine—but I could never be content with being a mere animal for you, and your love I can never awaken.

JULIE. Are you sure of that?

JEAN. You mean that it might be possible!—My ability to love you, yes, without doubt! You are beautiful, you are refined— [*Goes up to her and takes her hand.*] cultivated, amiable when you like, and the flame that is roused by you in a man will probably never be quenched. [*Puts his arm round her waist.*] You 're like mulled wine with strong spices in it, and a kiss from you . . .
          [*He tries to lead her out ; but she frees herself gently.*

JULIE. Leave me! You won't win me in that fashion!

JEAN. *How* then?—Not in that fashion! Not by caresses and pretty speeches; not by thought for the future, by saving you from disgrace! *How* then?

JULIE. How? How? I don't know. Not in any way! I loathe you as I loathe rats, but I can't escape you!

JEAN. Escape *with* me!

JULIE. [*Drawing herself up.*] Escape? Yes, we must escape! But I 'm so tired! Give me a glass of wine.
          [*Jean fills her glass.*
[*Looking at her watch.*] But we must talk first; we 've still a little time left.
          [*Drinks the wine and holds out her glass for more.*

JEAN. Don't drink so immoderately—it will go to your head!

JULIE. What if it does?

JEAN. What if it does? It 's vulgar to get drunk! What was it you wanted to say?

JULIE. We must fly! But we must talk first; that is, I must talk; so far you have done all the talking. You 've told me the story of your life; now I want to tell you mine; then we shall know each other thoroughly before we begin our travels together.

JEAN. One moment! Pardon me! Consider whether you won't regret it afterwards when you 've laid bare the secrets of your life.

JULIE. Aren't you my friend?

JEAN. Yes, sometimes. But don't rely on me.

JULIE. You don't really mean that. Besides, my secrets are already common property. You see, my mother was of plebeian birth, the daughter of quite simple people. She was brought up according to the theories of her time as regards equality, woman's liberty, and all that sort of thing; and she had a decided objection to marriage. So when my father made love to her, she said she could never marry him, but . . . she did marry him all the same. I came into the world— against my mother's wishes, so far as I can make out. My mother wanted to bring me up as a child of nature: I was even to learn everything a boy learns, to become a proof that a woman is as good as a man. I had to go about dressed as a boy and learn how to handle a horse; but I wasn't allowed in the cowshed, I was made to groom and harness and go out hunting; I even had to try and learn farming! On our estate men were given women's work to do, and women men's—the result being that the property was on the verge of ruin and we became the laughing-stock of the neighbourhood. In the end my father must have wakened from the spell; he rebelled, and everything was altered to suit his wishes. My mother was taken ill—what it was I don't know—but she frequently had convulsive attacks, used to hide in the attic or in the garden, and sometimes stayed out all night. Then came the great fire which you have heard about. The house, the stables, and the farm-buildings were burnt down, and in circumstances which led one to suspect that the fire was no accident; for the disaster occurred the very day after the quarterly insurance premium had expired, and the new premium sent by my father was delayed by the messenger's carelessness, so that it arrived too late.   [She fills her glass and drinks.

JEAN. Don't drink any more!

JULIE. Oh, what does it matter? We had absolutely nowhere to go, and had to sleep in the carriages. My father didn't know where to get money for rebuilding the house. Then my mother advised him to try and borrow from a friend whom she had known in her youth, a brick manufacturer near here. My father borrowed the money, without having to pay any

interest, which surprised him.   And so the estate was rebuilt.
[*Drinks again.*] Do you know who burnt it down?

JEAN. The countess, your mother!

JULIE. Do you know who the brick manufacturer was?

JEAN. Your mother's lover?

JULIE. Do you know who the money belonged to?

JEAN. Wait a little—no, I don't know!

JULIE. It was my mother's!

JEAN. The count's, then—if there was no settlement?

JULIE. There was no settlement.   My mother had a little money
of her own, which she didn't want to be under my father's
control, so she deposited it with—her friend!

JEAN. Who pinched it!

JULIE. Quite so! He kept it! All this comes to my father's
knowledge; he can't bring an action; nor pay his wife's lover;
nor prove that the money was hers!   That was my mother's
revenge on him for assuming control over the household   At
that time he was on the point of shooting himself!   Rumour
said that he tried and failed.   But he took a new lease of life,
and my mother had to pay dearly for her conduct!   You can
imagine what those five years were for me!   I sympathized with
my father, but I took my mother's side nevertheless, because
I didn't know the circumstances.   From her I had learnt to
mistrust and hate men—for she hated men, as you know—
and I swore to her that I would never be the slave of a man.

JEAN. So you became engaged to the district attorney!

JULIE. Merely that he should be my slave.

JEAN. And that he wouldn't be?

JULIE. Oh, he wanted it all right, but he didn't get the chance.
I got bored with him!

JEAN. I saw that—in the stable yard!

JULIE. What did you see?

JEAN. What I did!—How he broke off the engagement.

JULIE. That is a lie! It was I who broke it off! Has he been
saying that he did it—the scoundrel?

JEAN. Oh, I don't think he was a scoundrel! You hate men,
Lady Julie?

JULIE. Yes, for the most part! But sometimes—when weakness
comes—oh, the shame of it!

JEAN. You hate me too?

JULIE. Beyond words! I should like to have you killed like a
wild beast.

JEAN. Just as one shoots a mad dog. Is that what you mean?

JULIE. Yes, just that!

JEAN. But now there's nothing here to shoot with—and no dog! What are we to do then?

JULIE. Travel!

JEAN. And plague each other to death?

JULIE. No—enjoy ourselves, for a day or two, for a week, for as long as one can enjoy oneself, and then—die——

JEAN. Die? How stupid! In that case I think it's better to start a hotel——

JULIE. [*Paying no attention.*]—by Lake Como, where the sun is always shining, where the laurels are green at Christmas and the oranges glow.

JEAN. Lake Como is a rainy hole, and I never saw any oranges there except at the grocer's. But it's a good place for strangers, as there are lots of villas to be let to loving couples, a most paying industry—do you know why? Why, because the contract is for six months and they leave after three weeks!

JULIE. Why after three weeks?

JEAN. They quarrel, of course! But the rent has to be paid just the same! Then one lets again. So it goes on and on, for there's love enough—even if it doesn't last very long!

JULIE. You don't want to die with me?

JEAN. I don't want to die at all! Not only because I am fond of life, but because I regard self-murder as a crime against the providence which has given us life.

JULIE. You believe in God—you?

JEAN. Certainly I do! And I go to church every other Sunday. And now, to tell the truth, I'm tired of all this and I'm going to bed.

JULIE. Indeed! And you think I shall be content with that? Do you know what a man owes the woman he has brought to shame?

JEAN. [*Takes out his purse and throws a silver coin on the table.*] There you are! I don't want to have any debts!

JULIE. [*Pretending not to notice the insult.*] Do you know what the law lays down?

JEAN. Unfortunately the law lays down no penalty for the woman who seduces a man!

JULIE. Do you see any way out other than going abroad, marrying, and then getting a divorce?

JEAN. And suppose I refuse to enter into this *mésalliance*?

JULIE. *Mésalliance*!

JEAN. Yes, for me! For, mark you! I'm better bred than you are; my pedigree contains no woman guilty of arson!

JULIE. Can you be sure of that?

JEAN. You can't be sure of the opposite, since we have no family records—except at the police-station! But your family records I have seen in a book on the drawing-room table. Do you know who the founder of your family was? A miller who let the king sleep with his wife one night during the Danish war. I have no ancestors of that sort! I haven't any ancestors at all, but I can become one myself!

JULIE. That's what I get for opening my heart to one who is unworthy of it, for sacrificing the honour of my family.

JEAN. Dishonour!—Now what did I tell you? People shouldn't drink—it makes them garrulous! And one must *not* be garrulous!

JULIE. Oh, how I regret what has happened!—how bitterly I regret it!—And if you had only loved me!

JEAN. For the last time—what do you mean? Do you want me to weep, to jump over your riding-whip, to kiss you? Do you want me to lure you away to Lake Como for three weeks, and then? . . . What am I to do? What do you want? This is getting rather painful! It always does when one goes and sticks one's nose into women's affairs! Lady Julie! I can see that you're unhappy: I know that you're suffering: but I cannot understand you. *We* don't have any of these whims; *we* don't hate one another! We make love for fun when our work gives us time; but we don't have time all day and all night, as you do! I think you're ill; I'm sure you're ill.

JULIE. Then you must be kind to me; and now you *are* talking like a human being.

JEAN. Yes, but be human yourself! You spit on me, and then forbid me to wipe it off—on you!

JULIE. Help me, help me! Only tell me what to do—where to go!

JEAN. O Lord! if I only knew myself!

JULIE. I've been mad—raving mad! But is there no possible escape?

JEAN. Keep still and be calm! Nobody knows anything.

JULIE. Impossible! The people know, and Kristin knows!

JEAN. They don't know: they could never believe such a thing!

JULIE. [*Hesitating.*] But—it might happen again!

JEAN. That is true!

JULIE. And the consequences?

JEAN. [*Frightened.*] The consequences?—Where *were* my wits, that I never thought of that? Yes, there's only one thing to do—you must go! At once! I shan't go with you or all would be lost. You must travel alone—abroad—anywhere!

JULIE. Alone? Where?—I can't do that!

JEAN. You must! And before the count comes back! If you stay here you know what will happen! Once one has done wrong one wants to go on with it, since the harm is already done. . . . So one gets more and more reckless and—at last one is found out! So you must go! Afterwards you can write to the count and confess everything, except that it was me! And that I don't think he'd guess! Nor do I think he'd be very pleased to know it!

JULIE. I'll go if you come with me!

JEAN. Are you mad, woman? Lady Julie running away with her valet! It would be in the papers the next day, and the count would never survive it!

JULIE. I can't go! I can't stay here! Help me! I am so tired, so unutterably tired. Order me! Set me in motion! I can no longer think, nor act! . . .

JEAN. There, now! What a wretched creature you are! Why do you give yourselves airs and turn up your noses as if you were the lords of creation? Very well then—I'll give you your orders! Go upstairs and dress; provide yourself with money for the journey, and then come down again!

JULIE. [*Half whispering.*] Come upstairs with me!

JEAN. To your room?—Now you're mad again! [*Hesitates a moment.*] No! Go, at once! [*Takes her hand and leads her out.*

JULIE. [*On her way out.*] Do speak kindly to me, Jean!

JEAN. An order always sounds unkind; you can feel that yourself now!

[*Jean alone; he gives a sigh of relief; sits down at the table; takes out a note-book and pencil; adds up figures aloud now and then. Dumb show, till Kristin comes in dressed for church, carrying a dicky and a white tie.*

KRISTIN. Good Lord, what a state the room's in! What have you been up to?

JEAN. Oh, it's the young lady been bringing the people in. Were you so sound asleep you couldn't hear anything?

KRISTIN. I 've slept like a log!

JEAN. And dressed for church already!

KRISTIN. Ye-es! Why you, promised to come to communion with me to-day!

JEAN. Why, so I did!—And I see you 've got the vestments there! Come along then!

> [*Sits down. Kristin begins putting on his dicky and white tie. A pause.*

[*Sleepily.*] What 's the gospel for the day?

KRISTIN. Something about the beheading of John the Baptist, I expect!

JEAN. Awfully long affair that 's sure to be!—Look out, you 're choking me!—Oh, I 'm so sleepy, so sleepy!

KRISTIN. Yes: what have you been doing, sitting up all night? Why, you 're quite green in the face!

JEAN. I 've been sitting here talking to Lady Julie.

KRISTIN. She doesn't know what 's proper, that creature!

> [*A pause.*

JEAN. I say, Kristin!

KRISTIN. Well?

JEAN. It 's queer anyhow, when one comes to think of it! She!

KRISTIN. What is so queer?

JEAN. Everything!
> [*A pause.*

KRISTIN. [*Looking at the glasses standing half empty on the table.*] Have you been drinking together too?

JEAN. Yes!

KRISTIN. For shame!—Look me in the face!

JEAN. Yes!

KRISTIN. Is it possible? *Is* it possible?

JEAN. [*After consideration.*] Yes! It is!

KRISTIN. Faugh! I could never have believed it! Shame! Shame!

JEAN. Surely you 're not jealous of her?

KRISTIN. No, not of her! If it had been Clara or Sophy I 'd have scratched your eyes out!—Yes, that 's how it is: why, I don't know! Oh, but it really was disgusting!

JEAN. Are you angry with her then?

KRISTIN. No, with you! It was wrong, very wrong! Poor girl! No, I tell you I won't stop in this house any longer—where one can't feel any respect for the people in it.

JEAN. Why should one feel respect for them?

KRISTIN. Yes, tell me that, my artful young fellow! But you wouldn't like to be in the service of people who don't live decently, would you? Eh! It lowers one, I think.

JEAN. Yes, but isn't it some consolation to find that the others aren't one scrap better than we are?

KRISTIN. No, I don't think so; for unless they *are* better there's no standard for us to aim at, so as to better ourselves. And think of the count! Think of all the sorrow he's had in his life! No, I won't stay here any longer! With a fellow like you too! If it had been the district attorney: if it had been somebody a little higher .

JEAN. What's that you say?

KRISTIN. Yes, yes! You may be all right in your own way, but there *is* a difference between one class and another all the same. No, this is a thing I can never get over. To think that a young lady who was so proud, so bitter against men, should go and give herself—and to such a man! She who almost had poor Diana shot for running after the lodge-keeper's pug!—Just fancy! But I won't stay here any longer; on the twenty-fourth of October I quit.

JEAN. And then?

KRISTIN. Well, talking of that, it's about time you looked round for a job, if we are going to marry after all.

JEAN. Yes, but what sort of a job? I can't get a place like this when I'm married.

KRISTIN. Of course not! But I suppose you could take a hall-porter's job, or try for a place as commissionaire in some institution. Government rations are scanty, but they're safe and there's a pension for the widow and children . . .

JEAN. [*With a grimace.*] That's all very fine, but it isn't in my line to start thinking so soon about dying for the sake of wife and children. I must admit that I really had slightly higher views.

KRISTIN. Your views indeed! Yes, and your duties too! Don't you forget them!

JEAN. Don't you go irritating me, talking about duties! I know well enough what I ought to do, without your telling me! [*Listens to some sound outside.*] However, we've plenty of time to think over that. Now go and get ready and we'll go to church.

KRISTIN. Who's that walking about upstairs?

JEAN. I don't know, unless it's Clara.

KRISTIN. [*Going out.*] Surely it can't be the count's come home without anybody hearing him?

JEAN. [*Frightened.*] The count? No it can't be him, or he'd have rung.

KRISTIN. [*Going out.*] God help us! I've never seen the like.

[*The sun has now risen and is shining on the tree-tops in the park; the light moves slowly till it falls obliquely through the windows. Jean goes to the doorway and makes a sign.*

[*Julie comes in in travelling dress, carrying a small bird-cage covered with a towel. She places it on a chair.*

JULIE. I'm ready now.

JEAN. Hush! Kristin's awake.

JULIE. [*Extremely nervous during the following scene.*] Did she suspect anything?

JEAN. She knows absolutely nothing! But, good heavens, what a sight you are!

JULIE. A sight? In what way?

JEAN You're as pale as a corpse, and—pardon me, but your face is dirty.

JULIE. Let me wash then!—There! [*Goes to the basin and washes her hands and face.*] Give me a towel! Oh—there's the sun rising!

JEAN. And then the troll bursts!

JULIE. Yes, there've been trolls about to-night! Now, Jean! Come with me: I've got the money.

JEAN. [*Doubtfully.*] Enough?

JULIE. Enough to begin with! Come with me! I can't travel alone to-day. Think of it—Midsummer Day, in a stuffy train, crowded with masses of people all staring at one; standing at stations when one wants to fly. No, I can't do it, I can't do it! And then memories will rise: childhood's memories of midsummer days with the church decked in green—birch leaves and lilac: dinner at the table spread for relations and friends: after dinner the park, with dancing, music, flowers, and games! Ah, one may fly and fly, but one's memories follow in the luggage-van, and remorse, and the pangs of conscience.

JEAN. I'll come with you—but at once, before it's too late. This moment!

JULIE. Go and get ready then! [*Takes up the cage.*

JEAN. No luggage though! That would betray us!

JULIE. No, nothing at all! Only what we can take in the carriage with us.

JEAN. [*Who has got his hat.*] What on earth have you got there? What is it?

JULIE. Only my greenfinch. I don't want to leave her behind!

JEAN. Well, I'm blowed! So we're to take a bird-cage with us, are we? You must be mad! Drop that cage!

JULIE. The only thing of mine I'm taking with me from my home: the only living creature that loves me since Diana proved faithless! Don't be cruel! Let me take her with me!

JEAN. Drop that cage, I tell you—and don't talk so loud! Kristin can hear us!

JULIE. No, I can't leave her in strange hands! I'd rather you killed her!

JEAN. Give me the little beast, then, and I'll wring its neck!

JULIE. Very well, but don't hurt her! Don't—no, I cannot!

JEAN. Bring it here; I can!

JULIE. [*Takes the bird out of the cage and kisses it.*] Oh, my little Serine, must you die then and leave your mistress?

JEAN. Please don't let's have any scenes; your life, your whole future is at stake! Quick now! [*Snatches the bird from her; carries it to the chopping-block, and picks up the kitchen chopper. Lady Julie turns her head away.*] You should have learnt how to kill chickens instead of revolver shooting. [*Brings down the chopper.*] Then you wouldn't faint at the sight of a drop of blood!

JULIE. [*Screaming.*] Kill me too! Kill me! You who can butcher an innocent creature without a quiver! Oh, how I hate you, how I loathe you! There is blood between us! I curse the hour when I first saw you; I curse the hour when I was conceived in my mother's womb!

JEAN. Oh, what's the good of your cursing? Let's go!

JULIE. [*Goes to the chopping-block, as though she were dragged there against her will.*] No, I won't go yet; I cannot . . . I must see . . . Hush! There's a carriage outside. [*Listens to the sounds outside, without taking her eyes off the block and the chopper.*] So you think I can't bear the sight of blood! You think I'm so weak. . . . Oh, how I should love to see your blood, your brains on a chopping-block—to see your whole sex swimming in a sea of blood, like that poor creature. . . . I believe I could drink out of your skull; I would gladly bathe my feet in your breast; I could eat your heart roasted whole! You think I am weak; you think I love you because the fruit of my womb thirsted for your seed; you think I want to carry your offspring beneath my heart, to nourish it with my blood—to bear your child and take your name! By the way, what *is* your name! I 've never heard your surname—probably you haven't got one. I should be 'Mrs. Gatekeeper,' or 'Madam Dunghill'—you dog who wear my collar; you lackey with my crest on your buttons! I to share you with my own cook, to be the rival of my own servant! Oh! Oh! Oh! You think I 'm a coward and want to run away! No, now I 'm going to stay—blow wind, come wrack! My father will come home . . . find his desk broken open . . . his money gone! Then he 'll ring—that bell there . . twice for the valet—and then he 'll send for the police . . . and I shall tell everything! Everything! Oh, how lovely to have an end to it all—if only it could be the end!—And then he 'll get a stroke and die! And that will be the end of all of us . . . and then there will be quiet . . . peace! . . . eternal rest! . . . And then the coat of arms will be broken on the coffin—the count's line is extinct—but the valet's line will continue, in an orphan asylum   win laurels in a gutter, and end in a prison!

JEAN. There speaks the royal blood! Bravo, Lady Julie! Now cram the miller into his sack!

[*Kristin comes in, dressed for church, with a hymn-book in her hand.*

[*Julie hastens up to her and throws herself into her arms, as though seeking protection.*

JULIE. Help me, Kristin! Help me against this man!

KRISTIN. [*Coldly and unmoved.*] What a sight for a holiday morning! [*Looks at the chopping-block.*] And what a filthy mess! What does it all mean? And all this shrieking and hullabaloo!

JULIE. Kristin! You 're a woman, and you 're my friend! Beware of that scoundrel!

JEAN. [*Rather awkward and embarrassed.*] While the ladies are discussing things I 'll go and shave.   [*Slips out to the right.*

JULIE. *You* will understand me; *you* will listen to me!

KRISTIN. No, I really don't understand this sort of underhand business! Where are you off to, dressed up for a journey like that? And he with his hat on! What is it? What is it?

JULIE. Listen, Kristin; listen to me and I 'll tell you everything . . .

KRISTIN. I don't want to know anything . . .

JULIE. You *shall* hear me . . .

KRISTIN. What is it about? Is it about your folly with Jean?

Well, I don't worry about that at all; I 've nothing to do with all that. But if you 're thinking of fooling him into running off with you, why, we 'll soon put a stopper on that!

JULIE. [*Extremely nervous.*] Now try to be calm, Kristin, and listen to me! I can't stay here, and Jean can't stay here—so we must go abroad. . . .

KRISTIN. H'm, h'm!

JULIE. [*Brightening up.*] I 've just got an idea, though—suppose we all three went off—abroad—to Switzerland, and started a hotel together. . . . I 've got money, you see, and Jean and I would be responsible for everything—and you, I thought, could look after the kitchen. . . . Won't that be splendid?. . . Say yes, now! And come with us; then everything will be settled! . . . Now do say yes!

> [*Embraces Kristin and pats her on the shoulder.*

KRISTIN. [*Coldly and thoughtfully.*] H'm, h'm!

JULIE. [*Presto tempo.*] You 've never been abroad, Kristin—you must have a look round the world. You can't imagine what fun it is travelling by train—new people continually—new countries—and then we 'll go to Hamburg and have a look at the Zoological Gardens on our way—you 'll like that—and go to the theatre and hear the opera—and when we get to Munich we shall have the picture galleries! There are Rubenses and Raphaels there—the great painters, you know. You 've heard of Munich, where King Ludwig lived—the king who went mad, you know. And then we 'll see his castle—he still has castles furnished just like they are in fairy tales—and from there it 's not far to Switzerland—and the Alps! Think of the Alps covered with snow in the middle of summer—and oranges grow there, and laurels that are green all the year round. . .

> [*Jean is seen in the right wing, stropping his razor on a strop which he holds between his teeth and his left hand; he listens amused to the conversation and nods approval now and then.*

[*Tempo prestissimo.*] And then we 'll take a hotel—and I shall sit in the office while Jean stands and receives the guests . . . goes out shopping . . . writes letters. There 's life for you! Whistling trains, omnibuses driving up, bells ringing in the bedrooms and the restaurant—and I shall make out the bills —and I know how to salt them too. . . . You can't imagine how timid travellers are when it comes to paying bills! And

you—you will sit in the kitchen as housekeeper in chief. Of
course you won't do any cooking yourself—and you 'll have
to dress neatly and stylishly when you see people—and you,
with your looks—no, I 'm not flattering you—why, you 'll be
able to catch a husband one fine day! A rich Englishman, I
shouldn't wonder—they 're the easy ones to—[*Slackens her
pace.*] catch—and then we 'll get rich—and build ourselves a
villa on Lake Como—of course it rains there a little occasionally
—but—[*Slower.*]—I suppose the sun shines sometimes—however gloomy it seems—and—then—otherwise we can come
home again—and come back—[*A pause.*]—here—or somewhere else——

KRISTIN. Now do you believe all that yourself?

JULIE. [*Crushed.*] Do I believe it myself?

KRISTIN. Yes!

JULIE. [*Wearily.*] I don't know; I don't believe anything now.
[*Sinks down on the bench; puts her head between her arms on the
table.*] I believe in nothing! Nothing whatever!

KRISTIN. [*Turning towards the right, where Jean is standing.*]
Aha, so you were going to run away!

JEAN. [*Disconcerted, putting the razor on the table.*] Run away?
That 's putting it rather strong! You 've heard the young
lady's plan, and though she 's tired now after being up all
night, the plan can quite well be carried out!

KRISTIN. Listen to me now! Did you think I was going to be
cook to that——

JEAN. [*Sharply.*] Kindly use decent language when you 're
speaking to your mistress! Do you understand?

KRISTIN. Mistress!

JEAN. Yes!

KRISTIN. Listen! Just listen to the man!

JEAN. Yes, listen yourself—it would do you good—and talk a
little less! Lady Julie *is* your mistress; you ought to despise
yourself for the same reason that you despise her now!

KRISTIN. I 've always had so much self-respect——

JEAN. That you were able to despise other people!——

KRISTIN. That I have never sunk below my station. You can't
say that the count's cook has had any dealings with the groom
or the swineherd! You can't say that!

JEAN. No, you 've had to do with a fine fellow—luckily for you!

KRISTIN. Yes, he must be a fine fellow to sell the oats from the
count's stable——

JEAN. You 're a nice one to talk about that—getting a commission on the groceries and accepting bribes from the butcher!

KRISTIN. What do you mean?

JEAN. So you can't feel any respect for your mistress now! *You* indeed!

KRISTIN. Are you coming to church now? A good sermon on your fine deeds might do you good!

JEAN. No, I 'm not going to church to-day; you can go alone and confess your own misdeeds.

KRISTIN. Yes, I shall; and I shall come back with enough forgiveness to cover yours too! Our Redeemer suffered and died on the Cross for all our sins, and if we draw nigh to Him in faith and with a penitent heart He will take all our guilt upon Himself.

JEAN. Including grocery peculations?

JULIE. Do you believe that, Kristin?

KRISTIN. That is my living faith, as sure as I 'm standing here; it 's the faith which I learnt as a child, which I have kept from my youth upwards, Lady Julie. Moreover, where sin aboundeth, grace aboundeth also!

JULIE. Oh, if I only had your faith! Oh, if——

KRISTIN. Ah, but you see one can't get that without God's especial grace, and it is not given to all men to obtain that.

JULIE. Who do obtain it then?

KRISTIN. That is the great secret of the operation of grace, Lady Julie. God is no respecter of persons, but the last there shall be first. . . .

JULIE. Well, but in that case He must have respect for the last?

KRISTIN. [*Continuing.*] And it is easier for a camel to go through the eye of a needle than for a rich man to enter the kingdom of heaven! Yes, there you have it, Lady Julie! However, I 'm going now—by myself, and on my way I shall tell the groom not to let anybody have the horses, just in case they should want to get away before the count comes back! Good-bye!

[*Goes.*

JEAN. What a little devil! And all this because of a greenfinch!

JULIE. [*Wearily.*] Never mind the greenfinch! Can you see any way out of this? Any end to it?

JEAN. [*After consideration.*] No!

JULIE. What would you do in my place?

JEAN. In your place? Let me think!—A woman, of noble birth, fallen! I don't know—yes, now I know!

JULIE. [*Takes the razor and makes a gesture.*] Like this?

JEAN. Yes, But I shouldn't myself—note that! There's a difference between us!

JULIE Because you're a man and I'm a woman? What difference does that make?

JEAN. The same difference—as—between a man and a woman!

JULIE. [*Still holding the razor.*] I should like to! But I can't! My father couldn't either, that time when he should have done it.

JEAN. No, he should *not* have done it! He had to get his revenge first.

JULIE. And now my mother gets her revenge, through me.

JEAN. Have you never loved your father, Lady Julie?

JULIE. Yes, most dearly, but I think I must have hated him too! I must have done so without being aware of it! But it was he who brought me up to despise my own sex, as half a woman and half a man! Whose fault is it—what has happened? My father's, my mother's, or my own? My own? But I *have* no own! I haven't a thought that I didn't get from my father, one passion that I didn't get from my mother, and this last idea—about all men being equal—that I got from *him*, my affianced husband—for that reason I call him a scoundrel! How can it be my own fault? To put the blame on Jesus, as Kristin did—no, I'm too proud to do that, and—thanks to my father's teaching—too sensible. And as to a rich man not being able to go to heaven—that is a lie; anyhow Kristin, who has money in the savings-bank, will certainly never get there! Whose fault is it?—What does it matter whose fault it is? After all, it is I who have to bear the blame, to bear the consequences. . .

JEAN. Yes, but——

[*Two sharp rings on the bell, Julie starts to her feet; Jean changes his coat.*

The count is back! Suppose Kristin——

[*Goes to the speaking-tube, taps it and listens.*

JULIE. Has he been to his desk yet?

JEAN. It's Jean, my lord! [*Listens. The audience cannot hear what the count says.*] Yes, my lord! [*Listens.*] Yes, my lord! In one moment! [*Listens.*] At once, my lord! [*Listens.*] Very good! In half an hour!

JULIE. [*Extremely anxious.*] What did he say? My God! What *did* he say?

JEAN. He wants his boots and his coffee in half an hour.

JULIE. In half an hour then! Oh, I 'm so tired; I haven't the strength to do anything: I can't repent, can't run away, can't stay, can't live—can't die! Help me now! Order me, and I 'll obey you like a dog! Do me this last service, save my honour, save his name! You know what I *ought* to will, but cannot. . . . Will it yourself, and command me to carry it out!

JEAN. I don't know—but now *I* can't either—I don't understand —it 's just as if this coat made me—I cannot order you—and now, since the count spoke to me—why—I can't really explain it—but—oh, it 's that devil the lackey working in my back-bone!—I really believe if the count came down now and ordered me to cut my throat I 'd do it on the spot.

JULIE. Then pretend you 're he, and I you!—You showed me how well you could act just now, when you were on your knees —you were the aristocrat then—or—have you never been to the theatre and seen the mesmerist? [*Jean nods.*] He says to his subject: Fetch the broom, and he fetches it. Then he says: Sweep, and the man sweeps——

JEAN. The other man has to be asleep, though!

JULIE. [*As if in a trance.*] I am asleep already—the whole room seems like smoke to me . . . and you look like an iron stove . . . a stove like a man in black clothes and a tall hat—and your eyes are shining like coals when the fire is going out—and your face is a white patch like the ashes—[*The sunlight has now reached the floor and is shining upon Jean.*]—it 's so warm and lovely—[*She rubs her hands as if she were warming them before a fire.*]—and so light—and so peaceful!

JEAN. [*Takes the razor and puts it into her hand.*] There is the broom! Now go, while it 's light—out to the barn—and . . .
[*Whispers in her ear.*

JULIE. [*Waking up.*] Thank you! Now I am going, to rest! But just say—that the first can also obtain the gift of grace. Say it, even if you don't believe it.

JEAN. The first? No, I can't say that!—But stay—Lady Julie —now I know! You 're no longer among the first—you 're among the—last!

JULIE. That is true.—I 'm among the very last; I *am* the last! Oh!—But now I can't go—tell me once more that I 'm to go!

JEAN. No, now I can't either! I can't!

JULIE. And the first shall be the last!

JEAN. Don't think! Don't think! Why, you're taking away all my strength too, and making me a coward—What! I fancied I saw the bell move!—No! Shall we stuff it up with paper?—Fancy being so afraid of a bell!—Yes, but it isn't only a bell—there's someone behind it—a hand that sets it in motion—and something else that sets the hand in motion—but just stop your ears—stop your ears! Yes, and then it rings worse! Just goes on ringing till you answer it—and then it's too late! and then the police come—and then—[*The bell rings twice violently. Jean shrinks at the sound; then straightens himself.*] It's horrible! But there's no other possible end to it! Go!

[*Julie walks out firmly through the door.*

CURTAIN

HANNELE
A DREAM POEM

By Gerhart Hauptmann

Translated from the German by
CHARLES HENRY MELTZER

THIS version of *Hannele* was used in the spring of the year 1894, at the Fifth Avenue Theatre, New York, when the play was performed for the first time on the English-speaking stage, with the approval of Gerhart Hauptmann, who was present.

CHARACTERS

HANNELE
GOTTWALD (afterwards THE STRANGER), *a schoolmaster*
SISTER MARTHA, *a deaconess*
TULPE ⎫
HETE (Hedwig) ⎬ *Inmates of an almshouse*
PLESCHKE ⎪
HANKE ⎭
SEIDEL, *a woodcutter*
BERGER, *a magistrate*
SCHMIDT, *a police official*
DR. WACHLER

APPARITIONS INTRODUCED DURING HANNELE'S DELIRIUM

MATTERN (*a mason*), *supposed to be Hannele's father*
THE FORM OF HANNELE'S DEAD MOTHER
A GREAT DARK ANGEL
THREE ANGELS OF LIGHT
THE DEACONESS
GOTTWALD
GOTTWALD'S PUPILS
PLESCHKE
HANKE AND OTHER PAUPERS
SEIDEL
A VILLAGE DOCTOR
FOUR YOUTHS, CLAD IN WHITE
NUMEROUS BRIGHT ANGELS, GREAT AND SMALL
MOURNERS
WOMEN, ETC.

'*Suffer the little children to come unto Me, and forbid them not
For of such is the Kingdom of Heaven.*'

55

ACT I

SCENE: *A room in the almshouse of a village in the mountains. Bare walls. A door at centre, back. To the left of this door is a small window. Before the window are a rickety table and a bench. Near the table and to the left of it is a stove.*

To the right of the door is a pallet with a straw mattress and a few ragged coverlets.

It is a stormy December evening.

At the table, seated and singing a hymn which she reads from a hymn book, by the light of a tallow candle, sits Tulpe, an old, ragged pauper.

The stage directions as to 'right' and 'left' are given from the actor's standpoint.

TULPE. [*Sings in a cracked, quavering voice.*]
       'Jesus, lover of my soul,
       Let me to Thy bosom fly,
       While the waves of tr-ouble . . .'

Enter Hedwig, familiarly known as Hete, a disreputable woman of about thirty, with curly hair. Round her head is wrapped a thick cloth. She carries a bundle under her arm. Her dress is light and shabby.

HETE. [*Blowing on her fingers.*] Mercy on us, nice weather we're havin'. [*Drops her bundle on the table and goes on blowing her fingers, standing alternately on each of her feet, which are shod in worn-out old boots.*] We ain't had such weather for an age.

TULPE. What have yer got in there?

HETE. [*Grinning and whining with pain, sits on the bench by the stove and tries to take off her boots.*] Oh, Lord! My blessed toes are just burnin'!

TULPE. [*Unties Hete's bundle, in which are seen a loaf, a packet of chicory, a bag of coffee, a few pairs of stockings, etc.*] Ain't there nothin' for me in your bundle?

HETE. [*At first too busy with her boots to mind Tulpe. Suddenly snatches at the bundle and collects its contents.*] Tulpe! [*One of Hete's feet is bare. She piles her belongings together and carries*

57

them off to the pallet.] Now you 'd best leave my things alone—
d' you think I 've been trampin' about and freezin' all the
bones in my body for *you,* eh?

TULPE. Ah, yer needn't make such a fuss about it, you fool!
[*Rises, closes her hymn book, and wipes it carefully with her
skirt.*] I don't want none of the rubbish you 've been beggin'
for.

HETE. [*Hiding her property under the mattress.*] Beggin'? I 'd
like to know who 's done most beggin'—you or me! You 've
done nothin' else all your life. And you 're no chicken,
neither.

TULPE. Don't you fly out about it. We know the sort er life
you 've led. Pastor told you what he thought of *you,* he did.
I didn't tramp about the streets when *I* was a girl. *I* was
respect'ble.

HETE. I s'pose that 's why you were sent to jail!

TULPE. You 'll get there fast enough, don't you fear, my beauty.
Just you let me get a sight of a *gendarme,* that 's all. I could
tell him a thing or two about you, sure 's yer live!

HETE. Oh, shut up! I don't care for your *gendarmes.* Let 'em
come and see if I don't tell 'em somethin' as 'll make you feel
uncomfort'ble.

TULPE. Yer can't say nothin' against me!

HETE. Oh, I can't, can't I? Who stole the overcoat from the
innkeeper's little boy, eh?

[*Tulpe makes as though to spit at Hete.*]

That 's what you call manners, I s'pose? Yer shan't have
nothin' now, just to spite yer.

TULPE. Ah, go on! I wouldn't take anythin' from the likes er
you, anyhow.

HETE. No, and you won't get nothin'.

[*Pleschke and Hanke appear outside the open door, against
which they have been literally blown by the howling wind.
Pleschke, a scrofulous, childish old man, in rags, bursts
out laughing. Hanke, a good-for-nothing blackguard,
blasphemes. They are seen to shake the snow off their
hats and cloaks. Each carries a bundle.*

PLESCHKE. Lord, how it do blow! One er these 'ere nights, you
see if the old shanty ain't smashed to bits!

[*At sight of the newcomers Hete hurriedly drags her bundle from
beneath the mattress, picks it up, and runs past the men
into the courtyard and up a flight of stairs.*

[*Calling after Hete.*] Hey! Hulloa! Yer in a hurry! Wot are yer runnin' away fur? We won't hurt yer, will we, Hanke?

Tulpe. [*Busy at the stove with a saucepan.*] Oh, she ain't right in her head. She thinks you'll steal her bundle.

Enter Pleschke

Pleschke. Lord save us! That's rough on us, that is! Evenin'! G'd evenin'! Good Lord, what weather! Hang me if I wasn't a'most blown off my feet!

[*Limps to the table, lays his bundle down, and wags his white-haired, feeble head at Tulpe. Pants from fatigue, coughs, and tries to warm himself. Meanwhile, Hanke enters, lays his beggar's bag against the door, and shivers with cold as he puts fuel into the stove.*

Tulpe. Where er you been?

Pleschke. [*Stuttering.*] W-where have I been? Quite a way, quite a way. Up in the hills.

Tulpe. Brought anythin' back?

Pleschke. Lots—lots of things. Th' priest giv' me this 'ere five-pfenniger, and down at th' inn they give me—er—give me—er—a bowl er soup——

Tulpe. Hand it over, and I'll warm it up.

[*Takes a pot out of the bundle, sets it on the table, and stirs the contents of the saucepan.*

Pleschke. I—I've got somethin' else in here—sausage. The butcher give it to me. Ay, the butcher.

Tulpe. Where's the money?

Plesckhe. Oh, the money's all right. Here's the money.

Tulpe. Give it t' me. I'll take care of it for yer.

Re-enter Hete

Hete. Yer blamed old fool, why d' yer let her have it?

[*She goes to the stove.*

Tulpe. You mind yer own business.

Hanke. Don't worry. He's her sweetheart.

Hete. Saints alive!

Hanke. It's only right he should being her home a trifle now and then, ain't it?

Pleschke. [*Stammering.*] Y-you ought-oughter know—better, you ought. Can't yer leave a poor old man alone an'—n-not make game of him?

* c 989

HETE. [*Mimicking Pleschke.*] W-why d-don't yer l-let the poor old man alone? Pleschke, yer gettin' shaky. You won't last much longer.

PLESCHKE. [*Threatening her with a stick.*] Y-you'd best c-clear outer this!

HETE. I'd like to see you make me clear out.

PLESCHKE. Clear out! D' ye hear?

TULPE. Catch her one on the head. It'll do her good.

PLESCHKE. Clear out!

HANKE. Oh, drop it! Leave her alone.

> [*Hete, taking advantage of Hanke's having turned his back to defend her from Pleschke, makes a grab at his bag and tries to steal something from it. Tulpe sees her and shakes with laughter.*

I don't see much to laugh about.

TULPE. [*Still laughing.*] He don't see nothin' to laugh at!

PLESCHKE. Oh, Lord, just look at her!

TULPE. Yer 'd best look arter yer bag, or maybe you'll miss somethin'.

HANKE. [*Turns and sees that he has been tricked.*] You would, would you, you devil! [*Rushes after Hete.*] Just you let me get at you!

> [*Tramping of feet, as Hanke runs up the staircase after Hete. Smothered cries.*

PLESCHKE. Well, well, well! She's a smart un.   [*He laughs.*

> [*Tulpe joins in his laughter, which is interrupted by the sound of the sudden opening and shutting of a door.*

W-what was that?

> [*Howling wind heard outside. Snow dashes against the window-panes. Then all is quiet for a moment. The schoolmaster, Gottwald, a man of two-and-thirty, with a dark beard, enters, carrying Hannele Mattern, a girl of about fourteen. The child whimpers. Her long red hair streams over the schoolmaster's shoulders. Her face is pressed against his throat, her arms hang straight and limp. The rags in which she is clothed barely cover her. Gottwald takes no notice of Pleschke and Tulpe, carries the child in tenderly, and lays her on the bed, which stands on the right near the wall. He is followed by Seidel, a woodcutter, who carries a lantern in one hand. He also carries a saw, an axe, and a bundle of rags. On his grey head he wears a shabby old hat.*

PLESCHKE. [*Staring stupidly at the newcomers.*] Hulloa, hulloa, hulloa! What—what's the matter?

GOTTWALD. [*Laying his overcoat and some blankets over Hannele.*] Hot bricks, Seidel! Quick.

SEIDEL. [*To Tulpe.*] Don't stand there doin' nothin'. Heat some bricks. Look sharp!

TULPE. What's the matter with the girl?

SEIDEL. I've no time for talkin'.   [*Exit with Tulpe.*

GOTTWALD. [*Trying to soothe Hannele.*] There, there, don't you fear. We'll soon put you right.

HANNELE. [*Her teeth chattering.*] I'm afraid! I'm afraid!

GOTTWALD. Fear nothing. We won't let any harm come to you.

HANNELE. It's father. It's father!

GOTTWALD. Why, he's not here, my dear.

HANNELE. I'm afraid of father. Oh, if he should come!

GOTTWALD. Ssh! Ssh! He won't come.

[*Hurried steps are heard on the staircase. Hete bustles in, with an iron grater in her hand.*

HETE. [*Holding up the grater.*] Just look what Hanke's got!

[*Hanke rushes in after Hete and tries to take the grater from her. She flings it into the middle of the room.*

HANNELE. [*Screams with terror.*] He's coming! He's coming!

[*She half rises, leans forward, with anguish on her pale, sick, pinched little face, and stares at the place from which the noise comes. Hete dodges away from Hanke and runs into the back room. Hanke goes to pick up the grater.*

HANKE. [*Astonished.*] I'll give you a taste of it presently, you slut, you!

GOTTWALD. [*To Hannele.*] It's all right, my child. [*To Hanke.*] What are you doing here?

HANKE. What am *I* doin' here?

HETE. [*Putting her head in at the back door.*] 'Tain't his! He stole it!

HANKE. [*Threatening.*] You wait a bit! I'll get even with you.

GOTTWALD. I beg you to be quiet. The child's ill.

HANKE. [*Picks up the grater and draws back abashed.*] Why, what's the matter?

SEIDEL. [*Enters with two bricks.*] These ought to do.

GOTTWALD. [*Examining the bricks.*] Are they warm enough?

SEIDEL. Oh, they'll warm her.

[*He puts one of the bricks under Hannele's feet.*

GOTTWALD. Put the other one there.   [*Points to another place.*

SEIDEL. She don't seem much warmer yet.

GOTTWALD. The child's shivering with cold.

TULPE. [*Has entered, following Seidel. Behind her enter Hete and Pleschke and several other paupers, who stand in the doorway whispering and fussing about inquisitively. Tulpe moves to the bedside and stands there with her arms akimbo.*] Brandy and hot water 'ud do her good.

SEIDEL. [*Pulls out a flask. So do Pleschke and Hanke.*] There's just a drop left.

TULPE. [*At the stove.*] Bring it here.

SEIDEL. Is the water hot?

TULPE. Scaldin'!

GOTTWALD. You'd better put in a lump of sugar.

HETE. Where d'yer s'pose we'd get sugar from?

TULPE. Ah, shut up! Yer know yer've got some stowed away.

HETE. Yer lie I ain't got no sugar.   [*Laughs nervously.*

TULPE. It's *you* that's lyin'. I saw yer bring it in.

SEIDEL. [*To Hete.*] Run and get it, can't you?

HANKE. [*To Hete.*] What are yer waitin' for?

HETE. [*Doggedly.*] Fetch it yerself.

PLESCHKE. Get the sugar!

HETE. Yer can get all yer want at the grocer's.   [*Exit.*

SEIDEL. And if you don't get some at the grocer's, double quick time—— Well, you'll see! That's all I've got to say. You won't want more nor I'll give you, my lass.

PLESCHKE. [*Who has been out, returns.*] Ah, she's a bad lot, she is.

SEIDEL. I'd like to have the handlin' of her. I'd take her down a bit, I would, if I was the burgomaster. She's got no business to be in an almshouse—a great, big, healthy slut like her Why don't she work?

PLESCHKE H-here's a—b-b-bit of sugar.

HANKE [*Sniffing the aroma of the grog.*] I'd like to be ill myself, I would!

[*Schmidt enters with a lantern. His manner is important and impressive.*

SCHMIDT Now then, make room there. The judge'll be here in a moment.

[*Berger, the magistrate, enters. His manner stamps him as a retired officer He wears a short beard. Although his hair is grizzled, he seems still youthful and good-looking.*

He wears a well-cut long overcoat. His cocked hat is set jauntily on his head. One of his characteristics is a boyish swagger.

THE PAUPERS. Evenin', judge. Evenin', captain!

BERGER. Evenin'. [*Takes off his hat and cloak and puts them down with his stick. With a commanding gesture.*] Out with you, the whole lot of you! [*Schmidt hustles the paupers into the back room.*] Evenin', schoolmaster. [*Holds out his hand.*] How are you getting on?

GOTTWALD. We've just pulled the child out of the water!

SEIDEL. [*Stepping forward.*] Excuse me, judge. [*Makes a military salute.*] I was working later than usual down at t' smithy. You see, I was puttin' a new clamp round my axe—and just as I was comin' out er t' smithy—down yonder by the pond, judge—you know the big pond—it's pretty nigh as big as a lake—— [*Berger makes an impatient gesture.*] Yes, judge. Well, there's a corner in that pond as never freezes over—I can call to mind when I was a boy——

BERGER. Never mind that. Go on with your story.

SEIDEL. [*Saluting again.*] Yes, cap'n. Well—as I was sayin', I'd just come out o' t' smithy and was standin' in th' moon-light, when I heard someone cryin' At first I thought it was only someone makin' believe, as you might say. But hap-penin' to look toward the pond, I saw somethin' in the water! Yes, judge. Where it never freezes over. I called out to say I was a-comin', but she'd fainted! Well, I just ran back and fetched a plank from t' smithy and laid it over the hole—and in a moment I had brought her safe to land again.

BERGER. Bravo, Seidel. We don't hear that sort of tale every day. We hear more about quarrelling and fighting, and head-breaking, down in the village. . . . And then, I suppose, you brought her straight up here?

SEIDEL. Excuse me, judge. It was the teacher——

GOTTWALD. I happened to be passing by on my way home from a lecture. So I took her to my house first and got my wife to find some warm clothes for her.

BERGER. What do you make of the affair?

SEIDEL. [*Hesitating.*] Well, you see—h'm. She's Mattern's stepdaughter.

BERGER. [*Seems shocked.*] That ragged little thing Mattern's stepdaughter?

SEIDEL. Ay. Her mother died six weeks ago. . . . There ain't much more to tell. She kicked and scratched because she thought I was her stepfather.

BERGER. [*Thinking of Mattern, mutters.*] The scoundrel!

SEIDEL. He 's bin sittin' at the inn, drinkin' hard, ever since yesterday. It takes a cask to fill *him* up, it does.

BERGER. He 'll have a score to settle with me, for this job. [*Bends over Hannele.*] Now, my child. Listen. You needn't cry about it. What 's the girl looking at me like that for? . . . I won't hurt you. What 's your name? . . . A little louder, please. I can't hear you—— [*He rises.*] The child seems very stubborn.

GOTTWALD. She 's only frightened . . . Hannele!

HANNELE. [*Gasping.*] Yes, sir!

GOTTWALD. Do as the judge bids you, child.

HANNELE. [*Shivering.*] Dear Lord, I 'm freezing!

SEIDEL. [*Bringing in the grog.*] There. Take a drop o' this, my lass.

HANNELE. [*As before.*] Dear Lord, I 'm hungry!

GOTTWALD. [*To the magistrate.*] It 's no use. We can't make her drink.

HANNELE. It hurts!

GOTTWALD. Where does it hurt you, little one?

HANNELE. Oh, I 'm afraid! I 'm afraid!

BERGER. Who 's frightening you, my dear? Come, come, now. Tell us all about it. Don't be afraid. What was that?— I can't understand a word you 're saying. Try and remember how it happened. Did your stepfather ill-treat you?—Did he beat you or lock you up or—turn you out into the street?— It 's hard to get anything out of her.

SEIDEL. Ay! She ain't fond er chatterin'! Choppin' trees is easier nur makin' *her* talk. She 's as still as a mouse, *she* is.

BERGER. If we only had facts to go on—we might have the fellow locked up.

GOTTWALD. She 's terribly afraid of him.

SEIDEL. 'Tain't the first time, neither, as he 's been caught at this sort of game. Jest you ask the folks about him. They 'll tell you what sort of man he is. It 's a wonder she wasn't killed years ago.

BERGER. What has he done to her?

SEIDEL. Done?—Druv her out o' doors o' nights. That 's what he 's done to her. Sent her out a-beggin' in the snow. That 's what he 's done. And if she didn't bring him back enough to get him roarin' drunk, out she 'd have to go agen. That 's

what he 's done.   Many 's the night she 's froze and cried her
eyes out, she has.

GOTTWALD. It wasn't quite so bad while her mother lived.

BERGER. Well, anyhow, we 'll have the man arrested.   He 's a
notorious drunkard.   Now, my little maid, just look me
straight in the face.

HANNELE. [*Imploringly.*] Oh please, please, please!

SEIDEL. 'Tain't no use your asking questions.   You won't
get nothin' out o' her.

GOTTWALD. [*Gently.*] Hannele!

HANNELE. Yes, sir.

GOTTWALD. Do you know me?

HANNELE. Yes, sir.

GOTTWALD. Who am I?

HANNELE. Teacher, sir—Teacher Gottwald.

GOTTWALD. That 's right.   We 're getting along famously.
Now, my dear child, tell us all about it.   Don't be afraid.
How is it you did not stay at home instead of going down to
the pond by the blacksmith's?   Eh?

HANNELE. I 'm afraid!   I 'm afraid!

BERGER. We 'll go away, and you can say all you have to say
to the schoolmaster.

HANNELE. [*Shyly and mysteriously.*] He called me!

GOTTWALD. Who called you, my dear?

HANNELE. The Lord Jesus.

GOTTWALD. Where did the Lord Jesus call you?

HANNELE. From the water.

GOTTWALD. Where?

HANNELE. Why, from the bottom of the water.

BERGER. [*Changing his mind and putting on his overcoat.*] We 'd
better have the doctor fetched.   I dare say he 's not left the
inn yet.

GOTTWALD. I have sent for one of the sisters.   The child needs
very careful nursing.

BERGER. I 'll go for the doctor at once.   [*To Schmidt.*] Bring the
policeman to me at the inn, Schmidt.   We 'll have the fellow
locked up.   Good night, schoolmaster.

                    [*Berger and Schmidt exeunt.   Hannele falls asleep.*

SEIDEL. [*After a pause.*] He won't lock him up.   Not much.

GOTTWALD. Why not?

SEIDEL. He knows why, he does.   *Who 's the girl's father*, eh?

GOTTWALD. Stuff, Seidel.   That 's all gossip.

SEIDEL. All right.   I knows what I knows.

GOTTWALD. You mustn't mind what people say.   Half are lies.
—I only wish the doctor would make haste.

SEIDEL. [*Softly.*] She won't get over it.   You 'll see.

Enter Dr. Wachler, a grave-looking man of four-and-thirty.

DR. WACHLER. Good evening.

GOTTWALD. Good evening, doctor.

SEIDEL. [*Helping the doctor to take off his fur overcoat.*] Good
evening, Herr Doctor.

DR. WACHLER. [*Warming his hands at the stove.*] I should like
another candle. [*The sound of a barrel-organ comes from the
adjoining room.*] They must have lost their wits!

SEIDEL. [*At the half-closed door of the back room.*] Can't you keep
quiet in there?   [*Noise ceases.   Seidel goes into the back room.*

DR. WACHLER. Herr Gottwald, I believe?

GOTTWALD. That is my name.

DR. WACHLER. I hear she tried to drown herself?

GOTTWALD. She saw no other way out of her troubles, poor child.
[*Short pause.*

DR. WACHLER. [*Watching Hannele beside her bed.*] Has she been
talking in her sleep?

HANNELE. Millions and millions of stars! [*Dr. Wachler and Gottwald watch the child.   Through the window the moonlight streams
on the group.*] Why are you pulling at my bones?   Don't!
Don't!   It hurts, oh, it *does* hurt so!

DR. WACHLER. [*Carefully loosening the collar of Hannele's
chemise.*] Her body is a mass of bruises!

SEIDEL. Ah, and that 's how her mother looked when she was
put in her coffin!

DR. WACHLER. Shocking!   Shocking!

HANNELE. [*In a changed, peevish voice.*] I won't go home.   I
won't!   I want to go to Dame Holle.—Let me go to the pond.
—Let me go!—Oh, that dreadful, dreadful smell!—Father,
you 've been drinking brandy again!—Hark! how the wind
blows in the wood!—There was a storm in the hills this morning.—Oh, I do hope there won't be a fire.—Do you hear?   Oh,
what a storm!—It 'll blow the tailor away, if he hasn't put his
goose in his pocket!

Enter Sister Martha

GOTTWALD. Good evening, sister.
[*Sister Martha bends her head in response.   Gottwald joins*

*her at the back of the stage, where she is getting everything
ready for nursing.*

HANNELE. Where 's mother? In heaven? How far away it is!
[*She opens her eyes, stares about her in a dazed way, rubs her
eyes slowly, and says in an almost inaudible voice.*] Where am I?

DR. WACHLER. [*Bending over her.*] You 're with friends,
Hannele.

HANNELE. I 'm thirsty.

DR. WACHLER. Water!

[*Seidel, who has brought in another candle, goes out to get some
water.*

Does it pain you anywhere?   [*Hannele shakes her head.*
No. That 's first-rate. We 'll soon put you right.

HANNELE. Please, sir, are you the doctor?

DR. WACHLER. Yes, my dear.

HANNELE. Am I very, very ill?

DR. WACHLER. No, no! Not *very* ill.

HANNELE. Are you going to make me well again?

DR. WACHLER. [*Examining her quickly.*] Does that hurt? No!
Does that? Ah, this is the place!—Don't be frightened! I
won't hurt you. Is this where the pain is?

GOTTWALD. [*Returning to the bedside.*] Answer the doctor,
Hannele.

HANNELE. [*Earnestly, imploringly, tearfully.*] Oh, *dear* teacher
Gottwald!

GOTTWALD. Come, come! Attend to what the doctor says and
answer his questions.   [*Hannele shakes her head.*
No? Why not?

HANNELE. Oh, do, *do* let me go to mother!

GOTTWALD. [*Deeply moved—strokes her hair gently.*] Don't, don't
say that, my child!   [*Short pause.*
[*The doctor lifts his head, draws a long breath, and reflects for a
moment. Sister Martha has brought the lighted candle
from the table and stands near by, holding it.*

DR. WACHLER. [*Beckons to Sister Martha.*] One moment, sister.
[*The doctor and Sister Martha retire to the table. The doctor
gives the sister some instructions in an undertone. Gottwald glances at Hannele, the sister, and the doctor alternately. He stands waiting, hat in hand. Dr. Wachler
ends his quiet talk with Sister Martha.*

I 'll look in again later on. I 'll have the medicine sent round.
[*To Gottwald.*] It seems they have arrested the man at the inn.

SISTER MARTHA. Yes. So they say.

DR. WACHLER. [*Putting on his overcoat. To Seidel.*] You 'd better come to the apothecary's with me.

[*The doctor, Gottwald, and Seidel take leave of Sister Martha quietly as they move toward the door.*

GOTTWALD. [*In a casual way.*] What do you think of the case, doctor?   [*Doctor, Gottwald, and Seidel exeunt.*

[*Sister Martha, who is now alone with Hannele, pours some milk into a bowl. Meanwhile, Hannele opens her eyes and watches her.*

HANNELE. Have you come from Jesus?

SISTER MARTHA. What did you say, dear?

HANNELE. Have you come from the Lord Jesus?

SISTER MARTHA. Why, Hannele, have you forgotten me? I 'm Sister Martha. Don't you remember coming to see us one day and praying and singing those beautiful hymns?

HANNELE. [*Nodding joyfully.*] Oh yes, yes. Such beautiful, beautiful hymns!

SISTER MARTHA. I 've come to nurse you, in God's name, till you get well.

HANNELE. I don't want to get well.

SISTER MARTHA. [*Bringing her the milk.*] The doctor says you must take a little of this milk, to make you strong again.

HANNELE. [*Turns away.*] I don't *want* to get well.

SISTER MARTHA. Don't want to get well? That 's not sensible, my dear. There, let me tie your hair up. [*She ties her hair.*

HANNELE. [*Crying quietly.*] I don't want to get well.

SISTER MARTHA. Well, I declare! Why not?

HANNELE. Oh, how I *long* to go to heaven, sister.

SISTER MARTHA. We all long for that, darling. But we must be patient and wait until God calls us, and then, if we repent of our sins——

HANNELE. [*Eagerly.*] I *do* repent, sister! Indeed, indeed I do!

SISTER MARTHA. —and if we believe in the Lord Jesus——

HANNELE. I *do* believe in Him!

SISTER MARTHA. Then you may wait in peace, my child.—Let me smooth your pillow for you.—There. Now go to sleep.

HANNELE. I can't sleep.

SISTER MARTHA. Oh yes, you can, if you try.

HANNELE. Sister Martha!

SISTER MARTHA. Well, dear?

HANNELE. Sister! Are there any—any unpardonable sins?

SISTER MARTHA. We won't talk about that now. You must
not excite yourself.

HANNELE. Please, please, please! Won't you tell me?

SISTER MARTHA. Yes, yes. There *are* sins that God won't
pardon—sins against the Holy Ghost!

HANNELE. Oh, do you think I've committed one?

SISTER MARTHA. Nonsense. Why, only very, *very* wicked people,
like Judas, who betrayed our Lord, could commit those sins.

HANNELE. You don't know—you don't know.

SISTER MARTHA. Hush. You must go to sleep.

HANNELE. I'm so afraid.

SISTER MARTHA. You need not be.

HANNELE. But if I have committed one?

SISTER MARTHA. Oh, but you haven't.

HANNELE. [*Clings to the sister and stares into the darkness.*
Sister! Sister!

SISTER MARTHA. Hush, dear, hush!

HANNELE. Sister!

SISTER MARTHA. What is it?

HANNELE. He's coming. Can't you hear him?

SISTER MARTHA. I hear nothing.

HANNELE. That's his voice—outside! Hark!

SISTER MARTHA. Whose voice?

HANNELE. Father's! Father's! There he is!

SISTER MARTHA. Where? I don't see him.

HANNELE. Look!

SISTER MARTHA. Where?

HANNELE. At the foot of the bed!

SISTER MARTHA. It's only this coat and hat, darling. We'll
take the nasty things away and give them to Daddy Pleschke.
And then I'll bring some water and we'll make a compress
for you You won't be afraid if I leave you alone for a few
moments, will you? Lie quite still till I come back.

HANNELE. Was it really only the coat and hat, sister? How
silly of me.

SISTER MARTHA. Keep quite still. I'll be back directly. [*She
goes out, but returns, as the courtyard is pitch dark.*] I'll put the
candle outside in the courtyard for a minute. [*Shaking her
finger tenderly at Hannele.*] Now mind! Keep still!

[*She goes out.*

[*It is almost dark in the room. As soon as the sister has gone
the figure of Mattern, the mason, appears at the foot of the*

bed. He has a drunken and unkempt look, tangled red hair, and a shabby old soldier's cap. In his left hand he holds his tools. Round his right wrist is a cord. He stares threateningly at Hannele as if about to strike. A pale light envelops the apparition and streams on to the bed. Hannele covers her face with her hands in terror. She writhes and moans piteously

THE APPARITION. [*In a hoarse and exasperated voice.*] Where are you? Loafin' agen, as usual, eh? I'll teach yer to skulk, you little devil, you. So you 've been tellin' tales, have you? Tellin' the folks I ill-uses you, eh? I beats you, eh? Aren't you ashamed to tell such lies? You ain't no child of mine. Get up, you lazy baggage. I don't want to have nothin' more to do with you. I've half a mind to turn you out into the gutter. Get up and light the fire. D' ye hear? If I keeps you it 's out o' charity. Now then, up with you! You won't, won't you? Well then, look out——

[*Hannele, with an effort, rises. Her eyes remain closed. She drags herself to the stove, opens the stove-door, and falls senseless as Sister Martha returns with a lighted candle and a jug of water. The apparition vanishes. Sister Martha staggers, stares at Hannele as she lies among the ashes, and exclaims.*

SISTER MARTHA. Saints alive! [*She puts down the candle and the jug, hastens to Hannele, and lifts her from the floor. Hearing her cry, the inmates of the almshouse rush in.*] I just left her for a moment to fetch some water and she got out of bed. Here, Hedwig, give me a hand!

HANKE. You 'd best be careful, or you 'll hurt her.

PLESCHKE. It d-don't seem nat'ral to me, sister. Someone must a' bewitched the girl.

TULPE. That 's what 's wrong wi' her.

HANKE. [*Loudly.*] She won't last long, she won't.

SISTER MARTHA. [*When with Hedwig's assistance she has put Hannele to bed again.*] That may be all very true, my good man, but you really must not excite the child.

HANKE. You 're makin' quite a fuss about her, ain't you?

PLESCHKE. [*To Hanke.*] You 're a bad lot you are—a reg'lar out an' out bad lot. Ain't you got sense enough to know—as—as —s-sick folk mustn't be excited?

HETE. [*Mimicking him.*] S-sick folk mustn't be excited——

SISTER MARTHA. I really must request you——

TULPE. Quite right, sister.—You get out o' here!

HANKE. When we wants to go we 'll go, and not before.

HETE. The stable 's good enough for the likes of *us*.

PLESCHKE. Don't you make no fuss—you 'll find a place to sleep in, you will. [*The inmates of the almshouse go out.*

HANNELE. [*Opens her eyes. She seems terrified.*] Has he gone?

SISTER MARTHA. They 've all gone, Hannele. Did they frighten you?

HANNELE. [*Still terrified.*] Has father gone?

SISTER MARTHA. He hasn't been here.

HANNELE. Oh yes, he has, sister!

SISTER MARTHA. You dreamt it, my dear.

HANNELE. [*Sighing deeply.*] Oh, dear Lord Jesus! Dear, dear Lord Jesus! Won't you please, please, take me away from here? [*Her tone changes.*

> 'Oh, would He but come
>   And guide my way home!
> I 'm worn and I 'm weary,
>   No more can I roam!'

Yes, yes. I 'm sure He will, sister.

SISTER MARTHA. What, dear?

HANNELE. He 's promised to take me to Him, sister.

SISTER MARTHA. H'm. [*Coughs.*

HANNELE. He 's promised.

SISTER MARTHA. Who has promised?

HANNELE. [*Whispering mysteriously into the sister's ear.*] The dear Lord—Gottwald!

SISTER MARTHA. Get off to sleep again, Hannele, that 's a good girl

HANNELE. Isn't he handsome, sister? Don't you think teacher 's handsome? His name is Heinrich!—Did you know that? What a beautiful name! [*Fervently.*] Dear, good, kind Heinrich! Sister, when I grow up we 're going to be married!

> 'And when the priest had made them one,
>   The bride grew pink as heather;
> The bridegroom kissed her trembling lips,
>   And off they rode together.'

He has such a lovely beard. [*Entranced.*] And, oh, his head 's covered with such sweet white clover!—Hark! He 's calling me! Don't you hear?

SISTER MARTHA. Do go to sleep, my pet. No one is calling.

HANNELE. It was the voice of—Jesus. Hark! He's calling me again. Oh, I hear Him quite plainly. 'Hannele! Hannele!'—Let us go to Him!

SISTER MARTHA. When God calls He will find me ready!

HANNELE. [*Her head is now bathed in moonlight. She makes a gesture as though she were inhaling some sweet perfume.*] Don't you smell them, sister?

SISTER MARTHA. No, Hannele.

HANNELE. Lilacs! [*Her ecstasy increases.*] Listen! Listen! [*A sweet voice is faintly heard in the far distance.*] Is that the angels singing? Don't you hear?

SISTER MARTHA. Yes, dear, I hear. But now you must turn round and have a good long sleep.

HANNELE. Can you sing that, too?

SISTER MARTHA. Sing what, my child?

HANNELE. 'Sleep, darling, sleep!'

SISTER MARTHA. Would you like me to?

HANNELE. [*Lies back and strokes the sister's hand.*] Mother, mother! Sing to me!

SISTER MARTHA. [*Extinguishes the light, bends over the bed, and softly intones the following verses to the accompaniment of distant music.*

> 'Sleep, darling, sleep!
> In the garden goes a sheep.
> [*She sings the rest in darkness.*
> A little lamb with thee shall play,
> From dawn to sunset, all the day.
> Sleep, darling, sleep!'

[*Twilight fills the room. Sister Martha has gone. The pale and ghostly form of a woman appears and seats itself on the side of the bed. She is slightly bent and seems to rest on her thin bare arms. Her feet are bare. Her long white locks stream over her shoulders and on to the bed. Her face seems worn and wasted. Her sunken eyes, though closed, seem fixed on Hannele. Her voice sounds as the voice of one speaking in her sleep. Before she speaks, her lips are seen to move, as though it cost her a great effort to get the words out. She is prematurely aged. Her cheeks are hollow, and she is clad in miserable clothes.*

THE FEMALE APPARITION. Hannele!

HANNELE. [*Her eyes, also, are closed.*] Mother, dearest mother! Is it you?

THE FEMALE APPARITION. It is I.—I have washed the feet of my Saviour with my tears, and I have dried them with my hair.

HANNELE. Do you bring me good tidings?

THE FEMALE APPARITION. Yes!

HANNELE. Have you come far?

THE FEMALE APPARITION. Hundreds of thousands of miles, through the night!

HANNELE. How strange you look, mother!

THE FEMALE APPARITION. As the children of earth look, so I look!

HANNELE. There are buttercups and daisies on your lips. Your voice rings out like music.

THE FEMALE APPARITION. It is no true ring, my child.

HANNELE. Mother, dear mother, your beauty dazzles me!

THE FEMALE APPARITION. The angels in heaven are a thousand-fold more radiant!

HANNELE. Why are you not like them?

THE FEMALE APPARITION. I suffered for your sake.

HANNELE. Mother mine, won't you stay with me?

THE FEMALE APPARITION. [*Rising.*] I cannot stay!

HANNELE. Is it beautiful where you have come from?

THE FEMALE APPARITION. There the wide meadows are sheltered from the wind and storm and hail. God shields them.

HANNELE. Can you rest there when you are tired?

THE FEMALE APPARITION. Yes!

HANNELE. Can you get food to eat there, when you are hungry?

THE FEMALE APPARITION. There is meat and fruit for all who hunger, and golden wine for those who thirst.

[*She shrinks away.*

HANNELE. Are you going, mother?

THE FEMALE APPARITION. God calls me!

HANNELE. Does He call loudly?

THE FEMALE APPARITION. He calls *me* loudly!

HANNELE. My heart is parched within me, mother!

THE FEMALE APPARITION. God will cool it with roses and with lilies

HANNELE. Mother, will God redeem me?

THE FEMALE APPARITION. Do you know this flower I hold here in my hand?

HANNELE. It 's golden sesame![1] The key of heaven!

THE FEMALE APPARITION. [*Puts it into Hannele's hand.*] Take it and keep it as God's pledge. Farewell!

HANNELE. Mother! Mother, don't leave me!

THE FEMALE APPARITION. [*Shrinks away.*] A little while and ye shall not see me, and again a little while and ye shall see me.

HANNELE. I 'm afraid!

THE FEMALE APPARITION. [*Shrinking still farther away.*] Even as the snowdrifts on the hills are swept away by the winds, so shall thy troubles be lifted from thee.

HANNELE. Don't go!

THE FEMALE APPARITION. The children of heaven are as lightnings in the night. Sleep!

[*The room gradually grows dark. Pretty voices of young children are heard singing the second verse of 'Sleep, darling, sleep.'*

'Sleep, darling, sleep!
Bright guests their vigils keep——

[*A gold-green light suddenly floods the room. Three radiant Angels, crowned with roses, and having the forms of beautiful winged youths, appear and take up the song. In their hands they hold music. The Female Apparition has vanished.*

The guests who guard thee thro' the night
Are angels from the realms of Light.
Sleep, darling, sleep!'

HANNELE. [*Opens her eyes and gazes rapturously at the angels.*] Angels! [*Her joy and her amazement grow, but she seems still in doubt.*] Angels!! [*Triumphantly.*] Angels!!!

[*Short pause. Then the Angels sing the following strophes from the music in their hands.*

FIRST ANGEL

The sunlight that glints on the mountain
No gladness, or gold, had for thee.
For thee there was sorrow and sadness
In valley and forest and lea.

---

[1] In the German the flower is *Himmelsschlüssel*, that is 'Key of heaven,' but in English, cowslip. 'Sesame' seems more appropriate and suggestive.—C. H. M.

SECOND ANGEL

Thy hunger cried out to the reaper
   In vain, as he garnered the grain.
For milk thy poor lips went a-thirsting—
   They thirsted again and again.

THIRD ANGEL

The buds and the blossoms of springtide,
   In scarlet and purple arrayed,
For others had savour and sweetness:
   And faded—as thou, too must fade.

[Brief pause.

FIRST ANGEL

From out of the darkness of space
   A greeting we bring.
A message of love and of grace
   We bear on our wing.

SECOND ANGEL

In the hem of our raiment we bring thee
   The fragrance of May.
The rose of the morn, newly born,
   Illumines our way.

THIRD ANGEL

A glory of green and of glamour
   We leave in the skies.
The splendour of God is reflected
   And shines in our eyes!

END OF ACT I

ACT II

The scene is as it was before the appearance of the angels.

The Deaconess (Sister Martha) sits beside Hannele's bed. She lights the candle again and Hannele awakes. Her inward rapture is still shown in the expression of her face. As soon as she recognizes Sister Martha she breaks into joyous talk.

HANNELE. Sister! Sister Martha! Do you know who has been here? Angels! Angels, sister!

SISTER MARTHA. Aha! You 're wide awake again.

HANNELE. Yes, yes. Only think of it. [*Impulsively.*] Angels! Angels! Real angels, from heaven, Sister Martha, with great, big wings!

SISTER MARTHA. What sweet dreams you must have had, dear.

HANNELE. Why do you speak of dreams? Look, look! See what I have in my hand!

                [*She holds out an imaginary flower to her.*

SISTER MARTHA. What is it, dearest?

HANNELE. Can't you see?

SISTER MARTHA. H'm.

HANNELE. Look at it, sister. Only look!

SISTER MARTHA. I see, dear.

HANNELE. Smell how sweet it is!

SISTER MARTHA. [*Pretending to smell.*] Beautiful!

HANNELE. Take care, take care. You 'll crush it.

SISTER MARTHA. Oh no, I mustn't do that, my dear. What do you call this wonderful flower?

HANNELE. Why, golden sesame, of course!

SISTER MARTHA. Oh!

HANNELE. Of course it is. Can't you see? Bring the light here. Quick! Quick!

SISTER MARTHA. Ah! Now I see.

HANNELE. Isn't it beautiful?

SISTER MARTHA. Yes, yes. But you mustn't talk so much, my child. You must keep quite, quite still, or else the doctor will be angry. Now you must take the medicine he sent for you.

HANNELE. Oh, sister, why will you worry so much about me? You don't know what has happened—do you, now? Who do

you think it was gave me this lovely golden sesame? Guess,
guess—What 's sesame for? Don't you know, sister?

SISTER MARTHA. Ssh! You can tell me all about it in the morning, when you are strong and bright and well again.

HANNELE. I *am* well.

> [*She tries to rise and puts her feet out of bed.*

SISTER MARTHA. You mustn't do that, Hannele, dear.

HANNELE. [*Waving her away, gets out of bed and walks a few
steps.*] Please—please do leave me alone. I must go away—
away. [*She starts and stares fixedly at something.*] Oh, dear
Lord Jesus!

> [*The figure of an angel, clad in black and with black wings,
> appears. The angel is tall, majestic, and beautiful. In
> his hands he holds a long, wavy sword, the hilt of which is
> wrapped in crape. The angel is seated near the stove.
> He is silent and serious. He gazes steadily and calmly
> at Hannele. A supernatural white light fills the room.*

HANNELE. Who are you? [*Pause.*] Are you an angel? [*No
answer.*] Is it me you want? [*No answer.*] I am Hannele
Mattern. Have you come for *me*?   [*Again no answer.*

> [*During this incident Sister Martha has stood looking on,
> perplexed and thoughtful, with folded hands. She slowly
> passes out of the room.*

HANNELE. Has God made you dumb? Are you an angel? [*No
answer.*] Are you one of God's good angels? [*No answer.*]
Will you be kind to me? [*No answer.*] Are you an enemy?
[*No answer.*] Why have you hidden that sword in the folds
of your dress? [*Silence.*] I 'm so cold, so cold. Your look
chills me. You 're icy cold. [*Still silence.*] Who are you?
[*No answer. Terror suddenly overmasters her. She screams
and turns as if appealing for help to someone behind her.*]
Mother! Mother!

> [*A figure, dressed like the deaconess, but younger and more
> beautiful, and with great white wings, enters the room.
> Hannele hurries toward the figure, and clutches at her
> hand.*

Mother, mother! There 's someone in the room!

DEACONESS Where?

HANNELE There—there!

DEACONESS. Why do you tremble so?

HANNELE. I 'm afraid.

DEACONESS. Fear nothing. I am with you.

HANNELE. My teeth are chattering I can't *help* it, mother!
He terrifies me!

DEACONESS. Fear not, my child He is your friend.

HANNELE. Who is it, mother?

DEACONESS. Do you not know him?

HANNELE. Who is he?

DEACONESS. He is Death!

HANNELE. Death! [*She stares fixedly and fearfully at the angel
for a moment.*] Must it—must it be?

DEACONESS. Death is the gate, Hannele!

HANNELE. Is there no other, mother dear?

DEACONESS. There is no other

HANNELE Will you be cruel to me, Death?—He won't answer!
Why won't he answer any of my questions, mother?

DEACONESS. The voice of God has answered you already

HANNELE. Oh, dear Lord God, I have so often longed for this.
But now—now I am afraid!

DEACONESS. Get ready, Hannele.

HANNELE. For death, mother?

DEACONESS. For death

HANNELE. [*Timidly, after a pause.*] Shall I have to wear these
ragged clothes when they put me into the coffin?

DEACONESS God will clothe you
     [*She produces a small silver bell and rings it. In response
     there enters—silently, like all the following apparitions—
     a little humpbacked village tailor, carrying on his arm a
     bridal dress, a veil, and a wreath. In one hand he has a
     pair of crystal slippers. He has a comical, see-saw gait,
     bows silently to the angel and the deaconess, and lastly,
     and obsequiously, to Hannele.*]

THE VILLAGE TAILOR. [*Bobbing and bowing.*] Johanna Katherina Mattern, your most obedient. [*Clears his throat.*] Your
father, his excellency the count, has done me the honour of
ordering this bridal robe for you.

DEACONESS. [*Takes the dress from the tailor and attires Hannele.*]
I will help you to put it on, Hannele.

HANNELE. [*Joyfully.*] Oh, how it rustles.

DEACONESS. It's white silk, Hannele.

HANNELE. Won't the people be astonished to see me so beautifully dressed in my coffin!

THE VILLAGE TAILOR. Johanna Katherina Mattern. [*He clears
his throat.*] The village is full of it. [*He clears his throat.*]

It's full of the good luck your death is bringing you. [*Clears his throat.*] Your father, his excellency the count—[*Coughs.*] has just been talking to the burgomaster about it.

DEACONESS. [*Puts wreath on Hannele's head.*] Lift up your head, you heavenly bride!

HANNELE. [*Trembling with childish pleasure.*] Oh, Sister Martha, I'm so glad I am to die. [*Breaking off suddenly and doubtfully.*] You *are* Sister Martha, are you not?

DEACONESS. Yes, my child.

HANNELE. No, no. You're not Sister Martha. You are my mother!

DEACONESS. Yes.

HANNELE. Are you both of them?

DEACONESS. The children of heaven are all one in God.

THE VILLAGE TAILOR. If I may say so, Princess Hannele— [*He kneels to put on the slippers.*]—these slippers are the smallest in the land. Hedwig, and Agnes, and Liese, and Martha, and Minna, and Anna, and Käthe, and Gretchen, and the rest of them all have such very large feet [*He puts on the slippers.*] But they fit you—they fit you! We've found the bride! Princess Hannele's feet are the smallest!—Is there anything else I can do for you? [*Bows and scrapes.*] Your servant, princess. Your servant   [*He goes.*

HANNELE Who would have dreamt it, mother?

DEACONESS. Now you need not take any more of that nasty physic.

HANNELE. No.

DEACONESS. Soon you will be as bright and blithe as a lark, now, darling.

HANNELE. Oh, yes!

DEACONESS. Come, dear, and lie down on your death-bed.
    [*She takes Hannele by the hand, leads her gently to the bed, and waits while Hannele lies down.*

HANNELE. Now I'll soon know what death is, won't I?

DEACONESS. You will, Hannele

HANNELE. [*Lying on her back and playing with an imaginary flower.*] I have a pledge here!

DEACONESS. Press it closely to your breast.

HANNELE. [*Growing frightened again and glancing at the angel.*] Must it—must it be?

DEACONESS. It must.
        [*Sounds of a funeral march heard in the remote distance.*

HANNELE. [*Listening.*] That's Master Seyfried and the musicians announcing the funeral.

[*The angel rises.*

Oh, he's getting up!

[*The storm outside gains strength. The angel draws nearer to Hannele.*

Sister! Mother! He's coming to me! Where are you? I can't see you! [*Appealing to the angel.*] Make haste, thou dark and silent spirit! [*Speaking as though a heavy weight oppressed her.*] He's pressing me down!

[*The angel solemnly lifts up his sword.*

He'll crush me to pieces! [*With anguish.*] Help, sister, help!

[*The Deaconess steps majestically between the angel and Hannele, and lays her hands protectingly on the child's heart. She speaks softly, impressively, and with authority.*

DEACONESS. He dare not. I lay my consecrated hands upon thy heart.   [*The dark angel vanishes. Silence.*

[*The Deaconess lapses into meditation and her lips move as if in prayer. The sound of the funeral march has continued through this scene. A noise as of many tramping feet is heard. The form of the schoolmaster, Gottwald, appears in the central doorway. The funeral march ceases. Gottwald is dressed in mourning and bears a bunch of lovely bluebells in his hand. He takes off his hat reverently, and on entering makes a gesture as though he would have silence. Behind him are ranged his pupils—boys and girls, in Sunday clothes. At the gesture of the schoolmaster, they stop chattering, and seem afraid to cross the threshold. Gottwald approaches the Deaconess with a radiant look upon his face.*

GOTTWALD. Good day, Sister Martha.

DEACONESS. Good day, Teacher Gottwald.

GOTTWALD. [*Shakes his head sadly as he looks at Hannele.*] Poor little maid.

DEACONESS. Why are you so sad, Teacher Gottwald?

GOTTWALD. Is she not dead?

DEACONESS. Is that a thing to grieve over? She has found peace at last. I envy her.

GOTTWALD. [*Sighing.*] Ay, she is free from care and sorrow now. It is all for the best.

DEACONESS. [*Looking steadfastly at Hannele.*] How fair she seems.

GOTTWALD. Yes, very fair. Death seems to have clothed her
with beauty.

DEACONESS. God has made her beautiful, because she loved
Him.

GOTTWALD. Yes, she was always good and pious.

[*Sighs heavily, opens his hymn book, and peers into it sadly.*

DEACONESS. [*Peering into the same hymn book.*] We should not
repine. We must be patient.

GOTTWALD. And yet my heart is heavy.

DEACONESS. You do not mourn to know that she is saved?

GOTTWALD. I mourn to think that two fair flowers have withered.

DEACONESS. I do not understand you.

GOTTWALD. I have two faded violets in this book. How like
they are to the dead eyes of my poor little Hannele.

DEACONESS. They will grow bright and blue again in Heaven.

GOTTWALD. Oh, Lord, how long must we still wander in this vale
of tears! [*His tone changes abruptly. He becomes bustling and
business-like. Produces a hymn book.*] I thought it would be
a good idea to sing the first hymn here—in the house—' Jesus,
my Guide——'

DEACONESS. It is a beautiful hymn and Hannele Mattern was a
pious child.

GOTTWALD. And then, you know, when we get to the churchyard, we can sing 'Now lettest Thou thy servant.' [*He turns
to the schoolchildren and addresses them.*] Hymn No. 62! [*Intones hymn, slowly beating time.*] 'Now let-test-Thou-thy-
servant, De-pa-ar-art-in-peace——' [*The children chime in.*
Children, have you all warm clothes on? It will be cold out
yonder in the churchyard. Come in and take one last look at
our poor Hannele.

[*The children enter and range themselves about the bed.*
See how beautiful death has made the child. Once she was
clad in rags. Now she wears silken raiment. She went bare-
footed once. Now she has crystal slippers on her feet. Ere
very long she will be taken to a house all built of gold, where
she will never more know thirst or hunger.

Do you remember how you used to mock at her and call her
Princess Rag-Tag?—Now she is going away from us to be a
real princess in heaven. If any of you have offended her, now
is the time to beg for her forgiveness. If you do not, she will
tell her Heavenly Father how unkind you were to her, and it
will go hard with you.

A CHILD. [*Stepping forward.*] Dear Princess Hannele, please, please forgive me and don't tell God that I used to call you Princess Rag-Tag.

ALL THE CHILDREN. [*Together.*] We are all very, very sorry.

GOTTWALD. That's right, children. Hannele will forgive you. Now, boys and girls, go inside and wait till I join you.

DEACONESS. Come into the back room with me and I will tell you what you must all do if you want to join the bright angels some day, like Hannele.

[*She goes out. The children follow. The door closes.*

GOTTWALD. [*Alone with Hannele. He lays his flowers at her feet.*] My dear, dear Hannele, here are the violets I have brought you. [*Kneels by the bedside. His voice trembles.*] Do not forget me in your new felicity. [*He sobs and lays his head against the folds of her dress.*] My heart is breaking at the thought of parting from you.

[*Voices are heard without. Gottwald rises and lays a covering over Hannele. Two ageing women, dressed as if for a funeral, and with handkerchiefs and yellow-edged hymn-books in their hands, push their way into the room.*

FIRST WOMAN. [*Glancing round.*] We're ahead of them all.

SECOND WOMAN. No, we ain't. There's the teacher. Good day, Teacher.

GOTTWALD Good day.

FIRST WOMAN. You're takin' it to heart, Teacher. Well, well, I allow she was a sweet child. My, what a busy little thing she was, to be sure.

SECOND WOMAN. Say, Teacher, we've heard as how she killed herself. It ain't true, is it?

THIRD WOMAN. [*Appears.*] 'T'ud be a mortal sin!

SECOND WOMAN. Ay. that it would.

THIRD WOMAN. The minister, *he* says, there ain't no pardon for it.

GOTTWALD. The Saviour said: 'Suffer little children to come unto me, and forbid them not.'

Enter Fourth Woman

FOURTH WOMAN. Dear, dear, what weather we're havin'. We'll all be froze, I guess, before we've done. I hope the parson won't keep us long in the churchyard. The snow's a foot deep in the churchyard.

Enter Fifth Woman

FIFTH WOMAN. Th' parson won't have no prayers read over her. He says as how consecrated ground ain't no place for the likes er her.

Enter Pleschke

PLESCHKE. Ha' yer heard the news? A grand stranger's bin to see the parson. He says that Mattern's Hannele 's a saint.

HANKE. [*Hurrying in.*] They bringin' her a crystal coffin.

SEVERAL VOICES. [*Together.*] A crystal coffin!

HANKE. Reckon it 'll cost a pretty sum.

SEVERAL VOICES. [*Together.*] A crystal coffin!

Enter Seidel

SEIDEL. Thur 's strange goin's on down in the village. An angel 's bin thur—an angel as big 's a poplar, they do say. An' thur 's more of 'em down at th' blacksmith's—little uns, they be, no bigger nor babies. [*Looking at Hannele.*] She don't look like a beggar, she don't.

SEVERAL VOICES. [*Scattered.*] No, she don't look like a beggar.—A crystal coffin!—Did you ever hear the like!—And angels in the village!

[*Four youths clad in white enter, bearing a crystal coffin, which they put down close to Hannele's bed. They whisper to each other excitedly and curiously.*

GOTTWALD. [*Slightly raising the cloth.*] Would you like to have a look at the dead child?

FIRST WOMAN. [*Peeping at Hannele.*] Just look at her hair. Why, if it ain't shinin' just like gold!

GOTTWALD. [*Drawing the cloth completely from the body which is flooded with a pale light.*] Have you seen her silk dress and crystal slippers?

[*All utter exclamations of surprise, and draw back.*

SEVERAL VOICES. [*Confusedly.*] Lord, how beautiful!—
Why, that ain't our Hannele!—
That can't be Mattern's Hannele!—
Well, if it ain't wonderful!

PLESCHKE. She 's a saint, sure enough.

[*The four youths lay Hannele reverently in the crystal coffin.*

HANKE. I told you there wouldn't be no buryin for *her*.

FIRST WOMAN. I reckon they 'll put her into the church.

SECOND WOMAN. I don't believe the girl's dead at all. She looks too lifelike for that.

PLESCHKE. G-gi' me—gi' me—a feather.—We'll soon see if she's dead.—Just gi' me a feather——

[*They give him a feather. He holds it before her lips.*
It don't stir! The girl's dead, sure enough, she is. There ain't no life left in her.

THIRD WOMAN. I'd kinder like to give her this bit o' rosemary.
[*She puts a sprig into the coffin.*

FOURTH WOMAN. She can have my lavender, too.

FIFTH WOMAN. Why, where's Mattern?

FIRST WOMAN. Ay, where's Mattern?

SECOND WOMAN. Where he allus is, drinkin' down at th' inn.

FIRST WOMAN. Maybe he don't know what's happened.

SECOND WOMAN. He don't know nothin' when he's full o' drink.

PLESCHKE. Wot? Ain't no one told him there's a dead body in the house?

THIRD WOMAN. He might er found that out for hisself.

FOURTH WOMAN. I ain't accusin' any one, I ain't. But it *do* seem odd the man who killed the child, as you might say, shouldn't know nothin' about it.

SEIDEL. That's what I say, and every one in th' village 'ud say the same. Why, she's got a bruise on her as big as my fist.

FIFTH WOMAN. He's the devil's own child, is Mattern.

SEIDEL. I saw that there bruise when I was helpin' to put her to bed. I tell yer, it was as big as my fist. That's what settled her business.

FIRST WOMAN. He's the man as done it.

ALL. [*Whispering angrily to one another.*] That's what he is.

SECOND WOMAN. I call him a murderer.

ALL. He's a murderer, a murderer!

[*The drunken voice of Mattern, the mason, is heard without.*

MATTERN. [*Without.*] Lemme in, d'ye hear. Lemme in! I ain't done no harm to nobody. [*He appears in the doorway and bawls.*] Where are you hidin', you good-for-nothin' hussy? [*He staggers.*] I'll give you till I count five. Then look out. Now then One—two—three—and one makes—— Come out, damn you, you hussy. What d'ye mean by makin' me lose my temper? Lemme get a sight of you, that's all, and I'll break every bone in your body. [*He stumbles, recovers, and*

stares stupidly at the silent bystanders.] What are you starin'
at me for? [*No answer.*] What d' ye want? Devil take
you all. I ain't done nothin' to the girl. Come out, d' ye
hear? And mighty quick about it, too. [*He chuckles to himself.*] I know what I 'm about, if I *have* had a drop too much.
What, you ain't gone yet—— [*Savagely.*] Don't stand there
glarin' at me or I 'll——

    [*A man wearing a long, shabby, brown robe enters. He is about
    thirty years old. His hair is long and dark. His face
    is the face of the schoolmaster, Gottwald. In his left hand
    he holds a soft hat. He has sandals on his feet. He
    seems weary and travel-stained. He interrupts the mason
    by laying his hand gently on his arm. Mattern turns
    round roughly. The stranger looks him steadily and
    calmly in the face.*

THE STRANGER. [*Gently.*] Mattern, the mason, God's peace be
with thee.

MATTERN. Where do *you* come from? What do you want?

THE STRANGER. [*Appealing.*] My feet are weary and blood-
stained. Give me water wherewith to wash them. The
burning sun has parched my tongue. Give me wine wherewith to cool it. No food has passed my lips since early morn.
Give me bread wherewith to still my hunger.

MATTERN. It 's none of my business. If you 'd been working,
like an honest man, instead o' trampin' up and down the
country roads, you 'd be all right. *I* have to work for my
livin'.

THE STRANGER. I am a workman.

MATTERN. You 're a vagabond, you are. Honest workmen
don't starve.

THE STRANGER. For *my* work no man pays me.

MATTERN. You 're a vagabond.

THE STRANGER. [*Faintly, submissively, but pressingly.*] I am a
physician. Hast thou not need of me?

MATTERN. Not I. I 'm not sick. No doctors for me.

THE STRANGER. [*His voice trembling with emotion.*] Mattern, the
mason, bethink thee! Though thou hast denied me water, I
will heal thee. Though thou hast refused me bread, yet I can
make thee well. God is my witness.

MATTERN. Be off with you, d' ye hear? Be off. My bones are
sound. I don't want nothin' to do with doctors. Will you
clear out?

THE STRANGER. Mattern, the mason, bethink thee well. I will
wash thy feet. I will give thee wine. Thou shalt have sweet,
white bread to eat. Set thy foot upon my head, and I will
still heal thee, as God liveth.

MATTERN. You won't go, won't you, eh? I'll have to throw
you out?

THE STRANGER. [*Impressively.*] Mattern, the mason, dost thou
not know what lies within this house?

MATTERN. There ain't nothin' lyin' here but what belongs to the
place, 'ceptin' you. Off you go, damn you!

THE STRANGER. [*Simply.*] Thy daughter lies here, sick.

MATTERN. She don't want no doctors to cure her complaint.
She's lazy. That's wot's the matter with her. I'll cure
her, and mighty quick, too, if she don't stop skulkin'.

THE STRANGER. [*Loftily.*] Mattern, the mason, I come to thee
as a messenger.

MATTERN. A messenger? Who sent you, eh?

THE STRANGER. I come from the Father, and I go unto the
Father. What hast thou done with His child?

MATTERN. P'raps you know where she's hidin' herself better
than I do. What are His children to me? He don't seem to
trouble Himself much about them.

THE STRANGER. [*Directly.*] There is one dead within these walls.

MATTERN. [*Sees Hannele, approaches the coffin silently, and looks
in, muttering.*] Where the devil did she get all them fine
clothes and that 'ere crystal coffin?

[*The coffin-bearers whisper together angrily, 'Murderer!
Murderer!'*]

[*Softly and stammering.*] I—n-never did ye n-no harm. I
was kind to you, I was. I didn't deny you nothin'—[*Brutally,
to the Stranger.*] Wot d' yer want? Come, speak out and ha'
done with it? 'Tain't no business of mine.

THE STRANGER. Mattern the mason, hast thou nothing to say
to me?

[*The coffin-bearers grow more and more excited, and frequent
exclamations of 'Murderer!' 'Murderer!' are heard.*]

Hast thou not sinned? Hast thou never dragged her from
her sleep at night and beaten her till she grew faint with pain
and anguish?

MATTERN. [*Frenzied with excitement.*] May Heaven strike me
dead if I have!

[*Faint blue lightning and distant thunder.*

ALL. [*Scattered voices.*] It's thundering!—
Thunder in mid winter!—
He's perjured himself!—
The murderer's perjured himself!

THE STRANGER. [*Gently and persuasively.*] Hast thou still
nothing to confess, Mattern?

MATTERN [*Panic-struck.*] Those whom the Lord loveth, He
chasteneth. That's what I did to the girl. I treated her as
though she was my own child, I did.

THE WOMEN. [*Rushing at him.*] Murderer! Murderer!

MATTERN. She lied to me and cheated me.

THE STRANGER. Is this the truth?

MATTERN. So help me God!

> [*The golden sesame appears in Hannele's clasped hands. A
> mystic greenish-yellow light streams from it. The sight
> dismays Mattern, who recoils in terror.*

THE STRANGER. Mattern the mason, thou hast lied to me.

ALL. [*Scattered voices.*] A miracle! A miracle!

PLESCHKE. The girl's a saint, sure He's perjured hisself, he
has.

MATTERN. [*Shouting.*] I'll go hang myself!

> [*He presses his hands to his temples and goes.*

THE STRANGER. [*Advances to the coffin and turns to the bystanders, who draw back in awe of His now noble and imposing
form.*] Be not afraid! [*He stops and presses Hannele's hand.
Then in a gentle tone.*] The maiden is not dead. She sleepeth.
[*Earnestly.*] Johanna Mattern!

> [*A golden-green light steals into the room. Hannele opens her
> eyes and, with the help of the Stranger's hand, rises, not
> yet daring to fix her eyes on him. She leaves the coffin
> and sinks upon her knees before the Stranger. The by-
> standers flee in consternation. The Stranger and Han-
> nele remain alone. The Stranger's shabby gown falls from
> His shoulders. Beneath it is a robe of white and gold.*

THE STRANGER. [*Tenderly.*] Hannele!

HANNELE. [*With rapture, bending her head low.*] 'Tis He!

THE STRANGER. Dost thou know me?

HANNELE. I have waited for thee.

THE STRANGER. Canst thou name my name?

HANNELE [*Trembling with awe.*] Holy! Holy! Holy!

THE STRANGER. I know thy sorrow and thy pain.

HANNELE. I have longed for thy coming.

THE STRANGER. Arise!

HANNELE. Thy dress is spotless. I am ashamed.

THE STRANGER. [*Laying his right hand on Hannele's head.*] Thy shame I take from thee. [*He lifts her face gently and touches her eyelids.*] I fill thine eyes with everlasting light. Thy soul shall be all sunshine. Eternal brightness shall be thine, from dawn till eve and then till dawn again. Receive all radiant things, and feast thine eyes on all the glories of the deep blue sea and azure sky and fair green trees, for ever and for ever. [*He touches her ears.*] Let thine ears be opened to the music of the millions upon millions of God's angels. [*He touches her lips.*] Thus do I loose thy stammering tongue and quicken it with the life of thine own soul and My soul, and the soul of God Almighty. [*Hannele, trembling convulsively with rapture, tries to rise, but cannot. She sobs and buries her head in the Stranger's robe.*] With these thy tears I cleanse thee from the dust and stain of earth. I will raise thee high above the stars of God.

> [*The Stranger lays His hand on the child's head and speaks the following lines to the accompanying strains of soft music. As He speaks, the forms of many angels appear, crowding through the doorway. Some are tall, some short. Some are radiant winged boys and girls. They swing censers and strew flowers, and spread rich stuffs on the floor.*

THE STRANGER. The Realm of Righteousness is filled with light and joy.

God's everlasting peace reigns there without alloy.

> [*Harps are heard, at first played softly, then gradually swelling louder and louder.*

Its mansions are marble, its roofs are of gold,
Through its rivulets ripple wines ruddy and old.
In its silver-white streets blow the lily and rose,
In its steeples the chiming of joy-bells grows.
The beautiful butterflies frolic and play
On its ramparts, rich-robed in the mosses of May.
Swans, twelve, soft as snow, ring them round in the sky,
And their wings thrill the air with sweet sounds as they fly
And louder and louder the symphonies swell
Till their resonance reaches from heaven to hell.
For ever and ever, through aeons unending,
With music majestic their progress attending,

They soar above Zion and meadow and sea,
And their path is made lambent with mystery.
The blessèd below, in the regions of Light,
Wander on, hand in hand, and rejoice in their flight.
In the depths of the radiant, the ruby-red waves,
Swan dives down after swan, as its plumage it laves.
So they wash themselves clean in the clear, deep red
Of the blood that the Lord, their dear Saviour, had shed
And they pass from the glory of flood and of foam,
To the rest and the bliss of their heavenly home.

[*The Stranger turns to the angels, who have ended their work.
    With timid joy they draw near and form a semicircle
    round Hannele and the Stranger.*

Bring hither finest linen, children mine—
My fair, my pretty turtle-doves, come hither.
Surround her weak and wasted little frame
With comfort and with warmth, to keep her free
From frost and fever, pain and weary woe.
Be tender with her.   Shield her from rude touch,
And bear her swiftly up, on pinions light.
Above the waving grasses of the lea,
Beyond the shimmering wastes of moonlit space
Beyond the meads and groves of Paradise,
Into the cool and shade of boundless peace.
Then, while she rests upon her silken bed.
Prepare for her, in alabaster bath,
Water from mountain brook, and purple wine, and milk of
    antelope,
To wash away the stain of earthly ill!
From off the bushes break the budding sprays,
Lilac and jessamine, with dew bent low,
And let their moisture from the petals flow
Softly upon her, as the showers in May.
Take linen rare and fine, to dry her limbs
With loving hands, as ye would lily-leaves.
From jewell'd chalices pour the reviving wine,
Pressed from the patient heart of fragrant fruit.

.   .   .   .   .   .

Delight her lips with sweets, her heart delight
With all the dazzling splendours of the morn.
Enchant her eyes with stately palaces.

Let humming-birds, in iris hues arrayed,
From walls of malachite flash gold and green.
Beneath her feet spread velvets, richly wrought,
And strew her path with daffodils and tulips.
To fan her cheek let palms in cadence sway
And make her life unceasing holiday.
Where the red poppies rear their beauteous heads
And happy children dance to meet the day,
Bid her repose, free now from tear and sigh,
And witch her soul with gentle harmony.

THE ANGELS. [*Sing in chorus.*]

> We bear thee away to the Heavenly Rest,
> Lullaby, into the Land of the Blest,
> Lullaby, into the Land of the Blest!

[*The stage grows gradually dark, as the angels sing. Out of the darkness the sound of their song is heard more and more faintly. Then the stage grows light. The interior of the almshouse is seen exactly as before the first apparition. Hannele—a poor, sick child, once more lies on the bed. Dr. Wachler bends over her, with a stethoscope. The Deaconess (Sister Martha) stands by, watching anxiously, and holding a candle in her hand. The angels' song ceases.*]

DR. WACHLER. [*Rising.*] You are right!

DEACONESS. Is she dead?

DR. WACHLER. [*Sadly.*] She is dead.

CURTAIN

THE LIFE OF THE INSECTS

Comedy in Three Acts with
Prelude and Epilogue
by
JOSEF AND KAREL ČAPEK

Sole authorized translation from the Czech by
PAUL SELVER

CHARACTERS

PRELUDE

VAGRANT
PEDANT

ACT I

The Butterflies

APATURA IRIS
APATURA CLYTHIA
FELIX
VICTOR } *Butterflies*
OTAKAR

ACT II

The Marauders

CHRYSALIS
MALE BEETLE
FEMALE BEETLE
ANOTHER MALE BEETLE
ICHNEUMON FLY
ITS LARVA
MALE CRICKET
FEMALE CRICKET
PARASITE
BAND OF PILLAGERS

ACT III

The Ants

FIRST ENGINEER, *Dictator*
SECOND ENGINEER, *Head of the
  General Staff*
BLIND ANT
INVENTOR
MESSENGER

93

ACT III—*contd.*

The Ants

QUARTERMASTER GENERAL
JOURNALIST
PHILANTHROPIST
TELEGRAPHIST
COMMANDER-IN-CHIEF OF THE YELLOWS
ANT WORKERS AND SOLDIERS, OFFICIALS
MESSENGERS, OFFICERS, STRETCHER-BEARERS,
    WOUNDED, etc
ARMY OF THE YELLOWS

EPILOGUE

Life and Death

FIRST ⎫
SECOND ⎬ MOTH
THIRD ⎭
CHORUS OF MOTH-DANCERS
FIRST SNAIL
SECOND SNAIL
A WOODCUTTER
AN AUNT
A SCHOOLGIRL
A WANDERER

The insects wear human clothing   The Butterflies have drawing-room attire, the Marauders are dressed as citizens, the Ants are dressed in black or yellow close-fitting workmen's garb with belts, the Moths in gauze veils   The insect characteristics are expressed chiefly by pantomime gestures.

PRELUDE

Scene: *A green forest glade*

VAGRANT. [*Staggers from the wings, stumbles, and falls.*]
Ha, ha, ha. What fun, eh? Never mind. You needn't
laugh. I haven't hurt myself. [*Propping himself on his
elbow.*] You—you—you think I'm drunk? Oh no. I'm
stretched out quite firmly. You saw how steadily I fell. Like
a tree. Like a hero. I was performing—the fall—of man.
What a spectacle! [*He sits up.*] Why, I'm not staggering.
Not me, but everything else is drunk, everything's staggering
about, whirling around—round and round the whole time
in a circle. Ha, ha, that's enough, it makes me feel bad.
[*Looks round.*] What's that? Everything's whirling round
me. The whole earth. The whole universe. Doing me
too great an honour. [*Smooths his clothing.*] Excuse me,
I'm not dressed for the part of acting as centre of the harmony of the spheres. [*Throws his cap to the ground.*] There's
the centre. Whirl around my cap, it won't come to any
harm. Let's see, where did I leave off?

Oh yes, I know. I fell down beneath my load. And you,
crocus, thought I was drunk? Speedwell, veronica, don't
get so puffed up with your sobriety. They put your leaves,
veronica, on wounds; wait, speedwell, I'll lay my heart on
you. I don't say I'm not drunk; if I had roots like you I
wouldn't wander all over the world like a vagabond. That's
how it is. Why, I was in the Great War; I know Latin too,
and now I can turn my hand to all sorts of things. Clear
manure, sweep the streets, mount guard, draw beer, and what
not. Everything that others don't like doing. Now you see
who I am. Let's see, where did I leave off?

Ah, I know. Yes, that's me. They know me everywhere.
I'm a man. Nobody calls me anything else. They say to
me: 'Man, I'll have you arrested,' or 'Man, tidy up, do this for
me, bring that to me,' or 'Clear off, man.' And I'm not
offended at being a man. If I were to say to somebody: 'Man,
give me sixpence,' he'd be offended. If he doesn't like it,
well and good. I'll regard him as a butterfly, or a beetle, or
an ant, just as he prefers. It's all the same to me, man or

insect, I don't want to put any one in his place. Neither insect nor man. I just look on.

I just look on. If I had roots or a bulb in the earth, I'd look at the sky. [*Rises to his knees.*] At the skies. To my dying day I'd look straight at the sky. [*Stands up.*] But I'm a man, I must look at people. [*Looks round.*] And I see them.

PEDANT. [*Runs in with a net.*] Ha, ha. Oh, oh, oh. What fine specimens. Apatura Iris. Apatura Clythia. The painted lady and the light-blue butterfly. Ha, ha, what magnificent creatures Oh, just you wait, I'll have you. Ha, ha, they're off again. Ha, ha, cautiously, careful, hush, softly, softly, ah, ah, gently, gently—aha, oho, careful, careful, ah, oho, oho——

VAGRANT. Hi, what are you catching butterflies for? Good day to you, kind sir.

PEDANT. Softly, softly, careful. Don't move. They've settled on you. Butterflies. Nymphalidae. Careful, keep still. They settle on everything that smells. On mud. On offal. On garbage. Careful, they've settled on you. Oho, oho.

VAGRANT. Let them be. They're playing.

PEDANT. What, playing? Their play is only the overture to pairing. The male pursues the female, the bride slips away, lures him on, the pursuer tickles her with his feelers, sinks down exhausted, the female flits off, a new, stronger, sturdier male will come, the female slips away, entices the lover after her, aha, aha. Do you catch my meaning? That's the way of nature. The eternal contest of love. The eternal mating. The eternal round of sex. Rush, softly.

VAGRANT. And what will you do with them when you catch them?

PEDANT. What will I do? Well, the butterfly must be identified, recorded, and assigned a place in my collection. But the pollen mustn't be rubbed off. The net should be of delicate texture. The butterfly should be carefully killed by crushing its breast. And then impaled on a pin. And fastened down with paper strips. And placed in the collection when it's properly dried. It should be protected against dust and moth. Put a small sponge of cyanide into the case.

VAGRANT. And what's all that for?

PEDANT. Love of nature. Man alive, you've no love of nature! Aha, there they are again. Ha, ha, careful, careful, softly. You won't escape me, ha, ha.   [*Runs off.*

VAGRANT. Eternal mating, love's eternal contest,
    'Tis even so; 'tis ever pairing time,
    As said the pedant.   Kindly pardon me
    For being drunk. Why, I can see quite well.
    Everything 's twofold, everything 's in pairs,
    Here, there, and here again, and everywhere,
    All things in pairs.   Clouds, gnats, and trees,
    All things embrace and fondle, dally, provoke and pursue,
    Birds in the tree-tops, I see you, I see you,
    I see all.   And you two, yonder in the shadow,
    I see you linking your fingers, struggling hotly and softly,
    Let none of you think I don't see you from here.
    That 's eternal mating.   Kindly pardon me.
    I 'm drunk, but I 'm a sport. [*Covers his eyes.*] I see nothing.
    Do what you will.   I 'll shout before I uncover my eyes.
                                              [*Darkness.*
    All things strive to pair.   Only you, standing here in the
        darkness,
    Alone, alone, alone you wander your crooked way,
    Vainly, vainly, vainly would you lift your hands
    In love's hide-and-seek.   Enough   But ye shall take joy of
        each other,
    Wherefore I applaud you, that 's a goodly thing
    And nature's wise order, as the pedant said.
    —All things strive to pair.   Now do I behold
    The blissful garden of love bedecked with flowers.
                                     [*The back curtain rises*
    Wherein young pairs, beauteous twin beings,
    Butterflies swept along by the gust of love,
    In rapturous flight, as though they were at play,
    Unendingly they bear eternal matings
    For all things strive to pair.
                        [*He uncovers his eyes.   The scene is lit up.*
                    Where am I?

ACT I

THE BUTTERFLIES

A radiant, azure space, bedecked with flowers and cushions; mirrors, a small table with coloured glasses containing cold drinks and straws. High seats, as in a bar.

VAGRANT. [*Rubs his eyes and looks around.*] Hallo, how lovely, how beautiful! Why, it 's just like—like being in paradise. A painter couldn't have made a better picture. And how nice it smells!

[Clythie runs in laughing.

OTAKAR. [*Running after her.*] I love you. Clythie.

[Clythie runs off laughing, Otakar after her.

VAGRANT. Butterflies. Aha, butterflies. They 're playing. I 'd have a look at 'em, if I wasn't so—— [*Brushes his clothes.*] Oh, let 'em kick me out. I 'll lie down here. [*Arranges the cushions.*] I 'll lie down. I 'm blowed if I won't! [*Arranges a bed in the proscenium.*] And if we don't like it, we 'll close our eyes and have forty winks. [*Lies down.*] That 's the way.

Enter Felix

FELIX. Where is Iris? I saw her quaff the scent of the flowers —Iris, Iris. If I could at least find a rhyme to you [*Sits down among the cushions.*] 'Beauteous Iris, who as pure as fire is'—No. Something else: '—a diamond buckler my love's attire is, and has filled me with angel strength—Iris. Iris, Iris.' That would do. But where is Iris? How can she always be with that fellow Victor? Oh dear. 'Upon thy lips divine, grows not oft bitter, Iris, thy smile of victory, when sorrow's gesture dire is—' I 'll make an elegy of this, in regular alexandrines when she has let me down. Ah, 'tis a poet's lot to suffer. [*Laughter behind the scene.*
That 's Iris.

[Behind, by the entrance, a picture of delicate grief, he props his head in his hands. Iris enters, Victor after her.

IRIS. Felix, is that you there by yourself? And so interestingly sad?

98

FELIX. [*Turning round.*] You, Iris? Ah, I didn't imagine——

IRIS. Why aren't you playing outside? There are such lots of girls there.

FELIX. [*Jumping up.*] You know, Iris, that—that they don't interest me.

IRIS. Oh, poor fellow! Why not?

VICTOR. Not yet?

FELIX. No longer.

IRIS. [*Sitting down among the pillows.*] Do you hear that, Victor? And he says that right to my face. Come here, you rude man. Sit down here, nearer, still nearer. Tell me, darling, don't women interest you any longer?

FELIX. No. I'm tired of them.

IRIS. [*With a huge sigh.*] Oh, you men. What cynics you are. You just have your enjoyment, as much enjoyment as you can, and then you all say: I'm tired of them. How terrible it is to be a woman.

VICTOR. Why?

IRIS. *We* are never tired. What sort of a past have you had, Felix? When did you love for the first time?

FELIX. I don't know now. It's too long ago. And even then it wasn't for the first time. I was a schoolboy——

VICTOR. Ah, you were still a caterpillar. A green caterpillar, devouring the leaves.

IRIS. Felix, was she dark? Was she beautiful?

FELIX. Beautiful as the day, as the azure, as——

IRIS. As what? Quickly.

FELIX. As beautiful as you.

IRIS. Felix, dearest, did she love you?

FELIX. I don't know. I never spoke to her.

IRIS. Good heavens, what did you do to her then?

FELIX. I looked at her from afar——

VICTOR. Sitting on a green leaf——

FELIX. And wrote poems; letters; my first novel——

VICTOR. It's appalling the number of leaves such a caterpillar uses up.

IRIS. You're horrid, Victor. Look, Felix has his eyes full of tears. Isn't that nice?

VICTOR. Tears? Why——

FELIX. It isn't true. I haven't got tears in my eyes. On my honour I haven't.

IRIS. Let's see. Look into my eyes, quickly.

VICTOR. One, two, three, four—I knew he wouldn't hold out any longer.

IRIS [*Laughing.*] Now then, Felix, tell me at once what sort of eyes I have.

FELIX. Azure blue.

IRIS. That's a fine thing to say! They're brown. Ah, someone told me that they are golden. I don't care for blue eyes. They're so cold, so devoid of passion. Poor Clythie has blue eyes, hasn't she? Do you like her eyes, Felix?

FELIX. Clythie's? I don't know. Yes, she has beautiful eyes.

IRIS. Get along with you, she has such thin legs. Oh, you're such bad judges of women, you poets.

VICTOR. Have you read the last poem that Felix wrote? [*Taking a book out of his pocket.*] It came out in the Spring Almanac.

IRIS. Quick, read it to me.

FELIX. No, I won't let you read it to her. [*Trying to stand up.*] It's bad. It's old. I've long since got past that stage.

IRIS. [*Holding him back.*] Sit down quietly, Felix.

VICTOR. It's called *Eternal Downfall.*

FELIX. [*Putting his hands over his ears.*] But I don't want you to read it to her.

VICTOR. [*Reads with emphasis*]

> 'Downwards, downwards, swift and fleet
>   The pace at which we fly.
> The world desires deceit, deceit—
>   Woman desires to lie.'

IRIS. That's witty, isn't it, Victor? Felix, you naughty man, what made you write *that?*

VICTOR   'The dream be not frustrated—
>   Let love be consummated.
> All ever falls pell-mell;
>   Darling, let's fall as well.'

IRIS. Fall, I understand that; but what is 'consummated'?

VICTOR. That's Latin. It means love which, h'm, has achieved its aim.

IRIS. What aim?

VICTOR. Well, its usual one.

IRIS. Oh, how shocking. Felix, how could you write such a thing? I'm afraid of you How depraved you are. Is Latin always so immoral?

FELIX. Have pity, Iris. It's such a bad poem.

IRIS. Why bad?

FELIX. It still lacks the—the—real thing.

IRIS. Aha. Victor, you'll find my fan in the garden.

VICTOR. Oh, pray don't let me disturb you.   [*Exit.*

IRIS. Quick, Felix. Tell me the truth. You can tell me everything.

FELIX. Iris, Iris, how can you bear him about you? Such an old fop. Such a back-number. Such a washed-out lecher.

IRIS. Victor?

FELIX. How basely he looks upon you, upon love, upon everything. How shamelessly. How . . . how . . . how uncouthly. How can you put up with it?

IRIS. Poor Victor. He's so soothing. No, Felix, talk about poetry. I'm so fond of poetry. 'The dream be not frustrated . . .' [*Sits down among the pillows.*] Felix, you're awfully talented. 'Darling, let's fall as well.' Heavens, how passionately it's expressed. Tell me, Felix, poets are fearfully, fearfully passionate, aren't they?

FELIX. Oh, Iris, I've long since got past what's in that poem.

IRIS. If only the Latin wasn't so vulgar. I can put up with anything, anything, but it mustn't have a horrid name. Felix, you must be delicate towards women. If you were to kiss me now, would you give that a horrid name too?

FELIX. Iris, how could I dare to kiss you?

IRIS. Come, come, you men are capable of anything. Felix, bend down towards me. To whom did you write that poem? To Clythie?

FELIX. No, I assure you——

IRIS. To whom then?

FELIX. To nobody, upon my honour, to nobody. Or rather, to all the women in the world.

IRIS. [*Leaning on her elbow.*] Good gracious, have you con . . . con—what do you call it?—so many of them?

FELIX. Iris, I swear to you——

IRIS. [*Sinking down among the pillows.*] Felix, you're a terrible lady-killer. Tell me, who was your mistress?

FELIX. Iris, you won't tell anybody? You really won't?

IRIS. No.

FELIX. Well then—I haven't got one.

IRIS. What?

FELIX. Not yet. Upon my honour.

IRIS. Oh, what a fib. How many women have you told that to,

you innocent creature? Felix, Felix, I see through you. What a dangerous man you are.

FELIX Iris, you mustn't laugh at me. I've had terrible experiences in my imagination. Awful disappointments Love affairs without number, but only in my dreams. Dreams are the poet's life. I know all women, and haven't known one. Upon my honour, Iris.

IRIS. [*Leaning on her elbow.*] Then why do you say that you are tired of women?

FELIX. Oh, Iris, every one disparages the thing he loves the most.

IRIS. Brunettes?

FELIX. No, dreams. Eternal dreams.

IRIS. 'The dream be not frustrated.' You have such passionate eyes. You're fearfully talented, Felix. [*Sinks down among the pillows.*] What are you thinking of now?

FELIX. Of you. Woman is a riddle.

IRIS. Solve her then. But gently, Felix, please.

FELIX. I cannot see into the depths of your eyes.

IRIS. Then begin elsewhere.

FELIX. I . . . Iris . . . really . . .

IRIS. [*Abruptly sitting up.*] Felix, I'm in such a queer mood to-day. How silly it is to be a woman. To-day I should like to be a man, to conquer, to allure, to embrace. . . . Felix, I should be such a fearfully passionate man I should . . . I . . . I should snatch every one away wildly, savagely . . . what a pity that you aren't a girl. Let's pretend, shall we? You will be Iris and I will be your Felix.

FELIX. No Iris. It's too venturesome to be Felix. That means desiring, desiring something . . .

IRIS. [*In a faint voice.*] Oh, Felix, everything.

FELIX There is something greater than to desire everything.

IRIS. And that is——

FELIX. To desire something impossible.

IRIS. [*Disappointedly.*] You're right. You're always right, poor Felix. [*Stands up.*] What can be keeping Victor so long? Would you mind calling him?

FELIX. [*Jumping up.*] Iris, how have I offended you? Oh, I said too much.

IRIS. [*Turning round in front of the mirror.*] Oh, I wouldn't call it too much.

FELIX. To desire the unattainable. Iris, I was mad to talk to you like that.

IRIS. Bad-mannered, anyhow. Really, you know, it 's appalling the trouble I 'm taking with you. When we 're in the company of ladies, we mustn't behave as if we were longing for something which isn't there.

FELIX. The unattainable is there.

IRIS. [Looking round.] Where?

FELIX. [Pointing to the mirror.] Your reflection, Iris.

IRIS. [Laughing.] My reflection? Have you fallen in love with my reflection? [Stretching out her hands towards the mirror.] Look, my reflection has heard you. Embrace it. Kiss it, quickly.

FELIX. It is as unapproachable as you.

IRIS. [Turning to him.] I am unapproachable? How do you know?

FELIX. If I did not know, I should not love you.

IRIS. Felix, what a pity that I am so unapproachable.

FELIX. Ah, Iris, there is no true love except in the unapproachable

IRIS. Do you think so? [Pulls him by the hair and sings.] 'Darling, let 's fall as well.'

FELIX. Don't repeat that poem.

IRIS. Make one up for me, quickly. Something passionate.

FELIX.   'When in the final moment I cried;
              Death, hark to a mournful lover,
              Lay your hand where my heart once was,
              And a single wound you 'll discover—
              I am filled with angel-strength, for
              A diamond buckler my love's attire is.
              I am filled with angel-strength, by
              Iris, Iris, Iris.'

IRIS. Iris—attire is. How beautiful it is.

CLYTHIE [Behind the scene.] Iris, Iris.

IRIS. There she is again. And with that horrible husband of hers Just as we——

CLYTHIE. [Runs in laughing.] Just fancy, Iris, Otakarek says —Ah, you 've got Felix here How are you, Felix? Iris, you 've been teasing him, haven't you? He 's quite red.

OTAKAR [Runs in.] I 've got you now, Clythie. . . . Oh, I beg your pardon. Good day, Iris. How are you, old chap?

FELIX. [Sitting down among the pillows.] Whew!

IRIS. How hot you are, Clythie.

CLYTHIE. Otakarek chased me.

OTAKAR. Clythie flew away, and I had to follow her.

VICTOR. [Entering.] Hallo, there's quite a company here.

[Greets Clythie.

CLYTHIE. Oh, I'm so thirsty.

[Drinks from a glass through a straw.

IRIS. Take care of yourself, dearest. Victor, see how thin she's got again. You look ghastly.

CLYTHIE. Thanks, darling, you're so motherly.

VICTOR. Were you at the garden party yesterday?

CLYTHIE. Pooh, yesterday. That's ancient history.

VICTOR. Marvellous weather.

IRIS. [To Clythie.] Just a moment, dearest. [Arranges her bodice.] What have you been doing? Your bodice is torn.

CLYTHIE. Perhaps Otakarek trod on me.

IRIS. Trod on you? Up to your throat?

CLYTHIE. Look at him, he's all foot. Aren't you, toot?

OTAKAR. Eh?

VICTOR. And what am I?

CLYTHIE. You're all tongue.

IRIS. Oh, Clythie. And what is Felix?

CLYTHIE. Poor fellow, he's so sad. [Kneels down to him.] What is the matter with you, prince?

FELIX. I'm thinking.

CLYTHIE. Go on! What do you keep thinking about?

FELIX. Men's minds were given them to use.

CLYTHIE. And women?

FELIX. To misuse.

IRIS. Oh, very good, Felix!

CLYTHIE. [Standing up.] The horrid creature hates me.

VICTOR. Be careful, Clythie, that's the first step towards love.

OTAKAR. Eh?

IRIS. Felix and love? The idea. Why, he wrote something about women—wait . . .

FELIX. Iris I implore you.

IRIS.   'Downwards, downwards, swift and fleet
             The pace at which we fly.
             The world desires deceit, deceit—
             Woman desires to lie.'

CLYTHIE. Desires what?

IRIS. To lie.

VICTOR. Felix, you rascal, how many women have you already caused to lie?

OTAKAR. Ha, ha, ha. To lie. I see, of course. To lie. Ha, ha, ha.

IRIS. [*Goes on reciting.*] 'The dream be not frustrated.'

CLYTHIE. Wait, Otakarek is going to laugh again.

OTAKAR. Ha, ha, ha.

FELIX. I won't allow you to read it out. I've got past that stage.

IRIS. Felix is frightfully talented None of you could find a rhyme to 'Iris.'

CLYTHIE. 'Iris, than whom none slyer is.'

FELIX. Oh, ye gods, do stop it.

OTAKAR. Ha, ha, ha, that's splendid. Iris—slyer is.

IRIS [*Keeping her temper.*] Darling, you have such strange ideas of poetry. But you'd never believe what a beautiful rhyme Felix made to my name. Guess.

VICTOR. I give it up.

CLYTHIE. Oh, tell us, Iris.

IRIS. [*Triumphantly.*] 'A diamond buckler my love's attire is.'

VICTOR. What?

IRIS. '. . . my love's attire is.'

OTAKAR. Ha, ha, ha. Attire is. What fun!

IRIS. Oh, you're horrid. You've no sense of art I've got no patience with you.

VICTOR. Felix O, he kicks so.

IRIS. [*Claps her hands.*] Splendid, Victor You're frightfully witty

CLYTHIE. Good heavens, Victor's managed to produce a rhyme.

OTAKAR. Ha, ha, ha.   Felix O, he kicks so. That's good.

VICTOR. Pooh, poetry, what is it? Lying or fooling.

IRIS. Oh no. It stirs the feelings. I'm fearfully fond of it.

OTAKAR. Guitar.

CLYTHIE. What guitar?

OTAKAR. Rhymes with Otakar, ha, ha, ha. Good, eh?

IRIS. You're fearfully talented, Otakar. Why don't you write poems?

OTAKAR. Me? H'm. What about?

IRIS. About love. I adore poetry.

OTAKAR. Lovely star.

IRIS What lovely star? Who do you mean?

OTAKAR. Ha, ha, ha. That's a rhyme.

IRIS. Otakar, you have such a fearfully poetic soul.

CLYTHIE. [*Yawning.*] Do stop talking about literature. I'm so heartily sick of it.

VICTOR. Heartily? Fancy, poor Clythie imagines she's got a heart somewhere.

IRIS. Ha, ha, ha. Victor, you're awfully good company. I could give you a kiss. I do so admire witty people. See if you can catch me. [*Runs out. Victor runs after her.*

CLYTHIE. Oh, what a silly creature. What a perfect fright. What an awful figure. Felix?

FELIX. [*Jumping up.*] Yes?

CLYTHIE. How ever could you fall in love with her?

FELIX. With whom?

CLYTHIE. With that old frump.

FELIX. Whom do you mean?

CLYTHIE. Iris, of course.

FELIX. I? What can you be thinking of. That's all done with, long ago.

CLYTHIE. I understand. Iris is so fearfully ignorant. Such awful feet. Oh, Felix, at your age, you still have so many illusions about women. [*Sits down among the pillows.*

FELIX. I? I assure you, Clythie—upon my honour, I've long since got past that stage.

CLYTHIE. No, Felix, you don't know women. Sit down beside me, will you? You've no idea of what they're like. Their opinions. Their minds. And their bodies. Ugh. You are so young . . .

FELIX. Oh, no. I'm not young now. I've had so much experience.

CLYTHIE. You must be very young. That's the fashion now. To be young, to be a butterfly, to be a poet. Is there anything more beautiful in the whole world?

FELIX. No, Clythie. The lot of youth is to suffer. And the lot of a poet is to suffer a hundredfold. Really and truly.

CLYTHIE. The lot of a poet is to be frightfully happy. To enjoy life. Ah, Felix, you remind me of my first love.

FELIX. Who was that?

CLYTHIE. Nobody. None of my loves was the first. Ugh, that Victor. I do hate men so. Let's be friends, Felix, like two women together.

FELIX. Like two women?

CLYTHIE. Love means nothing to you. Love is so common.
Ah, I'd like something quite special and pure. Something
out of the ordinary. Something new.

FELIX. A poem?

CLYTHIE. Yes, that would do. You see how much you mean to me.

FELIX. Wait.   [*Jumps up excitedly.*

> 'Into my heart took flight
> As into the eye of a child
> A ray of light.
> When I met her, as a poppy she glowed,
> A bloom to the sight,
> And her shyness upon me she bestowed.'

CLYTHIE. [*Standing up.*] What's that?

FELIX. A poem. The beginning.

CLYTHIE. And how does it go on?

FELIX. I'll bring you the end in a moment. Now I've got past
the stage of everything I've written till now.   [*Flies off.*

CLYTHIE. Bah! [*Turns to Otakar who, in the meanwhile, has been
twirling his moustache in vast annoyance.*] Now then, can't
you leave those whiskers alone?

OTAKAR. Be mine. Be mine now.

CLYTHIE. Don't touch!

OTAKAR. Be mine. We are betrothed. I . . . I . . .

CLYTHIE. Otakarek, you are so handsome.

OTAKAR. I love you madly.

CLYTHIE. I know. It's delightful the way your heart is beating.
Say 'ha.'

OTAKAR. Ha.

CLYTHIE. Again.

OTAKAR. H'm. Ha.

CLYTHIE. How that rumbles in your chest. Like thunder.
Otakarek, you're fearfully strong, aren't you?

OTAKAR. Cly . . . Cly . . . Cly . . .

CLYTHIE. What is it now?

OTAKAR. Be mine.

CLYTHIE. Don't be tiresome, please.

OTAKAR. I . . . I . . .

CLYTHIE. So do I . . .

OTAKAR. [*Catching hold of her.*] Be mine. I adore you.

CLYTHIE. [*Running away.*] Not a bit of it. I should only spoil
my figure.

OTAKAR. [*Pursuing her.*] I . . . I . . . I want . . .

CLYTHIE. [*Laughs and flies off.*] Wait, only wait. You mustn't
be impatient.

OTAKAR. [*Flies after her.*] Clythie, be mine.   [*Exeunt.*

VAGRANT. [*Standing up.*]

> Whew, Off they go, love's motley crew.
> How they ogled, how they dallied and dallied;
> Ha, ha, the hunted female. Ha, ha, the insect legs.
> Ha, ha, the greedy little bodies behind the silken wings
> Leave me in peace, I know it, I 'll warrant you:
> That 's—what—they—call—love

CLYTHIE. [*Flies in from the other side, puts on make-up, and
powders herself by the mirror.*] Whew! I managed to get
away from him. Ha, ha.

VAGRANT. Ha, ha, drawing-room society. Ha, ha, ha, poetry.

> Sipping at life's enjoyments through the thinnest of straws,
> These low-neck delights, these thrills and soft ticklings,
> Eternal lie of eternal lovers eternally unappeased,
> What insects they are!

CLYTHIE. [*Flies up to him.*] Are you a butterfly?

                              [*Vagrant throws his cap at her.*

CLYTHIE. [*Flying away.*] Aren't you a butterfly?

VAGRANT. I am a man.

CLYTHIE. What is that? Is it alive?

VAGRANT. Yes.

CLYTHIE. [*Flying up.*] Does it love?

VAGRANT. Yes. It 's a butterfly.

CLYTHIE. How interesting you are. Why do you wear a black
gown?

VAGRANT. That 's dirt.

CLYTHIE. Oh, how nice you smell.

VAGRANT. That 's sweat and dust.

CLYTHIE. Your fragrance intoxicates me. It is so new.

VAGRANT. [*Throwing his cap at her.*] Shoo, you hussy.

CLYTHIE. [*Flying away.*] Catch me. Catch me.

VAGRANT. Flighty jade, worthless baggage——

CLYTHIE. [*Approaching him.*] Let me just smell. Let me just
taste. You are so unusual.

VAGRANT. I 've met the likes of you before, you minx. Why did
I love her? [*Catches hold of Clythie.*] I caught hold of her

insect hands like that, and begged her to smile at me, and then I let her go.   Oh, if I had only killed her. [*Lets her go.*] Fly away, you wench, I don't want you.

CLYTHIE. [*Flies away.*] Ugh, how strange you are.

[*Powders herself in front of the mirror.*

VAGRANT. Scented wanton, strumpet, skinny truoll, hag——

CLYTHIE. [*Coming close to him.*] Again, again.   It's so lovely, so coarse, so violent.

VAGRANT. What, you pest, isn't that enough for you, you white-faced harridan?

CLYTHIE. I love you!   Oh, I adore you!

VAGRANT. [*Flinching from her.*] Go, go, go.   You make me sick.

CLYTHIE. How tiresome you are.   Wretch!

[*Combs her hair by the mirror.*

IRIS. [*Returns beaten.*] Something to drink, quick.

CLYTHIE. Where have you been?

IRIS. [*Drinking through a straw.*] Outside.   Oh, it's so hot.

CLYTHIE. Where did you leave Victor?

IRIS. Victor?   Which Victor?

CLYTHIE. Why, you went with him——

IRIS. With Victor.   Oh no.   Aha, I see. [*Laughs.*] No, that was only fun.

CLYTHIE. With Victor?

IRIS. Of course.   Wait, it'll make you laugh.   He kept running after me, ha, ha, ha.

CLYTHIE. Where did you leave him.

IRIS. I'm telling you.   He kept running after me like mad, and suddenly, ha, ha, ha, a bird flew along and ate him up.

CLYTHIE. Never!

IRIS. As true as I'm standing here.   Oh, it did make me laugh.

[*Throws herself down among the pillows and hides her face.*

CLYTHIE. What's the matter with you?

IRIS. Ha, ha, ha.   Oh, these men.

CLYTHIE. Do you mean Victor?

IRIS. No, Otakar.   Victor was eaten by a bird.   Just fancy, immediately afterwards, your Otakarek came flying up, oh, the look in his eyes, all on fire, and then, ha, ha, ha——

CLYTHIE. What then?

IRIS. He came right after me.   Be mine.   I love you madly, ha, ha, ha.

CLYTHIE. Iris, what did you do?

IRIS. Ha, ha, ha.   I l-l-love you fearfully.   You mu-mu-must be m-m-mine.

FELIX. [*Flies up with a poem in his hands.*] Clythie, here it is. Listen.   [*Reads with boundless emotion.*

> 'Into my heart took flight
>   As into the eye of a child
>   A ray of light.'

IRIS. [*With her head among the pillows, laughing hysterically.*] Ha, ha, ha.

FELIX. [*Stops reading.*] What is it?

IRIS. [*Sobbing.*] What a coarse fellow.   Fie, for shame.   I would have strangled him.

CLYTHIE. Otakar?

FELIX. Listen, Clythie.   This is quite a new style:

> 'When I met her, as a poppy she glowed,
>   A bloom to the sight,
>   And her shyness upon me she bestowed.
> "'Tis I," she said, "you know me not.
> What I am, I myself cannot tell,
> I 'm a child and I blossom, I 'm life and I swell,
> I 'm a woman and lure, so bewildered am I——"'

IRIS. [*Standing up.*] Is my hair fearfully untidy?

CLYTHIE. Fearfully.   Wait, dearest.   [*Puts her hair straight. Aside.*] Beast.

IRIS. You 're angry, aren't you?   Ha, ha, ha, Otakar loves wond—er—ful—ly.   [*Flies off.*

FELIX. Now, Clythie, this is the best part:

> 'I 'm a child and I blossom, I 'm life and I swell,
> I 'm a woman and lure, so bewildered am I——'

CLYTHIE. Leave off.   The beast! [*Flies away.*] Where is somebody new?

FELIX. [*After her.*] Wait, wait.   This is just where love comes in.

VAGRANT. Fool.

FELIX. What 's that?   Ah, here 's somebody.   That 's good. I 'll read you the end.

> 'I 'm a woman and lure, so bewildered am I,
> Great world, what does it signify . . .?'

VAGRANT. [*Throwing his cap at him.*] Shoo.

FELIX. [*Flying about.*]

> '. . . What does it signify,
> That to-day my blood is all aglow?
> I 'm a woman, I love.   I am lite and I bloom.
> I 'm a child, and love for the first time I know.'

Do you understand?   That is Clythie, Clythie, Clythie.

[Flies off.

VAGRANT. [*Stretching out his hands to the auditorium.*] Ha, ha, ha, butterflies.

END OF ACT I

ACT II

THE MARAUDERS

The scene represents a sandy hillock, with a scanty growth of grass, the size of a tree trunk. On the left side the lair of the Ichneumon Fly, on the right side the deserted cavity of a cricket. The Vagrant lies asleep in the proscenium. A Chrysalis is fastened to a blade of grass. The Chrysalis is attacked by a gang of rapacious insects. From the left a small Beetle runs in and unfastens it from the blade of grass. From the right a second one runs out, chases the first one off, and tries to snatch the Chrysalis away. From the prompt-box a third leaps forth, chases the second one away, and drags the Chrysalis off.

CHRYSALIS. I ... I ... I ...

    [The third rapacious Beetle plunges headlong into the prompt-box. From the left the first Beetle, and from the right the second, run in and wrangle about the Chrysalis. The third darts out of the box and chases them both away, whereupon it takes the Chrysalis itself.

The whole earth is bursting. I am being born.

VAGRANT. *[Raising his head.]* What's that?

    [The third Beetle rushes into the box.

CHRYSALIS. Something great is at hand.

VAGRANT. That's good.   *[Lays his head down. Pause.*

MAN'S VOICE. *[Behind the scenes.]* What are you up to?

WOMAN'S VOICE. Me?

1ST VOICE. Yes, you.

2ND VOICE. Me?

1ST VOICE. Yes, you.

2ND VOICE. Me?

1ST VOICE. Yes, you. Clumsy slattern.

2ND VOICE. You wretch.

1ST VOICE. Fathead!

2ND VOICE. Dolt!

1ST VOICE. Slut! Frump!

2ND VOICE. Mud-pusher!

1ST VOICE. Take care. Look out.

2ND VOICE. Slowly.

1st Voice. L-l-look out.

> [*A large ball of manure rolls on to the stage, pushed by a pair of beetles.*

Male Beetle. Nothing 's happened to it?

Female Beetle. Oh dear, I do hope not.   I 'm all of a tremble.

Male Beetle. Ha, ha, that 's our capital.   Our nest-egg.   Our stock-in-trade.   Our all.

Female Beetle. Oh, what a lovely little pile, what a treasure, what a beautiful little ball, what a precious little fortune.

Male Beetle. It 's our only joy.   To think how we 've saved and scraped, toiled and moiled, denied ourselves, gone without this, stinted ourselves that——

Female Beetle. And worked our legs off and drudged and plodded to get it together and——

Male Beetle. And seen it grow and added to it, bit by bit. Oh, what a boon it is.

Female Beetle. Our very own.

Male Beetle. Our life.

Female Beetle. All our own work.

Male Beetle. Just sniff at it, old girl.   Oh, how lovely.   Just feel the weight of it.   And it 's ours.

Female Beetle. What a godsend.

Male Beetle. What a blessing.

Chrysalis.   The fetters of the world are rended,
                Now another life is blended.
                I am being born.

> [*The Vagrant raises his head.*

Female Beetle. Husband!

Male Beetle. What is it?

Female Beetle. Ha, ha, ha, ha.

Male Beetle. Ha, ha.   Ha, ha.   Wife!

Female Beetle. What is it?

Male Beetle. Ha, ha, ha, it 's fine to own something.   Your property!   The dream of your life!   The fruit of your labours!

Female Beetle. Ha, ha, ha.

Male Beetle. I 'm going off my head with joy.   I 'm . . . I 'm . . . I 'm . . . going off my head with sheer worry. Upon my soul, I 'm going off my head.

Female Beetle. Why?

Male Beetle. With worry.   Now we 've got out little pile. I 've been so much looking forward to it, and now we 've got it, we 'll have to make another one. Nothing but work, work, work.

FEMALE BEETLE. Why another one?

MALE BEETLE. You stupid creature, so that we can have two, of course.

FEMALE BEETLE. Ah, two. Quite right.

MALE BEETLE. Ah, just fancy, two of them. At least two. Let 's say even three. You know, every one who 's made one pile has to make another.

FEMALE BEETLE. So that he can have two.

MALE BEETLE. Or even three.

FEMALE BEETLE. Husband!

MALE BEETLE. Well, what is it?

FEMALE BEETLE. I 'm scared. Suppose someone was to steal it from us.

MALE BEETLE. What?

FEMALE BEETLE. Our little pile. Our joy. Our all.

MALE BEETLE. Our p-pile? My goodness, don't frighten me.

FEMALE BEETLE. We . . . we . . . we can't roll it about with us, till we 've made another one.

MALE BEETLE. I tell you what, we 'll invest it. In-vest it. We 'll store it up. We 'll bury it nicely. Wait a bit, in some hole, in some cranny. Out of harm's way, you know. It must be put aside.

FEMALE BEETLE. I only hope nobody 'll find it.

MALE BEETLE. Eh? Not likely. What, steal it from us? Our little pile. Our treasure. Our little round nest-egg.

FEMALE BEETLE. Our precious little store. Our life. Our whole concern.

MALE BEETLE. Wait, stay here and watch—watch it. Keep an eye on it.   [*Runs off.*

FEMALE BEETLE. Where are you off to now?

MALE BEETLE. To look for a hole . . . a little hole . . . a deep hole . . . to bury it in. Our precious gold . . . out of harm's way. [*Exit.*] Be care . . . ful.

FEMALE BEETLE. Husband, husband, come here. . . . Wait a bit. . . There 's . . . Husband. . . . He can't hear me. And I 've found such a nice hole. Husband. He 's gone. And I 've found such a beautiful little hole. What a stupid he is. The booby. The fool. If only I could just have a look at it. No, I mustn't leave you, little pile. If I could . . . only . . . peep. Little pile, dear little pile, wait a moment,

I 'll be back at once. I 'll only have just a peep, and I 'll be back again. [*Runs to the back and turns round.*] Little pile, you 'll be good and wait for me, won't you? I 'll be back at once, little pile——   [*Enters the lair of the Ichneumon Fly.*

CHRYSALIS. Oh, to be born, to be born. The new world.
                                        [*Vagrant stands up.*

STRANGE BEETLE. [*Runs in from the wings, where he has been lurking.*] They 've gone. Now 's my chance.
                                        [*Rolls the pile away.*

VAGRANT. Here, don't knock me over.

STRANGE BEETLE. Out of the way, citizen.

VAGRANT. What 's that you 're rolling along?

STRANGE BEETLE. Ha, ha, ha. That 's my pile. Capital. Gold.

VAGRANT. [*Flinching.*] That gold of yours smells.

STRANGE BEETLE. Gold don't smell. Roll along, pile, off you go. Bestir yourself. Come on. Possession 's nine points of the law. Ha, ha, ha, my boy.

VAGRANT. What 's that?

STRANGE BEETLE. Ah, it 's nice to own something. [*Rolls the pile to the left.*] My treasure. You lovely nest-egg. My jewel. My all. What a thing to possess. A little fortune to invest. To bury carefully. L-l-look out.   [*Exit.*

VAGRANT. To possess? Why not. Every one likes something of his own.

FEMALE BEETLE. [*Returns.*] Oh dear, oh dear. Someone 's living there. A little chrysalis. We can't put you there, pile. Where is the pile? Oh, where has my pile gone to? Where is our dear little pile?

VAGRANT. Why, just this minute——

FEMALE BEETLE. [*Rushing upon him.*] Thief, thief. What have you done with my pile?

VAGRANT. I 'm telling you, just this minute——

FEMALE BEETLE. You villain, give it here. Hand it back.

VAGRANT. Just this minute some gentleman rolled it over there.

FEMALE BEETLE. What gentleman? Who?

VAGRANT. A pot-bellied fellow, a fat, round man——

FEMALE BEETLE. My husband.

VAGRANT. A surly chap with crooked feet, a vulgar, conceited person——

FEMALE BEETLE. That 's my husband.

E 989

VAGRANT. And he said it was nice to own something and to bury something.

FEMALE BEETLE. That's him. He must have found another hole. [*Calls out.*] Husband, wait a bit. Husband. Darling. Where is the stupid creature?

VAGRANT. That's where he rolled it to.

FEMALE BEETLE. The booby. Couldn't he have called me? [*Rushes to the left.*] Husband, wait a bit. The pile. [*Exit.*] The p-p-pile.

VAGRANT.

This is a different one, that's as clear as mud!
This one belongs to the steadier classes.
Excuse me, I was a little drunk.
I quite thought they were all butterflies.
Beautiful butterflies, a little bit grazed.
Cream of the world, always pairing.
Those interesting ladies and their wooers,
Ha, ha, those insects panting after a morsel of bliss.
I can't abide such gentry.
These others at least smell of honest labour.
They don't want to enjoy, they only want to possess something.
They aren't gallant, but then they are human.
Wisely earth behaves, trusting only in what lasts,
Humbly building its happiness, even if it were of manure;
If work is not fragrant, fragrant is the gain,
You love for yourself, you build for all,
You labour for others, and if you're stingy,
Well, stinginess is a virtue, when it's for the family.
The family has its rights, the family sanctifies everything,
Even theft, if need be, for after all, there are children.
That's how it is, I tell you, and that's the whole point:
A man will do anything to preserve his kindred.

CHRYSALIS. [*Shouts.*]:

Upon the world prepare more space
Something huge will now take place.

VAGRANT. [*Turning to it.*] What's that?

CHRYSALIS. I'm being born.

VAGRANT. That's good. And what are you going to be.

CHRYSALIS. I don't know.   I don't know.   Something great.
VAGRANT. Aha.   [*Lifts it up and fastens it on to a blade of grass.*
CHRYSALIS. I'll do something amazing.
VAGRANT. What's that?
CHRYSALIS. I'm being born.
VAGRANT

I commend you, Chrysalis, for that.   In fervid urge
All things in the world are toiling for their birth,
Desiring to be, desiring to live, desiring to last, and let them
    feel what they will,
'Tis only one thing: the dire bliss of being.

CHRYSALIS.   Let the whole world give ear,
                 The mighty moment is here,
                 When I . . . when I . . .

VAGRANT. What?
CHRYSALIS. Nothing.   I don't know yet.   I desire to do something great.
VAGRANT.

Great?   Something great?   Good, make yourself drunk with
    that:
These good folk with their pile won't understand you.
The pile is small and full, promises are great and empty . . .

CHRYSALIS. Something unbounded.
VAGRANT.

And yet, Chrysalis, this somehow pleases me in you.
Something great, come to pass!   Only it must be great.
What will crawl from you, Chrysalis?   Why don't you bestir
    yourself?

CHRYSALIS. The whole world will be astounded when I am
born.
VAGRANT. Do it then.   I'll wait.   [*Sits down.*
ICHNEUMON FLY. [*From behind, with long quiet strides, drags the
    corpse of a cricket into its lair.*]   Look, Larva, daddy's bringing
    you something nice.   [*Enters the hole.*
CHRYSALIS. [*Shouting.*]

                 What pain!   The pangs of birth!
                 Now bursts the mighty earth
                 That it may set me free.

VAGRANT. Be born.

ICHNEUMON FLY. [*Returning from the hole.*] No, no, daughter, you must eat. You mustn't come out, it wouldn't do at all. Daddy 'll soon be here and he 'll bring you something nice, eh? What would you like, you greedy little girl?

LARVA. [*In front of the hole.*] Daddy, I feel bored here.

ICHNEUMON FLY. Ha, ha, that 's a nice thing. Come and give me a kiss. Papa 'll bring you something tasty. What, you want another cricket? Ha, ha, not at all a bad idea of yours.

LARVA. I should like . . . I don't know what.

ICHNEUMON FLY. Good heavens, how clever of you, Larva. I must give you something for that. Ta-ta, my child, daddy must go to work now, and get something for his darling, for his pretty little baby. Go in now, my pet. Have a nice feed.

[*Exit Larva.*

[*Approaching the Vagrant with long strides.*] Who are you?

VAGRANT. [*Jumps up and retreats.*] Me.

ICHNEUMON FLY. Are you eatable?

VAGRANT. No—I don't think so.

ICHNEUMON FLY. [*Sniffing at him.*] You 're not fresh enough. Who are you?

VAGRANT. A vagabond.

ICHNEUMON FLY. [*Bowing slightly.*] Have you any children?

VAGRANT. No, I don't think so.

ICHNEUMON FLY. Ah, did you see her?

VAGRANT. Who?

ICHNEUMON FLY. My Larva. Charming, eh? A smart child. And how she grows. What an appetite she has, ha, ha. Children are a great joy, aren't they?

VAGRANT. Every one says so.

ICHNEUMON FLY. Yes, to be sure. When you have them, you do at least know who you 're working for. If you have a child then you must strive, work struggle. That 's real life, eh? Children want to grow, to eat, to feast, to play, don't they? Aren't I right?

VAGRANT. Children want a lot.

ICHNEUMON FLY. Would you believe that I take her two or three crickets every day?

VAGRANT. Who to?

ICHNEUMON FLY. To my child. Charming, eh? And so clever. Do you think she eats them all up? No, only the softest bits, while they 're still alive, ha, ha. A splendid child, eh?

VAGRANT. I should think so.

ICHNEUMON FLY. I'm proud of her. Really proud. Just like her daddy, eh? She takes after me, you know. Ha, ha, and I'm gossiping here, instead of getting to work. Oh, the fuss and running about. But as long as we do it for somebody, what does it matter? Aren't I right?

VAGRANT. I suppose you are.

ICHNEUMON FLY. A pity you aren't eatable. Really it's a pity, you know. I must take her something, mustn't I? [*Fingering the Chrysalis*] What's this?

CHRYSALIS. [*Shouting.*] I proclaim the rebirth of the world.

ICHNEUMON FLY. Not ripe yet. No good, is it?

CHRYSALIS. I'll create something.

ICHNEUMON FLY. It's a worry to bring up children. A great worry, isn't it? To rear a family, just imagine. To feed those poor little mites. To provide for them, to secure their future, eh? It's no trifle, is it? Well, I must be off now. Good day to you. Pleased to have met you, sir. [*Runs off.*] Ta-ta, baby, I'll be back soon.   [*Exit.*

VAGRANT.

To provide for them. To feed these hungry little mouths.
That's the demands of a family. And to take live crickets to
    them.
And yet even a cricket wants to live, and kills nobody.
The good creature, he extols life with his humble melody.
This sticks in my gizzard.

LARVA. [*Crawling out of the hole.*] Daddy, daddy.

VAGRANT. So you're the Larva? Let's have a look at you.

LARVA. How ugly you are.

VAGRANT. Why?

LARVA. I don't know. Oh, how bored I am. I should like . . . I should like . .

VAGRANT. What?

LARVA. I don't know. To tear something apart, something alive. . . Ah, it makes me wriggle.

VAGRANT. What's the matter with you?

LARVA. Ugly, ugly, ugly.   [*Crawls away.*

VAGRANT.

Feeding a family like that. This sticks in my gizzard.
This is a thing about insects that a man can't help frowning at

Enter the Male Beetle

MALE BEETLE. Come along, old girl, I 've found a hole. Where are you? Where 's my pile? Where 's my wife?

VAGRANT. Your wife? Do you mean that old harridan? That fat, ugly chatterbox——

MALE BEETLE. That 's her. Where 's my pile?

VAGRANT That bad-tempered, dirty rag-bag.

MALE BEETLE. That 's her, that 's her. She had my pile. What has she done with my pile?

VAGRANT. Why, your better half went to look for you.

MALE BEETLE. And where 's my pile?

VAGRANT. That large stinking ball?

MALE BEETLE. Yes, yes, my nest-egg. My capital. My savings. Where 's my beautiful pile. I left my wife with it.

VAGRANT. There, was a gentleman who rolled it away yonder. He acted as if it was his.

MALE BEETLE. I don't care what he did with my wife. But where 's my pile?

VAGRANT. I keep telling you. The gentleman rolled it away. Your wife wasn't here at the time.

MALE BEETLE. Where was she? Where is she?

VAGRANT. She went after him. She thought it was you. She was shouting for you.

MALE BEETLE. My pile?

VAGRANT. No, your wife.

MALE BEETLE. I 'm not asking about her. Where 's my pile, I say?

VAGRANT. The gentleman rolled it away.

MALE BEETLE. What, rolled it away? My pile? God in heaven! Catch him! Catch him! Thief! Murder! [*Flings himself to the ground.*] My hard-earned fortune. They 've killed me. I 'd rather give up my life than that ball of golden manure. [*Jumps up.*] Help. Catch him. Mur—der.

[*Dashes off to the left.*

VAGRANT.

Ha, ha, ha. Murder. Crime. Burst, O ye clouds,
For the stolen pile. In such appalling grief
There is only one solace: That the beetle's pile
Will never belong to any one but another mud-pusher.

[*Sits down on one side.*

VOICE. [*Behind the scenes.*] Look out, woman, take care you don't stumble. Here we are, here we are. This is where we 'll live, this is our new little home. Oh, look out, you haven't hurt yourself, have you?

FEMALE VOICE. No, Cricket, don't be absurd.

MALE VOICE. But darling, you must be careful. When you 're expecting——

Enter a Male Cricket with a pregnant Female Cricket

MALE CRICKET. And now open the peep-hole. There. How do you like it?

FEMALE CRICKET. Oh, Cricket, I 'm *so* tired.

MALE CRICKET. Sit down, sit down, darling, sit down. Take great care of yourself now.

FEMALE CRICKET. [*Sits down.*] What a long way. And all that moving, too. No, Cricket, really it 's not right of you.

MALE CRICKET. Oh, darling, come, come. Look, darling, look.

FEMALE CRICKET. Now don't get angry, you horrid man.

MALE CRICKET. I won't say another word, really I won't. Fancy, Mrs. Cricket won't take care of herself, and in her state, too! What do you think of her?

FEMALE CRICKET. [*Tearfully.*] You naughty man, how can you joke about it?

MALE CRICKET. But darling, when I 'm so happy. Just fancy, all those little crickets, the noise, the chirping, ha, ha, ha. Darling, I 'm mad with joy.

FEMALE CRICKET. You . . . you . . . silly boy. Look, daddy, ha, ha.

MALE CRICKET. Ha, ha, ha. And how do you like it?

FEMALE CRICKET. It 's nice. Is this our new house?

MALE CRICKET. Our little nest, our villa, our own little place, our, ha, ha, our residence.

FEMALE CRICKET. Will it be dry? Who built it?

MALE CRICKET. Why, goodness me, another cricket has been living there.

FEMALE CRICKET. Fancy! And why did he move?

MALE CRICKET. Ha, ha, ha, he moved away. He moved away Don't you know where to? Have a guess.

FEMALE CRICKET. I don't know. Oh dear, what a long time you are before you say anything. Do hurry up and tell me.

MALE CRICKET. Well then—yesterday a shrike came and fastened him on to a thorn. Honour bright, darling, from end to end. Just imagine. His feet were wriggling there, ha, ha, he's still alive. And when I came along I at once saw that it would suit us. So we're moving into his house. By Jove, what a slice of luck! Ha, ha, what do you think of it?

FEMALE CRICKET. And he's still alive? Ugh, how horrible.

MALE CRICKET. Eh? Oh, what a godsend for us. Tralala, tratra, tralala tra. Wait a bit, we'll hang up our door-plate. [*From a bag he takes out a plate with the inscription 'Cricket, Music Dealer.'*] Where shall we hang it? Up there? More to the right? More to the left?

FEMALE CRICKET. A little higher. And you say that his feet are still wriggling?

MALE CRICKET. [*Knocks and points.*] I'm telling you; like that.

FEMALE CRICKET. Brr. Where is he?

MALE CRICKET. Would you like to see it?

FEMALE CRICKET. Yes, I would. No, I wouldn't. Is it horrible?

MALE CRICKET. Ha, ha, ha, I should think so. Is it hanging properly?

FEMALE CRICKET. Yes. Cricket, I have such a queer feeling——

MALE CRICKET. [*Running up to her.*] Good heavens, perhaps it's ... it's already ...

FEMALE CRICKET. Oh dear, I'm so frightened.

MALE CRICKET. But darling, why be frightened? Every lady——

FEMALE CRICKET. It's all very well for you to talk. [*Bursts into tears.*] Cricket, will you always love me?

MALE CRICKET. Of course, darling. Dear me, don't cry. Come, come.

FEMALE CRICKET. [*Sobbing.*] Show me how his feet wriggled.

MALE CRICKET. Like this.

FEMALE CRICKET. Ha, ha, how funny that must be.

MALE CRICKET. Well, well, you see there's nothing to cry about. [*Sits down beside her.*] We'll furnish this place beautifully. And as soon as we can manage it we'll put up some——

FEMALE CRICKET. Curtains.

MALE CRICKET. Curtains as well. Ha, ha, ha, curtains, of course. How clever of you to think of it. Give me a kiss.

FEMALE CRICKET. Never mind that now. Give over, you're so silly.

MALE CRICKET. Of course I am. [*Jumps up.*] Guess what I've bought.

FEMALE CRICKET. Curtains.

MALE CRICKET. No, something smaller. [*Searches in his pockets.*] Where did——

FEMALE CRICKET. Quick, quick, let me see.

[*The Male Cricket takes from his pocket a child's rattle and shakes it with both hands.*

Oh, how sweet.   Cricket, give it to me.

MALE CRICKET. [*Shakes it and sings.*]

'There was born a little
Cricket, Cricket, Cricket.
By his little bed there stood
Mamma, mamma, daddy.
Their two heads together
They banged, banged, banged—
Prettily his lullaby they
Twanged, twanged, twanged.'

Ha, ha, ha.

FEMALE CRICKET. Lend it to me, quickly.   Oh, daddy, I 'm so pleased.

MALE CRICKET. Listen then, darling . . .

FEMALE CRICKET. [*Shakes it and sings.*]

'Cricket, Cricket, Cricket.'

MALE CRICKET. Now I must run round a little.   Let people know I 'm here.   Knock at the doors.

FEMALE CRICKET. [*Shakes it and sings.*] 'They twanged, twanged, twanged.'

MALE CRICKET. I must get some introductions, fix up orders, have a look round.   Give me the rattle, I 'll use it on my way.

FEMALE CRICKET. And what about me? [*Tearfully.*] You won't leave me?

MALE CRICKET. Rattle for me.   And I dare say some neighbour will be coming along.   You must have a little chat with him, ask about the children, and all that, you know.   And we will wait for the thingumabob.   Till I come back.

FEMALE CRICKET. You bad boy.

MALE CRICKET. Ha, ha, ha.   Now, darling, be careful.   It won't be long now, my pet.   [*Runs off.*

FEMALE CRICKET. [*Shakes the rattle, the Male Cricket answers in the distance.*] 'There was born a little . . . Cricket' . . . I feel so frightened.

VAGRANT. [*Standing up.*] Don't be frightened. Small things are born easily.

FEMALE CRICKET. Who's there? Ugh, a beetle. You don't bite?

VAGRANT. No.

FEMALE CRICKET. And how are the children?

VAGRANT.

> I have none. I have none. Never have I in wedlock
> Hatched the tender love of a family.
> Nor have I known the joy of my own roof above me,
> Nor even the warm delight at another's ill success.

FEMALE CRICKET. Oh, dear, haven't you any children? That's a pity. [*Shakes the rattle.*] Cricket, Cricket. Oh, he doesn't answer. And why did you never marry, beetle?

VAGRANT.

> Selfishness, dear madam, selfishness. I ought to be ashamed of it.
> > The egoist finds ease in his solitude.
> > He need not love so much, or hate so much,
> > Or grudge others their small share of space.

FEMALE CRICKET. Yes, yes, these men. [*Rattles.*] Cricket, Cricket, Cricket.

CHRYSALIS. [*Shouting.*] Within me I bear the future. I . . . I . . .

VAGRANT. [*Approaching.*] Be born.

CHRYSALIS. I will achieve something illustrious

FEMALE BEETLE. [*Running in.*] Isn't my husband there? Where is the stupid man? Where is our pile?

FEMALE CRICKET. Oh, madam, can you play ball with it? Do let me see it.

FEMALE BEETLE It's not to play with, it's our future, our nest-egg, our all My husband, the clumsy creature, has gone off with it.

FEMALE CRICKET. Oh, dear, perhaps he's run away from you.

FEMALE BEETLE. And where is yours?

FEMALE CRICKET. He's away on business. [*Rattles.*] Cricket, Cricket.

FEMALE BEETLE. Fancy him leaving you all alone like that, poor thing. And you're expecting . . .

FEMALE CRICKET. Oh, dear.

FEMALE BEETLE. So young, too.   And aren't *you* making a pile?

FEMALE CRICKET. What for?

FEMALE BEETLE. A pile, that's for the family. That's the future. That's your whole life.

FEMALE CRICKET. Oh no. My whole life is to have my own little house, my nest, a little place of my own. And curtains. And children. And to have my Cricket. My own home. That's all.

FEMALE BEETLE. How can you live without a pile?

FEMALE CRICKET. What would we do with it?

FEMALE BEETLE. Roll it about with you everywhere. I tell you, there's nothing like a pile for holding a man.

FEMALE CRICKET. Oh no, a little house.

FEMALE BEETLE. A pile, I tell you

FEMALE CRICKET. A little house.

FEMALE BEETLE. Dear me, I should so much like to have a chat with you. You're so nice . . .

FEMALE CRICKET. And what about your children?

FEMALE BEETLE. If only I had my pile. [*Exit.*] P-p-p-pile. P-p-p-pile——

FEMALE CRICKET. Ugh, what a frump. And her husband's run away from her, ha, ha, ha. 'They twanged, twanged, twanged.' I—I—have such a queer . . . [*Clearing up by the door.*] Ha, ha, ha, how his feet wriggle.

ICHNEUMON FLY. [*Runs in from the wings.*] Aha. [*Approaches her with long, quiet strides, takes a dagger from his coat-tails, pierces the Female Cricket with a great lunge, and drags her to his lair.*] Out of it.

VAGRANT. [*Flinches.*] Oh . . oh. Murder.

ICHNEUMON FLY. [*In the entrance to his lair.*] Look, daughter. Come quick and have a look at what daddy's bringing you.

VAGRANT. He's killed her. And I . . . I stood there like a log. Good heavens, she didn't even utter a sound. And nobody shouted with horror. Nobody ran to help her.

PARASITE. [*Entering from the back.*] Bravo, comrade, that's just my opinion too.

VAGRANT To perish so defenceless.

PARASITE. That's just what I say. I've been looking on for quite a while, but *I* couldn't do a thing like that. No, I couldn't. Every one wants to live, don't they?

VAGRANT. Who are you?

PARASITE. I! Oh, nothing really. I'm a poor man. An orphan. They call me a parasite.

VAGRANT. How can any one dare to kill like that?

PARASITE. That's exactly what *I* say. Do you think he needs it? Do you think he's hungry, like me? Not a bit of it. He kills to add to his store. He collects things. It's a scandal, isn't it? Isn't this a piece of injustice? Why has one got a store while another starves? Why has he got a dagger while I've only got these bare hands? Aren't I right?

VAGRANT. I should say so.

PARASITE. That's what *I* say. There's no equality. For instance, I don't kill any one. My jaws are too tender. I haven't got the necessary attupt—appart—appurtenances. I'm merely hungry. Is that right?

VAGRANT. Killing shouldn't be allowed.

PARASITE. My very words, comrade. Or, at any rate, collecting things shouldn't be allowed. You eat your fill and you've got enough. Collecting things is robbing them who can't collect things. Eat your fill and have done with it. Then there'd be enough for all, wouldn't there now?

VAGRANT. I don't know.

PARASITE. But I'm telling you.

ICHNEUMON FLY. [*Returning from his lair.*] Eat it up, baby, eat it up. Choose what you like. Haven't you a nice daddy, eh?

PARASITE. Good day to you, sir.

ICHNEUMON FLY. How are you? How are you? Eatable?
                                                    [*Sniffs at him.*

PARASITE. Ha, ha, you're joking, sir. Why me?

ICHNEUMON FLY. Get out, you filthy creature. You scamp. What do you want here? Clear off!

PARASITE. Ha, ha, that's what *I* say, sir.   [*Cowers.*

ICHNEUMON FLY. [*To the Vagrant.*] Good day, sir.—Well, did you see that?

VAGRANT. Yes.

ICHNEUMON FLY. A fine piece of work, eh? Ha, ha, it's not every one who could do that. Ah, my boy, for that you want [*Taps his forehead.*] expert knowledge. Enterprise. I—ni—tiative. And foresight. And love for work, let me tell you.

PARASITE. [*Approaching.*] Just what *I* say.

ICHNEUMON FLY. My good sir, if you want to keep alive, you've got to fight your way. There's your future. There's your family. And then, you know, there's a certain amount of

ambition. A strong personality is bound to assert itself.
Aren't I right?

PARASITE. That's what *I* say, sir.

ICHNEUMON FLY. Of course, of course. Make your way in the
world, use the talent that's in you, that's what I call a useful
life

PARASITE. Absolutely, sir.

ICHNEUMON FLY. Hold your tongue, you disgusting object, I'm
not talking to you.

PARASITE Just what *I* say, sir.

ICHNEUMON FLY. And how it cheers you up, when you fulfil
your duty like that. When you perform your job. When
you feel that you're not living in vain. It's so elevating,
isn't it? Well, good day to you, sir. I must be off again.
My best respects. [*Runs off.*] Larva, *au revoir*.   [*Exit.*

PARASITE. The old murderer. Believe me, it was all I could do
not to fly at his throat. Yes, sir, I'd work, too, if need be.
But why should I work when someone else has more than he
can consume? I've got initiative, too, ha, ha, but here [*Pats
his stomach.*] I'm hungry, that's what I am, hungry, I tell
you. A fine state of things, eh?

VAGRANT. Anything for a piece of meat.

PARASITE. That's just what *I* say. Anything for a piece of
meat, and a poor man's got nothing. It's against nature.
Every one should have what he can eat, eh?

VAGRANT. [*Picks up the rattle and shakes it.*] Poor creature, poor
creature, poor creature.

PARASITE. That's it Every one wants to live.

          [*Behind the scenes there is a chirping in reply.*

MALE CRICKET. [*Runs in shaking a rattle.*] Here I am, my pet,
here, here here. Where are you, darling? Guess what
hubby's bought you.

ICHNEUMON FLY. [*Appearing behind him.*] Aha!

VAGRANT. Look out! Look out!

PARASITE. [*Stopping him.*] Don't interfere, mate. Don't get
mixed up in it. What must be, must be.

MALE CRICKET. But mummy?

ICHNEUMON FLY. [*With a great lunge pierces him and carries him
off.*] Daughter! Larva, what's your kind daddy bringing
you now, eh?   [*Enters his lair.*

VAGRANT. [*Raising his fist.*] Oh, Almighty God. How can you
allow it?

PARASITE. Just what *I* say. That 's the third cricket he 's had already, and me nothing. And that 's what the likes of us are expected to put up with.

ICHNEUMON FLY. [*Runs out from his lair.*] No, no, baby, I 've got no time. Daddy must go back to work. Eat, eat, eat. Be quiet now, I 'll be back in an hour.   [*Runs off.*

PARASITE. I 'm simply boiling over. The old scoundrel! [*Approaching the lair.*] What injustice! What a disgrace! I 'll show him, that I will. Just you wait? Has he gone? I must have a look.   [*Enters the lair.*

VAGRANT.

Murder and again murder. Heart, cease your beating,
They are only insects, they are only beetles,
It is only a tiny drama between blades of grass,
Nothing but insect-war, nothing but beetle-behaviour;
Insects live one way, human beings another.
Ah, to be among human beings again. Then a man can at least see
That there is, after all, something better than this insect crew.
Man does not crave merely to devour, he craves to create and build.
He indeed has some aim, and raises his pile.
No, that 's the beetles again, ugh. I can't get it out of my head.
A pile for the beetles, but for human beings there are humaner ideals.
Peaceable man extols life by his whole life.
So little suffices for happiness. To have a home, however small,
To harm nobody, to have few worries and to beget children,
For indeed, life desires only life, and sweet it is to regard
How you are living, and how your neighbour's . . . feet . . . are wriggling.
No, that 's the crickets again. Why do I keep getting muddled,
I 'm confusing him with the beetles. The narrow, paltry existence,
The paltry joy of crickets would not satisfy man.
Man desires something more than just to eat his fill
And gratefully, contentedly to munch a morsel of happiness.
Life calls for men, life calls for heroes, life calls for struggle;
If you would overcome life, seize it with a strong grip,

If you would be fully a man, you dare not be puny and weak,
If you would live, then rule, if you would eat, then . . . kill . . .
No, that 's the Ichneumon Fly again.   Silence.   Do you not hear
How throughout the world feverish jowls are working,
Chew-chew-chew, the blood-stained, sated smacking of lips
Over the still living morsel.   Life is the prey of life.

CHRYSALIS. [*Tossing to and fro.*] I feel something great.   Something great.

VAGRANT. What is great?

CHRYSALIS. To be born.   To live.

VAGRANT. Chrysalis, Chrysalis, I will not desert you.

PARASITE. [*Rolls out of the lair, enormously fat, and hiccups.*] Ha, ha, ha.   Ha, ha, ha, hup, ha, ha, ha.   Ha, ha, ha.   Hup, that 's—ha, ha, ha, hup, the old miser, he—hup, had stores—hup—for that white-faced—hup—daughter of his.   Hup, ha, ha, ha.   Ha, ha, ha, hup.   I feel quite—hup.   I 'm going to burst. [*Hiccups.*] Why, what a—hup—confounded fit of the hiccups.   Sir, I 'm some—somebody, too.   It 's not every one who could, eh—hup—eh?   Eat as much as that, eh?

VAGRANT. And what about the Larva?

PARASITE. Ha, ha, ha, hup, ha, ha, ha.   Ha, ha, ha, I, hup—I gobbled her up, too.   The table of nature is spread for all.   Hup, hup, hup.

END OF ACT II

ACT III

THE ANTS

SCENE: *A green forest*

VAGRANT. [*Seated, in thought.*]

Enough, you have seen enough.   You have seen all creatures
Sucking like lice at the great body of creation
In a fearful craving to increase their share
By depriving others.   You have seen enough.   [*Pause.*
And am I myself any different from the insects?
I am a cockroach, and from the dust I gather crumbs
That others have left.   That is your life;
Fit for nothing, for nothing, not even fit
To be devoured by somebody.

CHRYSALIS. [*Shouting.*]

Make room.   Make room.   I 'm being born
From my prison I 'll set the whole world free.
What a gigantic thought.

VAGRANT.

This eternal wrangling about one's tiny self,
This greedy bustle, this insect desire
To perpetuate one's own insignificance in one's own species—
I will not, I will not!   An accursed spell
Prompts me to tread human paths again,
Ah, human paths!   After my wandering,
When will ye greet me again, ye signboards
Which in human speech betoken
Parish and district, province and state,
State.   Brain, tarry a while.   First the parish,
Then the district, then the land, the nation
And native country and mankind, and all this is greater
Than any self.   Yes, this is the whole gist of it—
That insect selfishness knows only itself
And comprehends not that there is something more,
Parish and district, the whole commonalty.

130

CHRYSALIS.

> O pangs of creation!
> O tormenting thirst
> For a mighty deed.

VAGRANT. [*Jumping up.*]

The whole commonalty.   Now I have found you,
Concept of humanity.   We are only corn-grains.
Of a great harvest which belongs to all.
Tiny self, there is something above you,
Call it nation, mankind, or state,
Call it how you will, if only you serve it:
You are naught   The greatest worth of living
Is to sacrifice one's life   [*Sits down.*

CHRYSALIS.

> The hour of salvation draws nigh.
> Great tokens and great words
> Herald my advent.

VAGRANT.

Great is man by his great indebtedness,
He is only whole where he is part of a whole,
And lives humanly if he gives his life
For something greater than himself.   Call it how you will,
If only you serve this end.

CHRYSALIS. [*Tossing about.*]

> See what wings I have,
> What boundless wings.

VAGRANT. If only I knew the way to the nearest parish.   What 's
that biting me?   Is that you ant?   And there 's another.
And a third.   Why, good heavens.   I 've sat on an ant-heap.
[*Stands up.*] Fools, what are you crawling on to me for?
Look at them running after me, look—one, two, three, four.
And here 's another one, two, thre . .
> [*In the meanwhile the back curtain rises and displays the
> entrance to an ant-heap, a red building of several storeys.
> By the entrance sits a Blind Ant and counts continuously.
> Ants with sacks, joists, shovels, etc., enter and run across
> the storeys of the building in time to the Blind Ant's
> counting.*

BLIND ANT. [*Continuously.*] One two three four, one two three four . . .

VAGRANT. What 's that? What are you counting, old boy?

BLIND ANT. One two three four . . .

VAGRANT. What 's this here? A warehouse or a factory, isn't it? Hi, what 's this factory for?

BLIND ANT. One two three four . . .

VAGRANT. What 's this factory for, I 'm asking? Why is this blind fellow counting? Ah, he 's giving them the time. They all move in time as he counts. One two three four. Like machines. Bah, it makes my head swim.

BLIND ANT. One two three four . . .

1ST ENGINEER. [*Running in.*] Quicker, quicker. One two three four.

BLIND ANT. [*More quickly.*] One two three four, one two three four.   [*They all move more quickly.*

VAGRANT. What 's that? I 'm asking, sir, what that factory 's for.

ENGINEER. Who 's that?

VAGRANT. Me.

ENGINEER. From which of the ants?

VAGRANT. From the humans.

ENGINEER. This is an ant-realm. What do you want here?

VAGRANT. I 'm having a look round.

ENGINEER. Are you trying to find work?

VAGRANT. I don't mind.

2ND ENGINEER. [*Running in.*] A discovery! A discovery!

1ST ENGINEER. What is it?

2ND ENGINEER. A new method of speeding up. Don't count one two three four. Count O two three four. That 's shorter. Saves time. O two three four. Blind fellow, hallo!

BLIND ANT. One two three four.

2ND ENGINEER. Wrong. O two three four.

BLIND ANT. O two three four. O two three four.
    [*They all move more quickly.*

VAGRANT. Not so quickly. It makes me feel giddy.

2ND ENGINEER. Who are you?

VAGRANT. A stranger.

2ND ENGINEER. Where from?

1ST ENGINEER. From the humans. Where is the humans' ant-heap?

VAGRANT. What?

1st Engineer. Where is the humans' ant-heap?

Vagrant. Oh, yonder. And yonder again. Everywhere.

2nd Engineer. [*Yelping.*] Ha, ha. Everywhere. Fool!

1st Engineer. Are there many humans?

Vagrant. Yes. They're called the masters of the world.

2nd Engineer. Ha, ha! Masters of the world!

1st Engineer. *We*'re the masters of the world.

2nd Engineer. The ant-realm.

1st Engineer. The largest ant-state.

2nd Engineer. A world-power.

1st Engineer. The largest democracy.

Vagrant. What's that?

1st Engineer. All must obey.

2nd Engineer. All have to work. All for the One.

1st Engineer. As the One orders.

Vagrant. Who?

1st Engineer. The Whole. The State. The Nation.

Vagrant. Why, that's just like us. For instance, we have M.P.s. An M.P., that's democracy. Have you got M.P.s too?

1st Engineer. No. We have the Whole.

Vagrant. And who speaks for the Whole?

2nd Engineer. Ha, ha! He knows nothing.

1st Engineer. The One who orders. The Whole only issues commands.

2nd Engineer. And abides in the laws. And is nowhere else.

Vagrant. And who rules over you?

1st Engineer. Reason.

2nd Engineer. Law.

1st Engineer. The interests of the state.

2nd Engineer. That's it, that's it.

Vagrant. I like that. Yes, indeed, all for the Whole.

1st Engineer. For its greatness.

2nd Engineer. And against enemies.

Vagrant. What's that? Against who?

1st Engineer. Against all.

2nd Engineer. We are surrounded by enemies.

1st Engineer. We defeated the Black ants.

2nd Engineer. And starved out the Tawnies.

1st Engineer. And subjugated the Greys. Only the Yellows are left. We must starve out the Yellows.

2ND ENGINEER We must starve out all

VAGRANT. Why?

1ST ENGINEER In the interests of the Whole.

2ND ENGINEER. The interests of the Whole are the highest.

1ST ENGINEER Interests of race.

2ND ENGINEER. Industrial interests.

1ST ENGINEER Colonial interests

2nd ENGINEER World interests

1ST ENGINEER Interests of the Whole.

2ND ENGINEER Yes, yes, that 's it

1ST ENGINEER The Whole has nothing but interests.

2ND ENGINEER. None can have as many interests as the Whole.

1ST ENGINEER. Interests preserve the Whole.

2ND ENGINEER. And wars nourish it.

VAGRANT. Aha, you 're—you 're the warlike ants.

2ND ENGINEER Tut, tut. He knows nothing.

1ST ENGINEER. Our ants are the most peaceful ants.

2ND ENGINEER A nation of peace.

1ST ENGINEER. A labour state

2ND ENGINEER. They wish only for world-power——

1ST ENGINEER. Because they wish for world-peace

2ND ENGINEER. In the interests of their peaceable labour.

1ST ENGINEER And in the interests of progress.

2ND ENGINEER In the interests of their interests. When we rule over the world——

1ST ENGINEER. We shall conquer time. We wish to rule over time.

VAGRANT. Over what?

1ST ENGINEER. Time. Time is greater than space.

2ND ENGINEER. Time has found no master yet.

1ST ENGINEER. The master of time will be master of all.

VAGRANT Slowly, for heaven's sake slowly. Let me think.

1ST ENGINEER. Speed is the master of time.

2ND ENGINEER. The taming of time

1ST ENGINEER He who commands speed will be ruler of time.

2ND ENGINEER. O two three four   O two three four.

BLIND ANT. [*More quickly.*] O two three four. O two . . .

[*All move more quickly.*

1ST ENGINEER. We must quicken the pace.

2ND ENGINEER. The pace of output.

1ST ENGINEER. The pace of life

2ND ENGINEER. Every movement must be quickened.

1ST ENGINEER. Shortened.

2ND ENGINEER. Reckoned out.

1ST ENGINEER. To an instant.

2ND ENGINEER. To a hundreth of an instant.

1ST ENGINEER. So as to save time.

2ND ENGINEER. So as to increase output.

1ST ENGINEER. Work has been proceeding too slowly. Too ponderously. The ants were being destroyed by fatigue.

2ND ENGINEER. Wastefully.

1ST ENGINEER. Inhumanely. Now they're being destroyed only by speed.

VAGRANT. And what are they hurrying after like that?

1ST ENGINEER. The interests of the Whole.

2ND ENGINEER. A question of output. A question of power.

1ST ENGINEER. There is peace. Peace is rivalry.

2ND ENGINEER. We are waging the battle of peace.

BLIND ANT. O two three four.

[*An ant official approaches the two engineers and reports something to them.*

VAGRANT.

O two three four. Quicker still. O!
Flog this old slow time with the whip of speed,
Lash and hound it, make it surge forward more speedily,
For speed is progress. The world desires to rush more speedily onwards,
Desires to surge on to its goal, even if it surge to its ruin,
If only it be more quickly. Blind fellow, count: O.

BLIND ANT. O two three four . .

1ST ENGINEER. Quicker, quicker.

AN ANT. [*Collapsing beneath his load.*] Whew!

2ND ENGINEER. Tut, tut. What's that? Get up!

ANOTHER ANT. [*Bending over the one who has collapsed.*] Dead.

1ST ENGINEER. You two, carry him away. Quickly!

[*Two ants lift up the corpse.*

2ND ENGINEER. What an honour. He fell on the field of speed.

1ST ENGINEER. How are you lifting him? Too slowly. You're wasting time. Drop him. [*The two ants drop the corpse.*] Head and feet together. O two three. Wrong. Drop him. [*The two ants drop the corpse.*] Head and feet O two three four. Take him away, quick march. O two, O two, O . . .

2ND ENGINEER. —two three four. Quicker.

VAGRANT. Anyhow, he died quick enough.

1ST ENGINEER. To work, to work. He who has more must work more.

2ND ENGINEER. He requires more.

1ST ENGINEER. He has more to defend.

2ND ENGINEER. And more to gain.

1ST ENGINEER. We are a nation of peace. Peace means work.

2ND ENGINEER. And work strength.

1ST ENGINEER. And strength war.

2ND ENGINEER. Yes, yes.

VOICE. Look out, look out. Step aside.

Enter an Inventor, groping

2ND ENGINEER. Hallo, our Inventor.

INVENTOR. Take care, take care. Don't knock against my head. It is huge, it is of glass, it is fragile. It is greater than I am. Keep out of the way, it would burst, it would be smashed—bang. Look out. I'm carrying a head. Don't knock against it. Step aside.

2ND ENGINEER. Hallo, how goes it?

INVENTOR. It's hurting, it's bursting. It'll knock against the walls—bang. No, no, I can't get my two hands round it. No, no, I can't even carry it now. Look out, do you hear? Whew, whew, whew!

1ST ENGINEER. What is it?

INVENTOR. A machine, a new machine. In my head. Do you hear it working? It'll smash my head. Oh, oh—a huge machine. Out of the way. Out of the way. I'm carrying a machine.

1ST ENGINEER. What sort of machine?

INVENTOR. A war machine. An enormous one. The swiftest, most effective crusher of lives. The greatest progress. The acme of science. Whew, whew, whew, do you hear it? Ten thousand, a hundred thousand dead. Whew, whew! It keeps on working. Two hundred thousand dead. Whew, whew, whew, whew!

1ST ENGINEER. A genius, eh?

INVENTOR. Oh, oh. What pain! My head's splitting. Out of the way, out of the way. Take care I don't knock against you. [*Exit.*] Whew, whew, whew . . .

1ST ENGINEER. A great intellect. The greatest of scientists.

2ND ENGINEER. Nothing serves the state so much as science.

1ST ENGINEER. Science is a great thing. There will be war.

VAGRANT. Why war?

1ST ENGINEER. Because we shall have a new war-machine.

2ND ENGINEER. Because we still need another bit of the world.

1ST ENGINEER. A bit of the world from the birch-tree to the pine-tree.

2ND ENGINEER. And a road between two blades of grass.

1ST ENGINEER. The only open road to the south.

2ND ENGINEER. A question of prestige.

1ST ENGINEER. And trade.

2ND ENGINEER. The greatest national idea.

1ST ENGINEER. Either us or the Yellows.

2ND ENGINEER. Never was war more honourable or more urgent——

1ST ENGINEER. —than the one we must wage.

2ND ENGINEER. We are prepared.

1ST ENGINEER. We must only have a cause.

BLIND ANT. O two three four.   [*A gong.*

1ST ENGINEER. What's that?

VOICES. A messenger. A messenger.

MESSENGER. [*Runs in.*] I beg to announce myself. I am the guard of the southern army.

1ST ENGINEER. Good.

MESSENGER. In accordance with orders we crossed the frontier of the Yellows.

1ST ENGINEER. What then?

MESSENGER. The Yellows captured me and took me to their commander.

1ST ENGINEER. And?

MESSENGER. Here is the commander's letter.

1ST ENGINEER. Show it me. [*Takes the paper and reads.*] 'The government of the Yellow Ants calls upon the Ant-Realm, within three minutes to withdraw its army lying between the birch-tree and the pine-tree on the road between two blades of grass.'

2ND ENGINEER. Listen, listen.

1ST ENGINEER. 'This territory comprises the historical, vital

industrial, sacred and military interests of our state, so that it
rightfully belongs to us.'

2ND ENGINEER An insult! We shall not tolerate it.

1ST ENGINEER 'At the same time we are instructing our regiments to start advancing.' [*Drops the paper.*] War! War at
last!

2ND ENGINEER At last a war that is forced upon us.

1ST ENGINEER To arms.

NEW MESSENGER. [*Runs in.*] The Yellows are marching across
our frontiers.

1ST ENGINEER. [*Runs into the ant-heap.*] To arms! To arms!

2ND ENGINEER. [*In another passage.*] Mobilization! To arms!

BOTH MESSENGERS. [*In different passages.*] To arms! To arms!

 [*Alarm sirens From all sides the ants scramble into the
 ant-heap.*]

BLIND ANT. O two three four. O two three four.

          [*An increasing uproar within.*

VAGRANT.

To arms! To arms! The road between the blades of grass
Is threatened. Do you hear? The cranny from blade to
 blade,
A span of earth from grass to grass, your sacred rights,
The greatest interests of the state, the greatest problem in the
 world,
All is at stake. Ants, to arms
How could you live, if another possessed
The world between two husks If another carried
Ant-baggage into a strange ant-heap
A hundred thousand lives for these two blades of grass
Are too few I was in the war, oh,
That's a handiwork for insects, indeed. Dig trenches,
Root yourself in clay, hurrah, an attack in extended order.
At the double over stacks of corpses, fix bayonets,
Fifty thousand dead, to capture
Twenty yards of latrines. Hurrah, to arms!
The interest of the whole is concerned, the heritage of your
 history is concerned,
Nay more, the freedom of your native land, nay more, world-
 power,
Nay more, two blades of grass. Such a mighty cause
Can be settled only by the dead. To arms! To arms!

CHRYSALIS   The whole earth is quivering
Something mighty it is delivering,
I am being born.

[*To the beating of a drum the troops of the ants advance with rifles, bayonets, and machine-guns, with metal helmets on their heads, and line up in ranks. Enter the 1st Engineer with the badge of a commander-in-chief, his staff, the 2nd Engineer as head of the general staff, and a retinue of officers.*

VAGRANT. [*Passing along the ranks.*]

See what good training does.   Attention!   Sound the roll-call.
Soldiers, your country is sending you to war,
That you may fall.   Two blades of grass
Are watching you.

1ST ENGINEER. [*On an elevation.*] Soldiers!   We find ourselves compelled to call you to the colours.   A dastardly enemy has treacherously attacked us, for the purpose of outwitting our pacific preparations.   At this grave hour I have appointed myself dictator.

2ND ENGINEER. Three cheers for the dictator.   Shout, boys, or——

SOLDIERS. Three cheers for the dictator.

1ST ENGINEER DICTATOR. [*Saluting.*] Thank you.   You have realized the demand of the moment.   Soldiers, we are fighting for liberty and right . . .

2ND ENGINEER. And for the greatness of the state . . .

DICTATOR. And for the greatness of the state.   We shall wage war for civilization and military honour.   Soldiers, I am with you to the last drop of blood.

2ND ENGINEER Long live our beloved commander-in-chief!

SOLDIERS Long may he live!

DICTATOR I know my soldiers.   We will fight until the final victory   Long live our gallant men, hurrah!

SOLDIERS. Hurrah, hurrah!

DICTATOR. [*To the 2nd Engineer.*] First and second divisions attack.   Fourth division surround the pine-tree and break into the ant-heap of the Yellows.   Women and embryos to be slaughtered.   Third division in reserve.   No quarter.

[*2nd Engineer, head of the general staff, salutes.*

DICTATOR. May God assist us in this.   Soldiers, right turn, quick march.   [*Beating of drums.*

HEAD OF THE GENERAL STAFF. One two.   War forced upon us,
One two, one two.   In the name of justice.   Give no quarter.
For your hearths and homes.   One two.   One two.   We are
only defending ourselves.   War for the world.   For a greater
native land.   One two.   An inveterate enemy.   Will of the
nation.   To battle, strike hard.   Historical claims.   Brilliant
spirit of the army.   One two.   One two.
    [*Fresh troops continue to march past to the beating of drums.*
DICTATOR. Good luck, soldiers.   I shall be behind you.   Fifth
regiment, hurrah!   The conqueror of the pine-cones.   A mighty
epoch!   To victory!   Conquer the world!   Magnificent daring.
One two.   One two.   Seventh regiment, hurrah.   Beat them,
soldiers.   The Yellows are cowards.   Burn and slash, heroes.
MESSENGER. [*Running in.*] The Yellows have invaded the stretch
of country between the roots of the pine-tree and the stone.
DICTATOR. Entirely according to plan.   Faster, soldiers.   One
two.   War forced upon us for honour and glory needs of the
state spare nobody conception of justice soldiers show your
bravery victory is ours greatest moment in history quick march
quick march quick march. [*In the distance dull thuds: bang,
bang.*] The battle is beginning.   Second levy.
        [*Inspects the battlefield through a pocket telescope.*
BLIND ANT. O two three four, O two . . .
                                                [*An increasing din.*
CHRYSALIS. [*Shouting.*]

        The earth is bursting.   Hearken to my sign.
        The depths of the world
        Are toiling in pain for the birth that is mine.

DICTATOR. Second levy.   Third levy.   To arms!   To arms!
    [*To the quartermaster-general.*] Issue a report.
QUARTERMASTER-GENERAL. [*In a loud voice.*] The battle has
started at last amid favourable weather conditions.   Our
heroic men are fighting in magnificent spirits.
    [*New troops march past to the beating of drums from the ant-
    heap.*
DICTATOR. Right turn, quick march.   One two, one two.
Faster, boys.
MESSENGER. [*Running in.*] Our right wing is retreating.   The
fifth regiment is completely destroyed.
DICTATOR. According to plan.   Sixth regiment replace them.
                                                [*Messenger runs off.*

VAGRANT.

Ha, ha, according to plan.   So it's all right,
When death himself serves on the staff as a general
And carries out orders: I beg to report
The fifth regiment is destroyed, according to plan.
Oh, I know all about this, and I've seen it before,
I've seen broad fields bestrewn with corpses,
Slaughtered human flesh frozen in the snow,
I've seen the supreme staff, and Death himself with galloons,
With a breast full of medals, with a fluttering plume,
Survey the fallen, to see whether they are heaped according
    to plan
On the chart of the dead.

> [*Stretcher-bearers run in with wounded.*

WOUNDED MAN. [*Screams.*] The fifth regiment.   Our regiment.
We're all killed.   Stop, stop.

> [*The telegraph instrument clatters.*

TELEGRAPH OFFICER. [*Reads dispatch.*] 'Fifth regiment destroyed.   We await orders.'

DICTATOR. Sixth take their places. [*To the quartermaster-general.*]
Issue a report.

QUARTERMASTER-GENERAL. [*In a loud voice.*] The battle is
developing successfully.   The fifth regiment specially dis-
tinguished itself, heroically repelling all attacks, whereupon it
was relieved by the sixth.

DICTATOR. Bravo.   I will decorate you with the great order of
merit.

QUARTERMASTER-GENERAL. Thank you.   I am only doing my
duty.

LAME JOURNALIST. [*Approaching with a note-book.*] I am a
journalist.   Sha-sha-sha-shall we announce a vi-vi-vi-victory?

DICTATOR. Yes.   Successful operations.   Thanks to our plans
prepared long ago.   The admirable spirit of our forces.   Irre-
sistible advance.   The enemy demoralized.

LAME JOURNALIST. W-w-we . . . w-w-we . . . we, we, we . . . w-
w-we . . .

DICTATOR. Eh?

LAME JOURNALIST. We will pr-print ev-ev-everything.

DICTATOR. Good.   We rely upon the co-operation of the press.
Don't forget the admirable spirit.

LAME JOURNALIST. The press is per-per-performing its du-
du-duty.   [*Runs off.*

PHILANTHROPIST. [*With collecting-box.*] Help the wounded   All for the wounded.   Gifts for the wounded.   Give to the wounded. Help for the cripples.   All for the cripples.   Aid the cripples.

DICTATOR [*To officer.*] Second division attack.   It must break through.   Whatever the sacrifice.

PHILANTHROPIST. For our heroes.   Help your brothers   Help for the wounded.

VAGRANT. All for the wounded.   War for the wounded   All for their wounds.

PHILANTHROPIST. Help for the cripples.   Give to the wounded.

VAGRANT [*Tears off a button and puts it into the collecting-box.*] All for the wounded.   My last button for the war

ANOTHER WOUNDED MAN. [*Groaning in the ambulance.*] Oh, oh, oh. put me out of my misery   Oh, oh, oh.

PHILANTHROPIST. [*Going out.*] Aid the wounded . .

[*The telegraph instrument rattles.*

TELEGRAPHIST. The right wing of the Yellows is retreating

DICTATOR. Pursue them !   Finish them off !   Don't be bothered with prisoners

QUARTERMASTER-GENERAL. [*In a loud voice.*] The enemy retiring in confusion.   Our regiments, in defiance of death, dogging his footsteps with splendid daring.

DICTATOR. Fourth levy.

[*Quartermaster-general runs into the ant-heap.*

TELEGRAPHIST. Sixth regiment destroyed to the last man.

DICTATOR. According to plan.   Tenth take their place.   Fourth levy.   [*New detachments of armed troops march up.*

DICTATOR. At the double.

[*Ants advance to the battle-field at the double.*

TELEGRAPHIST. The fourth division has invested the pine-tree and made a rear attack on the ant-heap of the Yellows   The garrison is slaughtered.

DICTATOR. Raze it to the ground.   Kill the women and embryos.

TELEGRAPHIST. The enemy is overwhelmed.   They have evacuated a foot of the gorse-patch.

DICTATOR. Victory is ours. [*Falls down on his knees and removes his helmet.*] Great God of the ants, thou hast granted victory unto justice.   I appoint thee colonel [*Jumps up.*] Third division forward against the enemy.   All reserves forward against them.   Spare nobody !   No prisoners !   Forward ! [*Flings himself down on his knees.*] Righteous God of strength, thou knowest that our holy cause—— [*Jumps up.*] After them, after them. Attack them. Hunt them down. Slaughter all. The issue of world-power is settled. [*Kneels.*] God of the ants, in this significant hour . . . [*Prays to himself.*

VAGRANT. [*Bending over him, softly.*] World-power? Wretched ant, you call this patch of clay and grass the world, do you? This miserable, dirty span of earth? Trample down all this ant-heap of yours, and you with it, and not a tree-top will rustle above you, fool that you are

DICTATOR. Who are you?

VAGRANT Now only a voice; yesterday perhaps a soldier in another ant-heap What do you think of yourself, conqueror of the world? Do you feel great enough? Doesn't it seem to you that this heap of corpses is too small, upon which your glory is established, you poor wretch?

DICTATOR. [*Rises.*] It does not matter I proclaim myself emperor.   [*The telegraph instrument clatters.*

TELEGRAPHIST. The second division is asking for reinforcements. Our troops are worn out.

DICTATOR. What? They must hold out. Drive them with whips.

TELEGRAPHIST The third division has been thrown into confusion.

AN ANT. [*Escapes across the stage*] We're running away.

DICTATOR Fifth levy. All to arms!

A SHOUT. [*Behind the scenes.*] Stop! No, no! Back!

A PIERCING OUTCRY. Save yourselves!

DICTATOR Fifth levy. The unfit to the front. All to the front.

SOLDIER [*Fleeing from the left.*] They're beating us. Run!

TWO SOLDIERS. [*Running from the right.*] They've surrounded us. Escape!

SOLDIER [*From the left.*] To the west! Escape to the west!

SOLDIERS. [*From the right.*] They've surrounded us from the west. Run to the east!

DICTATOR [*Yells.*] Back! Back to your ranks! To the front!

SQUAD FROM THE RIGHT. [*In a mad stampede.*] Let's get out of it! Flames are spurting!

SQUAD FROM THE LEFT. To the west! Save yourselves! Make way!

THRONG FROM THE RIGHT. Escape, they're hunting us down. To the east!

THRONG FROM THE LEFT. To the west! Make way. They're here.

[*The two streams begin to scuffle and fight in a panic.*

DICTATOR. [*Jumps towards them and strikes at them.*] Back, you cowards! You cattle, I am your emperor.

SOLDIER. Hold your row! [*Strikes him down.*] Escape!

2ND ENGINEER. [*Runs in wounded and jumps on to the elevation.*] They've taken the city. Put out the lights.

YELLOWS. [*Penetrating from both sides.*] Hurrah, hurrah. The ant-heap is ours.

[*The lights go out. Darkness, turmoil, confusion.*

VOICE OF THE 2ND ENGINEER. Fight, fight. A-a-ah.

VOICE OF THE YELLOW LEADER. Into the passages after them. spare nobody. Slaughter all the men.

SHOUT OF THE SLAUGHTERED MEN. A-a-ah.

BLIND ANT. O two. O two. O two.

YELLOW LEADER. Slaughter the women and embryos.

SHOUT OF THE WOMEN. O-o-o-o-o.

BLIND ANT. O two. O two. O two.

YELLOW LEADER. After them. Murder. Murder them all.

[*The din becomes more remote.*

BLIND ANT. O two. O two. O-o-o.

YELLOW LEADER. Light! [*The lights are lit. The foreground is empty. The Yellows are penetrating into the passages and flinging ants down from the top storeys. Corpses heaped up on all sides.*] Excellent, Yellows. All are slaughtered.

VAGRANT. [*Reeling amongst the heaped-up corpses.*] Enough, general!

YELLOW LEADER. The victory of the Yellows. The victory of justice and progress. Ours is the path between two blades of grass. The world belongs to us Yellows. I proclaim myself ruler of the universe.

[*The din becomes remoter amid the passages.*

CHRYSALIS. [*Tossing about.*] I . . . I . . . I . . .

YELLOW LEADER. [*Falls down on his knees and removes his helmet.*] Most righteous God, thou knowest that we fight only for justice. Our history, our national honour, our commercial interests . . .

VAGRANT. [*Rushes out and kicks him over, tramples and grinds him to pieces with his boot.*] Bah, you insect. You stupid insect.

END OF ACT III

EPILOGUE

LIFE AND DEATH

The interior of a forest. Pitch-black night. The Vagrant sleeping in the foreground.

VAGRANT. [*Dreaming and talking in his sleep.*] Enough, general. [*Wakes up.*] What, have I been sleeping? Where am I? This awful darkness. I can't—can't—I can't see my hand before my eyes. [*Stands up.*] Why is it so dark? I can't see a step before me. Who's speaking? Who's there? [*Shouts.*] Who's there? [*Gropes about him.*] Nothing . . . nothing . . . nothing . . . [*Shouts.*] Is anything there? Is anything there at all? An abyss, everywhere this awful abyss. On which side does it begin to fall? If I had something to hold on to. There's nothing. There's nothing. O God, I'm frightened. Where's the sky got to? If at least the sky were left. Or a single will-o'-the-wisp. A single human glimmer. If—at least—some direction were left. Where am I? [*Kneels.*] I'm frightened. Light! If only there were light!

VOICE. [*From the darkness.*] There is light. Light enough.

VAGRANT. [*Lying on the ground.*] A single human glimmer. Only one ray.

ANOTHER VOICE. This hunger! This thirst!

ANOTHER VOICE. I'm calling you. Come! I'm seeking you I'm calling: Come!

THIN VOICE. A drink, a drink, drink.

VAGRANT. For God's sake. Only a tiny spark of light. What's that? Where am I?

VOICE OF THE MALE BEETLE. [*Far off.*] My little pile. Where is my little pile?

VAGRANT. Light!

VOICE. This hunger! This thirst!

DYING VOICE. Put me out of my misery.

ANOTHER VOICE. Be mine!

ANOTHER VOICE. Aha, aha, I've got him.

VAGRANT. Light! What's here? Ah, a stone.

VOICE. This thirst! This thirst!

ANOTHER VOICE. Mercy!

145

VAGRANT. If I can only strike a small spark out of it. [*Beats a stone against the stone.*] A single spark of light. The last tiny spark.

[*Sparks burst from the stone. The interior of the forest is lit up with a spectral radiance.*

[*Standing up.*] Light!

VOICES. [*Vanishing.*] Escape, there's light! Flee!

VAGRANT. Ah, what beauty!

VOICES. [*Approaching from behind the scenes.*] Light Light!

CHRYSALIS. Who is calling me?

VAGRANT. Light, praise God.

[*An increasing gleam and soft music.*

CHRYSALIS.   Upon your knees. Upon your knees.
         I—I—I the chosen one
         Am entering the world.

VOICES. [*Approaching.*] Behold, there's light!

CHRYSALIS.   In travail of birth
              Bursts my prison's girth.
              Seen, heard by none
              A deed is done.
              I shall be.

[*A bevy of moths fly into the midst of the radiance and dance.*

VAGRANT Where are you from with your transparent wings?

1ST MOTH. [*Flies from the centre of the others and whirls round.*]
              O-o-o.   [*Stands still.*
              Like a ray from the gloom
              Has burst forth the radiant, eternal,
              Mighty life of the moths.
              Dance, my sisters. O-o-o.   [*Whirls round.*

CHORUS OF MOTHS. Life we encircle.
              Life we dance through.
              We are life itself.
              Life.   Life.

1ST MOTH. [*Standing still.*]

From throbbings of rays our wings are woven,
From star unto star from glittering threads
An age-old divine weaver wove them. We dance through the universe,
We, the spirit of life, born from light,
Images of God, who——   [*Sinks down dead.*

2ND MOTH. [*Comes forward and whirls round.*]

> Who in us beholds himself,
> O-o-o. Eternal, eternal is life.

VAGRANT. [*Reeling towards her.*] How . . . how then, is it eternal?

2ND MOTH.

> To live, to encircle, to whirl. From depths of the universe
> Responds to us the creative, unbounded
> Whirling of moth-wings. To us is given
> The mysterious task of eternally whirling,
> From our wings is showered the harmony of the spheres.
> Oh what a duty and what creative joy
> To be a moth. To live is to rotate.
> O-o-o. [*Whirls round.*

CHORUS OF MOTHS. Eternal, eternal is life!

VAGRANT. [*Amongst them.*] Oh, what a duty and what creative joy——

CHORUS OF MOTHS. To rotate. Sisters, dance around

2ND MOTH. [*Standing still.*]

> Unravel life. What are we else,
> We, woven from daintiest fabrics,
> But thought and soul of creation?
> We are transparent. We are without weight or wrack.
> We are life itself. Like sparks from God's furnace
> Have we burst forth and we glorify—— [*Falls dead.*

VAGRANT. See, she is dead.

3RD MOTH. [*Comes forward and whirls.*]

> O-o-o. [*Stands still.*
> With us the whole world circles, its thanks and praises blending,
> It glorifies, leaps and rotates
> Before thee, mighty, lovely, unending
> Moth-gift of life.
> Breathless delight, eternal ecstasy
> Hail to thee, life's roundelay,
> Fiery dance, to which no end can be,
> All—— [*Falls dead.*

VAGRANT. [*Raising his hands and turning.*] O-o-o——

CHORUS OF MOTHS. All hail! All hail.!

VAGRANT. Life, life, you have cast a spell upon us. For even I, old, battered moth that I am, whirl and shout, O life . . .

CHORUS OF MOTHS. All hail, all hail!

VAGRANT. Let us live, all of us! Each of us desires to live. Each of us defends himself, and each one fights on his own. If only we were to act thus together. If you yourself were to lead us against—against destruction, against death.

CHORUS OF MOTHS. All hail, be glorified:

[Moth after moth falls dead.

VAGRANT. We all would follow you! All moths and all mortals, and thoughts, and works, and the creatures in the water, and ants, and grass, all unite with you. But first we ourselves must unite, all of us who live, into one regiment. And you will lead us, O omnipotent life . . .

CHORUS OF MOTHS. All hail to life!

CHRYSALIS. *[In a piercing shriek.]* Make room! *[Rends its husk and leaps forth as a moth.]* Here I am!

VAGRANT. *[Staggering towards it.]* You, Chrysalis? You? Show yourself! At last you have been born.

CHRYSALIS-MOTH. *[Whirling.]*

> O-o-o. *[Standing still.]* I
> Proclaim sway over life. I
> Enjoin creation; live, for the empery
> Of life has come. *[Whirling.]* O-o-o.

THE FEW OF THE LAST MOTHS. Eternal, eternal is life.

[They fall dead.

CHRYSALIS-MOTH. *[Standing still.]*

> The whole of life surged up to bring me forth,
> And it burst in its throes. Hearken, O hearken,
> I bear a mighty mission; I proclaim
> Immense tidings; silence, silence,
> I will utter great words.   *[Falls dead.*

VAGRANT. *[Kneeling down.]* Rise up, moth. Why have you fallen? *[Lifts her up.]* She is dead. Alas, delightful countenance, alas, clear and serene eyes. Dead! Do you hear, Chrysalis? What did you desire to say? Speak yet. *[Carries her in his arms.]* Dead. How light she is, O God, how beautiful. Why had she to die? Wherefore this fearful lack of meaning? *[Lays her on to the ground.]* Dead! *[Creeps along the*

ground and examines the dead moths, lifting their heads.] And
you too are dead, you who danced? And you who sang?
And you, who were so young? Ah, these lips will utter no
more sound. Dead! Do you hear, green moth? If only she
opened her eyes. It is so good to live. Awake, live! All—
hail—to—life! [*Crawls forward on his hands and knees.*] All
hail! Ugh! Who clutched at me? Away with you. [*The
light goes out, only a sharp ray falls on to the Vagrant.*] Who is
here? Ugh, stop, I feel a chillness. . . . Who are you?
[*Brandishes his hands in the void.*] Away with you, cold hand.
I desire not . . . [*Stands up.*] Don't touch! Who are you?
[*Defends himself.*] Stop, why are you strangling me? Ha, ha,
wait, I know who you are. You are . . . you are Death. So
many times have I seen you to-day. But I—will—not.
Stop, skeleton, eyeless and loathsome. [*Struggles in the void*]
Cease!   [*From the right two Snails crawl in*
1st Snail. Stop.[1] Someone.'s making a noise.
2nd Snail. You fool, come back.
Vagrant. [*Struggling.*] That's for you, rattle-bones! Ha, ha,
ha, you felt that, eh? [*Thrust down to his knees.*] Leave me
alone. Don't smother me. Come now, I only want to live.
Is that so much? [*Rises and waves his hands.*] I won't give you
my life, you old death's-head, I won't. That's for you.
[*Falls.*] Oh, you'd trip me up, would you?
1st Snail. I say, Snail.
2nd Snail. What?
1st Snail. He's struggling with death.
2nd Snail. We'll have a look, eh?
Vagrant. [*Rising.*] Let me live. What will it matter to you?
Only this time. At least till to-morrow. Let . . . only . . .
breathe . . . [*Struggles.*] Stop, don't strangle. I don't want
to die. I've had so little out of life. [*Shouts.*] Ah!
                                   [*Falls on his face.*
1st Snail. What fun, eh?
2nd Snail. I say, Snail.
1st Snail. What?
2nd Snail. He's done for.
Vagrant. [*Rises to his knees.*] You strangle a man when he's
down, do you, coward? Stop now, let me tell—all—I want—
another moment. [*Rises and staggers.*] Let me—live. Only

---

[1] In the original the snails are made to lisp.

live. [*Shrieks.*] No! Go away! There 's still so much for me to say. [*Sinks on to his knees.*] Now—I know—how to live.

                               [*Falls on his back.*

1ST SNAIL [*Crawls slowly forward.*] Well, it 's all up with him.

2ND SNAIL. Jesus, Jesus, what a blow! Oh dear, oh dear. What a misfortune!

1ST SNAIL. What are you complaining about? It 's nothing to do with us.

2ND SNAIL. But you know that 's what people say when some-one dies.

1ST SNAIL. Oh yes. Well, we 'll lie low.

2ND SNAIL. Oh yes. That 's the way of the world.

1ST SNAIL. It 's a pity there aren't fewer snails and more cauliflowers.

2ND SNAIL. Hi, Snail, look.

1ST SNAIL. What?

2ND SNAIL. What a lot of dead moths!

1ST SNAIL. It 's a pity they can't be eaten.

2ND SNAIL. Yes! Well, we 'll lie low, eh?

1ST SNAIL. As long as we 're alive. That 's what matters.

2ND SNAIL. That 's about it. I say, Snail . . .

1ST SNAIL. What?

2ND SNAIL. Life 's pleasant

1ST SNAIL. Rather! Nothing like life, you know.

2ND SNAIL. Then we 'll lie low.   [*They enter the wings.*

1ST SNAIL. That was funny, wasn't it?

2ND SNAIL. Rather! As long as—we 're—alive.   [*Exeunt.*

                 [*Pause. It becomes light. Birds awaken.*

WOODCUTTER. [*Enters from the back with his axe on his shoulder. Sees the Vagrant's corpse behind a bush, and bends down to it.*] Who 's this? Do you hear, old man? Come on, old fellow, wake up. What 's the matter with you? [*Stands up, takes off his cap, and crosses himself.*] He 's dead. Poor old man. [*Pause.*] Anyhow—his troubles are over.

AUNT. [*Enters from the left. She is carrying a newly born child to be baptized.*] Good day to you. What have you there, Uncle?

WOODCUTTER. Good day, Aunt. Someone 's died here. It 's a tramp.   [*Pause.*

AUNT. Poor man!

WOODCUTTER. And what about you, Aunt? To a baptism? To a baptism?

AUNT. That's my sister's baby. Tk, tk.

WOODCUTTER. One is born and another dies.

AUNT. And there are always people enough.

WOODCUTTER. [*Tickling the baby under the chin.*] Ks, ks, laddie. Wait till you grow up.

AUNT. If only he's better off than we are, Uncle.

WOODCUTTER. Why, as long as a man's got something to do the whole time.

SCHOOLGIRL. [*Enters from the right with a bag on her back.*] Praised be the Lord . . .

AUNT. For ever and ever.

WOODCUTTER. For ever and ever. [*The Schoolgirl passes across the stage and exit.*] It's fine weather to-day, Aunt, eh? More than words can tell.

SCHOOLGIRL'S VOICE. Praised be the Lord . . .

MAN'S VOICE. [*Behind the scenes.*] For ever and ever.

AUNT. Yes, it's a fine day we're having.

WANDERER. [*Enters from the left.*] Good day.

AUNT. Good day.

WOODCUTTER. A happy good day to you.

CURTAIN

THE INFERNAL MACHINE

By Jean Cocteau

Translated from the French by
CARL WILDMAN

La Machine Infernale was first performed at the
Comédie des Champs-Élysées (Théâtre Louis Jouvet)
On 10th April 1934, with scenery and custumes by
Christian Bérard.

CHARACTERS
(in order of appearance)

THE VOICE
THE YOUNG SOLDIER
THE SOLDIER
THE CAPTAIN
JOCASTA, *the queen, widow of Laïus*
TIRESIAS, *a soothsayer, nearly blind*
THE GHOST OF LAÏUS, *the dead king*
THE SPHINX
ANUBIS, *Egyptian God of the Dead*
THE THEBAN MATRON
A LITTLE BOY
A LITTLE GIRL
OEDIPUS, *son of Laïus*
CREON, *brother of Jocasta*
THE MESSENGER FROM CORINTH
THE SHEPHERD OF LAÏUS
ANTIGONE, *daughter of Oedipus*

ACT I

THE GHOST OF LAÏUS

THE VOICE

'He will kill his father.   He will marry his mother.'

To thwart this oracle of Apollo, Jocasta, Queen of Thebes, leaves her son on the mountain side with his feet pierced and bound. A shepherd of Corinth finds the nursling and carries it to Polybius. Polybius and Merope, king and queen of Corinth, were bemoaning a sterile marriage.   The child, Oedipus, or *Pierced-feet*, respected by bears and wolves, is to them a heaven-sent gift. They adopt him.

When a young man, Oedipus questions the oracle of Delphi.

The god speaks: *You will murder your father and marry your mother*.   He must therefore fly from Polybius and Merope.   The fear of parricide and incest drives him on towards his fate.

One evening, arriving at the cross-roads of Delphi and Daulis, he meets an escort.   A horse jostles him; a quarrel starts; a servant threatens him; he replies with a blow from his stick. The blow misses the servant and kills the master.   This dead man is Laïus, the old king of Thebes.   Parricide!

The escort, fearing an ambush, took to its heels.   Oedipus, unsuspecting, passed on.   Besides, he is young, enthusiastic; this accident is soon forgotten.

During one of his halts he learns of the scourge of the Sphinx. The Sphinx, 'the Winged Virgin,' 'the Singing Bitch,' is killing off the young men of Thebes.   This monster asks a riddle and kills those who do not guess it.   Queen Jocasta, widow of Laïus, offers her hand and her crown to the conqueror of the Sphinx.

Like the young Siegfried to come, Oedipus hurries on.   He is consumed with curiosity and ambition.   The meeting takes place.   What was the nature of this meeting?   Mystery.   Be that as it may, Oedipus enters Thebes a conqueror, he marries the queen.   Incest!

For the gods really to enjoy themselves, their victim must fall from a great height.   Years come and go in prosperity. Two daughters and two sons complicate the monstrous union. The people love their king.   But the plague suddenly descends upon them.   The gods accuse an anonymous criminal of infecting the country and demand that he shall be driven out.   Going from one discovery to another, and as if intoxicated by

misfortune, Oedipus, in the end, finds himself cornered.   The trap
shuts.   All becomes clear.   With her red scarf Jocasta hangs
herself.   With the golden brooch of the hanging woman Oedipus
puts out his eyes.

Spectator, this machine, you see here wound up to the full in
such a way that the spring will slowly unwind the whole length
of a human life, is one of the most perfect constructed by the
infernal gods for the mathematical destruction of a mortal.

ACT I[1]

THE GHOSTS

A patrol path round the ramparts of Thebes. High walls. A stormy night. Summer lightning. The din and bands of the popular district can be heard.

YOUNG SOLDIER. They 're having a good time!

SOLDIER. Trying to.

YOUNG SOLDIER. Well, anyway, they dance all night.

SOLDIER. They can't sleep, so they dance.

YOUNG SOLDIER. Never mind, they 're getting tight and going with women, and spending their nights in all sorts of dives, while I am here tramping up and down with you. Well I, for one, can't stick it any longer! I can't stick it! I can't! That 's clear enough, isn't it? I 've had my bellyful!

SOLDIER. Desert then.

YOUNG SOLDIER. Oh, no! I 've made up my mind. I 'm going to put my name down for the Sphinx.

SOLDIER. What for?

YOUNG SOLDIER. What for? Why, to do something, of course. To put an end to all this creepy business and ghastly hanging about.

SOLDIER. You wouldn't get scared, though?

YOUNG SOLDIER. Scared? How d' you mean?

SOLDIER. Oh, just scared, you know! I 've seen brighter and tougher lads than you who got the wind up. Unless this gent is going to kill the Sphinx and draw the first prize.

YOUNG SOLDIER. And why not? Oh, I know the only man who came back alive from the Sphinx had become a gibbering idiot. But supposing what he gibbers is true? What if it is a riddle? What if I guess the answer? What——

SOLDIER. Now listen here, you poor bastard. Don't you realize that hundreds upon hundreds of chaps who 've been to the stadium and college and everything have left their carcasses

[1] The four scenes should be planted on a little platform in the centre of the stage, surrounded by nocturnal curtains. The slope of the platform varies according to the requirements of the scenes. Besides the lighting of details, the four acts should be flooded in the livid mythical light of quicksilver.

behind there, and you, a poor little private soldier like you wants to——

YOUNG SOLDIER. I shall go! I shall, because I can't bear any longer counting the stones of this wall, hearing that band, and seeing your rotten mug, and——   [*He stamps.*

SOLDIER. That's the stuff, my hero! I was waiting for this explosion. I like it better that way. Now . . . now . . . enough blubbering. . . . Take it easy . . . there, there, there . . .

YOUNG SOLDIER. To hell with you!

[*The Soldier bangs his spear against the wall behind the Young Soldier who becomes rigid.*

SOLDIER. What's up?

YOUNG SOLDIER. Didn't you hear anything?

SOLDIER. No . . . where?

YOUNG SOLDIER. Ah! . . . I seemed to . . . I thought for a moment——

SOLDIER. You're like a sheet. . . . What's the matter? Are you going to pass out?

YOUNG SOLDIER. It's silly . . . I seemed to hear a knock. I thought it was him!

SOLDIER. The Sphinx?

YOUNG SOLDIER. No, him, the ghost, the phantom, you know!

SOLDIER. The ghost? Our dear old ghost of Laïus? And is that what turns your stomach over? Really!

YOUNG SOLDIER. I'm sorry.

SOLDIER. You're sorry, mate? What are you talking about? To start with, there's a good chance that our ghost will not appear again after last night's business. So that's that. And besides, what are you sorry about? Look at things squarely. We can hardly say this ghost scared us. Oh, well . . . the first time perhaps! . . . But, after that, eh? . . . He was a decent old ghost, almost a pal, a relief. Well, if the idea of this ghost makes you jumpy, it's because you're in a real state of nerves, like me, like everybody in Thebes, rich or poor alike, except a few big pots who make something out of everything. There's not much fun in war, anyway, but we don't know a blind thing about the enemy we're up against. We're beginning to get fed up with oracles, happy deaths, and heroic mothers. Do you think I should pull your leg as I do if my nerves weren't on edge, and do you think you'd start blubbering, and that lot over there'd get tight and dance? No, they'd be in bed and fast asleep, and we'd be playing dice while waiting for friend phantom.

YOUNG SOLDIER. I say . . .

SOLDIER. Well? . . .

YOUNG SOLDIER. What d' you think it's like . . . the Sphinx?

SOLDIER. Oh! give the Sphinx a rest. If I knew what it was like I shouldn't be here doing guard duty with you to-night.

YOUNG SOLDIER. Some make out it's no bigger than a hare, and is timid, and has a tiny little face, like a woman's. But I think it has a woman's head and breasts, and sleeps with the young men.

SOLDIER. Oh, turn it up! Shut up and forget it!

YOUNG SOLDIER. Perhaps it doesn't ask anything and doesn't even touch you. You meet it, look at it, and die of love.

SOLDIER. All we needed was for you to go and fall in love with the public scourge. After all, public scourge . . . between ourselves, do you know what I think about this public scourge? . . . It's a vampire! Yes, a common or garden vampire! Someone in hiding from the police, and who they can't lay their hands on.

YOUNG SOLDIER. A vampire with a woman's head?

SOLDIER. Can't you turn it up? No, not him! A real old vampire with a beard and moustache, and a belly. He sucks your blood and that's how it is they bring corpses back home, all with the same wound in the same place: the back of the neck! And now, go and see for yourself if you're still keen.

YOUNG SOLDIER. You say that . . .

SOLDIER. I say that . . . I say that . . Hi! . . . The captain.

[*They stand up to attention. The Captain enters and folds his arms.*

CAPTAIN. Easy! . . . Well, my lads. . . . Is this where we see ghosts?

SOLDIER. Sir——

CAPTAIN. Silence! You will speak when I ask you. Which of you two has dared——

YOUNG SOLDIER. I did, sir!

CAPTAIN. Good Lord! Whose turn to speak is it? Are you going to keep quiet? I was asking: which of you two has dared to make a report about a service matter, without it passing through the normal channels? Right over my head. Answer.

SOLDIER. It wasn't his fault, sir, he knew——

CAPTAIN. Was it you or him?

YOUNG SOLDIER. Both of us, but *I*——

CAPTAIN. Silence! I want to know how the high priest came to hear of what happens at night at this post, while I myself heard nothing.

YOUNG SOLDIER. It's my fault, sir, my fault. My comrade here didn't want to say anything about it. But I thought I ought to speak and, as this incident didn't concern the service ... and, well ... I told his uncle everything; because his uncle's wife is sister to one of the queen's linen-maids, and his brother-in-law is in Tiresias's temple.

SOLDIER. That's why I said it was my fault, sir.

CAPTAIN. All right! Don't burst my ear-drums. So ... this incident doesn't concern the service. Very good, oh, very good! ... And it seems ... this famous incident which doesn't concern the service is a ghost story?

YOUNG SOLDIER. Yes, sir.

CAPTAIN. A ghost appeared to you one night when you were on guard duty, and this ghost said to you ... Just what did this ghost say to you?

YOUNG SOLDIER. He told us, sir, he was the spectre of King Laïus, and he had tried to appear several times since his murder, and he begged us to find some way of warning Queen Jocasta and Tiresias with all speed.

CAPTAIN. With all speed! Fancy that! What a nice old ghost he must be! And ... didn't you ask him, say, why *you* had the honour of this visit and why he doesn't appear directly before the queen or Tiresias?

SOLDIER. Yes, sir, I asked him, I did. His answer was that he wasn't free to put in an appearance anywhere, and that the ramparts were the most favourable spot for people who had died violent deaths, because of the drains.

CAPTAIN. Drains?

SOLDIER. Yes, sir. He said drains, meaning because of the fumes which rise there.

CAPTAIN. Hoho! A very learned spectre, and he doesn't hide his light under a bushel. Did he scare you much? And what did he look like? What was his face like? What clothes did he wear? Where did he stand, and what language did he speak? Are his visits long or short? Have you seen him on different occasions? Although this business doesn't concern the service, I must say I am curious to learn from your lips a few details about the manners and customs of ghosts.

YOUNG SOLDIER. Well, he did scare us a bit the first night, I admit. You see, sir, he appeared very suddenly, like a lamp lighting up, there in the thickness of the wall.

SOLDIER. We both saw him.

YOUNG SOLDIER. It was hard to make out the face and the body; the mouth, when it was open, was clearer, and a white tuft of his beard, and a large red stain, bright red, near the right ear. He spoke with difficulty and couldn't somehow manage to get out more than one sentence at a time. But you'd better ask my comrade here about that, sir. He explained to me how it was the poor fellow couldn't manage to get it over.

SOLDIER. Oh! you know, sir, there's nothing very complicated about it! He spent all his energy in the effort to appear, that is, in leaving his new shape and taking on the old, so that we could see him. That's the reason why each time he spoke a little better, he began to disappear, became transparent like, and you could see the wall through him.

YOUNG SOLDIER. And as soon as he spoke badly you could see him very well. But you saw him badly as soon as he spoke well, and began saying the same thing over again. 'Queen Jocasta. You must ... you must ... Queen ... Queen ... Queen Jocasta. ... You must. ... You must warn the queen. ... You must warn Queen Jocasta. ... I ask you, gentlemen, I ask you, I ... I ... Gentlemen ... I ask ... you must ... you must ... I ask you, gentlemen, to warn ... I ask you ... The queen ... Queen Jocasta ... to warn, gentlemen, to warn ... Gentlemen ... Gentlemen ...' That's how he went on.

SOLDIER. And you could see he was afraid of disappearing before he'd said his piece right to the end.

YOUNG SOLDIER. Oh yes, and then, you know, remember, eh? Every time the same business. The red stain went last. Just like a ship's light on the wall, it was, sir.

SOLDIER. But the whole thing was over in a minute!

YOUNG SOLDIER. He has appeared in the same place five times, every night, a little before dawn.

SOLDIER. But last night it was different, we ... well, we had a bit of a fight, and my comrade here decided to tell the royal house everything.

CAPTAIN. Well! Well! And how was this night 'different,' which, if I'm not mistaken, caused a dispute between you . . .?

SOLDIER. It was like this, sir. . . . You know, guard duty isn't exactly all beer and skittles.

YOUNG SOLDIER. So really we were waiting for the ghost to turn up, like.

SOLDIER. And we laid the odds.

YOUNG SOLDIER. Will come . . .

SOLDIER. Won't . . .

YOUNG SOLDIER. Will come . . .

SOLDIER. Won't . . . and it may seem a funny thing to say, but it was a comfort to see him.

YOUNG SOLDIER. A habit, as you might say.

SOLDIER. We ended by imagining we saw him when he wasn't there. We'd say to each other: 'It's moving! The wall is lighting up. Don't you see anything? No. But you must do. Over there, I tell you. . . . The wall isn't the same. Don't you see, look, look!'

YOUNG SOLDIER. And we looked and stared our eyes out. We didn't dare move.

SOLDIER. We watched for the least change.

YOUNG SOLDIER. And when, at last, he turned up, we could breathe again, and weren't the least bit afraid.

SOLDIER. The other night we watched and watched and stared ourselves nearly blind; we thought he'd never show up, but he appeared stealthily . . not at all quickly like on the first nights. And once he was visible, he said new things and told us as well as he could that something fearful had happened, a thing of death which he couldn't explain to the living. He spoke of places where he could go and places where he couldn't go, and that he had been where he shouldn't and knew a secret which he shouldn't know, and that he would be discovered and punished, and afterwards he wouldn't be allowed to appear, he wouldn't be able to appear any more. [*Solemn voice.*] 'I shall die my last death,' he said, 'and it will be finished, finished. You see, gentlemen, there is not a moment to lose. Run! Warn the queen! Find Tiresias! Gentlemen! Gentlemen, have pity! . . .' He was begging away and day was breaking. And there he stuck!

YOUNG SOLDIER. Suddenly we thought he'd go mad.

SOLDIER. We understood from sentences without beginning or

end that he had left his post, as it were, . . . didn't know how
to disappear, and was lost.   We saw him going through the
same performance to disappear as to appear, and he couldn't
manage it.   So then he asked us to swear at him, because, he
said, swearing at ghosts is the way to make them go.   The
silliest thing about it was that we hadn't the guts to do it.
The more he repeated: 'Come on! young men, insult me!   Let
yourselves go, do your best. . . .   Oh, come on!'—the softer
we looked.

YOUNG SOLDIER. And the less we could lay our tongue to! . . .

SOLDIER. Yes, that was the limit!   And yet, it's not for lack of
blackguarding our superiors.

CAPTAIN. Very nice of you, men, I'm sure!   Thank you on
behalf of the superiors.

SOLDIER. Oh! I didn't mean that, sir. . . .   I meant . . . I
meant the princes, crowned heads, ministers, the government,
what . . . the powers that be.   In fact, we'd often talked
over wrongs which are done. . . .   But he was such a decent
sort, the ghost of poor old King Laïus, the swear-words wouldn't
come.   There he was, urging us on and we kept dithering:
'Go on then!   Buzz off, you old bastard!'   In short, we gave
him bouquets!

YOUNG SOLDIER. Because, you see, sir, 'you old bastard' is a
kind of friendly way of speaking among soldiers.

CAPTAIN. It's as well to know.

SOLDIER. Go on!   Go on then! . . . you bleeding . . . you old
. . . Poor ghost.   He hung there between life and death and
he was beside himself with fear because of the cocks and the
sun.   When, all of a sudden, we saw the wall become the wall
again, and the red stain go out.   We were dog-tired.

YOUNG SOLDIER. It was after that night that I decided to speak
to his uncle as he refused to speak himself.

CAPTAIN. Your ghost doesn't seem to be very punctual.

SOLDIER. Oh, you know, sir, he may not show himself again.

CAPTAIN. I am in his way, no doubt.

SOLDIER. No, sir, I mean after last night . . .

CAPTAIN. But I understand from what you say that your ghost
is very polite.   He will appear, I'm quite sure.   In the
first place, the politeness of kings is punctuality, and the
politeness of ghosts consists in taking on human form,
according to your ingenious theory.

SOLDIER. Possibly, sir, but it's also possible that with ghosts there are no more kings, and they may mistake a century for a minute. So if the ghost appears in a thousand years instead of this evening . . .

CAPTAIN. You're a clever sort of chap, but patience has its limits. I tell you this ghost will appear. I tell you my presence is upsetting him, and I tell you that no one outside the service must come along this patrol path.

SOLDIER. Yes, sir.

CAPTAIN. [*In an outburst.*] So, ghost or no ghost, you are to stop any one turning up here without the password. Those are orders. Is that clear?

SOLDIER. Yes, sir.

CAPTAIN. And don't forget to patrol. Dismiss!

[*The two soldiers stand stiffly at the slope.*

[*False exit.*] Don't try any clever tricks! I've got my eye on you.   [*He disappears. Long silence*

SOLDIER. As you were!

YOUNG SOLDIER. He thought we were trying to pull his leg.

SOLDIER. Don't you believe it! He thought someone was trying to pull ours.

YOUNG SOLDIERS. Ours?

SOLDIER. Yes, chum. I get to know lots of things, I do, through my uncle. The queen is nice, you know, but she isn't really liked; they think she's . . . [*He taps his head.*] They say she is eccentric and has a foreign accent, and is under the influence of Tiresias. This Tiresias advises the queen to do everything that will harm her. Do this . . . and do that. . . . She tells him her dreams, and asks him if she ought to get up right foot or left foot first; he leads her by the nose and licks her brother's boots, and plots with him against his sister. They are a low lot there. I wouldn't mind betting the captain thought our ghost was out of the same bag as the Sphinx. A priests' trick to attract Jocasta and make her believe anything they want.

YOUNG SOLDIER. No?

SOLDIER. Shakes you, doesn't it? But that's how it is. . . . [*In a very low voice.*] Listen, I believe in the ghost myself, take it from me. But, for that very reason, because I believe in him and they don't, I advise you to keep your mouth shut. You've already succeeded in making a fine hash of things. Take down this report: 'Has given proof of an intelligence well above his rank. . . .'

Young Soldier. Still, if our king . . .

Soldier. Our king! . . . Our king! . . . Steady on! . . . A dead king isn't a living king. It's like this, if King Laïus were living, well, between ourselves, he would manage on his own and wouldn't come looking for you to act as his A.D.C.

[*They move off towards the right by the patrol path.*

Voice of Jocasta. [*At the bottom of the steps. She has a very strong accent : the international accent of royalty.*] Still another flight! I hate steps! Why all these steps? We can see nothing! Where are we?

Voice of Tiresias. But, Majesty, you know what I think of this escapade, and *I* didn't——-

Voice of Jocasta. Stop it, Zizi. You only open your mouth to say silly things. This is not the time for moral lessons.

Voice of Tiresias. You should have taken another guide. I am nearly blind.

Voice of Jocasta. What is the use of being a soothsayer, I wonder! Why, you don't even know where the steps are. I shall break my leg! It will be your fault, Zizi, your fault, as usual.

Voice of Tiresias. My fleshly eyes have gone out to the advantage of an inner eye which has other uses than counting steps.

Voice of Jocasta. And now he's cross all over his eye! There, there! We love you, Zizi; but these flights of steps upset me so. We had to come, Zizi, we simply had to!

Voice of Tiresias. Majesty——

Voice of Jocasta. Don't be obstinate. I had no idea there were all these wretched steps. I am going to go up backwards. You will steady me. Don't be afraid. *I* am leading you. But if I looked at the steps, I should fall. Take my hands. Forward!   [*They appear on the set.*

There . . . there . . . there . . . four, five, six, seven . . .

[*Jocasta arrives on the platform and moves to the right. Tiresias treads on the end of her scarf. She utters a cry.*

Tiresias. What is it?

Jocasta. It's your foot, Zizi! You're walking on my scarf.

Tiresias. Forgive me . . .

Jocasta. Ah! he's cross! But it isn't you that I am annoyed with, it's the scarf! I am surrounded by objects which hate me! All day long this scarf is strangling me. At one time it catches in the branches, at another it gets wound on to the hub of a carriage, another time you tread on it. It's a positive

fact.   And I am afraid of it, but I dare not be separated from
it!   Awful!   It will be the death of me.

TIRESIAS. Look what a state your nerves are in.

JOCASTA. And what is the use of your third eye, I should like to
know?   Have you found the Sphinx?   Have you found the
murderers of Laïus?   Have you calmed the people?   Guards
are stationed at my door and I am left with things that hate
me, that want my death!

TIRESIAS. From mere hearsay——

JOCASTA. I feel things.   I feel things better than all of you!
[*She puts her hand on her belly.*]   I feel them there!   Was every
possible effort made to discover the murderers of Laïus?

TIRESIAS. Majesty, you know very well the Sphinx made further
searches impossible.

JOCASTA. Well, I for one don't care a jot about your fowls'
entrails. . . .   I feel, there . . . that Laïus is suffering and
wants to be heard.   I am determined to get to the bottom
of this story, and to hear this young guard for myself; and
I *shall* hear him.   I am your queen, Tiresias, don't you
forget it.

TIRESIAS. My dear child, you must try and understand a poor
blind man who adores you, watches over you, and wishes you
were sleeping in your room instead of running after a shadow
on the ramparts.

JOCASTA. [*With mystery.*] I do not sleep.

TIRESIAS. You don't sleep?

JOCASTA. No, Zizi, I don't sleep.   The Sphinx and the murder
of Laïus have put my nerves all on edge.   You were right
there.   And I am glad in a way, because if I fall asleep for so
much as a minute I have a dream, always the same, and I am
ill for the whole day.

TIRESIAS. Isn't it my business to interpret dreams? . . .

JOCASTA. The place of the dream is rather like this platform, so
I'll tell you.   I am standing in the night, cradling a kind of
nursling.   Suddenly this nursling becomes a sticky paste
which runs through my fingers.   I shriek and try to throw
this paste away, but . . . oh! Zizi . . . if only you knew, it's
foul. . . .   This thing, this paste stays hanging on to me, and
when I think I'm free of it the paste flies back and strikes me
across the face.   And this paste is living.   It has a kind of
mouth which fixes itself on mine.   And it creeps everywhere,
it feels after my belly, and my thighs.   Oh! Horrible!

TIRESIAS. Calm yourself.

JOCASTA I don't want to sleep any more, Zizi . . . I don't want
to sleep any more. Listen to that music. Where is it?
They don't sleep either. It's lucky for them they have that
music. They are afraid, Zizi and rightly. They must
dream horrible things, and they don't want to sleep. And
while I think of it, why this music? Why is it allowed? Do
I have music to keep me from sleeping? I didn't know these
places stayed open all night How is it there is this scandal,
Zizi? Creon must send out orders! This music must be
forbidden! This scandal must stop at once.

TIRESIAS. Majesty, I implore you to calm yourself and to give
up this idea. You 're beside yourself for lack of sleep We
have authorized these bands so that the people don't become
demoralized, to keep up their courage. There would be
crimes . and worse than that if there were no dancing in
the crowded parts of the town.

JOCASTA. Do I dance?

TIRESIAS. That's different. You are in mourning for Laius.

JOCASTA. So are they all, Zizi. All of them! Every one! And
yet they can dance and I can't. It's too unfair . . I shall——

TIRESIAS. Someone coming, madam.

JOCASTA. I say, Zizi, I 'm shaking. I have come out with all
my jewels.

TIRESIAS. There 's nothing to fear. You won't meet prowlers
on the patrol path. It must be the guards

JOCASTA. Perhaps the soldier I am looking for?

TIRESIAS. Don't move. We 'll find out.

                [*The soldiers enter. They see Jocasta and Tiresias.*

YOUNG SOLDIER. Steady, looks like somebody

SOLDIER. Where have they sprung from? [*Aloud.*] Who goes
there?

TIRESIAS. [*To the queen.*] This is going to be awkward. . . .
[*Aloud.*] Listen, my good men . . .

YOUNG SOLDIER. Password.

TIRESIAS. You see, madam, we ought to have the password.
You 're getting us into an awful mess.

JOCASTA. Password? Why? What password? How silly,
Zizi. I shall go and speak to him myself.

TIRESIAS. Madam, I implore you. They have instructions.
These guards might not recognize you, nor believe me. It 's
very dangerous.

JOCASTA. How romantic you are! You see dramas everywhere.

SOLDIER. They 're whispering together. Perhaps they 're going to spring on us.

TIRESIAS. [*To the soldiers.*] You have nothing to fear. I am old and nearly blind. Let me explain my presence on these ramparts, and the presence of the person who accompanies me.

SOLDIER. No speeches. The password!

TIRESIAS. One moment. Just a moment. Listen, my good men, have you seen any gold coins?

SOLDIER. Attempted bribery.

> [*He goes towards the right to guard the patrol path and leaves the Young Soldier opposite Tiresias.*

TIRESIAS. You 're wrong. I meant: have you seen the queen's portrait on a gold coin?

YOUNG SOLDIER. Yes!

TIRESIAS. [*Stepping aside and showing the queen, who is counting the stars, in profile.*] And . . . don't you recognize . . .?

YOUNG SOLDIER. If you 're trying to make out there 's a connection, I don't get it. The queen is so young, and this . . . er . . . lady . . . well! . . .

JOCASTA. What does he say?

TIRESIAS. He says he finds madam very young to be the queen. . . .

JOCASTA. How entertaining!

TIRESIAS. [*To the Soldier.*] Fetch your officer.

SOLDIER. No need. I have my orders. Clear off! Look sharp!

TIRESIAS. You 'll hear more of this!

JOCASTA. Zizi, what is it now? What does he say?

The Captain enters

CAPTAIN. What 's going on here?

YOUNG SOLDIER. Two people without the password, sir.

CAPTAIN. [*Going towards Tiresias.*] Who are you? [*He suddenly recognizes Tiresias.*] My lord! [*He bows.*] My profoundest apologies.

TIRESIAS. Phew! Thanks, Captain. I thought this young warrior was going to run us through.

CAPTAIN. I am extremely sorry, my lord! [*To the Young Soldier.*] Idiot! Leave us.

> [*The Young Soldier goes to his comrade on the extreme right.*

SOLDIER. [*To the Young Soldier.*] What a brick!

TIRESIAS. Don't scold him! He was obeying orders. . . .

CAPTAIN. Such a visit . . . in such a place!   What can I do for your lordship?

TIRESIAS. [*Standing back to show the queen.*] Her Majesty!
                                    [*The Captain starts back.*

CAPTAIN. [*Bows at a respectful distance.*] Majesty! . . .

JOCASTA. No ceremony, please!   I should like to know which guard saw the ghost.

CAPTAIN. Oh, the sorry young specimen who ill-used my lord Tiresias, and if Your Majesty . . .

JOCASTA. See, Zizi.   What luck!   I was right in coming. . . . [*To the Captain.*] Tell him to approach.

CAPTAIN. [*To Tiresias.*] My lord, I don't know if the queen fully realizes that this young soldier would explain himself better through his officer; and that, if he speaks for himself, Her Majesty will be in danger of——

JOCASTA. What now, Zizi? . . .

TIRESIAS. The Captain was pointing out that he is used to the men and he might serve as a kind of interpreter.

JOCASTA. Send the Captain away!   Has the boy a tongue, or not?   Let him come near.

TIRESIAS. [*Aside to the Captain.*] Don't insist, the queen is overwrought. . . .

CAPTAIN. Very well. . . . [*He goes to his soldiers.   To the Young Soldier.*] The queen wants to speak to you.   And control your tongue.   I 'll pay you out for this, young fellow-me-lad.

JOCASTA. Come here!
                    [*The Captain pushes the Young Soldier forward.*

CAPTAIN. Go along then!   Go on, booby, forward.   You won't be eaten.   Excuse him, Your Majesty.   Our lads are scarcely familiar with court ways.

JOCASTA. Ask that man to leave us alone with the soldier.

TIRESIAS. But, Majesty——

JOCASTA. And no 'but Majestys.' . . .   If this Captain stays a moment longer I shall kick him.

TIRESIAS. Listen, officer. [*He leads him aside.*] The queen wants to be alone with the guard who has seen something.   She has her whims.   She might have your record blotted for you, you know, and I couldn't do anything about it.

CAPTAIN. Right.   I 'll leave you. . . .   If I stayed it was because . . . well . . . I don't mean to give you advice, my lord. . . .   But, between you and me, be on your guard about this ghost story. [*He bows.*] My lord. . . . [*A long salute to the queen. He passes near the Soldier.*] Hi! The queen wishes to stay alone with your comrade.

JOCASTA. Who is the other soldier? Has he seen the ghost?

YOUNG SOLDIER. Yes, Your Majesty, we were on guard duty together.

JOCASTA. Then let him stop. Let him stay there! I'll call him if I want him. Good evening, Captain, that will be all.

CAPTAIN. [*To the Soldier.*] We'll have this out later!

[*He goes out.*

TIRESIAS. [*To the queen.*] You have mortally offended that officer.

JOCASTA. About time, too! Generally it's the men who are mortally offended and never the officers. [*To the Young Soldier.*] How old are you?

YOUNG SOLDIER. Nineteen.

JOCASTA. Exactly his age! He would be his age. . . . He looks splendid! Come nearer. Look, Zizi, what muscles! I adore knees. You can tell the breed by the knees. He would look like that too. . . . Isn't he fine, Zizi. Feel these biceps, like iron . . .

TIRESIAS. I am sorry, madam, but you know . . . I'm no authority. I can scarcely see what they're like.

JOCASTA. Then feel. . . . Test them. Thighs like a horse! He steps away! Don't be afraid. . . . The old grandpa is blind. Heaven knows what he's imagining, poor lad. He's quite red! He's adorable! And nineteen!

YOUNG SOLDIER. Yes, Your Majesty!

JOCASTA. [*Mocking him.*] Yes, Your Majesty! Isn't he just too delicious! Ah! what a shame! Perhaps he doesn't even know he's handsome. [*As one speaks to a child.*] Well . . . did you see the ghost?

YOUNG SOLDIER. Yes, Your Majesty!

JOCASTA. The ghost of King Laïus?

YOUNG SOLDIER. Yes, Your Majesty! The king told us he was the king.

JOCASTA. Zizi . . . what do you know with all your fowls and stars? Listen to this boy . . . And what did the king say?

TIRESIAS. [*Leading the queen away.*] Majesty! Be careful. These young people are hot-headed, credulous . . . pushful. . . . Be on your guard. Are you certain this boy has seen the ghost, and, even if he has seen it, was it really the ghost of your husband?

JOCASTA. Gods! How unbearable you are! Unbearable and a spoil-sport. Every time you come and break the spell you stop miracles with your intelligence and incredulity. Please let me question this boy on my own. You can preach afterwards. [*To the Young Soldier.*] Listen. . . .

YOUNG SOLDIER. Your Majesty! . . .

JOCASTA. [*To Tiresias.*] I'll find out straight away whether he has seen Laïus. [*To the Young Soldier.*] How did he speak?

YOUNG SOLDIER. He spoke quickly and a lot, Your Majesty, ever such a lot, and he got mixed up, and he didn't manage to say what he wanted to.

JOCASTA. That's he! Poor dear! But why on these ramparts? The stench. . . .

YOUNG SOLDIER. That's it, Your Majesty. . . . The ghost said it was because of the swamps and the rising fumes that he could appear.

JOCASTA. How interesting! Tiresias, you would never learn that from your birds. And what did he say?

TIRESIAS. Madam, madam, you must at least question him with some order. You'll muddle this youngster's head completely.

JOCASTA. Quite right, Zizi, quite right. [*To the Young Soldier.*] What was he like? How did you see him?

YOUNG SOLDIER. In the wall, Your Majesty. A sort of transparent statue, as you might say. You could see the beard most clearly, and the black hole of the mouth as he spoke, and a red stain on the temple, bright red.

JOCASTA. That's blood!

YOUNG SOLDIER. Fancy! We didn't think of that.

JOCASTA. It's a wound! How dreadful!   [*Laïus appears.* And what did he say? Did you understand anything?

YOUNG SOLDIER. It wasn't easy, Your Majesty. My comrade noticed that he had to make a big effort to appear, and each time he made an effort to express himself clearly he disappeared; then he was puzzled as to how to set about it.

JOCASTA. Poor dear!

GHOST. Jocasta! Jocasta! My wife! Jocasta!
     [*They neither hear nor see him during the whole of the scene.*

TIRESIAS. [*Addressing the Soldier.*] And were you not able to grasp anything intelligible?

GHOST. Jocasta!

SOLDIER. Well, yes, my lord. We understood he wanted to warn you of a danger, put you on your guard, both the queen and you, but that's all. The last time he explained he knew some secrets he ought not to have known, and if he was discovered he would not be able to appear again.

GHOST. Jocasta! Tiresias! Can't you see me? Can't you hear me?

JOCASTA. And didn't he say anything else? Didn't he say anything particular?

SOLDIER. Ah, well, Your Majesty! Perhaps he didn't want to say anything particular in our presence. He was asking for you. That is why my comrade tried to let you know about it.

JOCASTA. Dear boys! And I have come. I knew it all the time. I felt it there! You see, Zizi, with all your doubts. And tell us, Young Soldier, where the ghost appeared. I want to touch the exact spot.

GHOST. Look at me! Listen to me, Jocasta! Guards, you always saw me before. Why not see me now? This is torture! Jocasta! Jocasta!

[While these words are being uttered the Soldier goes to the place where the Ghost is. He touches it with his hand.

SOLDIER. There. [He strikes the wall.] There, in the wall.

YOUNG SOLDIER. Or in front of the wall. It was difficult to make out.

JOCASTA. But why doesn't he appear to-night? Do you think he will still be able to appear?

GHOST. Jocasta! Jocasta! Jocasta!

SOLDIER. I am sorry, Your Majesty, I don't think so, after what happened last night. I'm afraid there was a spot of bother and Her Majesty may be too late.

JOCASTA. What a shame! Always too late. Zizi, I am always the last person in the whole kingdom to be informed. Think of the time we have wasted with your fowls and oracles! We ought to have run, to have guessed. We shall learn absolutely nothing! And there will be disasters, terrible disasters. And it will be your fault, Zizi, your fault, as usual.

TIRESIAS. Madam, the queen is speaking in front of these men.

JOCASTA. Yes, I am speaking in front of these men! I suppose I ought to restrain myself? When King Laïus, the dead King Laïus, has spoken in front of these men. But he has not spoken to you, Zizi, nor to Creon. He hasn't been to the temple to show himself. He showed himself on the patrol path to these men, to this boy of nineteen who is so handsome and looks like——

TIRESIAS. I implore you——

JOCASTA. Yes, I am overwrought, you must try to understand. These dangers, this spectre, this music, this pestilential smell. . . . And there's a storm about. I can feel it in my shoulder. I am stifling, Zizi, stifling.

GHOST. Jocasta! Jocasta!

JOCASTA. I think I hear my name. Didn't you hear anything?

TIRESIAS. My poor lamb. You're worn out. Day is breaking. You are dreaming where you stand. Are you even sure this ghost business hasn't come from the fatigue of these young men on the watch who force themselves not to sleep and who live in this depressing, swampy atmosphere?

GHOST. Jocasta! For pity's sake, listen to me! Look at me! Gentlemen, you are kind. Keep the queen. Tiresias! Tiresias!

TIRESIAS. [*To the Young Soldier.*] Step aside a moment, I want to speak to the queen.

[*The Young Soldier goes to his comrade.*

SOLDIER. Well, old son! You've clicked! She's fallen for you! Petted by the queen, eh!

YOUNG SOLDIER. Look here! . . .

SOLDIER. You're made for life. Don't forget your pals.

TIRESIAS. . . . Listen! Cockcrow. The ghost will not return. Let us go home.

JOCASTA. Did you see how handsome he is?

TIRESIAS. Don't recall those sad things, my lamb. If you had a son . . .

JOCASTA. If I had a son, he would be handsome, brave, he would guess the riddle and kill the Sphinx. He would return victor.

TIRESIAS. And you would go without a husband.

JOCASTA. Little boys always say: 'I want to become a man so that I can marry mother.' It's not such a bad idea, you know, Tiresias. Is there a sweeter union, a union that is sweeter and more cruel, and prouder, than that couple: a son and a young mother? Listen, Zizi, just now, when I touched that young guard, heaven alone knows what he must have thought, the poor lad, and I myself nearly fainted. He would be nineteen, Tiresias, nineteen! The same age as this soldier. Can we be sure Laïus did not appear to him because of this likeness?

[*Cock crows.*

GHOST. Jocasta! Jocasta! Jocasta! Tiresias! Jocasta!

TIRESIAS. [*To the soldiers.*] My friends, do you think it is any use waiting?

GHOST. For pity's sake!

SOLDIER. Frankly, no, my lord. The cocks are crowing. He will not appear now.

GHOST. Gentlemen! Mercy! Am I invisible? Can't you hear me?

JOCASTA. Come along! I will be obedient. But I am very glad I questioned the boy. You must find out his name and where he lives. [*She goes towards the steps.*] I had forgotten these steps, Zizi! . . . That band is making me ill. Listen, we can go back through the higher town by the side streets, and we can see the night life.

TIRESIAS. Madam, you don't mean it.

JOCASTA. Oh! now he's beginning again! He'll send me simply raving! Mad and off my head. I've got my veils on, Zizi, how do you expect I should be recognized?

TIRESIAS. My child, you said yourself you have come out wearing all your jewels. Your brooch alone has pearls as large as an egg.

JOCASTA. I am a martyr! Others can laugh and dance and amuse themselves. Do you imagine I am going to leave this brooch at the palace where it's simply asking to be taken? Call the guard. Tell him to help me down these steps. And you can follow us.

TIRESIAS. But, madam, since the presence of this young man affects you so strongly . . .

JOCASTA. He is young and strong. He will help me, and I shan't break my neck. Obey your queen for once, at least.

TIRESIAS. Hi! . . . No, he. . . . Yes, you. . . . Help the queen down the steps. . . .

SOLDIER. You see, old man!

YOUNG SOLDIER. [*Approaching.*] Yes, my lord.

GHOST. Jocasta! Jocasta! Jocasta!

JOCASTA. He's shy! And flights of steps hate me. Steps, hooks, and scarves. Oh! yes, they do, they hate me! They're after my death. [*A cry.*] Ho!

YOUNG SOLDIER. Has the queen hurt herself?

TIRESIAS. No, silly! Your foot! Your foot!

YOUNG SOLDIER. What foot?

TIRESIAS. Your foot on the end of the scarf. You nearly strangled the queen.

YOUNG SOLDIER. Ye gods!

JOCASTA. Zizi, you are utterly ridiculous. Poor darling. There you go calling him a murderer because he walks, as you did, on this scarf. Don't upset yourself, my boy. My lord is absurd. He never misses an opportunity of hurting people's feelings.

TIRESIAS. But, madam——

JOCASTA. You are the one who is clumsy. Come along. Thank you, my boy. Send your name and address to the temple. One, two, three, four. . . . Marvellous! Zizi! Do you see how well I 'm getting down. Eleven, twelve. . . . Zizi, are you following? Two more steps. [*To the Soldier.*] Thank you. I can manage now. Help grandpa!

Jocasta disappears left, with Tiresias.   Cocks are heard.

VOICE OF JOCASTA. Through your fault I shall never know what my poor Laïus wanted.

GHOST. Jocasta!

VOICE OF TIRESIAS. That story is all very vague.

VOICE OF JOCASTA. What? very vague? What do you mean, vague? It 's you who are vague with your third eye. That boy knows what he has seen, and he has seen the king. Have you seen the king?

VOICE OF TIRESIAS. But——

VOICE OF JOCASTA. Have you seen him? . . . No. . . . Well . . . It 's amazing . . . it 's like . . .   [*The voices die away.*

GHOST. Jocasta! Tiresias! Have pity!

[*The two soldiers turn to each other and see the Ghost.*

THE SOLDIERS. Oh! the Ghost!

GHOST. Gentlemen, at last! I am saved! I kept calling, begging. . . .

SOLDIER. You were there?

GHOST. During the whole of your talk with the queen and Tiresias. Then why was I invisible?

YOUNG SOLDIER. I 'll run and fetch them!

SOLDIER. Halt!

GHOST. What? You stop him?

YOUNG SOLDIER. Let me go . . .

SOLDIER. When the joiner comes the chair stops wobbling; when you get to the shoemender your sandal stops hurting you; when you get to the doctor you no longer feel the pain. Fetch them! That would only make him disappear.

GHOST. Alas! Do these simple souls then know what the priests cannot divine?

YOUNG SOLDIER. I shall go.

GHOST. Too late. . . . Stay. It is too late. I am discovered.
They are coming; they are going to take me. Ah! they 're
here! Help! Help! Quick! Tell the queen a young man
is approaching Thebes, and on no account . . . No! No!
Mercy! Mercy! They 've got me! Help! Ended! I . . .
I. . . . Mercy . . I . . . I . . .

> [*Long silence. The two soldiers, back to the audience, con-
> template endlessly the place in the wall where the Ghost
> disappeared.*

SOLDIER. Good God!

YOUNG SOLDIER. Poor devil!

SOLDIER. These things are beyond us, old man.

YOUNG SOLDIER. But it 's clear that, in spite of death, that
fellow wanted, at all costs, to warn his wife of a danger which
is threatening her. My duty is to overtake the queen and the
high priest and repeat to them word for word what we have
just heard.

SOLDIER. You want the queen bădly, don't you?

> [*The Young Soldier shrugs his shoulders.*

Well . . . he only had to appear to them and talk to them, they
were there. We saw him all right ourselves and they didn't.
But, to crown all, they even prevented *us* from seeing him.
So there you have it! Dead kings become ordinary people.
Poor Laïus! Now he knows how easy it is to get into touch
with the great of the earth.

YOUNG SOLDIER. But us?

SOLDIER. Oh, us! It 's easy enough to get into touch with men,
you coon. . . . But, when it comes to officers, queens, and
high priests . . . they always go before it happens, or come
when it 's all over.

YOUNG SOLDIER. What 's 'it'?

SOLDIER. How should I know? . . . I understand myself,
that 's the chief thing.

YOUNG SOLDIER. And you wouldn't go and warn the queen?

SOLDIER. A word of advice: let princes deal with princes, ghosts
with ghosts, and soldiers with soldiers.   [*Flourish.*

END OF ACT I

ACT II

THE MEETING OF OEDIPUS AND THE SPHINX

THE VOICE

The coronation and nuptial celebrations have been going on since dawn The crowd has just acclaimed the queen and the conqueror of the Sphinx for the last time.

Every one goes home. In the little square of the royal palace now rises only the slight murmur of a fountain. Oedipus and Jocasta find privacy at last in the nuptial chamber. They are very tired and heavy with sleep. In spite of a few hints and civilities on the part of destiny, sleep will prevent them from seeing the trap which is closing on them for ever.

The Voice

Spectators, let us imagine we can recall the minutes we have just lived through together and relive them elsewhere. For, while the Ghost of Laïus was trying to warn Jocasta on the ramparts of Thebes, the Sphinx and Oedipus met on a hill overlooking the town. The bugle-calls, moon, stars, and crowing cocks will be the same.

THE SCENERY

An unpeopled spot on a hill overlooking Thebes, by moonlight. The road to Thebes (from right to left) passes over the fore-stage. It gives the impression of rounding a high leaning stone whose base is fixed at the lower end of the platform and forms the support for the wings on the right. Behind the ruins of a little temple is a broken wall. In the middle of the wall stands a complete pedestal which used to indicate the entrance to the temple and bears the trace of a chimera : a wing, a foot, a haunch.

Broken and overturned columns. For the Shades of Anubis and Nemesis at the end, a record by the actors can declaim the dialogue, whilst the actress mimes the part of the dead girl with the head of a jackal.

THE MEETING OF OEDIPUS AND THE SPHINX

When the curtain rises a girl in a white dress is seen sitting among the ruins. The head of a jackal lies in her lap, its body remaining hidden behind her. Distant bugle calls.

SPHINX. Listen.

JACKAL. Well?

SPHINX. That's the last call. We're free.

[*Anubis gets up, and the Jackal's head is seen to belong to him.*

JACKAL, ANUBIS. It's the first. There'll be two more before the gates are closed.

SPHINX. It's the last. I'm quite sure it's the last.

ANUBIS. You're sure because you want the gates closed, but I'm sorry duty forces me to contradict you; we're not free. That was the first bugle call. We'll wait.

SPHINX. I may have been mistaken, but——

ANUBIS. May have been mistaken! You were. . . .

SPHINX. Anubis!

ANUBIS. Sphinx?

SPHINX. I've had enough of killing, enough of dealing out death.

ANUBIS. We must obey. There are mysteries within mystery, gods above gods. We have our gods and they have theirs. That's what is called infinity.

SPHINX. You see, Anubis, there is no second call. It's you who are mistaken, let us go. . . .

ANUBIS. Do you mean you would like this night to pass without any deaths?

SPHINX. Yes! I do, indeed! Yes! Although it's growing late, I tremble to think someone may still come by.

ANUBIS. You're getting sensitive.

SPHINX. That's my business.

ANUBIS. Don't get cross.

SPHINX. Why must we always be acting without aim, without end, without understanding? Why, for example, should you have a dog's head, Anubis? Why have the god of the dead in the shape given to him by credulous people? Why must we have an Egyptian god in Greece and why must he have a dog's head?

ANUBIS. It 's marvellous, how like a woman you look when it comes to asking questions.

SPHINX. That is no answer!

ANUBIS. Well, my answer is: that logic forces us to appear to men in the shape in which they imagine us; otherwise, they would see only emptiness. Moreover, neither Egypt nor Greece nor death, neither the past nor the future has any meaning for us. Further, you know only too well to what use I must put this jaw. And finally, our masters prove their wisdom by giving me a material form which is not human and so preventing me from losing my head, however beastly it may be; for I am your keeper, remember. I can see that if they had given you a mere watchdog we should already be in Thebes with me on a leash and you sitting in the middle of a band of young men.

SPHINX. How stupid you are!

ANUBIS. Then try and remember that these victims who touch the girl-figure you have assumed are no more than noughts wiped off a slate, even if each of these noughts were an open mouth calling for help.

SPHINX. That may be. But here the calculations of gods are hard to follow. . . . Here we kill. Here the dead really die. Here I do kill.

[*While the Sphinx was speaking with her eyes on the ground Anubis pricked up his ears, looked round, and moved silently off over the ruins where he disappears. When the Sphinx raises her eyes, she looks for Anubis, and finds herself face to face with a small group of people who enter down stage right, and whom Anubis had scented. The group is composed of a Theban Matron, her little boy and girl. The Matron is dragging her daughter along. The boy is walking ahead.*]

MATRON. Look where you 're going! Get along now! Don't look behind you! Leave your sister alone! Go on. . . . [*She sees the Sphinx as the little boy stumbles into her.*] Look out! I told you to look where you 're going! Oh! I 'm so sorry, miss. . . . He never looks where he 's going. . . . He hasn't hurt you, has he?

SPHINX. No! not at all.

MATRON. I didn't expect to meet any one on my path at such an hour.

SPHINX. I 'm new to these parts, I haven't been long in Thebes;

I was on my way to a relative who lives in the country and got lost.

MATRON. Poor dear! And where does your relative live?

SPHINX. . . . Near the twelfth milestone.

MATRON. The very part I come from! I had lunch with my family, at my brother's place, you know. He made me stay to dinner. And then, you know, you begin gossiping and don't notice the time, and so here I am going home after curfew with my brats half asleep already.

SPHINX. Good night.

MATRON. Good night. [*She makes to go.*] And . . . I say . . . don't linger on the way. I know the likes of you and me haven't much to fear . . . but I wouldn't be too bold, if I were you, till I was inside the walls.

SPHINX. Are you afraid of thieves?

MATRON. Thieves! Ye gods, what could they get out of me? Oh, no, my dear! Where *do* you come from? Any one can see you 're not from the town. Thieves! I should think so! I mean the Sphinx!

SPHINX. Do you really, honestly and truly, believe in that nonsense yourself?

MATRON. That nonsense indeed! How young you are. Young people are so disbelieving these days. Oh, yes, they are! That 's how disasters happen. Let alone the Sphinx, I 'll give you a case from my family. . . . My brother that I 've just left. . . . [*She sits down and lowers her voice.*] He married a beautiful tall blonde from the north. One night he wakes up and what does he find? His wife in bed without head or entrails. She was a vampire. When he 'd got over the first fright what does my brother do? without a moment's hesitation he finds an egg and lays it on the pillow in the place of his wife's head. That 's how you stop vampires getting back into their body. All at once he hears a moaning. It was the head and entrails flying wildly across the room and begging my brother to take away the egg. My brother wouldn't, and the head went from moans to anger, from anger to tears, from tears to kisses. To cut a long story short, my idiot brother takes away the egg and lets his wife get back into her body. Now he knows his wife is a vampire and my sons make fun of their uncle. They maintain that he made up this entire vampire story to disguise the fact that his wife really did go out, but with her body, and that he let her come back, and that he 's a coward and ashamed of himself.   But *I* know very well my sister-in-law is a vampire. . . .   And my sons are in danger of marrying fiends from the underworld, all because they are obstinate and *disbelieving*.

And the same with the Sphinx—I 'm sorry if I hurt your feelings, but it 's only the likes of my sons and you who don't believe in it.

SPHINX. Your sons . . .?

MATRON. Not the little brat who just bumped into you.   I mean my boy of seventeen. . . .

SPHINX. You have several sons, have you?

MATRON. I had four.   Now I have three.   Seven, sixteen, and seventeen.   And I can tell you ever since that wicked beast appeared the house has been impossible.

SPHINX. Your sons quarrel . . .?

MATRON. I mean, my dear, that it 's impossible to live under the same roof.   The one who 's sixteen is only interested in politics.   According to him the Sphinx is a bugbear used to scare the poor and to impose on them.   There may have been something like your old Sphinx at one time—that 's how my son speaks—but now the old Sphinx is dead; and he 's merely a priest's demon and an excuse for police jobbery.   They fleece and loot and terrorize the masses, and then blame it all on the Sphinx.   It 's a good thing the Sphinx has broad shoulders. Whose fault is it that we starve to death, that prices go up, and that bands of looters swarm over the countryside?   Why, the Sphinx's, of course.   And the Sphinx is to blame because business is bad, and the government 's weak and one crash follows another; because the temples are glutted with rich offerings whilst mothers and wives are losing the bare necessities of life, and because foreigners with money to spend are leaving the town. . . .   Ah, you should see him, miss, how he gets up on the table, shouting, waving his arms, and stamping his feet; and then he denounces those who are responsible for it all, preaches revolt, eggs on the anarchists, shouting at the top of his voice names that are enough to get us all hanged. And between ourselves, miss . . . I know . . . you can take it from me . . . the Sphinx exists all right, but they 're making the most of it.   You can be sure of that.   What we want is a man, a dictator!

SPHINX. And . . . what about the brother of your young dictator?

MATRON. Oh! he's another kettle of fish. He despises his brother, he despises me, he despises the gods, he despises everything. He makes you wonder where he can get hold of all he comes out with. He says, if you please, that the Sphinx would interest him if it killed for killing's sake, but that this Sphinx of ours is in league with the oracles, and so it doesn't interest him.

SPHINX. And your fourth son? When was it . . .?

MATRON. I lost him nearly a year ago. He was just nineteen.

SPHINX. Poor woman. . . . What did he die of?

MATRON. Sphinx.

SPHINX. [*Gloomily.*] Ah! . . .

MATRON. It's all very well for his younger brother to maintain he was a victim of police intrigues. . . . Oh, no! There's no mistake, he died through the Sphinx. Ah, my dear! . . . if I live to a hundred I'll never forget that scene. One morning (he hadn't been home that night) I thought I heard him knock; I opened the front door and saw the underneath of his poor feet and then there followed a long way off, ever so far away, his poor little face, and in the back of his neck—look, just here—a large wound from which the blood had already stopped flowing. They brought him to me on a stretcher. Then I went: Ho! and fell, all of a heap. . . . A blow like that, you know, you don't get over in a hurry. You may be thankful you don't come from Thebes, thankful if you have no brothers. . . . You're lucky. . . . My other boy, the orator, wants to avenge him. What's the good? But he hates the priests, and my poor son was one of a series of human offerings.

SPHINX. Human offerings?

MATRON. To be sure. During the first months of the Sphinx the soldiers were sent to avenge the fine young men who were found dead all over the place, and they returned empty-handed. The Sphinx couldn't be found. Then, as there was a rumour that the Sphinx asked riddles, young people from the schools were sacrificed; and then the priests stated that the Sphinx demanded human offerings. At that, the youngest and weakest and fairest were chosen.

SPHINX. Poor woman!

MATRON. I tell you, my dear, what we want is a man of action. Queen Jocasta is still young. At a distance you would say she was twenty-nine or thirty. What we want is a ruler to fall from the sky, marry her, and kill the beast; someone to make an end of corruption, lock up Creon and Tiresias, improve the state of finance and liven up the people, someone who would care for the people and save us, yes, that's it, save us. . . .

SON. Mummy!

MATRON. Sh!

SON. Mummy . . . I say, mummy, what does the Sphinx look like?

MATRON. I don't know. [*To the Sphinx.*] And what d' you think is the latest? They're asking us to contribute our last farthings for a monument to those killed by the Sphinx! Will that bring them back to us, I should like to know?

SON. Mummy . . . what is the Sphinx like?

SPHINX. Poor little chap! His sister's asleep. Come along. . . .
                    [*The son clings to the skirt of the Sphinx.*

MATRON. Now don't worry the lady.

SPHINX. He's all right.   [*She strokes his neck.*

SON. I say, mummy, is this lady the Sphinx?

MATRON. Little silly. [*To the Sphinx.*] I hope you don't mind. At that age children don't know what they're saying. . . . [*She gets up.*] Oh my! [*She takes the little girl who is asleep in her arms.*] Come along now! Off we go, lazy-bones!

SON. Mummy, is that lady the Sphinx? I say, mummy, is the Sphinx that lady? Is that the Sphinx, mummy?

MATRON. Sh! Don't be silly. [*To the Sphinx.*] Well, good evening. Excuse my gossiping to you. I was glad to stop for a breather. . . . And . . . take care. [*Fanfare.*] Quickly. There's the second bugle. After the third we'll be shut out.

SPHINX. Go along, quickly. I'll hurry my way. You've put me on my guard.

MATRON. Believe me, we'll not feel safe until there comes a man who will rid us of this scourge.   [*She goes out left.*

SON'S VOICE. I say, mummy, what's the Sphinx look like? Why wasn't it that lady? Then what's he like?

SPHINX. A scourge!

ANUBIS. [*Coming from among the ruins.*] That woman *would* have to come along here just now.

SPHINX. I've been unhappy for the past two days, for two days now I've been carrying on in this miserable way in the hope that this massacre would come to an end.

ANUBIS. Don't worry. You're all right.

SPHINX. Listen. This is my secret wish and these the circumstances which would allow me to mount my pedestal for a last
time. A young man will climb the hill, I shall fall in love with
him. He 'll have no fear. And when I ask my question he
will answer as to an equal. He will give *the answer*, d' you
hear, Anubis, and I shall fall dead.

ANUBIS. Make no mistake: only your mortal form will fall dead.

SPHINX. And isn't that the form I should want to live in to make
him happy!

ANUBIS. It 's nice to see that human form doesn't make a great
goddess become a little woman.

SPHINX. You see how right I was. That bugle we heard was
the last after all!

ANUBIS. Daughter of men! One is never finished with you. I
tell you no! No! [*He leaves her side and mounts an overturned
column.*] That was the second. When I 've heard another
one you can go. Oh!

SPHINX. What is it?

ANUBIS. Bad news.

SPHINX. Someone coming?

ANUBIS. Yes.

   [*The Sphinx gets up beside Anubis and looks into the wings,
    right.*

SPHINX. I can't! I can't and I won't question this young man.
You needn't ask me to.

ANUBIS. I should say, if you 're like a young mortal, he 's like a
young god.

SPHINX. What grace, Anubis, and what shoulders! He's coming.

ANUBIS. I 'll hide. Don't forget you are the Sphinx. I 'm
keeping my eye on you. I 'll be with you at the first sign.

SPHINX. Anubis, listen . . . quickly. . . .

ANUBIS. Sh! . . . He 's here.   [*Anubis hides.*

   [*Oedipus enters up stage right. He is walking along with his
    eyes on the ground. He starts.*

OEDIPUS. Oh! I 'm sorry. . . .

SPHINX. I startled you.

OEDIPUS. Well . . . no . . . I was dreaming, I was miles away,
and suddenly, before me——

SPHINX. You took me for an animal.

OEDIPUS. Almost.

SPHINX. Almost? Almost an animal, that 's the Sphinx.

OEDIPUS. Yes, I know.

SPHINX. You admit you took me for the Sphinx.   Thank you.

OEDIPUS. Oh! I soon realized my mistake.

SPHINX. Too kind.   The truth of the matter is it can't be so amusing to find yourself suddenly face to face with the Sphinx, if you 're a young man.

OEDIPUS. And . . . if you 're a girl?

SPHINX. He doesn't attack girls.

OEDIPUS. Because girls avoid his haunts and are not supposed to go out alone when the light is failing.

SPHINX. You 'd do well to mind your own business, young man, and let me go my way.

OEDIPUS. Which way?

SPHINX. You 're simply amazing.   Must I give my reasons for being out to a complete stranger?

OEDIPUS. And suppose I guessed your reason?

SPHINX. You amuse me.

OEDIPUS. Aren't you moved by curiosity, the curiosity which is raging amongst all modern young women, the curiosity to know what the Sphinx looks like?   If he has claws, or a beak, or wings, and whether he takes after the tiger or the vulture?

SPHINX. Oh, come, come!

OEDIPUS. The Sphinx is the criminal of the day.   Who 's seen him?   No one.   Fabulous rewards are promised to the first person who discovers him.   The faint of heart tremble. Young men die. . . .   But a girl, couldn't she venture into the forbidden area, setting orders at defiance, and dare what no reasonable person would dare, to unearth the monster, surprise him in his lair, get a view of him?

SPHINX. You 're on the wrong tack, I tell you.   I 'm going back to a relative who lives in the country, and as I had forgotten the very existence of a Sphinx and that the outskirts of Thebes are not safe, I was resting a moment on the stones of these old ruins.   You see how far you 're out.

OEDIPUS. What a pity!   For some time now I 've only run across people as dull as ditch water; so I hoped for something more unusual.   Pardon me.

SPHINX. Good evening!

OEDIPUS. Good evening!

[*They pass each other.   But Oedipus turns back.*
I say!   I may appear unpleasant, but I honestly can't bring myself to believe you.   Your presence in these ruins still intrigues me enormously.

SPHINX. You 're simply incredible.

OEDIPUS. Because if you were like other girls you would already have made off as fast as your legs would carry you.

SPHINX. My dear boy, you 're quite absurd.

OEDIPUS. It seemed to me so marvellous to find in a girl a worthy competitor.

SPHINX. A competitor? Then you are looking for the Sphinx?

OEDIPUS. Looking for him? Let me tell you, I 've been on the march for a whole month. Probably that 's why I appeared ill-mannered just now. I was so wild with excitement as I drew near Thebes that I could have shouted my enthusiasm to the merest block of stone, when, instead of a block of stone, what stands in my path but a girl in white? So I couldn't help talking to her about what was uppermost in my mind and thinking she must have the same purpose as myself.

SPHINX. But surely, a moment ago, when you saw me spring out of the shadow, you didn't seem to me very much on the alert for a man who wants to measure his strength with the enemy.

OEDIPUS. That is true. I was dreaming of fame, and the beast would have caught me unawares. To-morrow in Thebes I shall equip myself and the hunt will begin.

SPHINX. You love fame?

OEDIPUS. I 'm not sure about that. I like trampling crowds, trumpet calls, flying banners, waving palm branches, the sun, gold and purple, happiness, luck—you know, to live!

SPHINX. Is that what you call living?

OEDIPUS. Don't you?

SPHINX. No, I must say I have quite a different idea of life.

OEDIPUS. What 's that?

SPHINX. To love. To be loved by the one you love.

OEDIPUS. I shall love my people and they me.

SPHINX. The public square is not a home.

OEDIPUS. The public square has nothing to do with it. The people of Thebes are looking for a man. If I kill the Sphinx I shall be that man. Queen Jocasta is a widow; I shall marry her. . . .

SPHINX. A woman who might be your mother!

OEDIPUS. The main thing is that she is not.

SPHINX. Do you imagine that a queen and her people would give themselves up to the first comer?

OEDIPUS. Would you call the vanquisher of the Sphinx a first comer? I know the promised reward is the queen. Don't laugh at me. Please listen. You must. I must prove that my dream isn't merely a dream. My father is King of Corinth. My father and mother were already old when I was born and I lived in a court of gloom. Too much fuss and comfort produced in me a feverish longing for adventure. I began to pine and waste away, when one evening a drunk shouted at me that I was a bastard and that I was usurping the place of a legitimate son. Blows and abuse followed, and the next day, despite the tears of Merope and Polybius, I decided to visit the sanctuaries and question the gods. They all replied with the same oracle: You will murder your father and marry your mother.

SPHINX. What?

OEDIPUS. Yes, I mean it. At first this oracle fills you with horror, but I 'm not so easily imposed on! I soon saw how nonsensical the whole thing was. I took into account the ways of the gods and the priests, and I came to this conclusion: either the oracle hid a less serious meaning which had to be discovered, or the priests who communicate from temple to temple by means of birds found it perhaps to their advantage to put this oracle into the mouth of the gods and to weaken my chances of coming into power. Briefly, I soon forgot my fears, and, I may say, used this threat of parricide and incest as an excuse to flee the court and satisfy my thirst for the unknown.

SPHINX. Now it 's my turn to feel dazed. I 'm sorry I rather made fun of you. Will you forgive me, prince?

OEDIPUS. Give me your hand. May I ask your name? Mine is Oedipus; I 'm nineteen.

SPHINX. Oh, what does it matter about mine, Oedipus? You must like illustrious names. . . . That of a little girl of seventeen wouldn't interest you.

OEDIPUS. That 's unkind.

SPHINX. You adore fame. Yet I should have thought the surest way of foiling the oracle would be to marry a woman younger than yourself.

OEDIPUS. That doesn't sound like you. That 's more like a mother of Thebes where marriageable young men are few.

SPHINX. And that 's not like you either. That was a gross, common thing to say.

OEDIPUS. So, I shall have walked the roads past mountain and

stream merely to take a wife who will quickly become a
Sphinx, worse than that, a Sphinx with breasts and claws!

SPHINX. Oedipus. . . .

OEDIPUS. No, thank you! I prefer to try my luck. Take this
belt: with that you will be able to get to me when I have killed
the beast. |Business.

SPHINX. Have you ever killed?

OEDIPUS. Yes, once. At the cross-roads of Delphi and Daulis.
I was walking along like a moment ago. A carriage was approaching driven by an old man with an escort of four servants.
When I was on a level with the horses one of them reared and
knocked me into one of these servants. The fool tried to
strike me, I aimed a blow at him with my stick, but he dodged
down and I caught the old man on the temple. He fell and
the horses bolted, dragging him along. I ran after them, the
servants were terrified and fled; I found myself alone with the
bleeding body of the old man and the horses who screamed as
they rolled about entangled, and broke their legs. It was
dreadful . . . dreadful. . . .

SPHINX. Yes, isn't it . . . it's dreadful to kill.

OEDIPUS. Oh, well, it wasn't my fault and I think no more
about it. The thing is to clear all obstacles, to wear blinkers,
and not to give way to self-pity. Besides, there is my star.

SPHINX. Then farewell, Oedipus. I am of the sex which is
disturbing to heroes. Let us go our ways, we can have little
in common.

OEDIPUS. Disturbing to heroes, eh! You have a high opinion
of your sex.

SPHINX. And . . . supposing the Sphinx killed you?

OEDIPUS. His death depends, if I'm not mistaken, on questions
which I must answer. If I guess right he won't even touch
me, he'll just die.

SPHINX. And if you do not guess right?

OEDIPUS. Thanks to my unhappy childhood I have pursued
studies which give me a great start over the riff-raff of Thebes.

SPHINX. I'm glad to hear it.

OEDIPUS. And I don't think this simple-minded monster is
expecting to be confronted by a pupil of the best scholars of
Corinth.

SPHINX. You have an answer to everything. A pity, for, I own,
Oedipus, I have a soft spot for weak people, and I should like
to have found you wanting.

OEDIPUS. Farewell.

> [*The Sphinx makes one step as if to rush in pursuit of Oedipus, stops, but cannot resist the call. Until her 'I! I!' the Sphinx does not take her eyes off those of Oedipus; she moves as it were round this immobile, steady, vast gaze from under eyelids which do not flicker.*

SPHINX. Oedipus!

OEDIPUS. Did you call me?

SPHINX. One last word. For the moment does nothing else occupy your mind, nothing else fire your heart, nothing stir your spirit save the Sphinx?

OEDIPUS. Nothing else, for the moment.

SPHINX. And he . . . or she who brought you into his presence. . . . I mean who would help you. . . . I mean who may perhaps know something to help bring about this meeting . . . would he or she in your eyes assume such prestige that you would be touched and moved?

OEDIPUS. Naturally, but what does all this mean?

SPHINX. And supposing I, I myself, were to divulge a secret, a tremendous secret?

OEDIPUS. You 're joking!

SPHINX. A secret which would allow you to enter into contact with the enigma of enigmas, with the human beast, with the singing bitch, as it is called, with the Sphinx?

OEDIPUS. What! You? You? Did I guess aright, and has your curiosity led you to discover . . .? No! How stupid of me. This is a woman's trick to make me turn back.

SPHINX. Good-bye.

OEDIPUS. Oh! Forgive me! . . .

SPHINX. Too late.

OEDIPUS. I 'm kneeling; a simple fool who begs forgiveness.

SPHINX. You 're a fatuous young man who is sorry to have lost his chance and is trying to get it back.

OEDIPUS. I am and I 'm ashamed. Look, I believe you, I 'll listen. But if you have played me a trick I shall drag you by the hair and grip you till the blood flows.

SPHINX. Come here. [*She leads him opposite the pedestal.*] Shut your eyes. Don't cheat. Count up to fifty.

OEDIPUS. [*With his eyes shut.*] Take care!

SPHINX. It 's your turn to do that.

> [*Oedipus counts. One feels that something extraordinary is happening. The Sphinx bounds across the ruins,*

*disappears behind a wall and reappears in the real
pedestal, that is, she seems to be fastened on to the pedestal,
the bust resting on the elbows and looking straight ahead,
whereas the actress is really standing, and only lets her bust
appear and her arms in spotted gloves with her hands grasping the edge; out of the broken wing suddenly grow two
immense, pale, luminous wings and the fragment of
statue completes her, prolonging her, and appearing to
belong to her. Oedipus is heard counting : 'Forty-seven,
forty-eight, forty-nine,' then he makes a pause and
shouts : 'Fifty.' He turns round.*

OEDIPUS. You!

SPHINX. [*In a high distant voice, joyous and terrible.*] Yes, I!
I, the Sphinx!

OEDIPUS. I 'm dreaming!

SPHINX. You are no dreamer, Oedipus. You know what you
want, and did want. Silence. Here I command. Approach.
    [*Oedipus, with his arms held stiffly by his body as if paralysed,
    tries frantically to free himself.*
Come forward.   [*Oedipus falls on his knees.*
As your legs refuse their help, jump, hop. . . . It 's good for
a hero to make himself ridiculous. Come along! Move
yourself! Don't worry, there 's nobody to see you.
    [*Oedipus, writhing with anger, moves forward on his knees.*
That 's it. Stop! And now. . . .

OEDIPUS. And now, I 'm beginning to understand your methods
what moves you make to lure and slay.

SPHINX. . . . And now, I am going to give you a demonstration,
I 'm going to show you what would happen in this place,
Oedipus, if you were any ordinary handsome youth from
Thebes, and if you hadn't the privilege of pleasing me.

OEDIPUS. I know what your pleasantries are worth.
    [*He knits up all the muscles of his body. It is obvious he is
    struggling against a charm.*

SPHINX. Yield! Don't try to screw up your muscles and resist.
Relax! If you resist you will only make my task more
delicate and I might hurt you.

OEDIPUS. I shall resist! [*He shuts his eyes and turns his head away.*

SPHINX. You need not shut your eyes or turn away your head.
For it is not by my look nor by my voice that I work. A blind
man is not so dexterous, the net of a gladiator not so swift, nor
lightning so fine, nor a coachman so stiff, nor a cow so weighty,

nor a schoolboy working at his sums with his tongue out so good, nor a ship so hung with rigging, so spread with sails, secure and buoyant; a judge is not so incorruptible, insects so voracious, birds so bloodthirsty, the egg so nocturnal, Chinese executioners so ingenious, the heart so fitful, the trickster's hand so deft, the stars so fateful, the snake moistening its prey with saliva so attentive. I secrete, I spin, I pay out, I wind, I unwind, I rewind, in such a way that it is enough for me to desire these knots for them to be made, to think about them for them to be pulled tight or slackened. My thread is so fine it escapes the eye, so fluid you might think you were suffering from a poison, so hard a quiver on my part would break your limbs, so highly strung a bow stroked between us would make music in the air; curled like the sea, the column, and the rose, muscled like the octopus, contrived like the settings of our dreams, above all invisible, unseen, and majestic like the blood circulating in statues, my thread coils round you in fantastic patterns with the volubility of honey falling upon honey.

OEDIPUS. Let me go!

SPHINX. And I speak, I work, I wind, I unwind, I calculate, I meditate, I weave, I winnow, I knit, I plait, I cross, I go over it again and again, I tie and untie and tie again, retaining the smallest knots that I shall later on have to untie for you on pain of death; I pull tight, I loosen, I make mistakes and go back, I hesitate, I correct, entangle and disentangle, unlace, lace up and begin afresh; and I adjust, I agglutinate, I pinion, I strap, I shackle, I heap up my effects, till you feel that from the tip of your toes to the top of your head you are wrapped round by all the muscles of a reptile whose slightest breath constricts yours and makes you inert like the arm on which you fall asleep.

OEDIPUS. [*In a weak voice.*] Let me be! Mercy! . . .

SPHINX. And you will cry for mercy, and you won't have to be ashamed of that, for you won't be the first. I have heard prouder than you call for their mothers, and I have seen more insolent than you burst into tears; and the more silent are even weaker than the rest: they faint before the end and I have to minister to them after the fashion of embalmers in whose hands the dead are drunk men no longer able to stand on their feet!

OEDIPUS. Merope! . . . Mother!

SPHINX. Then I should command you to advance a little closer,

and I should help you by loosening your limbs. So! And I
should question you. I should ask you, for example: What
animal is it that goes on four legs in the morning, in the afternoon on two, and in the evening on three? And you would
cudgel your brains, till in the end your mind would settle on a
little medal you won as a child, or you would repeat a number,
or count the stars between these two broken columns; and I
should make you return to the point by revealing the enigma.

Man is the animal who walks on four legs when he is a child,
on two when he is full-grown, and when he is old with the help
of a stick as a third leg.

OEDIPUS. How idiotic!

SPHINX. You would shout: How idiotic! You all say that.
Then, since that cry only confirms your failure, I should call
my assistant, Anubis. Anubis!

*[Anubis appears and stands on the right of the pedestal with
folded arms; and his head turned to one side.*

OEDIPUS. Oh, miss! ... Oh, Sphinx! ... Oh, Sphinx, please
don't! No! No!

SPHINX. And I should make you go down on your knees. Go
on. ... Go on ... that's right. ... Do as you're told.
And you'd bend your head ... and Anubis would bound
forward. He would open his wolf-like jaws!

[Oedipus utters a cry.

I said: *would* bend, *would* bound forward, *would* open. ...
Haven't I always been careful to express myself in that mood?
Why that cry? Why that horrified expression? It was a
demonstration, Oedipus, simply a demonstration. You're free.

OEDIPUS. Free!

*[He moves an arm, a leg. ... He gets up, he reels, he puts
his hand to his head.*

ANUBIS. Pardon me, Sphinx, this man cannot leave here without
undergoing the test.

SPHINX. But ...

ANUBIS. Question him.

OEDIPUS. But ...

ANUBIS. Silence! Question this man.

[A silence. Oedipus turns his back and remains motionless.

SPHINX. I'll question him. ... All right. ... I'll question
him. ... *[With a last look of surprise at Anubis.]* What animal
is it that walks on four legs in the morning, on two in the
afternoon, and on three in the evening?

OEDIPUS. Why, man, of course! He crawls along on four legs when he's little, and walks on two legs when he is big, and when he's old he helps himself along with a stick as a third leg.

[*The Sphinx sways on her pedestal.*

[*Making his way to the left.*] Victory!

[*He rushes out left. The Sphinx slips down into the column, disappears behind the wall, and reappears wingless.*

SPHINX. Oedipus! Where is he? Where is he?

ANUBIS. Gone, flown. He is running breathlessly to proclaim his victory.

SPHINX. Without so much as a look my way, without a movement betraying feeling, without a sign of gratitude.

ANUBIS. Did you expect anything else?

SPHINX. Oh, you fool! Then he has not understood a single thing.

ANUBIS. Not a single thing.

SPHINX. Kss! Kss! Anubis. . . . Here, here, look, after him, quickly, bite him, Anubis, bite him!

ANUBIS. And now it's all going to begin afresh. You're a woman again and I'm a dog.

SPHINX. I'm sorry. I lost my head, I'm mad. My hands are trembling. I'm like fire. I wish I could catch him again in one bound, I'd spit in his face, claw him with my nails, disfigure him, trample on him, castrate him, and flay him alive!

ANUBIS. That's more like yourself.

SPHINX. Help me! Avenge me! Don't stand there idle!

ANUBIS. Do you really hate this man?

SPHINX. I do.

ANUBIS. The worst that could happen to him would seem too good to you?

SPHINX. It would.

ANUBIS. [*Holding up the Sphinx's dress.*] Look at the folds in this cloth. Crush them together. Now if you pierce this bundle with a pin, remove the pin, smooth the cloth till all trace of the old creases disappears, do you think a simple country loon would believe that the innumerable holes recurring at intervals result from a single thrust of a pin?

SPHINX. Certainly not.

ANUBIS. Human time is a fold of eternity. For us time does not exist. From his birth to his death the life of Oedipus is spread flat before my eyes, with its series of episodes.

SPHINX. Speak, speak, Anubis, I'm burning to hear. What d' you see?

ANUBIS. In the past Jocasta and Laïus had a child. As the oracle gave out that this child would be a scourge. . . .

SPHINX. A scourge!

ANUBIS. A monster, an unclean beast. . . .

SPHINX. Quicker, quicker!

ANUBIS. Jocasta bound it up and sent it into the mountains to get lost. A shepherd of Polybius found it, took it away, and, as Polybius and Merope were lamenting a sterile marriage . . .

SPHINX. I can't contain myself for joy.

ANUBIS. They adopted it. Oedipus, son of Laïus, killed Laïus where the three roads cross.

SPHINX. The old man.

ANUBIS. Son of Jocasta, he will marry Jocasta.

SPHINX. And to think I said to him: 'She might be your mother.' And he replied: 'The main thing is that she is not.' Anubis! Anubis! It 's too good to be true. . . .

ANUBIS. He will have two sons who will kill each other, and two daughters, one of whom will hang herself. Jocasta will hang herself. . . .

SPHINX. Stop! What more could I hope for? Think, Anubis: the wedding of Jocasta and Oedipus! The union of mother and son. . . . And will he know soon?

ANUBIS. Soon enough.

SPHINX. What a moment to live! I have a foretaste of its delights. Oh, to be present!

ANUBIS. You will be.

SPHINX. Is that true? . . .

ANUBIS. I think the moment has come to remind you who you are and what a ridiculous distance separates you from this little body which is listening to me. You who have assumed the role of Sphinx! You, the Goddess of Goddesses! You, the greatest of the great! The implacable! Vengeance! Nemesis!   [*Anubis prostrates himself.*

SPHINX. Nemesis. . . . [*She turns her back to the audience and remains a while erect, making a cross with her arms. Suddenly she comes out of this hypnotic state and rushes up stage.*] Once more, if he is in sight, I should like to feed my hatred, I want to see him run from one trap to another like a stunned rat.

ANUBIS. Is that the cry of the awakening goddess or of the jealous woman?

SPHINX. Of the goddess, Anubis, of the goddess. Our gods have cast me for the part of the Sphinx, and I shall show myself worthy of it.

ANUBIS. At last!

[*The Sphinx looks down on the plain, leaning over to examine it   Suddenly she turns round.   The last trace of the greatness and fury which had transformed her has disappeared.*

Dog! you lied to me.

ANUBIS. I?

SPHINX Yes, you! Liar! Liar! Look along the road. Oedipus is coming back, he 's running, he 's flying, he loves me, he has understood!

ANUBIS You know very well of what goes with his success and why the Sphinx is not dead.

SPHINX. Look how he jumps from rock to rock, just as my heart leaps in my breast.

ANUBIS. Convinced of his triumphs and your death this young fool has just realized that in his haste he 's forgotten the most important thing.

SPHINX Mean wretch! Do you mean to tell me he wants to find me dead?

ANUBIS Not you, my little fury: the Sphinx. He thinks he 's killed the Sphinx; he will have to prove it. Thebes won't be satisfied with a fisherman's yarn.

SPHINX. You 're lying. I 'll tell him everything. I 'll warn him.   I 'll save him.   I 'll turn him away from Jocasta, from that miserable town. . . .

ANUBIS. Take care.

SPHINX. I shall speak.

ANUBIS He 's coming. Let him speak first.

[*Oedipus, out of breath, comes in down stage left.   He sees the Sphinx and Anubis standing side by side.*

OEDIPUS. [*Saluting.*] I 'm glad to see what good health the immortals enjoy after their death.

SPHINX. What brings you back here?

OEDIPUS. The collecting of my due.

[*Angry movement on the part of Anubis towards Oedipus, who steps back.*

SPHINX. Anubis! [*With a gesture she orders him to leave her alone. He goes behind the ruins.   To Oedipus.*] You shall have it. Stay where you are. The loser is a woman. She asks one last favour of her master.

OEDIPUS. Excuse me for being on my guard, but you 've taught me to distrust your feminine wiles.

SPHINX. Ah! I was the Sphinx. No, Oedipus. . . . You will bear my mortal remains to Thebes and the future will reward you . . . according to your deserts. No . . . I ask you merely to let me disappear behind this wall so that I may take off this body in which, I must confess, I have, for some little while, felt rather . . . cramped.

OEDIPUS. Very well. But be quick. At the last bugles . . .

[*The bugles are heard.*
You see, I speak of them and they are sounded. I must waste no time.

SPHINX. [*Hidden.*] Thebes will not leave a hero standing at her gates.

VOICE OF ANUBIS. [*From behind the ruins.*] Hurry, hurry. It looks as though you 're inventing excuses and dawdling on purpose.

SPHINX. [*Hidden.*] Am I the first, God of the Dead, whom you 've had to drag by the clothes?

OEDIPUS. You 're trying to gain time, Sphinx.

SPHINX. [*Hidden.*] So much the better for you, Oedipus. My haste might have served you ill. A serious difficulty occurs to me. If you bear into Thebes the body of a girl instead of the monster which the people expect, the crowd will stone you.

OEDIPUS. That 's true! Women are simply amazing; they think of everything.

SPHINX. [*Hidden.*] They call me: The virgin with the claws. . . . The singing bitch. . . . They will want to identify my fangs. Don't be alarmed. Anubis! My faithful dog! Listen, since our faces are only shadows, I want you to give me your jackal's head.

OEDIPUS. Splendid idea!

ANUBIS. [*Hidden.*] Do what you like, so long as this shameful play-acting may come to an end and you may become yourself once more.

SPHINX. [*Hidden.*] I shan't be long.

OEDIPUS. I shall count up to fifty as I did before. I 'll have my own back.

ANUBIS. [*Hidden.*] Sphinx, Sphinx, what are you waiting for?

SPHINX. Now I 'm ugly, Anubis. A monster! . . . Poor boy . . . supposing I frighten him . . .

ANUBIS. Don't worry, he won't even see you.

SPHINX. Is he blind then?

ANUBIS. Many men are born blind and only realize it the day a home-truth hits them between the eyes.

OEDIPUS. Fifty!

ANUBIS. [*Hidden.*] Go on. . . . Go on. . . .

SPHINX. [*Hidden.*] Farewell, Sphinx.

> [*From behind the wall comes the staggering figure of a girl with a jackal's head. She waves her arms in the air and falls.*

OEDIPUS. About time too! [*He rushes forward, not stopping to look, lifts the body, and takes a stand down stage right. He carries the body before him on his outstretched arms.*] No, not like that! I should look like that tragedian I saw in Corinth playing the part of a king carrying the body of his son. The pose was pompous and moved no one.

> [*He tries holding the body under his left arm; behind the ruins on the mound appear two giants forms covered with rainbow veils: the gods.*

No! I should be ridiculous. Like a hunter going home empty-handed after killing his dog.

ANUBIS. [*The form on the right.*] To free your goddess's body of all human contamination, perhaps it might be as well for this Oedipus to disinfect you by bestowing on himself at least a title of demigod.

NEMESIS. [*The form on the left.*] He is so young. . . .

OEDIPUS. Hercules! Hercules threw the lion over his shoulder! . . . [*He puts the body over his shoulder.*] Yes, over my shoulder. Over my shoulder! Like a demigod!

ANUBIS. [*Veiled.*] Isn't he simply *incredible*!

OEDIPUS. [*Moving off towards the left, taking two steps after each of his thanksgivings.*] I have killed the unclean beast.

NEMESIS. [*Veiled.*] Anubis . . . I feel very ill at ease.

ANUBIS. We must go.

OEDIPUS. I have saved the town!

ANUBIS. Come along, mistress, let us go.

OEDIPUS. I shall marry Queen Jocasta!

NEMESIS. [*Veiled.*] Poor, poor, poor mankind! . . . I can stand no more, Anubis. . . . I can't breathe. Let us leave the earth.

OEDIPUS. I shall be king!

> [*A murmur envelops the two huge forms. The veils fly round them. Day breaks. Cocks crow.*

END OF ACT II

ACT III

THE WEDDING NIGHT

ACT III

The platform represents Jocasta's bedroom, which is as red as a little butcher's shop amid the town buildings. A broad bed covered with white furs. At the foot of the bed an animal's skin. On the right of the bed a cradle.

On the right fore-stage a latticed bay window, looking on to the square of Thebes. On the left fore-stage a movable mirror of human size.

Oedipus and Jocasta are wearing their coronation costumes. From the moment the curtain rises they move about in the slow motion induced by extreme fatigue.

JOCASTA. Phew! I 'm done! You are so full of life, dear! I am afraid, for you, this room will become a cage, a prison.

OEDIPUS. My dear love! A scented bedroom, a woman's room, yours! After this killing day, those processions, that ceremonial, that crowd which still clamoured for us under our very windows. . . .

JOCASTA. Not clamoured for us . . . for you, dear.

OEDIPUS. Same thing.

JOCASTA. You must be truthful, my young conqueror. They hate me. My dress annoys them, my accent annoys them, they are annoyed by my blackened eyelashes, my rouge, and my vivaciousness!

OEDIPUS. It 's Creon who annoys them! The cold, hard, inhuman Creon! I shall make your star rise again. Ah! Jocasta! What a magnificent programme!

JOCASTA. It was high time you came. I 'm exhausted.

OEDIPUS. Your room a prison! Your room, dear . . . and our bed.

JOCASTA. Do you want me to remove the cradle? After the death of the child I had to have it near me, I couldn't sleep. . . . I was too lonely. . . . But now . . .

OEDIPUS. [*In an indistinct voice.*] But now . . .

JOCASTA. What?

OEDIPUS. I said . . . I said . . . that it 's he . . . he . . . the dog

... I mean ... the dog who won't ... the dog ... the
fountain dog. ....   [*His head droops.*

JOCASTA. Oedipus! Oedipus!

OEDIPUS. [*Awakens, startled.*] What?

JOCASTA. You were falling asleep, dear!

OEDIPUS. Me? Never.

JOCASTA. Oh, yes, you were, dear. You were telling me about
a dog who won't ... a fountain dog. And I was listening.
                    [*She laughs and herself seems to be becoming vague.*

OEDIPUS. Nonsense!

JOCASTA. I was asking you if you wanted me to remove the
cradle, if it worries you.

OEDIPUS. Am I such a kid as to fear this pretty muslin ghost?
On the contrary it will be the cradle of my luck. My luck
will grow in it beside our love until it can be used for our first
son. So you see! ...

JOCASTA. My poor love. .... You 're dropping with fatigue and
here we stand ... [*Same business as with Oedipus.*] ... stand
on this wall. ...

OEDIPUS. What wall?

JOCASTA. This rampart wall. [*She starts.*] A wall. ...   What?
I ... I ... [*Haggard.*] What 's happening?

OEDIPUS. [*Laughing.*] Well, this time it 's you dreaming.
We 're tired out, my poor sweet.

JOCASTA. I was asleep? Did I talk?

OEDIPUS. We *are* a pretty pair! Here I go telling you about
fountain-dogs, and you tell me about rampart walls: and this
is our wedding night! Listen, Jocasta, if I happen to fall
asleep again (Are you listening?), do please awaken me, shake
me, and if you fall asleep I 'll do the same for you. This one
night of all must not founder in sleep. That would be too sad.

JOCASTA. You crazy darling you, why? We have all our life
before us.

OEDIPUS. Maybe, but I don't want sleep to spoil the miracle of
passing this joyous night alone, unutterably alone with you.
I suggest we remove these heavy clothes, and as we 're not
expecting any one——

JOCASTA. Listen, my darling boy, you 'll be cross ...

OEDIPUS. Jocasta, don't tell me there 's still some official duty
on the programme!

JOCASTA. While my women are doing my hair, etiquette demands
that you receive a visit.

OEDIPUS. A visit? At this hour?

JOCASTA. A visit . . . a visit . . . a purely formal visit.

OEDIPUS. In this room?

JOCASTA. In this room.

OEDIPUS. From whom?

JOCASTA. Now don't get cross. From Tiresias.

OEDIPUS. Tiresias? I refuse!

JOCASTA. Listen, dear. . . .

OEDIPUS. That's the limit! Tiresias playing the part of the family pouring out their farewell advice. How comic! I shall refuse his visit.

JOCASTA. You crazy dear, *I* am asking you to. It's an old custom in Thebes that the high priest must in some way bless the royal marriage bonds. And besides, Tiresias is our old uncle, our watch-dog. I am very fond of him, Oedipus, and Laïus adored him. He is nearly blind. It would be unfortunate if you hurt his feelings and set him against our love.

OEDIPUS. That's all very well . . . in the middle of the night. . . .

JOCASTA. Do! Please, for our sake and the sake of the future. It's essential. See him for five minutes, but see him and listen to him. I ask you to.   [*She kisses him.*

OEDIPUS. I warn you I shan't let him sit down.

JOCASTA. I love you, dear. [*Long kiss.*] I shall not be long. [*At the right-hand exit.*] I am going to let him know he can come. Be patient. Do it for my sake. Think of me. [*She goes out. [Oedipus, alone, looks at himself in the mirror and tries attitudes. Tiresias comes in left, unheard. Oedipus sees him in the middle of the room and turns about face.*

OEDIPUS. I am listening.

TIRESIAS. Steady, my lord. Who told you I had saved up a sermon for your especial benefit?

OEDIPUS. No one, Tiresias, no one. But I don't suppose you find it pleasant acting as kill-joy. I suggest you are waiting for me to pretend I have heard your words of counsel. I shall bow, and you will give me the accolade. That would be enough for us in our tired state and at the same time custom would be satisfied. Have I guessed right?

TIRESIAS. It is perhaps correct that there is at the bottom of this procedure a sort of custom, but for that, it would be necessary to have a royal marriage with all the dynastic, mechanical, and, I admit, even irksome business which that entails. No, my lord. Unforeseen events bring us face to face with new

H 989

problems and duties.   And you will agree, I think, that your coronation, and your marriage, appear in a form which is difficult to classify, and does not fit into any code.

OEDIPUS. No one could say more graciously that I have crashed on Thebes like a tile from a roof.

TIRESIAS. My lord!

OEDIPUS. Let me tell you that things fitting neatly into categories reek of death.   What we want, Tiresias, is not to fit, but to make a new departure.   That's the sign of masterpieces and heroes.   And that's the way to astonish and to rule.

TIRESIAS. Right!   Then you will admit that I myself, by playing a part outside the ceremonial sphere, am also making a new departure.

OEDIPUS. To the point, Tiresias, to the point.

TIRESIAS. Very well.   I shall come straight to the point and speak with all frankness.   My lord, your auguries look black, very black.   I must put you on your guard.

OEDIPUS. There!   Just as I expected!   Anything else would have surprised me.   This is not the first time the oracles have been violently against me and my audacity has thwarted them.

TIRESIAS. Do you believe they can be thwarted?

OEDIPUS. I am the living proof of it.   And even if my marriage upsets the gods, what about your promises, your freeing of the town, and the death of the Sphinx?   And why should the gods have pushed me on as far as this room if this marriage displeases them?

TIRESIAS. Do you think you can solve the problem of free will in a minute!   Ah, power, I fear, is going to your head!

OEDIPUS. You mean, power is slipping from your hands.

TIRESIAS. Take care!   You are speaking to a high priest.

OEDIPUS. Take care yourself, high priest.   Must I remind you that you are speaking to your king?

TIRESIAS. To the husband of my queen, my lord.

OEDIPUS. Jocasta notified me a little while ago that her power is to pass into my hands, in full.   Run and tell that to your master.

TIRESIAS. I serve only the gods.

OEDIPUS. Well, if you prefer that way of putting it, say that to the person who is awaiting your return.

TIRESIAS. Headstrong youth!   You don't understand me.

OEDIPUS. I understand perfectly well: an adventurer is in your

way. I expect you hope I found the Sphinx dead on my path.
The real conqueror must have sold it to me, like those hunters
who buy the hare from a poacher.   And supposing I have paid
for the mortal remains, whom will you find ultimately as the
conqueror of the Sphinx?   The same type of person who has
been threatening you every minute and preventing Creon
from sleeping: a poor private soldier whom the crowd will
bear in triumph and who will claim his due . . . [*Shouting.*]
his duel

TIRESIAS. He would not dare.

OEDIPUS. Ah, you see! I have made you say it. That 's the
secret of the intrigue. There go your beautiful promises.
That is what you were counting on.

TIRESIAS. The queen is more to me than my own daughter. I
must watch over her and defend her. She is weak, credulous,
romantic. . . .

OEDIPUS. You are insulting her.

TIRESIAS. I love her.

OEDIPUS. She is in need of no one's love but mine.

TIRESIAS. About this love, Oedipus, I demand an explanation.
Do you love the queen?

OEDIPUS. With all my being.

TIRESIAS. I mean: do you love to take her in your arms?

OEDIPUS. I love most of all to be taken in her arms.

TIRESIAS. I appreciate that delicate distinction. You are
young, Oedipus, very young.   Jocasta might be your mother.
I know, oh, I know, you are going to reply——

OEDIPUS. I am going to reply that I have always dreamed of
such a love, an almost motherly love.

TIRESIAS. Oedipus, aren't you confusing love and love of glory?
Would you love Jocasta if she were not on a throne?

OEDIPUS. A stupid question which is always being asked.
Would Jocasta love me if I was old, ugly, and had not appeared
out of the unknown?   Do you fancy you cannot be infected
by love through touching purple and gold?   Are not the
privileges of which you speak of the very substance of Jocasta,
an organic part of her?   We have been each other's from all
eternity. Within her body lie fold after fold of a purple
mantle which is much more regal than the one she fastens on
her shoulders.   I love and adore her, Tiresias.   At her side
I seem to occupy at last my proper place.   She is my wife, she
is my queen.   I possess her, I shall keep her, I shall find her

again, and neither by prayers nor threats can you drag from me obedience to orders from heaven knows where.

TIRESIAS. Think it over again, Oedipus. The omens and my own wisdom give me every reason to fear this wild marriage. Think it over.

OEDIPUS. Rather late, don't you think?

TIRESIAS. Have you had experience of women?

OEDIPUS. Not the slightest. And to complete your astonishment and cover myself with ridicule in your eyes, I am a virgin.

TIRESIAS. You!

OEDIPUS. The high priest of a capital is astonished that a country boy should put all his pride in keeping himself pure for a single offering. You would, no doubt, have preferred a degenerate prince, a puppet, so that Creon and the priests could work the strings.

TIRESIAS. You are going too far!

OEDIPUS. Must I order you again? . . .

TIRESIAS. Order? Has pride sent you mad?

OEDIPUS. Don't put me into a rage! My patience is at an end, my temper is ungovernable, and I am capable of any unpremeditated act.

TIRESIAS. What arrogance! . . . Weak and arrogant!

OEDIPUS. You will have brought it on yourself.
    [He throws himself upon Tiresias, seizing him by the neck.

TIRESIAS. Let me go. . . . Have you no shame? . . .

OEDIPUS. You are afraid that I could, from your face, there, there, close up, and in your blind man's eyes, read the real truth about your behaviour.

TIRESIAS. Murderer! Sacrilege!

OEDIPUS. Murderer! I ought to be. . . . One day I shall probably have to repent for this foolish respect, and if I dared . . . Oh, oh! Why! Gods, look here . . . here . . . in his blind man's eyes, I had no idea it was possible.

TIRESIAS. Let me go! Brute!

OEDIPUS. The future! My future, as in a crystal bowl.

TIRESIAS. You will repent. . . .

OEDIPUS. I see, I see. . . . Soothsayer, you have lied! I shall marry Jocasta. . . . A happy life, rich, prosperous, two sons . . . daughters . . . and Jocasta still as beautiful, still the same, in love, a mother in a palace of happiness. . . . Now it 's not so clear, not clear. I want to see! It 's your fault, soothsayer. . . . I want to see!
    [He shakes him.

TIRESIAS. Accursed!

OEDIPUS. [*Suddenly recoiling, letting Tiresias go, and putting his hands over his eyes.*] Oh, filthy wretch! I am blind. He's thrown pepper at me. Jocasta! Help! Help! . . .

TIRESIAS. I threw nothing, I swear. You are punished for your sacrilege.

OEDIPUS. [*Writhing on the ground.*] You lie!

TIRESIAS. You wanted to read by force the secrets my diseased eyes hold and that I myself have not yet interpreted; and you are punished.

OEDIPUS. Water, water, quickly, it's burning me. . . .

TIRESIAS. [*Laying his hands over Oedipus's face.*] There, there. . . . Keep quiet. . . . I forgive you. Your nerves are on edge. Come, keep still. Your sight will return, I swear. I expect you got to the point which the gods wish to keep in darkness, or they may be punishing you for your impudence.

OEDIPUS. I can see a little . . . I think.

TIRESIAS. Are you in pain?

OEDIPUS. Less . . . the pain is going. Ah! . . . it was like fire, red pepper, a thousand pinpoints, a cat's paw scrabbling in my eye. Thank you. . . .

TIRESIAS. Can you see?

OEDIPUS. Not clearly, but I can see, I can see. Phew! I really thought I was blind for good and that it was one of your kind of tricks. In any case, I deserved it.

TIRESIAS. We like to believe in miracles when miracles suit us, and when they don't we like to believe in them no longer, but say it is a trick on the part of the soothsayer.

OEDIPUS. Forgive me. I am of a violent and vindictive disposition. I love Jocasta. I was waiting for her, impatiently, and this extraordinary phenomenon, all those images of the future in the pupil of your eyes bewitched me, fuddled me, as it were, and made me mad.

TIRESIAS. Can you see better now? It is an almost blind man asking you.

OEDIPUS. Quite, and I have no more pain. I'm really ashamed of my conduct towards you, a blind man and a priest. Will you accept my apologies?

TIRESIAS. I was only speaking for your own good and Jocasta's.

OEDIPUS. Tiresias, in a way I owe you something in return, a confession that is difficult to make, and which I had promised myself I would make to no one.

TIRESIAS. A confession?

OEDIPUS. I noticed during the coronation ceremony that you and Creon had some understanding between you. Do not deny it. Well, I wished to keep my identity secret; but I give it up. Listen carefully, Tiresias. I am not a wanderer. I come from Corinth. I am the only child of King Polybius and Queen Merope. A nobody will not soil this marriage bed. I am a king and son of a king.

TIRESIAS. My lord. [*He bows.*] A word from you would have cleared the atmosphere of the uneasiness created by your incognito. My little girl will be so glad. . . .

OEDIPUS. But wait! I ask you as a favour to safeguard at least this last night. Jocasta still loves in me the wanderer dropped out of the clouds, the young man stepping suddenly out of the shadows. It will unfortunately be only too easy to destroy this mirage to-morrow. In the meantime, I hope the queen will become sufficiently submissive for her to learn without disgust that Oedipus is not a prince fallen from the sky, but merely a prince.

I wish you good evening, Tiresias. Jocasta will be on her way back. I am dropping with fatigue . . . and we want to remain alone together. That is our desire.

TIRESIAS. My lord, excuse me.

[*Oedipus makes a sign to him with his hand. Tiresias stops at the left-hand exit.*

One last word.

OEDIPUS. [*Loftily.*] What is it?

TIRESIAS. Forgive my boldness. This evening, after the closing of the temple, a beautiful young girl came into the private chapel where I work and, without a word of excuse, handed me this belt and said: 'Give it to Lord Oedipus and repeat word for word this sentence: Take this belt: with that you will be able to get to me when I have killed the beast.' I had scarcely tucked away the belt when the girl burst out laughing and disappeared, I don't know how.

OEDIPUS. [*Snatching away the belt.*] And that's your trump card. You have already built up a whole system in order to destroy my hold on the queen's head and heart. How should I know? A previous promise of marriage. . . . A girl takes her revenge. . . . The temple scandal. . . . Tell-tale find. . . .

TIRESIAS. I was fulfilling my commission. That's all.

OEDIPUS. Miscalculation and bad policy. Go . . . and carry this bad news with all speed to Prince Creon.

[*Tiresias stays on the threshold.*

He reckoned he was going to scare me! But in point of fact, it is I who scare you, Tiresias, *I* scare you. I can see it written in large letters on your face. It wasn't so easy to terrorize the child. Confess that the child terrifies you, grandpa! Confess, grandpa! Confess I terrify you! Confess at least I make you afraid!

[*Oedipus is lying face down on the animal skin. Tiresias is standing like a bronze statue. Silence. Then thunder.*

TIRESIAS. Yes. Very afraid. [*He leaves, walking backwards. His prophetic voice can be heard.*] Oedipus! Oedipus, listen to me! You are pursuing classic glory. There is another kind: obscure glory, the last resource of the arrogant person who persists in opposing the stars.

[*Oedipus remains looking at the belt. When Jocasta comes in, in her nightdress, he quickly hides the belt under the animal skin.*

JOCASTA. Well now? What did the old ogre say? Did he torment you?

OEDIPUS. Yes . . . no. . . .

JOCASTA. He's a monster. Did he prove to you that you are too young for me?

OEDIPUS. You are beautiful, Jocasta! . . .

JOCASTA. That I am old?

OEDIPUS. He rather gave me to understand that I loved your pearls, and your diadem.

JOCASTA. Always spoiling everything! Ruining everything! Doing harm!

OEDIPUS. But you can take it from me, he didn't manage to scare me. On the contrary, I scared him. He admitted that.

JOCASTA. Well done! My love! You, dear, after my pearls and diadem!

OEDIPUS. I am happy to see you again without any pomp, without your jewels and orders, white, young, and beautiful, in our own room.

JOCASTA. Young! Oedipus! . . . You mustn't tell lies. . . .

OEDIPUS. Again! . . .

JOCASTA. Don't scold me.

OEDIPUS. Yes, I shall scold you! I shall scold you because a woman like you ought to be above such nonsense. A young girl's face is as boring as a white page on which my eyes can read nothing moving; whereas your face! ... I must have the scars, the tattooing of destiny, a beauty which has weathered tempests. Why should you be afraid of crows' feet, Jocasta? What would a silly schoolgirl's look or smile be worth beside the remarkable sacred beauty of your face; slapped by fate, branded by the executioner, and tender, tender and ... [*He notices that Jocasta is weeping.*] Jocasta! my dear little girl, you're crying! What ever's the matter? ... All right, then.... What have I done now? Jocasta!...

JOCASTA. Am I so old ... so very old?

OEDIPUS. My dear crazy girl! It's you who persist in——

JOCASTA. Women say things to be contradicted. They always hope it isn't true.

OEDIPUS. My dear Jocasta! ... What a fool I am! What a great brute!... Darling.... Don't cry. Kiss me.... I meant——

JOCASTA. Never mind.... I am being ridiculous.

[*She dries her eyes.*

OEDIPUS. It's all my fault.

JOCASTA. It isn't.... There ... the black is running into my eye now.   [*Oedipus coaxes her.* It's all over.

OEDIPUS. Quick, a smile.   [*Slight rumbling of thunder.* Listen.

JOCASTA. My nerves are bad because of the storm.

OEDIPUS. But look at the sky! It is full of stars, and clear.

JOCASTA. Yes, but there is a storm brewing somewhere. When the fountain makes a still murmur like silence, and my shoulder aches, there is always a storm about and summer lightning.

[*She leans against the bay window. Summer lightning.*

OEDIPUS. Come here, quickly....

JOCASTA. Oedipus! ... come here a moment.

OEDIPUS. What is it? ...

JOCASTA. The sentry ... look, lean out. On the bench on the right, he's asleep. Don't you think he's handsome, that boy? with his mouth wide open.

OEDIPUS. I'll throw some water in it! I'll teach him to sleep!

JOCASTA. Oedipus!

OEDIPUS. How dare he sleep when guarding the queen!

JOCASTA. The Sphinx is dead and you're alive. Let him sleep in peace! May all the town sleep in peace! May they all sleep every one!

OEDIPUS. Lucky sentry!

JOCASTA. Oedipus! Oedipus! I should like to make you jealous, but it isn't that. . . . This young guard——

OEDIPUS. What is so extraordinary about this young guard then?

JOCASTA. During that famous night, the night of the Sphinx, while you were encountering the beast, I had an escapade on the ramparts with Tiresias. I had heard that a young soldier had seen the ghost of Laïus, and that Laïus was calling for me to warn me of a threatening danger. Well . . . that soldier was the very sentry who is guarding us.

OEDIPUS. Who is guarding us! . . . Anyway . . . Let him sleep in peace, my kind Jocasta. I can guard you all right on my own. Of course, not the slightest sign of the ghost of Laïus?

JOCASTA. Not the slightest, I'm sorry to say. . . . Poor lad! I touched his shoulders and legs, and kept saying to Zizi, 'Touch, touch,' and I was in a state . . . because he was like you. And it's true, you know, Oedipus, he was like you.

OEDIPUS. You say: 'This guard was like you.' But, Jocasta, you didn't know me then; it was impossible for you to know or to guess. . . .

JOCASTA. Yes, indeed, that's true. I expect I meant to say my son would be about his age. [Silence.] Yes . . . I am getting muddled. It's only now that this likeness strikes me. [She shakes off this uneasy feeling.] You're a dear, you're good-looking, I love you. [After a pause.] Oedipus!

OEDIPUS. My goddess!

JOCASTA. I approve of your not telling the story of your victory to Creon or to Tiresias, or to everybody [With her arms round his neck.], but to me . . . to me!

OEDIPUS. [Freeing himself.] I had your promise! . . . And but for that boy——

JOCASTA. Is the Jocasta of yesterday the Jocasta of now? Haven't I a right to share your memories without anybody else knowing anything about it?

OEDIPUS. Of course.

JOCASTA. And do you remember you kept saying: 'No, no, Jocasta, later, later when we are in our own room.' Well, aren't we in our own room? . . .

OEDIPUS. Persistent monkey! Charmer! She always ends by getting what she wants. Now lie still. . . . I am beginning.

JOCASTA. Oh, Oedipus! Oedipus! What fun! What fun! I'm quite still.

> [*Jocasta lies down, shuts her eyes, and keeps still. Oedipus begins lying, hesitating, inventing, accompanied by the storm.*

OEDIPUS. Now. I was nearing Thebes. I was following the goat track which rounds the hill to the south of the town. I was thinking of the future, of you whom I imagined less beautiful than you are in reality, but still, very beautiful, painted, and sitting on a throne in the centre of a group of ladies-in-waiting. Supposing you do kill it, I said to myself, would you, Oedipus, dare to ask for the promised reward? Should I dare to go near the queen? . . . And I kept walking and worrying. All of a sudden I stopped dead. My heart was beating hard. I had just heard a sort of song. The voice that sang it was not of this world. Was it the Sphinx? My haversack contained a knife. I slipped the knife under my tunic and crept along. Do you know those ruins of a little temple on the hill, with a pedestal and the hind quarters of a chimera?   [*Silence.*
Jocasta . . . Jocasta. . . . Are you asleep?

JOCASTA. [*Awaking with a start.*] What? Oedipus. . . .

OEDIPUS. You were asleep.

JOCASTA. I wasn't.

OEDIPUS. Oh, yes, you were. There's a fickle little girl for you! She wants me to tell her a story and then goes and falls asleep in the middle of it, instead of listening.

JOCASTA. I heard it all. You're mistaken. You were speaking of a goat track.

OEDIPUS. I'd got a long way past the goat track! . . .

JOCASTA. Don't be angry, darling. Are you cross with me? . . .

OEDIPUS. Me?

JOCASTA. Yes, you are cross with me, and rightly. What a stupid silly I am! That's what age does for you.

OEDIPUS. Don't be sad. I'll start the story again, I promise you, but first of all you and I must lie down and sleep a little, side by side. After that, we shall be clear of this sticky paste, this struggle against sleep which is spoiling everything. The first one to wake up will wake the other. Promise.

JOCASTA. Promised. Poor queens know how to snatch a

moment's sleep where they sit, between two audiences. But give me your hand. I am too old. Tiresias was right.

OEDIPUS. Perhaps so for Thebes, where girls are marriageable at thirteen. But what about me? Am I an old man? My head keeps dropping and my chin hitting my chest wakes me up.

JOCASTA. You? That's quite different, it's the dustman, as children say! But as for me . . . You begin to tell me the most marvellous story in the world, and I go and doze away like a grandma beside the fire. And you will punish me by never beginning it over again, and finding excuses. . . . Did I talk in my sleep?

OEDIPUS. Talk? No. I thought you were being very attentive. You naughty girl, have you some secrets you are afraid you might give away?

JOCASTA. No, only those foolish things we sometimes say when sleeping.

OEDIPUS. You were lying as good as gold. Till soon, my little queen.

JOCASTA. Very soon, my king, my love.

[*Hand in hand, side by side, they shut their eyes and fall into the heavy sleep of people who struggle against sleep. A pause. The fountain soliloquizes. Slight thunder. Suddenly the lighting becomes the lighting of dreams. The dream of Oedipus. The animal skin is pushed up. It is lifted by the head of Anubis. He shows the belt at the end of his outstretched arm. Oedipus tosses about and turns over.*]

ANUBIS. [*In a slow mocking voice.*] Thanks to my unhappy childhood, I have pursued studies which give me a great start over the riff-raff of Thebes, and I don't think this simple-minded monster is expecting to be confronted by a pupil of the best scholars of Corinth. But if you have played a trick on me I shall drag you by the hair. [*Up to a howl.*] I shall drag you by the hair, I shall drag you by the hair, I shall grip you till the blood flows! . . . I shall grip you till the blood flows! . . .

JOCASTA. [*Dreaming.*] No, not that paste, not that foul paste! . . .

OEDIPUS. [*In a distant, muffled voice.*] I shall count up to fifty: one, two, three, four, eight, seven, nine, ten, ten, eleven, fourteen, five, two, four, seven, fifteen, fifteen, fifteen, fifteen, three, four. . . .

ANUBIS. And Anubis would bound forward.   He would open his wolf-like jaws!

[*He disappears under the platform.   The animal skin resumes its normal appearance.*

OEDIPUS. Help! Help! I'm here! Help me! Everybody! Come here!

JOCASTA. What? What is it? Oedipus, my darling! I was in a dead sleep! Wake up!   [*She shakes him.*

OEDIPUS. [*Struggling and talking to the Sphinx.*] Oh, miss! No! No, miss! Please don't! No! Let me go, miss! No! No! No!

JOCASTA. My pet, don't scare me so. It's a dream. This is me, me, Jocasta, your wife, Jocasta.

OEDIPUS. No, no! [*He awakens.*] Where was I? How ghastly! Jocasta, is that you? . . . What a nightmare, what a horrible nightmare!

JOCASTA. There, there, it's all over, you are in our room, dear, in my arms. . . .

OEDIPUS. Didn't you see anything? Of course, how silly of me, it was that animal skin. . . . Phew! I must have talked. What did I say?

JOCASTA. Now it's your turn. You were shouting: 'Oh no, miss! Please don't, miss! Let me go, miss!' Who was that wicked young woman?

OEDIPUS. I don't remember. What a night!

JOCASTA. How about me? Your shouts saved me from an unspeakable nightmare. Look! You're soaked through, swimming in perspiration. It's my fault. I let you go to sleep in all those heavy clothes, golden chains, clasps, and those sandals which cut your heel. . . . [*She lifts him up. He falls back.*] Come along! What a big baby! I can't possibly leave you in this state. Don't make yourself so heavy, help me. . . .

[*She lifts him up, takes off his tunic, and rubs him down.*

OEDIPUS. [*Still in a vague state.*] Yes, my little darling mother. . . .

JOCASTA. [*Mocking him.*] 'Yes, my little darling mother. . . .' What a child! Now he's taking me for his mother.

OEDIPUS. [*Awake.*] Oh, forgive me, Jocasta, my love, I am being so silly. You see I'm half asleep, I mix up everything. I was thousands of miles away with my mother who always thinks I am too cold or too hot. You're not cross?

JOCASTA. Silly boy! Let me see to you, and sleep away. All the time he's excusing himself and asking forgiveness. My word! What a polite young man! He must have been taken care of by a very kind mother, very kind, and then he goes and leaves her, yes. But I mustn't complain of that. I love with all the warmth of a woman in love that mother who petted you and kept you and brought you up for me, for us.

OEDIPUS. Sweet.

JOCASTA. I should say so! Your sandals. Raise your left leg. [*She takes off his sandals.*] And now the right.

> [*Same business; suddenly she utters a terrible cry.*

OEDIPUS. Hurt yourself?

JOCASTA. No . . . no. . . .

> [*She recoils, and stares like a mad creature at Oedipus's feet.*

OEDIPUS. Ah, my scars! . . . I didn't know they were so ugly. My poor darling, did they upset you?

JOCASTA. Those holes . . . how did you get them? . . . They must come from such serious injuries. . . .

OEDIPUS. From the hunt, it seems. I was in the woods; my nurse was carrying me. Suddenly from a clump of trees a wild boar broke cover and charged her. She lost her head and let me go. I fell and a woodcutter killed the animal while it was belabouring me with its tusks. . . . But she is really as pale as a ghost! My darling! I ought to have warned you. I'm so used to them myself, those awful holes. I didn't know you were so sensitive. . . .

JOCASTA. It's nothing. . . .

OEDIPUS. Weariness and sleepiness put us into this state of vague terror . . . you had just come out of a bad dream. . . .

JOCASTA. No, Oedipus. No. As a matter of fact, those scars remind me of something I am always trying to forget.

OEDIPUS. I always strike unlucky.

JOCASTA. You couldn't possibly know. It's to do with a woman, my foster-sister and linen-maid. She was with child at the same age as myself, at eighteen. She worshipped her husband despite the difference of age and wanted a son. But the oracles predicted so fearful a future for the child that, after giving birth to a son, she had not the courage to let it live.

OEDIPUS. What?

JOCASTA. Wait. . . . Imagine what strength of mind a poor woman must have to do away with the life of her life . . . the son from her womb, her ideal on earth and love of loves.

OEDIPUS. And what did this . . . woman do?

JOCASTA. With death in her heart, she bored holes in the feet of the nursling, tied them, carried it secretly to a mountain-side, and left it to the mercy of the wolves and bears.

[*She hides her face.*

OEDIPUS. And the husband?

JOCASTA. Every one thought the child had died a natural death, and that the mother had buried it with her own hands.

OEDIPUS. And . . . this woman . . . still lives?

JOCASTA. She is dead.

OEDIPUS. So much the better for her, for my first example of royal authority would have been to inflict on her, publicly, the worst tortures, and afterwards, to have her put to death.

JOCASTA. The oracles were clear and matter-of-fact. Before those things a woman always feels so stupid and helpless.

OEDIPUS. To kill! [*Recalling Laïus.*] Of course, it isn't infamous to kill when carried away by the instinct of self-defence, and when bad luck is involved. But basely to kill in cold blood the flesh of one's flesh, to break the chain . . . to cheat in the game!

JOCASTA. Oedipus, let's talk about something else . . . your furious little face upsets me too much.

OEDIPUS. Yes, let us talk about something else. I should be in danger of loving you less if you tried to defend this miserable wretch.

JOCASTA. You're a man, my love, a free man and a chief! Try and put yourself in the place of a child-mother who is credulous about the oracles, worn out, disgusted, confined, and terrified by the priests. . . .

OEDIPUS. A linen-maid! That's her only excuse. Would you have done it?

JOCASTA. [*With a gesture.*] No, of course not.

OEDIPUS. And don't run away with the idea that to fight the oracles requires a herculean determination. I could boast and pose as a wonder; I should be lying. You know, to thwart the oracles I only had to turn my back on my family, my longings, and my country. But the farther I got from my native town, and the nearer I came to yours, the more I felt I was returning home.

JOCASTA. Oedipus, Oedipus, that little mouth of yours which chatters away, that little wagging tongue, those frowning eyebrows and fiery eyes! Couldn't the eyebrows relax a little,

Oedipus, and the eyes close gently for once, and that mouth be used for softer caresses than words?

OEDIPUS. I tell you, I 'm just a brute! A wretched, clumsy brute!

JOCASTA. You are a child.

OEDIPUS. I 'm not a child!

JOCASTA. Now he 's off again! There, there, be a good boy.

OEDIPUS. You 're right. I 'm behaving very badly. Calm this talkative mouth with yours, and these feverish eyes with your fingers.

JOCASTA. One moment. I 'll close the grille gate. I don't like that gate being open at night.

OEDIPUS. I 'll go.

JOCASTA. You stay lying down.... I 'll take a look in the mirror at the same time. Do you want to embrace a fright? After all this excitement the gods alone know what I look like. Don't make me nervous. Don't look at me. Turn the other way, Oedipus.

OEDIPUS. I 'm turning over. [*He lies across the bed with his head on the edge of the cradle.*] There, I 'm shutting my eyes. I 'm not here.   [*Jocasta goes to the window.*

JOCASTA. [*To Oedipus.*] The little soldier is still asleep, he 's half-naked ... and it isn't warm to-night ... poor lad!

[*She goes to the movable mirror; suddenly she stops, listening in the direction of the square. A drunk is talking very loud with long pauses between his reflections.*

VOICE OF THE DRUNK. Politics! ... Pol—i—tics! What a mess! They just tickle me to death! ... Ho! Look, a dead 'un! ... Sorry, a mistake: 's a soldier asleep. ... Salute! Salute the sleeping army!

[*Silence. Jocasta stands on her toes, and tries to see outside. Politics! ... [Long silence.] It 's a disgrace ... a disgrace. ...*

JOCASTA. Oedipus, my dear!

OEDIPUS. [*In his sleep.*] H'm!

JOCASTA. Oedipus! Oedipus! There 's a drunk and the sentry doesn't hear him. I hate drunks. I want him sent away, and the soldier woken up. Oedipus! Oedipus! Please!
                              [*She shakes him.*

OEDIPUS. I wind, I unwind, I calculate, I meditate, I weave, I winnow, I knit, I plait, I cross ...

JOCASTA. What 's he saying? How soundly he sleeps! I might die, he wouldn't notice it.

DRUNK. Politics!

> [*He sings. As soon as the first lines are sung Jocasta leaves Oedipus, putting his head back on the edge of the cradle, and goes to the middle of the room. She listens.*
>
> > 'Majesty, what ever are you at?
> > Majesty, what ever are you at?
> > Your husband's much too young,
> > Much too young for you, that's flat! . . . Flat. . . .'
>
> Et cetera. . . .

JOCASTA. Oh! The beasts . . .

DRUNK. 'Majesty, what ever are you at
With this holy marriage?'

> [*During what follows Jocasta, bewildered, goes to the window on tiptoe. Then she returns to the bed, and leaning over Oedipus, watches his face, but still looking from time to time in the direction of the window, where the voice of the Drunk alternates with the murmur of the fountain and the cock-crows. She lulls the sleep of Oedipus by gently rocking the cradle.*

Now, if I were in politics . . . I'd say to the queen: Majesty! . . . a minor can't be your man. . . . Take a husband who's serious, sober, and strong . . . a husband like me. . . .

VOICE OF THE GUARD. [*Who has just awakened. He gradually recovers his self-assurance.*] Get along, there!

VOICE OF THE DRUNK. Salute the waking army! . . .

GUARD. Get a move on!

DRUNK. You might at least be polite. . . .

> [*As soon as the Guard is heard Jocasta leaves the cradle, having first muffled Oedipus's head in the muslin.*

GUARD. D' you want a taste of the cooler?

DRUNK. 'Always politics! What a mess!
Majesty, what ever are you at? . . .'

GUARD. Come on, hop it! Clear off! . . .

DRUNK. I'm clearing off, I'm clearing off, but you might be polite about it.

> [*During these remarks Jocasta goes to the mirror, She cannot see herself owing to the moonlight conflicting with the dawn. She takes the mirror by its supports and moves it away from the wall. The mirror itself stays fastened to the*

scenery. Jocasta drags the frame along, trying to get some light, glancing at Oedipus who sleeps on. She brings the piece of furniture carefully into the foreground, opposite the prompter's box, so that the public becomes her mirror and Jocasta looks at herself in full view of all.

DRUNK. [*Very distant.*]

'Your husband's much too young,
Much too young for you, that's flat! ...   Flat! ...'

[*Sound of the sentry's footsteps, bugle-calls, cock-crows, a kind of snoring noise from the rhythmic, youthful breathing of Oedipus. Jocasta, with her face up against the empty mirror, lifts her cheeks by handfuls.*

END OF ACT III

ACT IV

OEDIPUS REX
(Seventeen years later)

Seventeen years soon pass. The great plague in Thebes seems to be the first set-back to that renowned good luck of Oedipus. For their infernal machine to work properly the gods wanted all ill luck to appear in the guise of good luck. After delusive good fortune the king is to know true misfortune, the supreme consecration, which, in the hands of the cruel gods, makes of this playing-card king, in the end, a man.

ACT IV

OEDIPUS REX

(*Seventeen years later*)

*Cleared of the bedroom, the red hangings of which are pulled away
into the flies, the platform seems to be surrounded by walls which
grow in size. It finally represents an inner courtyard. By a
balcony high up Jocasta's room is made to communicate with this
court. One gets to it through an open door below, in the centre.*

*When the curtain rises Oedipus, aged, and wearing a little beard,
stands near to the door. Tiresias and Creon are standing on the
right and left of the court. Centre right, a young boy rests one
knee on the ground : he is the Messenger from Corinth.*

OEDIPUS. What have I done to shock people now, Tiresias?

TIRESIAS. You are enlarging on things, as usual. I think, and
I 'll say again, it might be more decent to learn of a father's
death with less joy.

OEDIPUS. Indeed. [*To the Messenger.*] Don't be afraid, boy.
Tell me, what was the cause of Polybius's death? Is Merope
so very terribly unhappy?

MESSENGER. King Polybius died of old age, my lord, and . . .
the queen, his wife, is barely conscious. She is so old she can't
fully realize even her misfortune.

OEDIPUS. [*His hand to his mouth.*] Jocasta! Jocasta!
[*Jocasta appears on the balcony ; she parts the curtain. She
is wearing her red scarf.*

JOCASTA. What is it?

OEDIPUS. How pale you are! Don't you feel well?

JOCASTA. Oh, you know, the plague, the heat, and visits to
hospitals—I 'm absolutely exhausted. I was resting on my
bed.

OEDIPUS. This messenger has brought me great news, worth
disturbing you for.

JOCASTA. [*Astonished.*] Good news? . . .

OEDIPUS. Tiresias blames me for finding it good: My father is
dead.

JOCASTA. Oedipus!

233

OEDIPUS. The oracle told me I should be his murderer, and that
I should be the husband of my mother.   Poor Merope! she is
very old, and my father, Polybius, has died a good natural
death!

JOCASTA. I never knew the death of a father was a subject for
rejoicing!

OEDIPUS. I hate play-acting and conventional tears.   To tell
the truth, I was so young when I left my father and mother
that I no longer have any particular feelings for them.

MESSENGER. Lord Oedipus, if I may . . .

OEDIPUS. You may, my boy.

MESSENGER. Your indifference is not really indifference.   I can
explain it to you.

OEDIPUS. Something new.

MESSENGER. I ought to have begun at the end of the story.   On
his deathbed the King of Corinth asked me to tell you that
you are only his adopted son.

OEDIPUS. What?

MESSENGER. My father, one of Polybius's shepherds, found you
on a hill, at the mercy of wild beasts.   He was a poor man; he
carried his find to the queen who used to weep because she
had no children.   This is how the honour of performing such
an extraordinary mission at the Theban court has fallen
to me.

TIRESIAS. This young man must be exhausted after his journey,
and he has crossed our town which is full of noxious vapours.
Perhaps it would be better if he took some refreshment and
rested before being questioned.

OEDIPUS. No doubt, Tiresias, you would like the torture to last.
You think my world is tottering.   You don't know me well
enough.   Don't you rejoice too soon.   Perhaps I am happy
to be a child of fortune.

TIRESIAS. I was only putting you on your guard against your
sinister habit of questioning, seeking to know and understand
everything.

OEDIPUS. Whether I am a child of the muses or of a common
tramp, I shall question without fear; I will know things.

JOCASTA. Oedipus, my love, he is right.   You get excited. . . .
You get excited . . . and you believe everything you 're told,
and then afterwards——

OEDIPUS. What! That's the last straw! Unflinchingly I
withstand the hardest knocks, and you all plot to make me

put up with these things and not try to find out where I
come from.

JOCASTA. Nobody is plotting . . . my love . . . but I know
you. . . .

OEDIPUS. You're wrong, Jocasta. Nobody knows me at
present, neither you, nor I, nor any one else. [*To the Messenger.*] Don't tremble, my lad. Speak up. Tell us more.

MESSENGER. That's all I know, Lord Oedipus, except that my
father untied you when you were half dead, hanging by your
wounded feet from a short branch.

OEDIPUS. Oh, so that's how we come by those fine scars!

JOCASTA. Oedipus, Oedipus, dear . . . come up here. . . . Anybody would think you enjoy opening old wounds.

OEDIPUS. And so those were my swaddling clothes! . . . My
story of the hunt is . . . false, like so many others. Well, if
that's the way things are . . . I may come of a god of the
woods and a dryad, and have been nourished by wolves.
Don't you rejoice too soon, Tiresias!

TIRESIAS. You do me an injustice. . . .

OEDIPUS. At any rate I haven't killed Polybius, but . . . now I
come to think of it . . . I have killed a man.

JOCASTA. You!

OEDIPUS. Yes! I! Oh, you needn't be alarmed! It was
accidental, and sheer bad luck! Yes, I have killed, soothsayer, but as for parricide, you'd better officially give it up.
During a brawl with the serving-men I killed an old man at
the cross-roads of Delphi and Daulis.

JOCASTA. At the cross-roads of Delphi and Daulis! . . .
                              [*She disappears as if drowning.*

OEDIPUS. There's marvellous material for you to build up a
really fine catastrophe. That traveller must have been my
father. 'Heavens, my father!' But incest won't be so easy,
gentlemen. What do *you* think, Jocasta? . . . [*He turns
round and sees Jocasta has disappeared.*] Splendid! Seventeen
years of happiness, and a perfect reign, two sons, two daughters,
and then this noble lady only has to learn that I am the
stranger whom, by the way, she first loved, and she turns her
back on me. Let her sulk! Let her sulk! I shall be left
alone with my fate.

CREON. Your wife, Oedipus, is ill. The plague is demoralizing
us all. The gods are punishing the town and desire a victim.
A monster is hiding in our midst. They demand he shall be

found and driven out.   Day after day the police have failed
and the streets are littered with corpses.   Do you realize
what an effort you are asking of Jocasta?   Do you realize
that you are a man and she is a woman, an ageing woman at
that, and a mother who is worried about the plague?   Instead
of blaming Jocasta for a movement of impatience, you might
have found some excuse for her.

OEDIPUS. I see what you are getting at, brother-in-law.   The
ideal victim, the monster in hiding. . . .   From one coincidence
to another . . . wouldn't it be a pretty job, with the help of
the priests and the police, to succeed in muddling the people
of Thebes and make them believe *I* am that monster!

CREON. Don't be absurd!

OEDIPUS. I think you 're capable of anything, my friend.   But
Jocasta, that 's another matter. . . .   I am astonished at her
attitude. [*He calls her.*]   Jocasta! Jocasta! Where are you?

TIRESIAS. She looked all to pieces.   She is resting . . . let her be.

OEDIPUS. I am going. . . . [*He goes toward the Messenger.*] Now,
let us come to the point. . . .

MESSENGER. My lord!

OEDIPUS. Holes in my feet . . . bound . . . on the mountain-
side. . . .   How did I fail to understand at once? . . .   And
then I wondered why Jocasta . . .

It 's very hard to give up enigmas. . . .   Gentlemen, I was
not the son of a dryad.   Allow me to introduce you to the son
of a linen-maid, a child of the people, a native product.

CREON. What 's this all about?

OEDIPUS. Poor Jocasta!   One day I unwittingly told her what
I thought of my mother. . . .   I understand everything now.
She must be terrified, and utterly desperate.   In short . . .
wait for me.   I must question her at all costs.   Nothing must
be left in the dark.   This horrible farce must come to an end.

[*He leaves by the middle door.   Creon immediately rushes to
the Messenger, whom he pushes out through the door on
the right.*]

CREON. He is mad.   What does all this mean?

TIRESIAS. Don't move.   A storm is approaching from out of the
ages.   A thunderbolt is aimed at this man, and I ask you,
Creon, to let this thunderbolt follow its capricious course, to
wait motionless and not to interfere in the slightest.

[*Suddenly, Oedipus is seen on the balcony, stranded and
aghast.   He leans on the wall with one hand.*]

OEDIPUS. You have killed her for me.

CREON. What do you mean, killed?

OEDIPUS. You have killed her for me. . . . There she is, hanging
. . . hanging by her scarf. . . . She is dead . . . gentlemen, she
is dead. . . . It's all over . . . all over.

CREON. Dead? I'm coming. . . .

TIRESIAS. Stay here. . . . As a priest I order you to. It's inhuman, I know; but the circle is closing; we must keep silent
and remain here. . . .

CREON. You wouldn't stop a brother from——

TIRESIAS. I would! Let the story be. Don't interfere.

OEDIPUS. [At the door.] You have killed her for me . . . she was
romantic . . . weak . . . ill . . . you forced me to say I was a
murderer. . . . Whom did I murder, gentlemen, I ask you?
. . . through clumsiness, mere clumsiness . . . just an old man
on the road . . . a stranger.

TIRESIAS. Oedipus: through mere clumsiness you have murdered
Jocasta's husband, King Laïus.

OEDIPUS. You scoundrels! . . . I can see it now! You are
carrying on your plot! . . . It was even worse than I thought.
. . . You have made my poor Jocasta believe that I was the
murderer of Laïus . . . that I killed the king to set her free
and so that I could marry her.

TIRESIAS. Oedipus, you have murdered Jocasta's husband, King
Laïus. I have known it for a long time, and you are telling lies.
I haven't said a word about it either to you or to her or to Creon
or to any one else. This is how you reward me for my silence.

OEDIPUS. Laïus! . . . So that's it. . . . I am the son of Laïus
and of the linen-maid. The son of Jocasta's foster-sister and
Laïus.

TIRESIAS. [To Creon.] If you want to act, now's the time.
Quickly. There are limits even to harshness.

CREON. Oedipus, through you, my sister is dead. I kept silence
only to protect Jocasta. I think it is useless to prolong
unduly the false mystery and the unravelling of a sordid
drama whose intrigue I have finally succeeded in discovering.

OEDIPUS. Intrigue?

CREON. The most secret of secrets are betrayed one day or
another to the determined seeker. The honest man, sworn
to silence, talks to his wife, who talks to an intimate friend,
and so on. [Into the wings.] Come in, shepherd.

[An old shepherd comes in, trembling.

OEDIPUS. Who is this man?

CREON. The man who carried you bleeding and bound on to the mountain-side, in obedience to your mother's orders.   Let him confess.

SHEPHERD. To speak means death to me.   Princes, why haven't I died before so as not to live through this minute?

OEDIPUS. Whose son am I, old man?   Strike, strike quickly!

SHEPHERD. Alas!

OEDIPUS. I am near to the sound of something that should not be heard.

SHEPHERD. And I . . . to the saying of something that should not be said.

CREON. You must say it.   I wish you to.

SHEPHERD. You are the son of Jocasta, your wife, and of Laïus, killed by you where the three roads cross.   Incest and parricide, may the gods forgive you!

OEDIPUS. I have killed whom I should not.   I have married whom I should not.   I have perpetuated what I should not.   All is clear. . . .

[*He goes out.   Creon drives out the Shepherd.*

CREON. Who was the linen-maid and foster-sister he was talking about?

TIRESIAS. Women cannot hold their tongues.   Jocasta must have made out that her crime had been committed by a servant to see what effect it had on Oedipus.

[*He holds his arm and listens with bent head.   Forbidding murmur.   The little Antigone, with hair dishevelled, appears on the balcony.*

ANTIGONE. Uncle!   Tiresias!   Come up, quickly!   Hurry, it's horrible!   I heard shrieks inside; mother, my darling mother, doesn't move any more, she has fallen like a log, and my dear, dear father is writhing over her body and stabbing at his eyes with her big golden brooch.   There's blood everywhere.   I'm frightened!   I'm too frightened, come up . . . come up, quickly. . . .

[*She goes in.*

CREON. This time nothing shall prevent me. . . .

TIRESIAS. Yes, I shall.   I tell you, Creon, the finishing touches are being put to a masterpiece of horror.   Not a word, not a gesture.   It would be improper for us to cast over it so much as a shadow of ourselves.

CREON. Sheer insanity!

TIRESIAS. Sheer wisdom. . . .   You must admit——

CREON. No! Besides, power falls once more into my hands.
> [*He frees himself, and at the very moment when he bounds forward the door opens. Oedipus appears, blind. Antigone is clinging to his clothes.*

TIRESIAS. Stop!

CREON. I shall go mad! Why, but why has he done that? Better have killed himself.

TIRESIAS. His pride does not desert him. He wanted to be the happiest of men, now he wants to be the most unhappy.

OEDIPUS. Let them drive me out, let them finish me off, stone me, strike down the foul beast!

ANTIGONE. Father!

TIRESIAS. Antigone! My soothsaying staff! Offer it to him from me. It will bring him some luck.
> [*Antigone kisses the hand of Tiresias and carries the staff to Oedipus.*

ANTIGONE. Tiresias offers you his staff.

OEDIPUS. Is he there? . . . I accept it, Tiresias. . . . I accept it. . . . Do you remember, seventeen years ago, I saw in your eyes that I should become blind, and I couldn't understand it? I see it all clearly now, Tiresias, but I am in pain. . . . I suffer. . . . The journey will be hard.

CREON. We must not let him cross the town, it would cause an awful scandal.

TIRESIAS. [*In a low voice.*] In a town of plague? And besides, you know, they saw the king Oedipus wished to be; they won't see the king he is now.

CREON. Do you mean he will be invisible because he is blind?

TIRESIAS. Almost.

CREON. Well, I can tell you I have had enough of your riddles and symbols. *My* head is firmly fixed on my shoulders and my feet planted firmly on the ground. I shall give my orders.

TIRESIAS. Your police may be well organized, Creon; but where this man goes they will not have the slightest power.

CREON. I——
> [*Tiresias seizes his arm and puts his hand over his mouth. . . . For Jocasta appears in the doorway. Jocasta, dead, white, beautiful, with closed eyes. Her long scarf is wound round her neck.*

OEDIPUS. Jocasta! You, dear! You alive!

JOCASTA. No, Oedipus. I am dead. You can see me because you are blind; the others cannot see me.

OEDIPUS. Tiresias is blind. . . .

JOCASTA. Perhaps he can see me faintly . . . but he loves me, he won't say anything. . . .

OEDIPUS. Wife, do not touch me! . . .

JOCASTA. Your wife is dead, hanged, Oedipus. I am your mother. It's your mother who is coming to help you. . . . How would you even get down these steps alone, my poor child?

OEDIPUS. Mother!

JOCASTA. Yes, my child, my little boy. . . . Things which appear abominable to human beings, if only you knew, from the place where I live, if only you knew how unimportant they are!

OEDIPUS. I am still on this earth.

JOCASTA. Only just. . . .

CREON. He is talking with phantoms, he's delirious. I shall not allow that little girl——

TIRESIAS. They are in good care.

CREON. Antigone! Antigone! I am calling you. . . .

ANTIGONE. I don't want to stay with my uncle! I don't want to, I don't want to stay in the house. Dear father, dear father, don't leave me! I will show you the way, I will lead you. . . .

CREON. Thankless creature.

OEDIPUS. Impossible, Antigone. You must be a good girl. . . . I cannot take you with me.

ANTIGONE. Yes, you can!

OEDIPUS. Are you going to desert your sister Ismene?

ANTIGONE. She must stay with Eteocles and Polynices. Take me away, please! Please! Don't leave me alone! Don't leave me with uncle! Don't leave me at home!

JOCASTA. The child is so pleased with herself. She imagines she is your guide. Let her think she is. Take her. Leave everything to me.

OEDIPUS. Oh! . . .   [*He puts his hand to his head.*

JOCASTA. Are you in pain, dear?

OEDIPUS. Yes, my head, my neck and arms. . . . It's fearful.

JOCASTA. I'll give you a dressing at the fountain.

OEDIPUS. [*Breaking down.*] Mother . . .

JOCASTA. Who would have believed it? That wicked old scarf and that terrible brooch! Didn't I say so time and again?

CREON. It's utterly impossible.   I shall not allow a madman to go out free with Antigone.   It is my duty to——

TIRESIAS. Duty!   They no longer belong to you; they no longer come under your authority.

CREON. And pray whom should they belong to?

TIRESIAS. To the people, poets, and unspoiled souls.

JOCASTA. Forward!   Grip my dress firmly . . . don't be afraid.
                                                    [*They start off.*

ANTIGONE. Come along, father dear . . . let's go. . . .

OEDIPUS. Where do the steps begin?

JOCASTA AND ANTIGONE. There is the whole of the platform yet. . . . [*They disappear . . . Jocasta and Antigone speak in perfect unison.*] Careful . . . count the steps. . . .   One, two, three, four, five. . . .

CREON. And even supposing they leave the town, who will look after them, who will admit them?

TIRESIAS. Glory.

CREON. You mean rather dishonour, shame. . . .

TIRESIAS. Who knows?

CURTAIN

THE MASK AND THE FACE

A Grotesque Comedy in Three Acts

BY LUIGI CHIARELLI

From the Italian
by
NOEL DE VIC BEAMISH

CHARACTERS

COUNT PAOLO GRAZIA, *aged 35*
LUCIANO SPINA, *a lawyer, aged 30*
CIRILLO ZANOTTI, *a banker, aged 50*
MARCO MILIOTTI, *a magistrate, aged 40*
GIORGIO ALAMARI, *a sculptor, aged 25*
PIERO PUCCI, *aged 25*

SAVINA GRAZIA, *aged 28*
MARTA SETTA, *aged 25*
ELISA ZANOTTI, *aged 30*
WANDA SERINI, *aged 20*

ANDREA
GIACOMO } *Servants*
TERESA

ACT I

Time, the present, on Lake Como

A large room in Count Grazia's house on Lake Como. Through wide french windows at the back one looks on a flowered terrace overlooking the lake and the opposite shores. On right and left stairs leading down to the shore. At the back of the terrace a few little tables, more in advance, near the windows, a card table.

The room well and tastefully furnished, is in semi-obscurity. The lake is bathed in moonlight.

At the rise of the curtain Marta is seated at the piano playing a tango. Wanda and Piero are dancing.

The others are talking and watching the dancers. Savina and Luciano are on the terrace.

Suddenly, continuing to play, Marta turns and looks at them.

ELISA. Charming! How well they dance.

GIORGIO. Beautifully. Quite a Tanagra.

ELISA. Was the man who invented the tango called Tanagra?

MARTA. [*Abruptly.*] It's immoral! It should be forbidden.

CIRILLO. My dear child, nothing is immoral. You would have to start by putting a ban on man.

MARTA. That is true.

CIRILLO. So that women could appear moral.

MARTA. How rude!

ELISA. Do you like dancing?

GIORGIO. No.

ELISA. What a pity.

WANDA. [*Suddenly stops dancing. To Marta.*] Stop! Stop! [*Marta stops playing. Wanda pointing to the lake.*] Listen! Do you hear? The Americans again.

ELISA. Oh! the lovers. [*A man's voice is heard rising from the lake in the slow rhythm of an American song. All are silent for a moment, listening.*] How they must adore each other!

CIRILLO. Who knows! It seems to me that those two young people are a bit too pretentious. Lake Como ... moonlight ... and sentimental songs.

ELISA. I won't allow you to say a word against them.

CIRILLO. I 'm not saying anything against them.   I 'm merely
  sorry for them.

ELISA. Heretic! [*To Giorgio.*] Aren't they too sweet?

[*Moves away talking to him.*

PIERO. Exportation love!

MARTA. Italy has become the sanatorium of fugitive adulterers!

WANDA. I heard they were forced to run away because her
  husband was such a brute.

PAOLO. A husband who has any self respect does not allow his
  wife to run away with a lover.

MARTA. What would you do?

[*Turns laughingly towards Savina.*

SAVINA. [*Annoyed.*] Marta!   [*She goes towards the terrace.*

MARTA. This is quite amusing.

PAOLO. What should I do?   Kill her.   Yes, kill her.   She
  knows that quite well. [*To Savina who turns round.*] Don't
  you, Savina?

SAVINA. Of course, darling.

PAOLO. You see . . .

MARTA. And what would you do with the lover?

PAOLO. Nothing.   A man should consider every other man as his
  wife's potential lover.

MARCO. Men are always in the right.

MARTA. Yes.   Duty was invented for women.

CIRILLO. To give more spice to their sins.

ELISA. And a stimulant to their imagination

CIRILLO. God help women if man had no imagination!   A poor
  lot of things they would appear.

WANDA. Look!   There they are.   I can see them quite clearly.
  Oh! how happy they must be.

ELISA. I think they are just too sweet!

WANDA. Do any of you know them?

ELISA. I saw them one evening on the beach.

WANDA. Is she beautiful?

ELISA. I can't say.

MARTA. Young?

ELISA. Very.   He is marvellous.   Just like one of those posters
  advertising the Olympic Games.

WANDA. They never leave each other.

ELISA. How perfectly marvellous.

WANDA. And the blinds of the villa are always drawn.

CIRILLO. Forging bank notes, probably.

WANDA. They only go out in the evening, and drift along in their boat.   Singing . . . dreaming . . .

CIRILLO. Yes, till one day they will wake up.   Just like those two last year.

MARTA. Last year?   What happened last year?   I was not here.

CIRILLO. Well.   Two young Americans came along here on the lake: lovers.   And one fine day the husband turned up.

MARTA. And then?

CIRILLO. Nothing, my dear, nothing.   He forgave her and took her back.

PAOLO. Damned idiot.

CIRILLO. Why?

PAOLO. Why?   Because a husband who forgives is ridiculous. A hundred times ridiculous.   And nothing is worse than ridicule.   For a husband like your American, there is only one solution.   Suicide!

PIERO. I heard that the lover paid the husband twenty thousand dollars, and his travelling expenses as well.

PAOLO. Of course if he makes a profession of it . . .

ELISA. I am sure that as soon as she arrived back she must have died of a broken heart.

WANDA. Oh, be quiet.   If you talk like that you will make us all lose any wish to have a husband.

PIERO. Alas!   A wish that vanishes only with matrimony.

WANDA. Idiot!

ELISA. For women a husband is a necessary misfortune.

WANDA. Tell me, Piero, if I was untrue to you, would you kill me?

PIERO. I suppose that means that you are quite certain I shall marry you?

WANDA. [Lowering her voice.] You know that nothing else is possible.

PIERO. My sweet, all is possible . . . even that I shall marry you.

WANDA. And that I shall scratch your eyes out!

CIRILLO. What are those two love-birds up to now?   They are always bickering.   It's stupid.   There won't remain anything for them to do when they are married.   It compromises their wedded bliss.

PIERO. She asked me if I would kill her if she was untrue to me.

CIRILLO. And what did you answer?   No, no.   To kill her would be to take the matter seriously, and that would be folly.   She is much too charming.

ELISA. Still talking about love and faithfulness.

PIERO. I have that unfortunate lack of taste, my dear.

ELISA. Faithfulness is not a virtue, it is ignorance.

MARTA. That is why it is necessary to give the unfaithful a lesson.

WANDA. By killing them? I hardly see how they would profit by the lesson.

MARCO. Others would.

CIRILLO. Oh, yes! With ideas like that what a damn lot of foolish things you could do in life, young man.

PIERO. But that is just what women love us for; our foolishness. It is only when we are really stupid that women forgive us for our enormous superiority over them.

SAVINA. Well, have you men finished pulling women to pieces? You are forgetting your game of poker this evening.

PIERO. You are laughing at us? It's true you have nothing to fear.

PAOLO. I should think not.

CIRILLO. [*To Savina.*] And what do you think of all the fine ideas put forth by these gentlemen?

SAVINA. Oh, just a little revolt of the slaves. [*Looking at her husband.*] Led by a tiny Spartacus.

PAOLO. Savina! The subject displeases me. Who's for a game of poker?

MARCO AND OTHER VOICES. I . . . I . . .

PAOLO. Too many . . . five only. [*Rings the bell.*] You?

MARCO. Yes.

PAOLO. [*To the manservant who enters.*] Get the table ready on the terrace. [*Servant goes out and re-enters with the cards and chips; goes on the terrace and prepares the table. Paolo to Piero.*] You?

PIERO. Yes. [*To Giorgio, who is talking to Elisa, and who answers in the affirmative.*] You? and——

WANDA. And I . . .

PAOLO. [*Hesitating.*] You . . . no . . .

WANDA. Yes, me. Last night I lost a hundred and twenty lire, and I want to pick up.

PAOLO. Oh, all right. Then we are complete now.

[*Goes, followed by several others, towards the terrace.*

ELISA [*To Giorgio in a low voice.*] You are leaving me for . . . poker?

GIORGIO. Yes.

ELISA. Charming.   So we understand each other?

GIORGIO. Perfectly.

[Goes on the terrace; the players take their places at the table.

ELISA. Alamari, the sculptor, has asked me if I will go to his studio and pose for him.   Just the head.   May I?

CIRILLO. Of course.   Go to his studio and pose . . . and repose.

ELISA. Thank you.   [Walks away.

CIRILLO. And I can also . . . repose.

[Lights a cigar, turns down the light, and stretches out comfortably in an arm-chair.   The only lamp which remains still alight hardly illuminates the room.   Meanwhile the players have started their game.   Elisa leans over Giorgio's shoulder, watching.   Marta turns over the pages of a magazine.   Luciano, smoking a cigarette, stands looking out upon the lake.

PAOLO. Play. [To Savina.] Savina, we are thirsty.

SAVINA. What would you like?

MARCO. Something cool.

PAOLO. Tea.

SAVINA. Cold tea?

MARCO. Good idea.   Twenty.

PIERO. Pass.   I would prefer orange juice.

WANDA. Oh, I never have any luck.   Pass.

MARCO. Flush.

PAOLO. That's the limit.   And you took three cards!

ELISA. You will never be lucky in love!

SAVINA. [After having asked the others.] I'll have the drinks brought in at once. [She enters the room. To Cirillo.] Hallo! What are you doing here, philosopher?

CIRILLO. Like all true philosophers ... nothing. [To Luciano, who strolls towards him.] What do you think of it?

LUCIANO. Of what?

CIRILLO. Of philosophy, of course.

LUCIANO. Oh! . . .

CIRILLO. Well?

LUCIANO. What did you say?

CIRILLO. You are extremely absent-minded, young man.

LUCIANO. I beg your pardon.   I was . . . thinking.

CIRILLO. Of a girl?

LUCIANO. Who said so?

CIRILLO. You must be an enthusiast.

LUCIANO. For what?   Philosophy?

CIRILLO. If you like. Good, very good. You know there is a certain resemblance between philosophy and women. Both have a tendency to complicate the most simple questions

LUCIANO. Do you think so?

CIRILLO. Well, you should know. You are a woman's lawyer, aren't you? How is it that this evening you never said a word in their defence?

LUCIANO. Defend them! useless fatigue! It is not even necessary in court.

CIRILLO. You are right. We men have our work cut out to defend ourselves from them.

SAVINA. [*Entering on left.*] Here is something for thirsty souls. [*To Cirillo and Luciano.*] What are you two plotting in the dark?

LUCIANO. We are discussing philosophy.

SAVINA. Tell me another! [*The servant enters carrying a tray with drinks. To the servant.*] Give one to Signor Cirillo. Philosophy makes one thirsty. What will you have?

CIRILLO. I really don't know. You embarrass me. I never know what I should drink.

SAVINA. Cold tea?

CIRILLO. It will prevent me from sleeping. I think it is more difficult to choose a drink than a wife.

SAVINA. Not really?

CIRILLO. Oh yes . . . wives are all the same . . . and——

SAVINA. You can't complain, you have a model wife.

CIRILLO. I don't deny it. . . . It is just philosophy talking.

SAVINA. Help yourself; [*Going towards Luciano.*] and you . . .

LUCIANO. Thanks, I'm not thirsty. [*Lowering his voice.*] I'm going now. Have you opened the door of the veranda?

SAVINA. Yes.

LUCIANO. I shall wait in your room. Come soon.

SAVINA. Be careful!

LUCIANO. Don't worry. [*Indicating Paolo.*] He'll be some time yet As usual! Poker before anything.

SAVINA. [*To Cirillo.*] Well?

CIRILLO. Cold tea! I shan't sleep a wink. [*Goes out on the terrace with Savina. The servant, after Cirillo has helped himself, goes out on the terrace and serves the others.*] I shall get my wife to sing me a lullaby.

ELISA How perfectly sweet!

MARTA. [*Advances, sipping her drink. To Luciano.*] You have not said a word to me all the evening.

LUCIANO. The others made up for it.

MARTA. You seem preoccupied.

LUCIANO. Nonsense.

MARTA. Why aren't you playing?

LUCIANO. I'm going.

MARTA. What, now?

LUCIANO. I promised the Savuccis to look in.

MARTA. At this time of night?

LUCIANO. They usually sit up till four in the morning.   Playing, dancing . . .

MARTA. So you won't see me home again to-night.

LUCIANO. On the contrary.   I shall be delighted if you are still here when I return.

MARTA. You behave as though we were already married.

LUCIANO. That remark would fit Piero.

MARTA. Piero is always near Wanda.

LUCIANO. Yes, a bit too much.

MARTA. Evil tongues.

LUCIANO. It's their business.

MARTA. Exactly.   But how about you and me?   Don't you think that you slightly exaggerate on the other side?   It was all arranged that we should be married now, in September. Instead, you talk of putting it off till next year.

LUCIANO. My dear girl, I have already explained to you that the state of my affairs at the present moment are not in a very favourable condition.

MARTA. Yes, yes.   You have told me all that   Meanwhile our marriage is always postponed to an indefinite date.

LUCIANO   The day will come . . .

MARTA. You do not seem to be particularly enthusiastic.

LUCIANO   I shall be when the moment arrives.

MARTA. Meanwhile——

LUCIANO. Meanwhile what?

MARTA. Meanwhile you are going to the Savucci's this evening.

LUCIANO. What have they got to do with it?

MARTA. Oh . .   nothing.

LUCIANO. [*Trying to hide his irritation.*] What on earth are you getting at?   Do explain yourself.

MARTA   Explain myself?   Are you or are you not going to the Savuccis'?

LUCIANO. Well?

MARTA. That's all. What do you want me to explain? Have a good time.

LUCIANO. They are clients of mine. It is a duty visit.

MARTA. At midnight?

LUCIANO. They invited me.

MARTA. I'll come with you.

LUCIANO. [*Alarmed.*] Where?

MARTA. No ... no. I won't come. Let us live in peace.

LUCIANO. I see no reason why it should be otherwise.

MARTA. That's right.

CIRILLO. [*Entering, sneezes violently.*] Ugh! This damp night air will be the death of me.   [*Returns to his arm-chair.*

LUCIANO. Well, I'll say good night.

CIRILLO. Going? What's the hurry?

LUCIANO. I shall probably see you later. [*To Marta.*] So long, darling.

MARTA. Bye-bye!

LUCIANO. [*Going on to the terrace. To Savina.*] Good night, Signora Savina.

SAVINA. Are you going?

PAOLO. Pass. [*To Luciano.*] So soon?

LUCIANO. I am just going over to the Savuccis'. We shall see each other later. I'll come to see Marta home.

SAVINA. You are sure to find these fanatics still here. We, on the contrary, shall meet to-morrow. I'm going to bed. I am so tired.

MARCO. I'm afraid we do rather overdo it, don't we?

SAVINA. Not at all. But you know I'm such a sleepyhead that there comes a moment when I just can't keep my eyes open. So, please forgive me.

LUCIANO. [*Nodding to the others. To the servant who enters.*] My hat and stick.

    [*The servant goes out and returns with the hat and stick.*

PAOLO. [*To Luciano.*] Then we shall expect you later. My regards to Signora Teresa.

LUCIANO. All right. Cheerio!   [*Goes out by the terrace.*

SAVINA. Well, good night all. Enjoy yourselves.

GIORGIO. One card.

PAOLO. Three cards. [*Kisses Savina on the cheek.*] Good night, my dear. Sleep well.

SAVINA. [*Entering the room, followed by Marta.*] Good night, Signor Cirillo.

CIRILLO. Good night, Signora Savina.   How I envy you.

SAVINA. Come and keep me company!

CIRILLO. It is quite evident that you have firmly made up your mind to remain an honest woman.

SAVINA. Oh, I wouldn't trust you.

CIRILLO. Thanks.   You leave me a few illusions.

MARTA. [*Who is smoking a cigarette, to Savina who goes towards left.*] I 'll come and finish my cigarette in your room.   Then you can show me those two hats you bought yesterday.

SAVINA. My dear! at this time of night?

MARTA. Why not?

SAVINA. No, I would prefer you to see them on.   To-morrow I am going to wear one of them, the mauve velvet, probably.

MARTA. Velvet!

SAVINA. All the fashion this year, my dear . . . a velvet in summer . . . not logical, I know . . . but anyway heads are not logical, so why should hats be?   Good night.

MARTA. One can at least change one's hat.

SAVINA. Alas! too often.   If you saw my milliner's bill.

MARTA. How can one help it?   We must please men.

SAVINA. We are slaves to fashion.

MARTA. Women's fashions are a little dictated by the taste of their lovers.

SAVINA. They are quite crazy in Paris.

MARTA. And here also.

SAVINA. [*Trying to get away from Marta.*] Well?

MARTA. Well . . . I think I 'll sit and read something till Luciano comes back.

SAVINA. A good idea. [*Handing her a magazine.*] Look, this came to-day.

MARTA. Who can tell at what time Luciano will come back.   He has gone to the Savuccis'.

SAVINA. Charming people.

GIORGIO. There!   I 'll pay and finish.   I 've had enough for to-night.

MARTA. Yes, charming.   And he has left me here to wait for him.

SAVINA. Well, you 're engaged to him, aren't you.   It 's natural that you should wait.   Thank goodness I haven't to sit up and wait for anybody.   I 'm dead with sleep.   Good night.   I 'm off.

[*Goes out quickly on left.   Marta watches her go, makes a gesture of disgust, and goes on to the terrace.*

GIORGIO. [*Followed by Elisa, enters the room. They do not see Cirillo stretched out in the arm-chair.*] Well, what news?

ELISA. Darling! My husband has given me permission to go to your place. Oh, I am so thrilled, I can hardly wait till to-morrow when I shall be in your arms.

GIORGIO. My sweet!

ELISA. At three then . . .

GIORGIO. At—— [*Turning, catches sight of Cirillo, who suddenly appears to be asleep.*] My God! your husband!

ELISA. Oh . . . asleep. . . . He is always asleep.

GIORGIO. If he has heard anything . . .

ELISA. No . . . besides . . . he is so good.

GIORGIO. You complain of that?

ELISA. Of course. Unfortunately it is the virtue of others that leads us to sin.

GIORGIO. Probably.

ELISA. A husband like that is not even worth betraying. To think that the only things that can give any spice to married life are just the necessary risks of deception, the lies, the subterfuges . . .

GIORGIO Therefore if you . . . the fault is his?

ELISA. Of course. I should have married a man like Savina's husband, Paolo. A man in love with me, ardent and cruel, who would have held me as a slave, subdued me with caresses and fear. A man who would have placed in my life a background of voluptuousness and tragedy. And instead . . . look at him there . . . asleep. Do you know, once I deliberately let him catch me, so as to provoke some terrible reaction, and what happened? Nothing. He forgave me. It is always the same. Drama recoils from my life, and without drama love is tame, sad, vulgar.

GIORGIO. I say, don't let us joke about it.

ELISA. Your kisses will compensate for all I have suffered.

PAOLO. Oh, this is the last straw. I'm not playing any more.

[*A burst of protest from the players, who wish to retain him.*

MARTA. [*In a state of suppressed nervousness, comes from terrace, crosses room, and goes out on left, passing before Cirillo.*] Sleep well?

CIRILLO. [*Pretending to start up half awake.*] Who? Oh! Ah! [*Sees his wife.*] I'm sorry, my dear, I must have dozed off.

ELISA. Rest, darling. Sleep. It does you so much good.

CIRILLO. Oh . . . er . . . yes.

MARCO. [*To Giorgio and Elisa.*] You two take a hand.   Just for half an hour. [*Elisa and Giorgio sit down at the table and play.*

PAOLO. [*Entering the room.*] Phew! that's enough for to-night. [*Seeing Cirillo.*] What are you doing?

CIRILLO. [*Rising.*] I . . . I was half asleep.

MARTA. [*Enters left and goes on terrace. She is growing more and more unnerved. Passes before Cirillo.*] Good morning! Did you sleep well?

CIRILLO. What on earth is the matter with Marta? She is running round like a lost soul.

PAOLO. She is waiting for Luciano.   Waiting for her fiancé. It's love!

CIRILLO. It's marriage.

PAOLO. It seems to me that marriage is a much maligned institution.   For example . . . I am happy.

CIRILLO. So am I.   It's just a question of getting reconciled. . . .

PAOLO. To what?

CIRILLO. To your own wife.

PAOLO. It is also a question of trying to understand women.

CIRILLO. There is only one way to understand woman. The more they are loved the more they feel they are understood.

PAOLO. Don't you love your wife?

CIRILLO. I . .   Oh . . . but——

PAOLO. What?

CIRILLO. I did not say that my wife feels herself to be misunderstood . . . in life.

PAOLO. Well . . . what then?

CIRILLO. Well, life is something more vast than matrimony. Life comprises . . . all . . . all.

PAOLO. I don't understand.   I don't know.

CIRILLO [*Smiling sadly.*] Go on! You understand quite well. Why pretend? Yes. You know, everybody knows. We all do.

PAOLO. What?

CIRILLO. Yes.

PAOLO. You mean——

CIRILLO. Of course.

PAOLO. Oh!

CIRILLO. Eh? . . .

PAOLO. Your wife?

CIRILLO. My wife.

PAOLO. And you?

CIRILLO. And I!

PAOLO. [*Ironically.*] Oh! Magnificent!

CIRILLO. H'm! magnificent? I should hardly call it that.

PAOLO. And you mean to say that you submit? . . .

CIRILLO. One adapts oneself to circumstances!

PAOLO. And you allow your wife to betray you like that?

CIRILLO. Let us be just. Who betrayed her in the first place? I did. I married her when I was twenty years older than she.

PAOLO. But . . . hang it all, man, she knew that when she married you. She should have thought of it before.

CIRILLO. But I knew it too. And it was I who should have thought of it first, because it was in my interest, because it was I who ran the risk of becoming . . . what I am.

PAOLO. So you married her already prepared for——

CIRILLO. And if I did? All men of spirit should marry with that idea. Then they know what to expect.

PAOLO. Oh! I should never have stood it.

CIRILLO. No? And what then? You see, if I had been one of those terrible husbands . . . she——

PAOLO. Would not have been untrue to you.

CIRILLO. She would have betrayed me just the same, and I should have looked ridiculous. And, after all, why . . . ridiculous?

PAOLO. What? Don't you feel ridiculous all the same?

CIRILLO. I? Good Lord! No. There are too many of us in the same box. And when you are a crowd you feel normal. I'm just a normal husband.

PAOLO. Oh, at the very first symptom of anything of the sort I should have been without mercy.

CIRILLO. I know. You would have killed her. But suppose I had killed her the first time. What then? To-day I should find myself again in precisely the same position with my second wife or my tenth mistress.

PAOLO. No. The other, or the others, would no longer have dared.

CIRILLO. My dear Paolo, women dare all. It is only danger that tempts them. The man who really attracts them is the man who knows how to incite them into committing the most irreparable follies. Ah, you don't know women!

PAOLO. I know myself, and I know that I would kill her.

CIRILLO. I know that, too, and I know you. But why?

PAOLO. Why? Because marriage is a pact for life, and it is

only justice that if a woman breaks it she should pay with her life.

CIRILLO. My dear boy, that sounds like Napoleon. You are the Napoleon of husbands. But even Napoleon was not particularly lucky in marriage. Nothing is sacred to women.

PAOLO. What vile cynicism. You almost make me . . .
[*Makes a gesture of repulsion.*

CIRILLO. I also . . . at times . . . almost. . . . But then when one looks closely at humanity one ends by being even indulgent with oneself. And besides what I have told you . . really at the bottom of my heart there is something which I do not say . . if I did . . . then probably I should become ridiculous. For her, too, will come the weariness, the nausea, and the disillusion. She will see that the ashes of love are a little sad . . . a little vile. And then . . . and then one day perhaps she will turn to me. From the first that was all I could hope for.

PAOLO. And so you, the husband, resign yourself to be the last? Even if you are.

CIRILLO. Yes. Women are so much wiser than we. In their feelings they have less pride. They always wish to be the last love of the man they love. Such exquisite delicacy on their part.

PAOLO. Oh, shut up, you disgust me. Ugh!

MARTA. [*Entering on Cirillo's last words. She is very agitated, but tries to control herself. To Paolo.*] Oh! You are here?

PAOLO. Yes.

MARTA. [*To Cirillo, indicating Paolo.*] What is wrong with him?

CIRILLO. Oh, he is a too susceptible husband.

MARTA. [*Pretending to have understood something else and simulating great surprise.*] Oh, what are you saying? You don't mean . . .

CIRILLO. You try and calm him.

MARTA. [*Hesitatingly.*] Come, come, Signor Paolo, it is nothing, you are wrong.

PAOLO. What?

MARTA. But, of course. Don't make a mountain out of a molehill.

PAOLO. Oh, you call it a molehill?

MARTA. What else? One must not judge by appearances.

PAOLO. [*Looking sharply at Marta, who turns her head away.*] Eh?

MARTA. It's so absurd. Perhaps a little foolishness, a little flirting, but from that to——

PAOLO. To what?

CIRILLO. [Uneasy at the turn the conversation is taking.] Signora Marta!

MARTA. [To Paolo.] No, no. You must not upset yourself like that. I assure you that you are mistaken. I know her so well. I can swear that she never——

[Meanwhile she has backed towards the second door on left, and stands before it, as though wishing, without his understanding her aim, to prevent Paolo entering Savina's room.

PAOLO. [Starting forward.] She. . . . Who?

CIRILLO. [To Marta.] What have you said?

MARTA. [As though amazed and bewildered.] But . . . weren't you speaking of——

PAOLO. Of?

CIRILLO. Oh, of no one!

PAOLO. Shut up! [To Marta.] Of whom?

MARTA. I don't know.

PAOLO. Speak!

MARCO [From the terrace.] I say, you people, do be quiet.

MARTA. [To Cirillo.] But . . . what did you tell me?

CIRILLO. I? You are crazy. [To Paolo.] Don't listen to her. Can't you see she doesn't know what she is talking about.

MARTA. Oh! I don't understand a thing.

PAOLO. [Advancing towards her. Hoarsely.] You were speaking . . . of . . . of her.

MARTA. But I thought that——

PAOLO. Of Savina.

CIRILLO. But it is all a mistake . . . don't you understand?

PAOLO. By God! I will know.

MARCO. Oh, do be quiet! What on earth is the matter with you all?

[The card players rise from the table and come to the threshold of the room.

PAOLO. [To Marta.] You know. You shall tell me.

MARTA. You are mistaken. No . . .

PAOLO. Ah, you won't. Then, by heavens, she will.

[Goes to enter Savina's room.

MARTA. [Barring the way.] No.

PAOLO [Stops short.] What?

CIRILLO. Paolo. [*Catches him by the arm.*] Don't be a fool.

PAOLO. Damn you! Let me pass. [*Shakes Cirillo off and rushes through second door on left. Slams the door behind him. All run after him anxiously with the exception of Marta, who remains alone, frightened and in a state of tension at what is going to happen. Voices and tumult from within, and dominating all the voice of Paolo shouting.*] Open, open . . . or I'll break the door in . . . open! [*Knocks furiously at the door of his wife's room. A few moments, then Paolo's voice again, frantically.*] Open, by God, open! [*Finally Paolo flings himself at the door, which crashes open. More cries, more tumult. Marta, who has remained motionless, grows rigid, then suddenly falls into an arm-chair beside her. After a few moments all re-enter on right. Paolo is in the midst of his friends, who are trying to calm him. He is still in a state of frenzied fury, uttering inarticulate sounds.*] My God! what more do you want of me? Haven't you given them all the time they wanted to get away.

MARCO. It is no use to go on raging now, you must think of some other means of avenging your honour.

[*Places the revolver he has wrested from Paolo on the table.*

PAOLO. My honour? Are you trying to be funny? It doesn't exist.

PIERO. Who is talking of honour? . . . why, only barbarians . . .

PAOLO. Be quiet. All of you. Not another word. You were all their accomplices. You all knew. Only I was blind like any other idiot of a husband . . . blind . . . ridiculous. . . . Yes, that's it . . . ridiculous.

MARCO. For heaven's sake, calm yourself, man. Later you can see what is best to do.

PAOLO. Yes . . . later . . . I shall go to court. That's right, isn't it? To court . . . to hear a judge tell me which article of the law authorizes an injured husband to be made a laughing-stock of. Meanwhile, she . . . she laughs at me. To think I had not even the satisfaction of seeing who the scoundrel was. . . . But, of course, he is only following his male instincts . . . and he is right, seeing that all women . . . all . . . all . . are open doors.

MARTA. [*To Elisa.*] Take me away. . . . Take me away. Take me home. Oh, my God! I can't stand it.

ELISA. Yes, of course. You shall come with us. Calm yourself.

PAOLO. [*To all.*] Well, what are you all doing here? You have condoled with me, haven't you? Counting, perhaps, on passing the night watching this corpse of a husband, what? [*To Cirillo.*] Are you satisfied? Pleased, eh?

CIRILLO. I? What are you talking about?

PAOLO. Well, aren't I the normal husband now? The Napoleon of normal husbands! Oh, you make me sick!

CIRILLO. Don't be absurd.

ELISA. What does he mean?

CIRILLO. He is suffering.

ELISA. Poor man!

CIRILLO. Yes, poor devil!

PAOLO. For God's sake leave me alone. Get out.

MARCO. Yes, yes. We are going . . . when you are calmer.

PAOLO. At once, I tell you.

MARCO. When you have promised not to do anything foolish.

PAOLO. At once, I said. My God, don't you realize that you exasperate me?

MARCO. Oh! all right, we'll go.

PIERO. [*Aside to Wanda.*] Take note for the future, my sweet.

WANDA. Take note yourself!

> [*Some shake hands with Paolo, the others, not quite sure what attitude they should assume, go away quietly. All go out by the terrace. Marta clings to Elisa's arm.*

PAOLO. [*When all have finally gone closes the big glass doors violently. The servant is seen outside clearing the table and putting out the lights.*] Oh! [*He walks excitedly about the room for a few moments, then suddenly in a hoarse, broken voice.*] But . . . why . . . why have I to suffer this? [*Flings himself into a chair, his head in his hands. A few moments pass. Suddenly Savina appears behind the glass doors and stands looking in at Paolo. Then opening the door quietly, enters, closes it again, and stands leaning against it. Paolo lifts his head, turns sharply round, sees his wife, jumps to his feet, and for a moment remains as though turned to stone, with staring eyes, gazing at her. Then suddenly he comes to life, springs at her, seizes her and pushes her brutally back a few steps.*] You . . . you. . . . [*She makes a gesture of entreaty, and seems as though she wishes to speak.*] Not a word! it is useless.

SAVINA. [*In a broken voice.*] Paolo!

PAOLO. Ah, so you have returned!

SAVINA. Listen. . . .

PAOLO. Have you come to laugh at me . . . you?——

SAVINA. To humble myself.

PAOLO. You succeeded in escaping me a few minutes ago, but you won't again, now I 've got you here.

SAVINA. If you love me . . . if——

PAOLO. I 'll show you how I love you!

[*Seizes her by the throat. Savina doesn't resist, she utters a little cry, he at once relaxes his grip and backs away from her with an instinctive gesture of horror at what he was about to do. They both remain gazing at each other. Paolo has clearly the conviction that he cannot commit this crime.*

SAVINA. [*After a long silence.*] Paolo!

[*With a violent gesture Paolo orders her to be silent. Another long silence.*

Paolo . . . do what you like with me.

PAOLO. [*Bitterly.*] Irony! . . . but don't imagine you are safe yet.

SAVINA. [*Who has understood that he can never kill her.*] No!

PAOLO. [*Looking at his hand, stretches it out towards her throat.*] God help me! I can't. [*With a gesture of horror he covers his face with his hands.*] The very touch of your skin . . . [*Shudders.*] Oh, why did they disarm me? [*Menacingly.*] But——

SAVINA. [*With great audacity takes the revolver from the table and hands it to him.*] Here 's your revolver, take it.

PAOLO. [*Makes a furious gesture to seize it, then his arm falls helplessly to his side. With rage.*] Oh, you vile woman!

[*Sinks down on a chair.*

SAVINA. No, no. . . . You will not kill me. . . .

PAOLO. No? Don't be too sure.

SAVINA. You will not kill me.

PAOLO. You 've risked everything . . . to . . . beat me.

SAVINA. I have risked less than you imagine.

PAOLO. Certainly your life isn't worth much at present.

SAVINA. Life! What does that matter? It is the least of things. I understand now that is perhaps the one thing I have never risked.

PAOLO. You are mad. I would have killed you.

SAVINA. No. Paolo, for heaven's sake, drop this mask. Be sincere with yourself. Look into your heart. Don't be a slave to your words and to your conventional ideas. At this moment all our future is at stake. Paolo, don't make matters worse . . . don't place an impassable barrier between us. Think, my dear, we can still save something . . . and be happy again.

PAOLO. No, no . . . you are dead to me.

SAVINA. It shall be as you wish . . . only think it over first.

PAOLO. [*To himself.*] For me . . . but for the others? Dead to me . . . an empty phrase.

SAVINA. [*With profound bitterness.*] And it's that which hurts you, not the fact that you have lost me!

PAOLO. [*Laughing harshly.*] Ridiculous!

SAVINA. [*Ironically.*] How terrible!

PAOLO. [*After a long silence.*] Well! there is only one thing to do. . . .

SAVINA. Anything you like.

PAOLO. You must go.

SAVINA. [*With pained surprise.*] Go?

PAOLO. You must disappear.

SAVINA. Exiled?

PAOLO. For ever.

SAVINA. For ever?

PAOLO. No one must suspect your departure. In less than an hour . . . in my car . . . we shall go to Switzerland. From there you will take the train to Paris . . . then to London. I shall see to the rest.

SAVINA. Paolo, what do you mean?

PAOLO. That is none of your business.

SAVINA. You make me afraid.

PAOLO. Afraid! You needn't be. . . . I am quite calm now.

SAVINA. It is not for myself . but for you.

PAOLO. For me? For me you should not have done what you have done.

SAVINA. What are you hiding from me? Let me leave to-morrow. Give me time to speak . . . to . . . to explain.

PAOLO. It is useless. . . . What do you hope for?

SAVINA Paolo . . . give me till to-morrow.

PAOLO. No. After what has happened have I not the right to turn you out of my house? It is the least I can do And . . . also . . . you will go far away and change your name You think I ask a lot? It is on that condition that I spare your life

SAVINA. Take another name?

PAOLO. I insist. I will see that you have what money you want for the moment. Later I shall arrange matters.

SAVINA. But . . . it's for ever, then?

PAOLO. What did you imagine? And understand this! No one must know . . not even he . . . so that he won't come to join you.

SAVINA. Would you mind?

PAOLO. Only because I do not wish any one to know where you are.   Remember you are dead . . . to all.

SAVINA. [*Disillusioned.*] Oh! you needn't have any doubt about that.   Does it really seem possible to you that I should be standing here before you if I still had a grain of feeling for that man?   No, no, all that is done with . . . finished.

PAOLO. Please keep your regrets to yourself.

SAVINA. It is not that which I regret.

PAOLO. I am not interested.   You see that I do not even ask his name.

SAVINA. What would be the use?

PAOLO. I have nothing more to say.

SAVINA. So you are adamant?

PAOLO. Absolutely.

SAVINA. Think, Paolo . . .

PAOLO. Go!

SAVINA. Paolo . . .

PAOLO. Be quiet!   And be sure that no one sees you.

SAVINA. [*Looking at him with great pity mixed with irony.*] My sentence of death commuted to one of exile!

[*Goes out slowly on left.*

PAOLO. [*Rings the bell, then sits down at a table and writes.   The servant enters by first door on right.*] Is there any one up but yourself?

ANDREA. No, Signor Count, Giacomo and Teresa have already gone to bed.

PAOLO. Bring the car round to the front door.

ANDREA. Shall I ring up the chauffeur?

PAOLO. No.   I shall drive myself.   When you have brought the car round take your bicycle and go at once to Como and send this telegram. [*Gives him the paper he has been writing.*] If you do not feel like coming back you can sleep in Como. . . .   Go.

[*The servant bows and exits by the first door on left.   Paolo watches him.*

It was all he could do to keep himself from laughing in my face!   So . . . it is beginning. . . .   Ah!

LUCIANO. [*Enters by the second door on left.   Tries to appear at ease.*] Hallo! have they all gone?   Where is Marta?

PAOLO. [*Assuming a tragic expression, goes towards him.*] Ah!   Heaven has sent you!

LUCIANO. What has happened?

PAOLO. I want your help.

LUCIANO. Why?

PAOLO. Why? Because [*Trying to produce the desired effect.*] I have killed my wife!

LUCIANO. [*Falling back.*] What?

PAOLO. She betrayed me . . . I killed her.

LUCIANO. Are you mad?

PAOLO. I killed her . . . killed her . . .

LUCIANO. [*Petrified.*] How? When?

PAOLO. An hour ago. Whilst we were all here, she . . . was in her room with a man.

LUCIANO. With a . . . man?

PAOLO. I surprised them . . . but . . . they had time to escape.

LUCIANO. [*Anxiously.*] And then?

PAOLO. Then . . . I was here alone . . . when . . . she . . . returned and entered, hoping, perhaps, that I would forgive her. [*Warming to his recital.*] Forgive her! . . . she could hope! She said something, I forget what. I flung myself at her . . . she uttered a cry. I dragged her on to the terrace and caught her by the throat . . . I can still feel my nails digging into her soft white flesh . . . she struggled . . . frantically. And I . . . at a moment . . . out of my mind, pushed her back, back against the balustrade . . . till she fell over into the lake. There was a cry . . . two white hands beating despairingly in the air . . . then circles . . . ever widening circles . . . and after . . nothing more . . . only silence. I had killed her.

[*He sinks back into the chair.*

LUCIANO. It 's atrocious! Horrible!

PAOLO. It was inevitable.

LUCIANO. [*After a silence . . . trying to steady his voice.*] And . . . he?

PAOLO. He . . . who? . . . the lover? I don't know who he is. I don't know anything. It doesn't interest me.

LUCIANO. [*With a sigh of relief.*] Ah!

PAOLO. And now this is where you come in.

LUCIANO. [*Starting.*] What?

PAOLO. Aren't you my best friend? To-morrow I am going to give myself up. You must defend me.

LUCIANO. No, no!

PAOLO. Why not?

LUCIANO. I . . . don't know. I . . . might fail.

PAOLO. On the contrary. You are the one man for the job.

You have known me for years. You know my character . . . my ideas. Only you can influence the jury and get me acquitted. My fate is in your hands.

LUCIANO. My God! [*Presses his hands to his head.*] No, no, I can't.

PAOLO. You can't? It is a question of saving me and you refuse. Why?

LUCIANO. Saving you? That's just it. I don't know if you will succeed.

PAOLO. I shall certainly be acquitted. Perhaps you think I had no right to kill that despicable woman?

LUCIANO. I don't know . . . I don't know.

PAOLO. Why do you defend her? Perhaps you have a reason? Explain yourself. . . .

LUCIANO. None at all, none. I agree. She was a shameless woman. All right. I accept. I 'll defend you.

PAOLO. At last! Then to-morrow morning we shall go to Como together and I shall give myself up. Good night! [*He holds out his hand to Luciano who, plunged in thought, does not see it.*] You won't shake hands with a murderer?

LUCIANO. Why, of course . . . with pleasure . . . I am so accustomed——

PAOLO. Till to-morrow then?

LUCIANO. [*Preparing to go.*] How calm you are.

PAOLO. After a great tragedy . . . one is numbed.

[*From the lake comes the sound of the Americans singing; it lasts till the end of the act.*

Sing! Sing! [*To Luciano.*] Will you go out by the gate? It will be quicker.

[*Opens the windows at the back, and stands aside to let Luciano pass. Luciano, seeing the lake, stops short, overcome by a vague timidity. He would like Paolo to precede him, and for a moment there is a scene of one inviting the other to pass. In the end Paolo, irritated, pushes past Luciano, and they both go out. The song drifts farther and farther away.*

SAVINA. [*Enters cautiously by the door on right. Takes a few steps. Looks out and leans against the window, then . . . with great bitterness.*] I have only been dead an hour, and already my lover calls me a shameless woman!

END OF ACT I

ACT II

Scene: *The same.   Ten months later.*

The room is crowded with flowers, bouquets, baskets, vases.   They are scattered about everywhere, on the furniture, on the floor.   To each offering is attached a card or ribbon.   A large flag flies from the terrace.   Through the big open windows comes the sound of a fête.   Andrea, Giacomo, and Teresa are on the terrace.

ANDREA. There. . . .   There. . . .   He is coming.

TERESA. Yes, yes!   Do you hear the music?
   [*The gay sound of a band and the cries and cheering of the crowd are heard.*

ANDREA. The town band is accompanying him!

TERESA. Every one is so delighted at his acquittal.

ANDREA. He must be happy to be coming home after all these months.

TERESA. While the countess . . .   Poor dear!

ANDREA. May her soul be at peace!

TERESA. Without Christian burial at the bottom of the lake.
   [*Wipes her eyes.*

ANDREA. If she had done her duty it would not have happened.

TERESA. Oh, you men are all alike!

ANDREA. Be quiet.   He is coming.   There he is!
   [*The music approaches mingled with the cries and plaudits of the crowd.   Andrea and Giacomo clap their hands enthusiastically.   Teresa, exulting, waves her handkerchief.   Andrea, Giacomo, and Teresa rush down the stairs one imagines on left, uttering cries of joy.   After a few moments Paolo appears, followed by the three servants.   He enters the room quickly, slightly annoyed at all this demonstration.*

PAOLO. [*To the servants.*]   Thank you, my friends.   Thank you.
   You are very kind.   [*Shake hands with the three who are greatly affected.*]   I also want to thank you for all you said in my favour at the trial.

ANDREA. Every word we said was gospel truth, Signor Count.

TERESA. Nothing but the truth!

PAOLO. Very good of you . . . very good of you, indeed.

ANDREA. [*Taking Paolo's hat and overcoat.*] Is there anything I can get you, Signor Count?

PAOLO. Oh! . . . just one moment.

ANDREA. We have an excellent lunch ready for you.

PAOLO. I've lunched already. [*Draws a deep breath.*] Oh! [*After a short silence.*] My God! Is that band going on all night! [*Takes notes from his pocketbook and gives them to Giacomo.*] Here, thank them from me, and tell them to go.

                        [*Giacomo goes out by terrace.*

And now . . . [*Perceives for the first time that the room is full of flowers.*] Heavens above! What on earth is all this?

ANDREA. Flowers that arrived for you this morning, Signor Count.

PAOLO. [*Dumbfounded.*] For me? . . . Good Lord! [*After remaining a few moments contemplating them in blank amazement he looks at the card attached to one of the baskets, then at another and another . . . and reads.*] 'From one great soul to another.' 'To one who dared!' 'To a hero!' Good God! [*He walks about the room shaking his head. The music ceases. A few cries and more applause. He sees the flag.*] And that?

ANDREA. We put it out as an expression of our joy, Signor Count. . . .

PAOLO. Oh, I see . . . a national fête.

ANDREA. Signor Count . . . may I present my wife.

PAOLO. Who? What, Teresa! You've married Teresa?

               [*Andrea and Teresa nod. Paolo is embarrassed.*

Oh, splendid! My congratulations.

ANDREA. Thank you, Signor Count.

TERESA. [*Curtseying.*] Thank you, Signor Count.

PAOLO. [*To change the conversation.*] And . . . what other news is there? Any letters?

ANDREA. Letters! Hundreds!

                    [*Goes out on left followed by Teresa.*

PAOLO. Ouf! I can't get the hang of all this. [*Looking at the flowers he makes a grimace.*] Might be a dancer's dressing-room! [*Sees Andrea and Teresa enter carrying a large basket piled up with letters.*] Now, what is this?

ANDREA. [*Placing the basket on a chair.*] Your correspondence, Signor Count.

PAOLO. What? All that? . . . [*Goes nervously to the basket, takes some letters, some telegrams, opens one and reads.*] 'I have seven million dollars, an ardent nature, a stainless past, an empty heart.—Emily.' Pah! [*Throws away the telegram in disgust. Opens a letter.*] 'I too have killed. I killed my husband because he betrayed me with a revolver.' H'm, the husband must have had exotic tastes! [*Sees Andrea and Teresa entering with another basket piled up with letters.*] What, another? No, no ... I've had enough. Take the damned things away ... burn them ... throw them in the lake ... anything!

       [*Andrea and Teresa go out again on left with baskets.*

Is there nothing serious in the world? They turn the most agonizing tragedy into farce! ... Buffoons! ... And it is for those people I.... Buffoons!

MARCO. [*Entering from terrace.*] May I?

PAOLO. Oh, it 's you?

MARCO. I felt I must come to tell you once again ...

PAOLO. That is nice of you.

MARCO. I don't know how to express all the joy I feel ...

PAOLO. Thank you ...

MARCO. But you do not look very happy.

PAOLO. Why should I not be?

MARCO. [*Seeing the flowers.*] All this enthusiasm, this admiration.... You must feel proud.

PAOLO. Up to a point.

MARCO. What? The homage of so many generous and admiring friends? ...

PAOLO. I know ... I know. It is very kind ... but ... rather embarrassing.

MARCO. Why?

PAOLO. Oh! I don't know.

MARCO. I understand. You did not expect it. A gust of wind blew you on to a pedestal, and to-day you are a celebrated man, famous and admired. A judge and jury and all the majesty of the law have legalized your act. So be at peace with your conscience as you are with the world.

PAOLO. All right. I 'll do as you say.

MARCO. My wife, too, who holds exactly the same opinion as I do on the question, will be here in a moment to congratulate you.

PAOLO. Your wife? ... You are married?

MARCO. Yes. I thought Luciano had told you.

PAOLO. No.   And . . . who is she?

MARCO. I have married Wanda.

PAOLO. What?

MARCO. Yes, Wanda.

PAOLO. [*Still more astonished.*] Wanda?

MARCO. But, of course, don't you remember her?

PAOLO. Oh, yes, I remember her very well.

MARCO. We were married six months ago.

PAOLO. [*After having looked at him a long time in silence, with a glance of subtle irony, holds out his hand.*] Congratulations!

MARCO. Thank you, old man.

PAOLO. My warmest congratulations!

MARCO. Thanks! . . . and I can say, without bragging, that it is an absolute success.

PAOLO. I am quite sure of that.

MARCO. We are ideally happy.

PAOLO. Of course.

MARCO. She is so pure . . . so enchanting.   I could never have found a better wife.

PAOLO. No doubt about that . . . and——

MARCO. Ah, you are thinking of Piero . . . the boy she was engaged to before?

PAOLO. Yes.

MARCO. Oh, he is a feather-brained young fool!   He would never have understood her.   He would have made her unhappy.

PAOLO. Quite true.

MARCO. They broke it off, but have remained very good friends. There is no harm when everything is done correctly.

PAOLO. Of course not.   Well. . . .   Well. . . .   I'm delighted to hear all this.

MARCO. Thank you. [*Wanda enters from the terrace, followed by Piero.*] Here she is!

PAOLO. [*Shaking hands with Wanda.*] How nice of you to come.

WANDA. Paolo . . . I am so happy to see you here again.

PAOLO. You are very kind.

PIERO. [*To Paolo.*] Hallo, old jail-bird!   We have already made all the flowery speeches, haven't we?

PAOLO. [*Annoyed.*] Thanks, thanks!

PIERO. I say! All these flowers!   Rather like a cocotte's boudoir.

PAOLO. Worse than that!

PIERO. Or an honest woman's then? [*Laughs.*] When are you going to marry again?

PAOLO. [*With intention.*] When you learn to respect women.

PIERO. Then you 'll have to wait till I 'm dead! It 's a pity!

> [*Laughs and turns to speak to Marco.*

PAOLO. [*To Wanda.*] So . . . I find you married! And with the last man I would have imagined.

WANDA. But——

PAOLO. Be wise! And . . . above all . . . prudent.

WANDA. Why do you say that to me?

PAOLO. Because in my long hours of solitude I have thought a lot, and now, I have understood, my dear, that life is not made up of formulas.

WANDA. I think I understand what you mean. . . .

PAOLO. That is already something! People should never be forced to face their own convictions. With thoughtless words and ideas we saddle ourselves with obligations, which, thank God! in the moment of necessity we forget, because . . if we remembered them they would lead inevitably to disaster. Men should have more courage, they should cast off the conventionalities which in their pride and vanity they have set up. They should forget all the lies they have uttered, so that finally they can be honest and sincere with themselves. It is not easy, especially when one is swept away by some violent emotion. Then . . . then . . . one follows what we call the programme of our life, and which, like all programmes, being perfectly logical, is completely inapplicable to life.

WANDA. [*Who has listened with deep interest.*] So . . . you——

PAOLO. I? I don't enter into the question. I was merely speaking for you and for others who are near you. . .

WANDA. Oh . . . that 's all over and done with now.

> [*She throws a glance at Piero.*

PAOLO. So much the better. And so——

WANDA. [*Shrugs her shoulders.*] And so——

> [*Goes towards Marco. From the terrace enter Cirillo and Elisa.*

ELISA. [*Running towards Paolo.*] Darling Paolo! Let me kiss you. [*Paolo passively submits to be embraced.*] I 'm so thrilled that I can't find one word to tell you how overjoyed I am. Oh, I do believe you have grown stouter.

PAOLO. [*Smiles.*] It 's the rest I 've been having.

ELISA. What a lamb! Have you received my flowers?

PAOLO. Yes, thank you so much.

ELISA. And then you must tell me all about what you went through . . . there. . . .

PAOLO. Yes, this winter. I think to simplify matters I 'll write a book: *My prisons!*

ELISA. How sweet! And in exchange I shall tell you all that has happened whilst you have been away. Quite a lot of weddings! Marco and Wanda. [*She turns to look at them, then lowering her voice.*] Poor soul!

PAOLO. Ssst! For heaven's sake . . . be quiet!

ELISA. You are right. Then Luciano, your lawyer, with Marta . . .

PAOLO. I know, and also my valet, Andrea, has married Teresa. My example does not seem to have deterred the aspirants to matrimony.

Giorgio enters from terrace.

GIORGIO. [*Advancing towards Paolo.*] My dear Paolo. Words are unnecessary.   [*He shakes hands heartily with Paolo.*

PAOLO. My dear fellow . . . a thousand thanks.

[*Moves away to get a cigarette.*

ELISA. [*To Giorgio.*] Can't I see you at least to-day? It 's a whole fortnight! What is wrong?

GIORGIO. Yes, to-day. I shall expect you at five o'clock. I have something to say to you.

ELISA. Why not now? What have you to tell me?

GIORGIO. At five o'clock.   [*Moves off.*

PAOLO. So . . . we were saying?

ELISA. I am very unhappy, Paolo, very——

PAOLO. Courage! courage. . . . In life there is always time to begin again.

ELISA. [*Shaking her head.*] Alas! . . .

PAOLO. Yes, yes. . . .

ELISA. Would you if you could?

PAOLO. I? . . . recommence? . . .

ELISA. If not in marriage at least in love.

PAOLO. Ah! . . . Now what is in your mind?

ELISA. But I, at present——

PAOLO. You, if not in love, at least in matrimony.

ELISA. [*Surprised.*] Why do you say that to me? [*Sighs.*] In marriage! . . . If I had married a man like you. . . . Yes. You were made for me! . . . You have all the qualities that . . . But fate!

PAOLO. [*Brusquely.*] Fate made me marry a woman like you . . . and . . . it was bad.

ELISA. [*Moves away, wounded.*] Heavens! How coarse you are
... [*Turns and looks at him.*] and yet you please me! ...
[*Goes towards the others.*

CIRILLO. [*Followed by Piero, comes towards Paolo.*] Cheer up!

PAOLO. Oh, it's you? ...

PIERO. [*To Paolo.*] I say, do you know that the mayor is
coming to-day to offer you his official congratulations on your
acquittal.

PAOLO. The mayor? ... But have they all gone mad in this
place? Don't they realize that all this ends by becoming
grotesque? I won't see any one.... I'm sick of congratulations.

CIRILLO. Courage, my friend!

PIERO. And this evening they are going to give a banquet in
your honour. The mayor will invite you to be present.

PAOLO. [*Scandalized.*] A banquet?

PIERO. Yes, at the Hôtel Splendide. There will be heaps of
people.

PAOLO. That is the limit! ... Don't let them dare to suggest
such a thing! ... Do they think I have become their buffoon?

PIERO. And the mayor will read a wonderful speech.

PAOLO. I don't wish to hear another word on the subject....

PIERO. He called on me this morning and asked me to write it.

PAOLO. A banquet! ... Oh, it's fantastic! ...

PIERO. Won't you go?

PAOLO. *Go?* My God! No.... Let them enjoy their damned
banquet. I don't want to serve as an excuse for their indi-
gestion! ...

PIERO. It's a pity; such a lovely speech! ...
[*Moves away smiling.*

PAOLO. But what do they want of me?

CIRILLO. These are the penalties of fame! ...   [*Smiles.*

PAOLO. You too? ...

CIRILLO. Yes, I too, necessarily!

PAOLO. Why?

CIRILLO. Because if I did not extol you ... I should have to pity
you.

PAOLO. And for what reason?

CIRILLO. For the same reason that you feel forced to be irritated
... so as not to pity yourself.

PAOLO. I beg of you not to torment me with a useless play on
words.

CIRILLO. My dear fellow, it is not to torment you . . . but to give you courage! . . .

PAOLO. Give me courage?

CIRILLO. Yes . . . you need it.

PAOLO. Why?

CIRILLO. To stand all this! . . . [*A silence.*] In certain cases the absolution of the court has something terrible about it: it abandons the accused to the crowd so that they can deliver justice in the way that pleases them most. . .   And you . . . they pelt with stones of enthusiasm   and you will not be able to escape.

PAOLO. And what do you think I should have done?

CIRILLO. Left at once, gone far away   But I know that it was impossible.

PAOLO. Yes, it was impossible.

CIRILLO. Why was it necessary for you to return here and show yourself to those ten friends who knew, and in whose honour you killed your wife, for fear that they would not have kept silent over the unfortunate incident which you that night were forced to admit?

PAOLO. What I did was right!

CIRILLO. Oh, the pity of it!

PAOLO. It was right.

CIRILLO. It is quite useless for you to go on repeating that word! What good does it do you now that this very day a judge and jury and the whole world have assured you of it? What good?   To convince yourself, perhaps?

PAOLO. Of what?

CIRILLO. That it was right? . . .

PAOLO. Don't let us speak about it.   You know how different our opinions are. .

CIRILLO. At present, not so different as you imagine, perhaps.

PAOLO. [*Mockingly.*] Ah?

CIRILLO. Tell me: If that night you had been alone in your house, and could have had the absolute certitude that no one would ever have known, would you have killed her?

PAOLO. Killed her?   You doubt it, perhaps?

CIRILLO. I doubt it.

PAOLO. What? . . do you forget my principles?

CIRILLO. No.   But you   have forgotten yourself, betrayed yourself, for your principles.

PAOLO. Do you mean to say that I am not sincere?

CIRILLO. Exactly . . . you acted in good faith, that I can believe.

PAOLO. Ah. . . . No. . .

CIRILLO. And so these flowers, the music, the flags, the speeches, the applause, the celebrity, the triumph, all are welcome! To-day you are certainly living the most wonderful moments of your life; enjoy it all to the full; and do you want a piece of advice? Go to the banquet to-night. It is logical that you should.

PAOLO. Oh . . . shut up!

CIRILLO. Ah, you see!

PAOLO. Look here, what are you trying to get at? What are you trying to prove?

CIRILLO. Nothing! . . . In life there is nothing to prove because everything is evident.

PAOLO. For example?

CIRILLO. That you are a weakling.

PAOLO. I? . . . after what I have done? . . . Ah, you perhaps——

CIRILLO. Leave me out of it. Perhaps some day you will also understand me! . . But now we are speaking of other things.

PAOLO. I, a weakling! . . .

CIRILLO. You lack the strength, the courage to overcome the terror of ridicule. You killed your wife from fear of being considered a ridiculous husband! And the joke is that ridicule always falls on those that fear it! . . .

PAOLO. I do not!

CIRILLO. Then you will go to the banquet to-night!

PAOLO. But don't you understand?

CIRILLO. What?

PAOLO. That I have a profound disgust for all to-day's absurd exaggerations?

CIRILLO. I love you for this one moment of sincerity. You feel the absurdity of all this glorification. You destroy your past!

PAOLO. It is not that, you misunderstand me.

CIRILLO. No, no, acknowledge that you are beaten. The husband who pardons is not always ridiculous; it can happen sometimes that it is the one who has killed, as you can see.

PAOLO. I don't understand anything! . . . [A silence.] The truth is that I have a sense of utter delusion.

CIRILLO. I understand! You begin to see the absurdity of our conventions!... But you must be prepared to face things even more subtle and painful.

PAOLO. Still more? It isn't possible!

CIRILLO. Yes. All this will blow over, and relatively soon; but ...

PAOLO. But ...

CIRILLO. But it is from to-day that you will really begin to kill your wife. In yourself you will kill her. Day by day, hour by hour, in every sentiment.... What you have already done is nothing. The crime was only a starting point.

PAOLO. You are hurting me!

CIRILLO. Forgive me. We shall not speak of it again.

[*He goes towards the terrace.*

PAOLO. [*After a long silence.*] I wonder what she is doing.

CIRILLO. [*On the threshold of the terrace to Luciano and Marta, who appear.*] Ah, here comes the hero of the day!

[*Luciano and Marta greet the friends who are on the terrace, Paolo turns, sees them, and makes a sharp gesture of annoyance. Luciano and Marta come towards Paolo.*

LUCIANO. Hallo! How are you? Well ... I hope to see your face a bit brighter to-day?

PAOLO. Why more to-day than yesterday?

LUCIANO. Why?

MARTA. [*Walking about the room looking at the flowers and reading the cards.*] What lovely flowers, and what a lot!... A real appreciation!

[*After wandering about the place for a while she rejoins the others on the terrace.*

PAOLO. [*Who has seen a paper in Luciano's hand.*] Ah, you have bought the special edition!

LUCIANO. Yes!

PAOLO. Quite natural! Of course they have printed the full text of your wonderful speech.

LUCIANO. Oh, I didn't buy it for that!

PAOLO. You are one of the leading lights at the Bar to-day! And you owe it to me!...

LUCIANO. I beg of you not to speak of it. Remember what I have had to go through for this. I did not want to do it, and if it had not been for our friendship—— But anyway I am not really satisfied.

PAOLO. Neither am I!

LUCIANO. [*Surprised.*] You?

PAOLO. Please send me your bill to-morrow.   I intend to pay you . . . at once.

LUCIANO. Pay me? . . . Oh, no!

PAOLO. No? Why?

LUCIANO. Because it would go against me to take money from you . . . from a friend! . . .

PAOLO. And it would go against me to owe you gratitude for an acquittal obtained by such means.

LUCIANO. What means?

PAOLO. Defaming that unfortunate woman . . . in open court. . . .

LUCIANO. I spoke the truth.

PAOLO. [*Starting.*] What?

LUCIANO. As a lawyer speaks in court to obtain the desired result! Oratorical necessity! . . .

PAOLO. You should have confined yourself to the thesis of the right, and nothing more.

LUCIANO. With the jury one had to sustain the thesis of sentiment.

PAOLO. Of the right!

LUCIANO. You would have been condemned!

PAOLO. You should have affirmed that I was in my right when . . . I killed.

LUCIANO. It was my duty to get you acquitted.

PAOLO. No: your duty was not to make matters worse for me. For that I chose a friend! . . . Instead you only thought of your own success! . . . Ah! . . .

MARTA. Well? What are you two squabbling over?

PAOLO. I shall expect your bill to-morrow.

[*Goes to the entrance of the terrace.*

MARTA. What a nice client. [*To Luciano.*] What is the matter? Are you upset?

LUCIANO. He says . . . he is displeased with me.

MARTA. What an idea! You got him acquitted! You have paid your debt.

LUCIANO. What debt?

MARTA. Of friendship.

LUCIANO. He pretends on the contrary . . . that I have not been his friend.

MARTA. How extraordinary! A better friend than you he could not have found.

LUCIANO. And he wants to pay me!

MARTA. That is only right.

LUCIANO. Ah, no! . . .

MARTA. You are too scrupulous! One would say that at present it is you who want an acquittal from him!

LUCIANO. [*Looking at her coldly.*] For you?

MARTA. It was not I who defended him, it is not I therefore who could have displeased him; so perhaps it is the contrary!

LUCIANO. Exactly; it seems to me that you go out of your way to be pleasant to him. One would say that it is you who want him to forgive you something!

MARTA. For having married you, perhaps?

[*They remain looking into each other's eyes, then suddenly Marta bursts into a strident laugh. Luciano makes a gesture of anger and walks away.*

PAOLO. [*Re-entering the room.*] I should like to know what that infernal crowd is doing at the gate? One would think they were waiting for the doors of a theatre to open.

MARTA. To see a great tragedian who has returned to us after a long sentence. . . .

PAOLO. Signora, I beg of you! . . .

MARTA. And my husband has announced you to the public with such flowery eloquence and rhetoric. . . .

PAOLO. Your husband . . . your husband! . . .

MARTA. My husband? . . . Isn't he your best friend?

PAOLO. My best friend? By heavens! . . . No! . . .

MARTA. No? You astonish me!

PAOLO. I know that what I am telling you is disagreeable . . . but . . .

MARTA. Disagreeable? . . . Not at all! . . . I have no wish that you should be my husband's friend.

PAOLO. [*With a laugh.*] Ah, you are afraid that I shall corrupt him? . . . Inspire him with my ideas? You are afraid for yourself?

MARTA. The day when it is a question of me, I shall not be in the least afraid . . . because there will be you to defend me! . . .

PAOLO. I?

MARTA. Because it could not be any one else but you.

PAOLO. [*After a silence, ironically.*] Indeed! . . .

MARTA. So I prefer that you should not be friends; as you see I am a highly moral person! . . .

PAOLO. Extremely . .

MARTA. And you? How have you passed all this time? What did you do in prison? . . .

PAOLO. Nothing.

MARTA. Nothing! That is certainly very little. . . . And then . . . the solitude! . . . Always alone, weren't you?

PAOLO. Your husband came . . . sometimes! . . .

MARTA. He cannot have been much comfort! . . . And always between those four walls! . . .

PAOLO. Nearly always!

MARTA. [*Provocatively.*] My God! . . . I can well imagine the enormous burden of desire accumulated in there which you carried away with you when you came out! [*Moving towards him.*] The desire for the sun, for movement, for life!

PAOLO. In my hurry to get out I left all that behind me!

MARTA. All?

PAOLO. [*Looks at her with mingled irony and curiosity, then walks slowly away, rings the bell, turns again and looks at her, then goes to the threshold of the terrace.*] My friends . . . will you excuse me if I leave you for a few minutes?

MARCO. My dear Paolo, if we are in the way, we 'll go.

PAOLO. No, no, please stay. [*To Andrea, who has entered on left.*] Is my room all in order?

ANDREA. Yes, Signor Count. [*Paolo walks slowly towards right.*] Do you require my help in any way?

PAOLO. No, thanks.

ANDREA. [*Takes a step nearer and lowers his voice.*] If you go into the . . . signora's room . . . you will see there are flowers. . . . Teresa puts fresh ones every day . . . and I have not prevented her . . . because the intention was good! . . . I don't know if we have done wrong. . . . If you do not . . .

PAOLO. [*Who has listened to him very moved, slaps him affectionately on the back.*] No, no.

> [*He takes a few steps, stops, hesitates, then forcing himself to dominate his feelings goes out by second door on right. Some of the people who were on the terrace have entered the room, and are looking after him in silence. Andrea has gone out quickly on left. The conversation is resumed. Among those who have entered the room are Piero and Wanda.*]

WANDA. [*To Piero in a low voice.*] What about those letters? When will you return them to me?

PIERO. When you come to fetch them.

WANDA. I? You are mad! . . .

PIERO. I shall be at home to-morrow at four o'clock; and I shall await you! . . .

WANDA. You will have to wait a long time! . .

PIERO. One of my qualities is . . patience!

WANDA. Is this a revenge?

PIERO. No, a favour!

WANDA. Idiot! You will return my letters to me at once, do you understand!

PIERO. I shall be at home to-morrow at four o'clock, and . . . I shall await you!

> [*Smiles and moves away. She makes a gesture of exasperation. Suddenly there is heard from the street a confused murmur of excited voices, which seem to be coming nearer and nearer to the house. The people on the terrace look down into the street with curiosity and surprise. Those in the room stop talking, listen, and go towards the terrace.*

CIRILLO. Something must have happened!

MARTA. Yes. . . . Let us go and see!

> [*All at once all on the terrace rush towards the left and disappear. The voices are now quite near. One can distinctly hear the words: 'It is she! It is she! Bring her here! . . . Here! . . .' Then the voices are hushed.*

ANDREA. [*After a moment enters and rushes on the terrace. He appears very agitated. Calls in a high-pitched voice.*] Signor Count! Signor Count!   [*He runs towards right.*

PAOLO. [*Entering from right.*] What has happened?

ANDREA. [*Confused and unable to hide his agitation.*] Signor Count!

PAOLO. Well? [*Now the voices are very distinct coming from a room on the left.*] What is going in in there? What is it?

ANDREA. It is . . . that they have . . .

PAOLO. Well?

ANDREA. A little while ago . . . on the lake, two boats passing before the house . . . felt something knock against the oar . . . and . . . and . . . then . . .

PAOLO. And then?

ANDREA. It was a corpse!

PAOLO. Ah! . . .

ANDREA. The corpse of a woman! . . .

PAOLO. Ah! . . .

ANDREA. A woman! . . .

PAOLO. Yes. Yes . . . I heard what you said!

ANDREA. The Signora Savina!...

PAOLO. [*Irritated and incredulous.*] What?

ANDREA. Signora Savina!... We recognized her!

PAOLO. [*Astounded.*] What? You have——?

ANDREA. It is she! There is no doubt of it!... and in what a state!... Unrecognizable!...

PAOLO. But you are crazy!...

ANDREA. I assure you!... It is she.... We all recognized her at once! And you will, too, as soon as you see her. . .

PAOLO. I do not wish to see anything.

ANDREA. What?

PAOLO. I tell you I will not see anything!

ANDREA. But, signor!...

PAOLO. Be quiet! Do you think I am going to be a party to all your fantastic flights of imagination?

ANDREA. But it is she!

PAOLO. It 's absurd!

ANDREA. Why? They recovered the body at the exact spot where ... she fell in!

PAOLO. [*Wringing his hands.*] Oh ... this is the limit!...

ANDREA. Come, signor, she is there!

PAOLO. Where?

ANDREA. In there.

PAOLO. Eh?... Is that the morgue?

ANDREA. The poor signora, we brought her into her own home. You would not have wished her to remain on the beach?

PAOLO. [*To Marco who has entered on left.*] Well?

MARCO. Ah, you know?...

PAOLO. I know that you are a crowd of lunatics, and that is all I know.

ANDREA. Don't you believe it is the Signora Savina?

MARCO. Not believe it? And who else could it be? It is evident that it is a question of a body that has been immersed for a considerable time. Her clothing undoubtedly has remained entangled in some rocks. ... But ... it is she ... it was unanimous ... there was not a doubt ... it is she ... and it is natural.

PAOLO. [*Miserably.*] Natural?

[*From left enter Cirillo, Piero, Elisa, and Wanda. The women are in tears.*]

MARCO. Come in there for a moment. I know it is a terrible ordeal for you ... but it is necessary that you should see her . . . that you identify her.   Then I shall arrange so that all the legal formalities can proceed at once.

PAOLO. [*With sad irony.*] I suppose it is necessary.

[*Goes out with Marco on left.*

WANDA. My God!   What an atrocious thing!

ELISA. Poor Savina!

PIERO. Are you sure that it is she?

ELISA. There is no doubt about it!   I recognized her at once!

PIERO. By what?

ELISA. By . . . everything!

PIERO. Oh, then! . . .

WANDA. How sensitive Luciano is!   He nearly fainted when he saw the body.

PIERO. His nerves are weak, poor chap! . . .

MARTA. [*Entering from left.*] Oh dear!   Oh dear!   What an awful thing! . . .   I can't remain here! . . .   I am going! . . . Good-bye!   My God! . . to think of it!   [*Goes out by terrace.*

WANDA. One can imagine Paolo's emotion at the sight of . . . his wife!

ELISA. It was really cruel to drag him into that room.

WANDA. What remorse!

ELISA. Here he comes!   He looks like a dying man! . . .

[*Paolo enters on left, followed by Marco.   He is not in the least upset; one could almost say that he wants to laugh!*

MARCO. So, there is no doubt?

PAOLO. But! . . .

MARCO. It is she.

PAOLO. [*With a large gesture of resignation.*] It is she!

MARCO. Good!   Now try and keep calm   I will see to everything.   [*To Piero.*] Will you come with me?

[*They go out together on left.*

ELISA. We shall see to everything, and——

PAOLO [*Walking about with a set face and taciturn, makes an imperative gesture asking her not to speak   Elisa and Wanda go out on left.   After a long silence during which he continues to walk about the room making gestures.*] The last straw! . . . God alone knows how it will end!   [*He stops on the threshold of the terrace.   The second door on left opens slowly, and cautiously a woman's head, heavily veiled, appears.   After a moment's hesitation she enters.   She is enveloped in an ample but light coat, grey in colour.   She takes a few light steps into the room Paolo turns round sharply.*]   Who are you? . . . Signora*

Were you looking for me? [*The woman inclines her head in assent.*] Me? Ah, I think I understand! . . . Perhaps you sent me flowers, perhaps you wrote me one of the many letters I found here when—— [*The woman has lifted her veil. It is Savino. Paolo recognizes her. For a moment he remains speechless with surprise. Then furious.*] My God! . . . You. . . . Here! . . . What for? . . . Why? . . . Have you forgotten. . . Are you mad?

> [*Looks hastily round terrified lest someone else should be about.*

SAVINA. [*In a low gentle voice.*] Don't be afraid! . . No one saw me! . . . I came by the veranda stairs . . . and besides . . . I am veiled.

PAOLO. What folly! [*Rushes and locks all the doors; closes the glass doors at back, and draws the blinds.*] What have you come here for?

SAVINA. To see you! . . Won't you ask me to sit down? . . . I am Madame Sévérine de Grèze, who lives in London. You see what a long journey I have taken just for the pleasure of seeing you for a moment. . .

PAOLO. Don't talk nonsense.

SAVINA. A few days ago I came as far as Chiasso, just over the frontier, so as to be able to follow your trial more closely. I heard you were acquitted, and so I came here! . . .

PAOLO. To do what?

SAVINA. I have told you! . . . and then I thought that on this day of your rejoicing it would be nice for you, in the midst of so much homage to receive also . . . the pardon of your victim.

PAOLO. But, wretched woman, don't you know that in there is . . . is your corpse? . . .

SAVINA. [*Stupefied.*] Mine?

PAOLO. Yes!

SAVINA. My corpse? . . I don't understand! . . .

PAOLO. A little while ago some boatmen fished up the body of a woman, just in front of our   of my villa, which had evidently been in the water a long time. It was unrecognizable   yet .   they all recognized you at once!

SAVINA. Me?

PAOLO. They took you, and carried you into the house, into that room, and now they are all in there round your body . . . weeping!

SAVINA. And you?

Paolo. I? . . . What could I do? They almost forced me to identify you! . . .

Savina. Ah!

Paolo. And now what are you going to do?

Savina. So . . . I am really dead?

Paolo. In a few hours the legal declaration will be made.

Savina. Dead. . . . Also for you? You identified me!

Paolo. What did you hope?

Savina. Who knows!

Paolo. It is absurd! . . .

Savina. At least this: that the thought that I was still alive could, I don't know, comfort you.

Paolo. It is quite a matter of indifference to me! . . .

Savina. As I was comforted when I heard you were acquitted.

Paolo. The case is totally different! . . .

Savina. And so I must go away again?

Paolo. Most certainly!

Savina. Return to London?

Paolo. Wherever you like!

Savina. And pass all my life alone?

Paolo. But! . . .

Savina. And never see you again?

Paolo. It is necessary. . . .

Savina. So be it! . . . I shall once more become Madame Séverine de Grèze! . . . And for the rest of my life! . . . Good-bye. . . . Good-bye, Paolo! . . .

Paolo. [*Very distressed and struggling with his feelings.*] Now? . . . No, not now. . . .

Savina. Why?

Paolo. It would be imprudent! . . .

Savina. Don't be afraid; as I came so I will go. And no one will recognize me with this veil! . . . Good-bye! . . .

Paolo. [*Taking her hand.*] No, you might be recognized.

Savina. Who would think of it? I am in there dead, and I have been dead for such a long time!

Paolo. All the more reason! If someone should recognize you, do you realize what would happen?

Savina. Ridicule?

Paolo. I have told you that I won't have it.

Savina. [*Mildly.*] Won't have it? . . . I am Madame Séverine de Grèze! . . .

Paolo. Anyway . . . you will wait till it is dark.

SAVINA. Where?

PAOLO. [*Still more distressed.*] There . . . in there! [*The handle of the second door on the left is heard to rattle.*] Go, go. . . .

SAVINA. [*Obediently.*] All right . . . don't be long, Paolo!

[*Goes out by second door on right.*

PAOLO. [*Staring.*] Eh! . . . what? [*After a moment he goes and opens the second door on left.*] What is it?

LUCIANO. [*Enters, his face is extremely pale.*] I can't stand it any longer! I can't stand it!

PAOLO. What is the matter with you?

LUCIANA. That corpse.

[*Paolo makes a gesture of grief.*

It is horrible! . . . Paolo . . . I must tell you all! . . .

PAOLO. All? . . . What is it now?

LUCIANA. It is more than I can bear! . . . I can't continue to live under such conditions! . . .

PAOLO. What has happened to you?

LUCIANA. It 's . . . You remember that night?

PAOLO. Which night?

LUCIANO. I was your greatest friend, the most sincere, the most devoted of friends.

PAOLO. That is all over now! . . .

LUCIANO. What is over?

PAOLO. Aren't you alluding to my annoyance at the way in which you conducted my case?

LUCIANO. No!

PAOLO. What then?

LUCIANO. Well, the friendship I had for you did not save me from myself! . . . The day that cursed madness seized me it seemed that the friend I loved above all others and . . . the husband had become two distinct personages! . . . To the friend I kept my whole heart, but . . . alas! . . .

PAOLO. What on earth are you telling me? . . .

LUCIANO. That night . . . it was I . . . in there . . . with her! . . .

PAOLO. You! . . .

LUCIANO. And it was I . . . who led her to her death! . . .

PAOLO. You? . . .

LUCIANO. And now do what you like with me! . . .

PAOLO. Ah! . . . You swine! . . .

LUCIANO. I had to confess to mitigate my remorse!

PAOLO. You? . . . You took my wife, my love, my honour! You, my friend! . . . Ah! . . .

LUCIANO. You are right! . . .

PAOLO. Blackguard! . . . And you had the face to assume my defence! . . . You went so far as to accuse her, to say infamous things about her! . . . And you had been her lover! . . . How could you? . . . You unspeakable cur! . . . Ah, no, she could not have loved you, she never loved you.

LUCIANO. [*Touched in his vanity.*] Why?

PAOLO. It must have been a moment of folly. . . . You make me sick!

LUCIANO. [*Wearily.*] Oh . . . enough!

PAOLO. [*With intentional cruelty.*] And now let me tell you something . . . to-day . . . your wife . . . offered herself to me! . . .

LUCIANO. What?

PAOLO. She is my revenge! . . .

LUCIANO. [*Trying to react.*] Ah, not that! . . .

PAOLO. It disgusts me! . . .

LUCIANO. [*Reassured.*] Oh, then! . . .

PAOLO. But for you it will be the same! . . . And now . . . get out!

[*Luciano slowly goes out by the terrace.   Paolo again closes the glass doors, then goes towards the second door on right. Savina appears on the threshold of the door, and enters the room.*

SAVINA. Well?

PAOLO. You heard? [*He flings himself at her, clearly urged by an idea of violence.*] Ah! . . .

SAVINA. [*Retreating quickly.*] What do you want to do? Kill me again? . . .

PAOLO. [*Stops as though struck.*] Again? . . .

SAVINA. Just think, my corpse is already in that room! . . .

PAOLO. [*Broken, wringing his hands.*] Ah, here I am caught in my own net! . . .

SAVINA. I am Sévérine de Grèze! . . .

PAOLO. Even that night I did not have the impression of your betrayal so clearly and laceratingly as at this moment! . . .

SAVINA. But you see quite well now that the man with whom I betrayed you was not worth the betrayal! . . .

PAOLO. Don't try to be clever! . . . Oh, why did I not really kill you that night?

SAVINA. You would feel very remorseful to-day!

PAOLO. Better remorse than to suffer like this!

SAVINA. You feel it more, because I am here!

PAOLO. Oh, go away, I never want to see you again!

SAVINA. If you had killed me . . . then . . . to-day your suffering would have been much greater.

PAOLO. It would have been a liberation.

SAVINA. What liberation? If you love me!

PAOLO. I? . . . Oh!

SAVINA. You love me!

PAOLO. I hate you!

SAVINA. You love me.

PAOLO. Oh! Go away. . . .

SAVINA. You do not want me to go away.

PAOLO. The sooner the better!

SAVINA. Only a little while ago you tried to detain me!

PAOLO. Because I did not wish there to be any scandal!

SAVINA. Because you love me! because you still want me . . . with you.

PAOLO. It 's a lie! . . . Who said so?

SAVINA. It was not necessary for you to say so! . . . I know that I shall remain with you . . . that you will want me again, as before! . . .

PAOLO. You are mistaken! . . . Listen, I don't give a damn for the scandal, the ridicule . . . or for anything! . . . Rather than have you here for another minute I prefer facing anything, whatever the consequence may be! . . . Even if they see you, recognize you, I don't care, but to have you here another minute, no! . . . Now do you understand?

SAVINA. Oh! . . . as you like . . . I shall go! . . .

PAOLO. At once! . . .

SAVINA. I am going, but——

PAOLO. Not another word, it is useless, I will not listen.

SAVINA. But . . . [*In a voice full of sincerity.*] Paolo, alone, without you . . . I cannot live! You shall have the liberty you desire, and very soon!

[*Paolo turns and looks at her.*

I prefer to kill myself, Paolo! . . . I shall kill myself! . . .

PAOLO. [*Seizing her by the hand.*] No! . . .

SAVINA. [*Quickly.*] Paolo! . . .

PAOLO. [*Trying to recover himself.*] No. . . . I don't want you to go now! . . . Wait till this evening, as we had arranged! . . . That is what I meant. . . .

SAVINA. [*With great pity.*] My poor darling! . . .

PAOLO. [*In a stifled voice.*] Please, leave me! . . .

SAVINA. I shall wait for you! . . .

> [*She goes away slowly, shaking her head; when she reaches
> the second door on right she turns again and looks at him,
> then goes out. Paolo remains alone, takes a few steps,
> he is miserable and broken. He drops into a chair, and
> buries his head in his hands. Suddenly the first door on
> the right opens, and Andrea and Giacomo appear, one
> behind the other, bearing four large candlesticks with
> lighted candles, one in each hand. They walk solemnly
> across the room, and disappear by the second door on left.
> Paolo jumps to his feet as though terrified. Then he
> remains petrified, looking after them in stunned silence.*

TRANSLATOR'S NOTE

Suggestion for curtain: *The door on right opens quietly and
Savina takes a step into the room.*

SAVINA. Paolo! . . .

> [*He swings round, utters a smothered exclamation, pushes
> her back into the room, follows her, and slams the
> door.*

END OF ACT II

ACT III

SCENE: *The same.*

Early afternoon. A day bathed in sunshine. The funeral is imminent. Cirillo, Marco, Giorgio, Piero, Elisa, and Wanda are together in the drawing-room, with many others. The women are all in deep mourning. The men in black frock-coats, top-hats, and black gloves. In the distance one hears the measured tolling of a bell. The servants come and go busily. The guests converse, but in low tones, so that one hears only a confused murmur of voices.

ELISA. [*Raising her voice.*] It will be a most impressive funeral!
           [*Several voices tell her to be silent: 'Sssst! . . .'*
CIRILLO. [*Indicating the second door on right, in a low voice.*] Paolo is in there! . . .
        [*The conversation resumes its murmured and confused tone. The women have handkerchiefs in their hands, with which from time to time they wipe their eyes. The men are extremely grave, the lugubrious expression befitting the occasion. Some are on the terrace looking down into the street. Paolo enters from second door on right, which he locks, putting the key in his pocket. He is dressed in a light grey suit. All gather round him and solemnly shake hands with him. He accepts their sympathy in silence, then goes out by second door on left. At his departure the conversation becomes more animated.*

ELISA. Did you notice Paolo's face! . . . He looked like death!
WANDA. Remorse!
CIRILLO. Poor chap! He is finished! . . .
PIERO. A corpse, even if it is only a woman's, is no light weight in a man's life! . . .
ELISA. He is so distraught that he has not even thought of putting on a black suit!
WANDA. Someone should tell him!
ELISA. [*To Wanda.*] Does my dress look all right? I had to have it made in such an awful hurry!
WANDA. It suits you beautifully. I had no time, I just had to put on this old thing I bought last year!

CIRILLO. What impresses me is that Paolo shut himself up in his room last night, and didn't leave it till now!

WANDA. Who knows what he is suffering?

MARTA. We must try to take him out of himself! . . .

ELISA. Yet the maid Teresa told me that she served him his meals in his room, and that his appetite was enormous. He ate enough for two, especially this morning for lunch.

MARCO. It 's a good thing he can eat!

WANDA. Do you know whom I saw this morning?

ELISA. Who?

WANDA. You remember those two Americans who were here last year, that couple who used to sing on the lake every evening?

ELISA. Oh, are they here again? How sweet!

WANDA. He has come alone! She isn't here.

ELISA. What can have happened? Perhaps they have separated?

WANDA. Perhaps! She was so charming. . . .

ELISA. Oh, but men, you know——
                                    [*Sighs and looks at Giorgio.*

MARCO. Probably the husband took her back. . .

ELISA. All the promises . . . the vows. . . .
                                    [*Sighs again and looks at Giorgio.*

PAOLO. [*Enters from left; there is an immediate silence.*] My friends, will one of you do me the favour to go down below; people are still coming in, and I have not the slightest wish to receive them! . . .

MARCO. Of course, of course; let us go down!

PAOLO. Thank you!
   [*Opens the second door on right, enters, and locks it behind him.*

CIRILLO. What is he doing locking himself in like that?

ELISA. Poor Paolo!

CIRILLO. [*Who is on the terrace.*] Still more flowers arriving! . . .
   [*Marco, Piero, Wanda, and the other guests go out slowly by the door on left.*

ELISA. [*Barring Giorgio's way, imploring.*] Giorgio!

GIORGIO. What, again?

ELISA. Giorgio! . . . we cannot part like this! . . .

GIORGIO. [*Annoyed.*] Good Lord! . . . I thought I had explained myself quite clearly, yesterday . . .

ELISA. I can't! I won't have it! . . .

GIORGIO. But I will; and that is sufficient!

[*Shrugs his shoulders and goes out by door on left. Elisa makes a gesture of despair.*

CIRILLO. [*Coming in from terrace.*] Elisa? What has happened to you?

ELISA. Oh, my friend! . . . my friend! . . .

CIRILLO. I know it is terrible . . but now all her suffering is over! . . . The one to pity at present is Paolo! . . He almost imposed the crime on himself! . . It is truly tragic, this moment in which he is forced to realize that he was deceived in his judgment of our feeling, and of our ideas; now he weeps for this fatal error! . . .

ELISA. Perhaps you are right! . . . What is the use of killing?

CIRILLO. [*After having looked at her for a moment ironically.*] Ah! Do you know I believe that is the only opinion we have in common!

ELISA. You are mistaken, Cirillo! I have always thought that if a woman was untrue to her husband he had every right to kill her! Now I know that as well as being right, it is great!

CIRILLO. [*With a tinge of bitter irony.*] Ah! Is that a reproach? . . . You are right! . . . If it is so, I have deceived you! . . . I have been a bad husband!   [*Gives a short laugh.*

ELISA. Why do you say that, now?

CIRILLO. Or at least I have been a profound egoist. I wanted to please myself rather than please you! . . . [*Laughs again.*

ELISA. You might spare me those bitter words! . . . Don't you see that I am suffering?

CIRILLO. For that?

ELISA. I beg of you!

CIRILLO. What then? A grief I know nothing about? Then it is a great pity that you should mention it to me at all!

ELISA. I am my own grief, Cirillo!

CIRILLO. [*Surprised.*] What?

ELISA. It was for that I asked you to weigh your words! . . . You who did not kill me, you will not now kill the possibility of a life together! . . .

CIRILLO. Explain yourself! . . .

ELISA. Do you really believe that you have not understood? If it can give you pleasure, well then Yes . . . you have guessed rightly.

CIRILLO. [*Puts a hand gently on her shoulder. After a silence, in a voice a little shaken by emotion.*] Elisa! . . .

ELISA. Oh, thank you, thank you! . . .   I want to explain to you——

CIRILLO. No, if you mean what you say you will not speak! It is better!

ELISA. I cannot be silent! . . .

CIRILLO. Don't speak! . . .   Imagine that a long time ago we agreed to meet here to-day! . . .   We shake hands, and continue our way together! . . .

ELISA. But I must open my whole heart to you! . . .

[*Cirillo makes a gesture of despair. Elisa continues with emphasis.*

I want to tell you all the torture of my soul for ever seeking a happiness which ever eludes me.   Ah, with what bitterness I have paid for all my foolish illusions, for all my errors! . . .

CIRILLO. Stop! . . .

ELISA. Forgive me if I have made you suffer! . . .   But I too have suffered so much and when I hurt you I hurt myself too! . . .   Forgive me! . . .   [*Weeps.*

CIRILLO. [*Sadly.*] Calm yourself!   Every one lives as best he can! . . .   If now you are really sincere the past does not count any longer! . . .

ELISA. Forgive me! . . .   You won't bear me any grudge?

WANDA. [*From left, loudly.*] Elisa?

ELISA. I 'm coming! . . .

CIRILLO. Go, go! . . .   You too are a poor thing! . . .

ELISA. [*Takes from her bag a little hand mirror and a powder box ; having wiped her eyes, she powders her face coquettishly ; then returns everything to the bag.*] Ah, my heart feels lighter!   It seems to me that only from to-day am I really beginning to live! . . .   You will know how to forget, won't you? . . .

CIRILLO. It is you who should forget.

ELISA. Oh, thank you, thank you! . . .

CIRILLO. Run away, they are waiting for you! . . . Cheer up! . . .

[*Elisa, her hand on the handle of door on left, turns to look at Cirillo, then goes out. Cirillo, leaning against a chair, remains looking for some moments at the door by which she has gone out, then shakes his head and remains thoughtful.*

PAOLO. [*Entering on right.*] Hallo!   What are you doing? . . .

CIRILLO. [*Following his train of thought.*] Who knows if she is really sincere . . . or? . . .

PAOLO. Who?

CIRILLO. My wife!   A few minutes ago she made a scene!...

PAOLO. One of the usual sort?...

CIRILLO. If it had been the usual sort you would not see me so worried. It was most unusual!...

PAOLO. What was it about?

CIRILLO. She spoke to me of repentance, of weariness, of delusions ... and of ... of sentimental plans for the future!... It is very serious!... But!...

PAOLO. Ah!... Perhaps you were right after all!

CIRILLO. Um!... She was a bit too emphatic!... We shall see! . Who knows?...   [Goes out on left.

SAVINA. [Half opens the door on right, puts her head out, and calls in a low voice.] Paolo?

PAOLO. [Turns round frightened.] What do you want?

SAVINA. Is there any one on the terrace?

PAOLO. No, but——   [Looks timidly around him.

SAVINA. [Enters; she is in a very smart light costume.] What, again!...

PAOLO. Someone may come in at any moment!...

SAVINA. I am sick of remaining shut up in that room!... I am longing so much to walk about freely in my own ... in our own, house!.. I seem to have forgotten it, and I love it so much!...

PAOLO. What are you saying?... Think!...if someone should see you!

SAVINA. Oh, not now!...

PAOLO. How?... The situation remains unchanged.

SAVINA. It is only for us to change it; and ... we have already done so!...

PAOLO. It is not the same thing!...

SAVINA. It is the only thing that has any value!... What do all those people matter to you? Why do you still think of subordinating your feeling, your life, your happiness to them? What have they given you? Only evil! And a few charitable words!...

PAOLO. It may be!... But our life is not made up of ourselves alone!..

SAVINA. But we, above all, have to exist, if we love our life!

PAOLO. That's it: but one must be able to love it!...

SAVINA. [With infinite tenderness.] Paolo!... We are both weak convalescents after great suffering!... Only remember one thing; that we must forget! . . . And only love can accomplish the great miracle of healing our memories. Why do you behave like this?

PAOLO. It is something that is beyond my control!

SAVINA. That is not true! You love me! . . . and nothing is stronger than love.

PAOLO. I don't know! . . . I am caught in a whirlpool! . . . And you, you triumph over me, over my life! . . .

SAVINA. It is not I, it is your love that triumphs!

PAOLO. Ah! . . . How is it that you are so sure of my love? You may be deceiving yourself! . . .

SAVINA. No, I do not deceive myself. Only for love have you been able to conquer yourself, only for love have you been able to free yourself of these monstrous phantoms of social prejudices.

PAOLO. It is possible that you are mistaken! . . .

SAVINA. And then the heart of a woman, of a woman who loves, Paolo, is a mirror of truth. And in my heart I feel mirrored all the frenzy of your love. No, Paolo, I am not deceiving myself. . . .

PAOLO. But maybe you are! . . . Perhaps your heart lies! Ah, you do not know all the torment that was unchained in me last night! . . .

SAVINA. I understood! . . .

PAOLO. When I held you again in my arms! . . . When I felt the beating of your heart against mine! . . .

SAVINA. I was yours! . . .

PAOLO. When I felt your trembling body responding to my passion! . . . I was filled with a madness to destroy! . . . I felt all the most primitive instincts, hatred, cruelty, all that was bestial and vile, rising within me. I wanted to tear you to pieces, crush and annihilate something in you for ever, for ever! . . . It was the beast leaping to recover what had been wrested from him by a childish trick, and who felt his talons caught in a veil woven in mystery! . . . Your memories, that was my despair! . . .

SAVINA. Paolo!

PAOLO. And then I felt myself flung down into the depths of an abyss, my whole being vanquished, without strength or will.

SAVINA. You put your head on my shoulder and sobbed like a child!

PAOLO. From humiliation! . . .

SAVINA. And you let me dry your tears! You went to sleep in my arms, lulled by the tenderness of my words! . . . Without wanting to, you sought refuge in me, against the wrong which I had done you! . . . One cannot love more than that, Paolo! . . . That is why I am sure.

PAOLO. I can only feel my own misery! . . .

SAVINA. You love me! . . .

PAOLO. No, I do not love you! . . . Try to understand me! . . . I want you to be wholly mine! . . . Only mine! . . . And that, now——

SAVINA. Oh! . . . If my sin has awakened in you the necessity of this cruel love I can forgive myself! . . .

PAOLO. What? . . .

SAVINA. Yes, because at first your love was dormant in your heart, you did not know it existed. But now that your body and soul are but one cry of desire, now I know that I am loved! . . .

PAOLO. Stop! Don't you see how I suffer?

SAVINA. A great love lives and thrives on pain.

PAOLO. Oh, be quiet, be quiet! . . .

SAVINA. And one can only understand the supreme beauty of love, when one feels the soul rent asunder by tears! . . .

PAOLO. You are cruel! . . .

SAVINA. I love you because you love me! . . .

PAOLO. You love me? . . . Ah! . . .

SAVINA. I have never loved any one else! . . .

PAOLO. Ah, but that. . . . How can I be sure?

SAVINA. Feeling how wholly I am yours! . . .

PAOLO. Wholly? Ah, I seem to see the traces of the past stamped on your body!

SAVINA. You will forget them! . . .

PAOLO. How?

SAVINA. Because I have forgotten. I remember nothing. Last night when I gave myself to you I was serenely happy. That is the proof which should make you regain your peace of mind.

PAOLO. Is it true? . . . Your lips . . . your hair. . . . [*With a stifled cry.*] Ah! . . .

[*He seizes her in his arms, straining her to him as though wishing to assure himself of his physical possession. Then after a moment he releases her and drops weakly back on to a chair.*

SAVINA. Think if I were not here beside you now! . . .   **Suppose**
I were dead.

> [*Paolo makes her a sign to stop.*

Think of that if you want to understand your love! . . .   And
instead, I am near you, loving you, eager and submissive
to please you, to do everything you wish, so that you
will love me, because if you do not I shall be a poor lost
creature with nothing left me to live for only to weep . .
and weep! .

> [*She kneels at his feet, her head on his knees, her body shaken
> with sobs.*

PAOLO. [*Caressing her hair.*] To love any one means to **suffer**
for them! . . . and I have suffered so much for you! . . .   I
have wanted you, longed for you, and I love you . . . **love**
you! . .

SAVINA. Paolo! . . .

PAOLO. So much! . . .

SAVINA. Forgive me! . . .

PAOLO. No, you must not say that now. . . .   Let us think **of**
the future! . . .   Get up and dry your eyes. . . .   All **is**
finished and done with! . .

SAVINA. [*Rising.*] The future. . . .   With you! . . .

PAOLO. With me, of course! . . .   You go in there now; I shall
go down and see what is happening! . . .

> [*He accompanies her to the door on right, she goes out. He
> crosses the room to go out by door on left.*

LUCIANO. [*Enters at back. He is in a black frock-coat, and carries
a top-hat in one hand and a bouquet of violets in the other. Seeing
Paolo he stops.*] You sent to say that I was not to miss the
funeral; so here I am! . .

> [*Paolo looks at him coldly and goes out by door on left. Luciano
> turns and looks after him.*

SAVINA. [*Entering from right.*] Paolo! Listen, darling! . . .

> [*Seeing Luciano she stops and would beat a retreat, but Luciano
> at the sound of her voice turns round and sees her. He
> gives a stifled yell of terror, his hat and flowers drop to the
> ground. Trembling he points at her . . . covers his eyes,
> looks again, utters inarticulate sounds, automatically
> backs a few steps till he is held up by the piano, where he
> remains as though nailed to the spot, his hands pressed
> back on the keys which sound discordantly at every start
> he makes. His eyes are starting out of his head. His*

*jaw has dropped.   He is a man who has seen a corpse
come back to life.   Savina, who has been watching
Luciano in his surprise and terror, smiles ironically, then
takes a few steps towards a little table which is near her.
Luciano makes another gesture of terror.   She takes a
paper, and begins to read in a cold ironic voice a passage
from Luciano's speech in court.   From time to time she
lifts her eyes from the paper, knowing Luciano's words
almost by heart.   He listens as if out of his mind . . .
numbed.*

'Well, gentlemen of the jury, this woman who employed
every subtle art to preserve the loving confidence of her husband while she dragged her wanton beauty in the febrilé
alcoves of vice and sin. this woman does not merit any pity
. . . any excuse; a woman greedy for sickly and perverse
sensations, lost to all decency, and lacking in every moral
sense.' [*Slowly crushing the paper in her hand she flings it at
Luciano's feet, looking mockingly into his face.*] Reptile! . . .
[*After a moment she bursts into a shrill laugh, and turns aside.
Luciano makes a violent effort to recover himself, moves
away from the piano, and rushes off terrified towards door
on left, but on the threshold he encounters Paolo, who is
entering.   For a moment Luciano vacillates, then darts
away by the back.*]

PAOLO. [*Irritated, turns to look after him, then in an excited voice
to Savina.*] Did you meet that man?

SAVINA. I found him here when I returned to the room.

PAOLO. And you spoke to him?

SAVINA. Didn't you see him? He was like a lunatic. I
annihilated him with his own words, his speech for the
defence! . . .

PAOLO. Ah . . . and now? . .

MARCO. [*Enters on left, followed by Cirillo and Piero.   Seeing
Savina. he gives a jump and remains a moment dismayed   Cirillo
and Piero are struck dumb   The three remain speechless.*]
What? . . .

CIRILLO. What? . . .

PIERO. What? . . .

MARCO. What is the meaning of this joke?

PAOLO. [*With calm indifference.*] What about it?

MARCO. She is alive?

PAOLO. It would seem so.

MARCO But .   . it 's enough to drive one crazy! . .

PAOLO. Well? . .

MARCO. And that corpse they are carrying away, whose is it then?   [*Paolo shrugs his shoulders.*
[*To Savina.*] And you . . . you! . .

SAVINA Well?

PIERO A voice from the tomb. . .

MARCO Well! . .   Well! .   That is not an answer. Explain yourselves! . . .

PAOLO Why explain, and what? You have eyes? .   That 's enough! . . .
[*Cirillo has sat down, and with difficulty restrains his mirth.*

MARCO. Ah! you think it is enough, do you? Too easy to get out of it like that! .

PAOLO. Excuse me, but who are you? What business is it of yours?   Be happy that she is alive, and that is all! .   .

MARCO Ah, no. .

SAVINA. [*Ironically.*] Thank you! . . .

MARCO. This is not the moment to be funny! . . . [*To Paolo.*]
Have you the right to fool people like that?

PAOLO. Do you want me to kill her for your pleasure?

MARCO. Ah, so you are trying to make light of the matter?

PAOLO. You are beginning to get on my nerves! .

MARCO. Indeed?

PIERO. [*Touches Savina to assure himself that she is alive ; in a low voice.*] I am delighted. [*Shakes the hand she holds out to him.*] There is no getting away from the fact; it is warm   .
quite warm! .   .   [*Savina slowly goes out on right.*

MARCO. And you think that you are allowed to make a mockery of the law in this way?

PAOLO. Oh! As to that, you magistrates! . . .

MARCO. All right! . . . but I warn you that this time you will not escape.

PAOLO. What?

MARCO. Yes, my dear sir . . . exactly what I say! Dissimulation of crime. [*Almost with cruel joy and with an air of triumph.*]
Article 211 of the Penal Code.   'Any person making a false statement to the judicial authorities, or, to a public official, who must refer the matter to same, a crime which he knows has not been committed,' etc. etc., 'up to thirty months.' . . Have you understood! . . . Up to thirty months! . . . What do you say to that? . . .

PAOLO. [*Extremely irritated.*] Say.... What do I say?... I killed her and was acquitted.... I did not kill her, and I am sent to prison!... It's absurd!...

MARCO. Article 211.

PIERO. Eh! The law.... I don't know the law!...

MARCO. Just a moment!... Now that I come to think of it ... it is not enough....

PAOLO. Ah, no?

MARCO. A false declaration before witnesses!... Do you understand?... A false declaration made in public!... You declared before a public official that your wife was dead; yesterday you identified the corpse as that of your deceased wife!... Article 279!... 'Any person making a false declaration to a public official before witnesses, concerning the identity and civil status of himself or another person,' etc. etc. 'is punished by imprisonment of from three months to a year.' Pay attention! 'From nine to thirty months if it is a question of falsifying a document of civil law or judicial authority.' Have you understood?

PAULO. It is fantastic!...

MARCO. Thirty and thirty, sixty months, which at the most might be reduced to forty-five!... Are you satisfied with your ... joke?

PAOLO. Look here! I've had enough of this!... To hell with the law, the penal code, the assize court, and all the rest of it.... I don't give a damn for any of them!

MARCO. It is not so easy as all that!... You have hoaxed the public; laughed at the law! You will be arrested immediately!...

PAOLO. I don't care!...

PIERO. What a delinquent!...

MARCO. And that corpse? Whose is it then?... It will be necessary to hold a new inquiry—an autopsy will have to be made!... Suicide or homicide?... That is the difficulty!

PAOLO. And what do you intend doing now?...

MARCO. Stop the funeral, and then proceed——

PAOLO. Proceed to what? You are crazy!... At present you will let them carry away that corpse, because I refuse to have it in my house any longer; once it is in the cemetery you can jolly well do what you please!...

MARCO. I can't waste any time! . . .

PAOLO. Are you afraid it will escape you? . . . Now just understand this, whatever is to happen will happen, but now there is to be no scandal, do you understand? . . . And not a word to any one, not even to friends; there will be plenty of time for them to know later.   At present nothing must happen to disturb the solemnity of the funeral. Do we understand each other?

MARCO. All right, all right. . . .   I pity you. . . .

PAOLO. [*Ironically.*] I am deeply touched! . . .

MARCO. [*Going out back.*] I wonder whose corpse it is. . . .

PIERO. How amusing life is! . . .

PAOLO. Oh, yes; [*To Cirillo.*] and what do you think about it?

CIRILLO. I?   I have been making superhuman efforts to awaken from my surprise! . . . [*Comes towards him.*] You have been really splendid.

PAOLO. Do you think I was wrong?

CIRILLO. Right or wrong have no importance now! . . .   I am delighted that things are so! . . .

PAOLO. But now there will be a scandal! . . .

CIRILLO. What does it matter? . . .   How many men who have killed their wives would not be overjoyed to see them come back to life again?

PAOLO. Just think how they will laugh! . . .

CIRILLO. They 'll soon get tired of that.

PAOLO. It is always the same! . . .   Even in the most tragic moments of our life we are pursued by ridicule! . . .

CIRILLO. Yes, it is true. . . .   In life next to the most grotesque buffoonery burns the most terrible tragedies; the grin of the most obscene mask covers the most searing passions! . . .   But we are not to blame if our joy or our pain does not suffice to fill even the smallest act of our lives.

PAOLO. And so we must accept?

CIRILLO. And learn to rise above our farces and our tragedies. . . .

PAOLO. Spectators of our own life! . . .

PIERO. Yes! . . .   But what about Article 211 and Article 279? . . .   It is not easy to be also the spectators of the penal code! . . .

CIRILLO. You have been once, you can be again! . . .

PAOLO. But how?   You understand, it is a question of immediate arrest! . . And I have had enough of prison. Return there? Ah, no! . . . And then . . . it will certainly not be Marco who will spare me! . . . You heard him! . . . What can I do?

CIRILLO. Escape! . . .

PAOLO. Where? . . .

CIRILLO. Where? . . . Anywhere! . . . Far away. . . . Take your Savina and fly.

PIERO. A good idea; so many thieves and murderers save themselves like that! . . .

PAOLO. Flight! . . . Ah! . . She and I wandering round the world like two fugitives.

CIRILLO. When one has plenty of money one escapes . . . as tourists! . A young couple on a pleasure trip! . . .

PAOLO. So that is what I am reduced to. I must go into hiding! change my name, my face, rush from country to country, trembling at the sight of every policeman! . . .

CIRILLO. It is an adventure! . . .

PAOLO. And we would have to conceal our legitimate love!

CIRILLO. My dear boy! You have lost a wife and gained a mistress! . What more could you wish for? . . .

ELISA. [Entering on left.] Well, what are you doing here? Are you coming? . . And you, Signor Paolo?

PAOLO. I? Oh, no, I couldn't bear it, it would hurt me too much!

ELISA. Poor dear! . . . Try to bear up! . . . [She approaches Piero.] What a lovely funeral! When I die will you remember to send me at least a flower? . .

PIERO. It will be impossible! . . . I shall follow you to the grave! .

ELISA. You make fun of everything! [Sighing.] You don't understand the value of sentiment! . . [She takes him by the arm.] Why don't you come and see me sometimes? . .

[Cirillo looks at her and makes a gesture of hopeless resignation. Cirillo, come along! . Good-bye, Paolo . . . bear up! . . . [She goes out by door on left.

CIRILLO. [Drops wearily into an arm-chair.] Again! . . .

SAVINA. [Entering from right.] Well then, Paolo?

PAOLO. [Rousing himself.] Oh, you were there? You heard?

SAVINA. Yes! . . .

CIRILLO. Signora Savina, when I saw you I was so amazed that

I was tongue-tied, I could not find words. . . .   But I am so happy things have turned out like this! . . .   I am sure that now you will both be very happy! . . .

SAVINA. Thank you! . . . but look what is happening now?

CIRILLO. If you love each other the rest does not matter. . . . When you are two! To feel alone, on the contrary . . . is sad! . . .   And hope, just hope, is not always sufficient to fill up our empty hours! . . .   To-morrow? Within a month? . . . a year? . . . Never? . . . Who knows? . . . It is sad! . . . [To Paolo.] Good-bye, and get off at once, you have no time to lose! . . . and, above all, do not kill her again! . . [To Savina.] Good-bye, signora, I am going to your funeral.

[He kisses her hand ; one can see he is greatly moved. He goes out slowly by the back.

SAVINA. Good-bye, Cirillo! . . .

PAOLO. He also! . . .   Poor old chap! . . .

SAVINA. Well, Paolo, have you decided anything?

PAOLO. Decided anything? There is little to decide; we must run away, and at once. . . . [He continues, getting more and more excited.] Run away, do you understand? Just like any two fugitives! . . .   And we have no time to waste, before the evening we must be out of this place, far away, because those gentlemen who represent the law will rush to reveal everything! . . .   We must be quick, quick! . .   In prison? Not if I know it. . . .   Ah, no . . . I have no longer the slightest desire to render an account of my life to any one, not to society, nor to my friends, nor to the law, nor to any one; I have had enough of it; I want to become——

[Suddenly from the street rises the solemn and measured notes of Chopin's Funeral March. Paolo, who had become even more excited, stops short, and remains immobile, listening. Savina, who is near the terrace, turns her head slightly towards the street, her hand grasps the blind ; she is seized with an acute anguish. Paolo with a cry, as though under the spell of some hallucination, stretches out his arms towards the procession which is slowly passing by.

Savina! . . .

SAVINA. [Turning, with tears in her voice.] Paolo!

[Together they watch with intense anguish, then, suddenly, she takes a few steps and opens her arms to Paolo in a gesture of supreme love.

PAOLO. [*Catching her to him and holding her desperately to him as though he would never let her go.*]   Ah, you are here, here, here!
[*He kisses her hair with great tenderness.*
[*The strains of the funeral march gradually die away in the distance.*

CURTAIN